E. Foxton

Herman

Young knighthood - Vol. 2

E. Foxton

Herman
Young knighthood - Vol. 2

ISBN/EAN: 9783337291839

Printed in Europe, USA, Canada, Australia, Japan

Cover: Foto ©Andreas Hilbeck / pixelio.de

More available books at **www.hansebooks.com**

HERMAN,

OR

YOUNG KNIGHTHOOD.

. FOXTON.

VOL. II.

BOSTON:
LEE AND SHEPARD.
1866.

Contents of Volume II.

HERMAN.

OR,

YOUNG KNIGHTHOOD.

———————

CHAPTER XVI.
THE KNIGHT'S CONQUEST.

> "Suffer me not, in any want,
>   To seek refreshment from a plant
>   Thou didst not set; since all must be
>   Plucked up, whose growth is not from Thee."
>   HENRY VAUGHAN.

> "Maid, choosing man, remember this:
>   You take his nature with his name;
>   Ask, too, what his religion is,
>   For you will soon be of the same."
>   THE ANGEL IN THE HOUSE.

HERMAN'S second letter, written on the second night after Constance's return, to Clara, crossed the latter on the road. On the receipt of his first, she had packed her travelling-trunk, bidden Sally to pack that of her obedient squire, Edward, and informed him, on his coming home from his club, that "she would trouble him to escort her to Baltimore the next day, to call on their younger sister."

She was astonished to find how happy she felt, after all her fears and misgivings. She did not know herself very well; or she would have marvelled less. Any one, who did know her well, could have seen that joy to either of her brothers must necessarily be joy to her, whatever she might have imagined beforehand; and it is scarcely necessary to say, that Herman's letter was jubilant to overflowing. Her eyes overflowed, too, and danced; and her heart bounded, over it. Disinterestedness is the truest self-interest, after all. Persons of large and generous sympathies can never be quite without prosperity; for, how poor or lonely soever their individual lot may be, there can scarcely ever come a time to them, when some of their friends will not be wealthy, some of them famous, some beautiful, and some beloved; and one generous, friendly soul takes to itself the wealth, fame, beauty, bliss, and each several welfare of all its several friends, and is thus the most wealthy, prosperous, and blessed, of them all.

Constance was just putting the last pretty touches to her *toilette*, a day or two after, and, as it happened, thinking of Clara, the only young female friend quite to her mind whom she had ever had, and conjecturing, fearing, and hoping, about the renewal of their intercourse, when Annette tapped at the door, said that a lady and gentleman wished to see her, and handed her two cards. She saw "Miss Arden" on the first one; and she saw no more. Her heart and she gave a great start simultaneously. She hurried to the parlour, longing to have the first meeting over, but trembling so that she could scarcely stand.

"My own precious sister!—how happy you have made Herman!" was Clara's sincerely grateful salutation; and Constance found herself in her arms.

In their soft, warm embrace, she rested a moment like a weary child, lost, but comforted by being found again. "I had no sister," whispered she in a voice choked with emotion, "to counsel me; or I could never have made him so unhappy! Kindest, dearest Clara, forgive me! Take care of me. Don't let me do so wrong again." From that time they were sisters, *comme il y en a peu.*

"Here is Edward," said Clara, as she released her; "you have not forgotten your elder brother?"

Edward, if not equally cordial,—for he had not yet quite forgiven the slight put upon his noble house, in the person of its noblest scion,—was courteous,—so courteous that, if he was at first somewhat cool, his coolness passed unnoticed. It did not last long; it could not. Constance had never been a person, whom it was possible to see often without strong feeling, of some kind, towards her; and, in her present mood, it was impossible to dislike her.

She was a creature of many phases; and the one which now appeared was,

> "To herself and all, a sweet surprise."

She became as a little child. "Let me be a child," she would say, "and begin my life afresh. Teach me. Blame me when I deserve it. Begin at the beginning with me. I have begun quite wrong; and I must pick out my work as well as I can, and do it all over again. I have never been properly trained; I never would be. Treat me as you do Jenny, dear Aunt Cora. Say, 'Constance, Constance, don't be foolish;—don't be wilful;—be gentle;—do as you would be done by!'"

In company, she was said, indeed, to be wonderfully unchanged; except that she endeavoured to learn, in imitation of Mrs. Ronaldson and Clara, to practise more of that general attention to others, courtesy, or, to speak plainly, kindness, in which she had piqued herself upon her deficiency, (which gave some discerning people occasion to say, that her loss of property had taken down her pride a little); but the dear domestic Constance, impetuous and imaginative still, yet docile and tender, disinterested and conscientious, yet gay and sportive, graceful and refined as ever, yet simple and natural, was something that neither bishop, relations, the brilliant and haughty Miss Aspenwall, nor the meek and mute Sister Agnes Alexis, had ever dreamed of before.

Many characters appear to attitudinize all through life, making *tableaux-vivans*, more or less cataleptic or grotesque, of some *beau idéal* of their own or other people's. A wonderful relief it would be to them, sometimes, if they could get their own, or other people's, leave to spring down from their pedestals, be themselves as God meant them to be, forget themselves and their posturing, and sit, stand, or walk, as harmless Nature dictates.

Such freedom and refreshment were now enjoyed by Constance. Satisfied with loving, she forgot to be imposing; and thus for the first time became,—it happens so sometimes, when the nature is a fine one,— truly admirable. She looked at our hero, and no longer thought or cared whether or not she looked a heroine. But there are many things in this world less heroic than devotion and humility.

Between this hero and heroine, there was now but one barrier left. Each wished it away; yet neither knew how to throw it down. All through the week, they walked, and sat, side by side. Both found it hard when Sunday came, that they must walk and kneel apart,—hard to be apart on that day of all others. One in love and in life, it was very hard to be two in faith and in prayer.

On Monday afternoon, Constance, who had remarkable skill in drawing outlines, was amusing herself and the children by sketching the profiles of different members of the family, and making them say, *which was who*. Perhaps it was partly a sly device, to give that wily young person an excuse for the study of certain features, which were, according to her impartial judgment, unspeakably regular, fine, and noble, and from the contemplation of which her eyes had fasted for years.

"There, children, run to the window; and guess who that is. Now, Herman, it is your turn. Look straight after them,—quick, while they are gone! You *are* altered, indeed," continued she, in a low voice; "those lines about your mouth and brow are new within four years. They are grave, earnest, commanding, powerful. They must have been stern sometimes in conflict, to be so strong when at rest. Herman, I never supposed before that I was cowardly; but, if you did not love me so, I could find it in me to be afraid of you."

"Constance, the queen, afraid of her champion?" said he, smiling and altering his outline very much, like a very bad sitter;—as he was, but his artist did not chide him. "Ariadne afraid of her panther? Are you afraid of its faring with you as it did with Paul Pry, when he ventured into the Zoölogical Gardens and

'Says the keeper, Observe this here tiger,—how tame!
But he bit Paul Pry's finger, who danced with the pain,
And vowed he'd ne'er meddle with tigers again?'"

1*

"You absurd youth, no! I am not afraid of anything on earth, when I see you smile;—except of your laughing at me, of which I think there *may* be some danger."

"There is not. I never shall laugh at you; unless it is for being afraid of so very tame and well broken a tiger as myself."

"Nor at my friends?"

"Not unless they're *very* queer. Couldn't you forgive the infirmity of human nature, in that case, and laugh too?"

"I do not know." She spoke absently, and then abruptly: "Herman, do you think it is quite impossible for you to become a Roman Catholic?"

"Quite; but I hope, that it is by no means impossible for you to cease to be a Roman Catholic."

"And shall you wish that?" asked she, with some anxiety and hesitation in her tone,—"if it goes against my conscience?"

"My dearest love, if it went against your conscience, what difference could my wishes, or those of any man, make to you?"

She clasped her hands, and was silent for an instant. Then, planting her little foot more firmly on the flowery floor, she resumed: "None, Herman!—after the example which you set me four years ago, they ought not,—they should not— make any. But, oh, I hope God, in His mercy, will remember how much weaker I am than you, and never call upon me to choose between my duty and my—love!"

"Amen, to that last clause. I shall never call upon you for such a choice, at any rate."

"I thought you would say so. I should be very sorry to apostatize, not only for shame at such changeableness, but because, though there are some things about Catholicism which are still irksome to me, I am sure that it suits me on the whole, and has done me the greatest good."

"'Catholicism,' or Christianity?"

"Why, Herman, you surely would not deny that Catholicism was, at least, one form of Christianity, if not the only form!"

"I certainly do not deny, that the doctrines of the Romish sect contain a certain infusion of Christianity; as do the doctrines of other so-called Christian sects."

"But, Herman, you are a liberal Christian. You do not think, do you, that it is of any consequence what people believe, if only they are good?"

"Yes; I do."

"You *do!* Oh, Herman, where is your liberality?"

"In its place, I hope. Do not look so disappointed, but listen, dearest Constance; and I will tell you why I think it is of consequence, and of what consequence I think it is. 'If only they are good,' as you say, *they* will be saved, I believe, in spite of their errors of doctrine; but their errors of doctrine, if they prevail, may do much,—it is fearful to consider how much,—to prevent their neighbours from being good. In the most superstitious and least Christian sects of Christendom, it is to be hoped, that there may be some soldiers of the cross strong enough to force their way, through all outworks of Man's word, into the full granary of God's word, and be fed; but how does it fare with the rest of the rank and file? The masses of whole sects are, I suspect, marked in the private characters of most of their members by the characteristics of their sectarian creeds, rather than by those of the Christianity, which their creeds undertake to embody. Those persons, for instance, whose creeds set forth to them Him after the pattern of whose perfection we are bidden to be perfect,—the Father,—as a Being, one of Whose chief attributes is a wide and arbitrary instinct of vengeance, seem to be generally harsh and implacable. Those, on the other hand, who consider Him as a Being of mild and weak benevolence, stripping Him of His attributes of judgment and strong empire, are apt to be themselves blandly indifferent to right and wrong. You may be strong and penetrating enough to get at the kernel of the nut, which the Reformation cracked, through all hindrances; but how can you seal it up again in shell and rind, for your neighbour to make wry faces at, or break his teeth upon? Is it 'good' for you to do so? He asks for bread,—that living bread, which came down from heaven,—which Christ lived a life of privation, and died a death of agony, to bring to him and us! Let us share it with him, to the best of our ability, in its pure and wholesome state,—not give him, either by precept or example, a stone which he can neither swallow nor digest. 'Offend not your brother with your meat,' nor even, unnecessarily, with your spiritual meat, 'for whom Christ died!' Do not let us insist upon having it served up seasoned with superfluous spices and condiments, which, however we may relish them, may weaken and sicken him."

"But, dearest Herman, I do not mean to offend or injure any one. If this faith is the best for me, but not for others, cannot I have and keep it for myself?— I need not be a propagandist."—

"No, my love; you shall keep it, as long as you think it right; but keep it to yourself, you cannot;

and a propagandist, I fear you must be. Every brilliant and distinguished man or woman, who becomes a convert to Romanism,—I do not think I exaggerate in saying so,—is of necessity more or less a propagandist of Romanism. When you 'let your light so shine before men, that, seeing your good works, they may glorify the Father,' they are too likely to glorify instead the Church of Rome. Thus the danger is, that your very virtues are enlisted against the cause of God's pure truth. You are bound to do what in you lies, to promote the coming of Christ's kingdom on earth; and Christ's kingdom on earth will be something very different from the dominion of the Papacy, unless the Papacy has been very much,—almost incredibly,—belied. I can understand that morbid, cowardly, self-centred souls may be glad to shuffle off, as they fancy, the risk of their own personal responsibility upon others, or selfish lovers of excitement, to obtain religious excitement at any hazard to their neighbours or country; but I do not believe that generous, high-hearted, patriotic persons, like you, have the least idea of what they may be doing, to overthrow religion and undermine the prosperity of their native land, when they throw their influence and example into the scale of this superstition. Spread out the map of Europe before you; and lay your finger, if you can, on that Roman Catholic country, which you would like to have this country resemble a few centuries hence. Consider how you would like to have either the clergy, or the laity, of these United States resemble those in general of the States of the Church.—Your eyes are saying something. Interpret, red lips."

"But, indeed, I think you must be prejudiced.

The bishop was a most wise and holy old man; and yet he upheld the Church of Rome." .

"And therefore you uphold it? A case in point! I beg your pardon, though. That was assertion, not argument. You will forgive me?"

"Yes, this once; because there are some little arrears of forgiveness, if I recollect right, to be made up on my part, before we can settle our accounts. But let me ask, if you have ever thoroughly examined the tenets of the Romish Church?"

"Constance, have you?"

"Ah, that is not fair! Never mind me just now. I will tell you by and by."

Now, it really had happened to Herman, as it does to many or most romantic young people, to be slightly threatened with the Roman fever himself, once upon a time. Feeling the symptoms coming on, but still retaining his reason so far as to suspect that the distemper might be a dangerous one, tò an American citizen and a Christian brought up to know better, he had had the good sense or good fortune to write for advice to his old friend, Dr. Lovel.

That spiritual potentate, according to his custom in dealing with those of his neophytes who possessed clear heads and good educations, had, instead of saving Herman the trouble of making up his own mind by making it up for him, (to be unmade again, very likely, by the next spiritual potentate who came in his way,) sent him word where he could find some materials for making it up for himself. .

Herman had thus read, by his recommendation, one or two solid church histories, and some numbers of Whateley's "Cautions for the Times," but chiefly the writings of past or present Romanists themselves. He had profanely chuckled over "the thrice happy St. Louis de Gonzague,"* rolling himself upon sharp-pointed thorns by night, instead of a salubrious mattress, and studied with a sadder and more indignant interest, on the one hand the melancholy account of the life and death of that splendid genius, Blaise Pascal, self-immolated to the gloomy spirit of self-torment, which, under the name of religion, he served, and, on the other, his masterly exposition, in the "Provincial Letters," of the principles of the confessional as expounded by the Jesuits,—and the later revelations of one or two abjuring Romish priests in Europe. But some of the discoveries, which, as he suspected, he thus had made, were too ugly to be imparted, except in case of the utmost need, to Constance. When a sensitive girl has unsuspectingly just sipped at the brim of a poisoned chalice, who would show her the spider lurking in the dregs, if by any means less shocking she can be kept from drinking more? Moreover,—whether rightly or wrongly I do not know, though I, too, would hope the former,—he rejoiced in hoping

---

* See the (Roman) "Catholic History of America," for an account of the singular blessedness of "the blessed Catharine Tegahkouita, illustrating the influence of Christianity on the domestic life of our Indians," from the guileless pen of her admiring confessor, in which are to be found these words:

"At another time, she strewed the mat on which she slept with large thorns, the points of which were very sharp; and, after the example of the holy and thrice happy St. Louis de Gonzague, she rolled herself for three nights in succession on these thorns, which caused her the most intense pain. In consequence of these things, her countenance was entirely wasted and pale, which those around her attributed to illness." .

If this beatific but restless gentleman was the same with St. Lewis Bertrand, I am inclined to hope that the quality of his bedding is above somewhat too severely impeached; for I learn from the Reverend Alban Butler, that the last named Saint "lay * * * usually on the ground, or on pieces of wood, which formed rather a rack than a bed."

that in this country, up to this time, the Church of
Rome, in the green tree instead of the dry, had borne
quite as many of her fair and sweet flowers as of her
baneful and bitter fruits. He believed that, with the
remarkable sagacity and power of adaptation for which
she has been justly commended, she had her uses for
good men as well as bad, and would hardly choose the
worst specimens of her manufacture to send into a new
and yet unconverted country. He had known one
excellent priest, and women, of her communion, who
might have been an ornament to any.

He ventured to suggest to Constance, however, that
setting up a claim to infallibility was generally a suspicious indication of spiritual as well as of medical
quackery; and to question whether such a claim sat
with any special grace upon a sect, some of whose
members had proved themselves capable of such little
mistakes,—to characterize them with the mildest
charity,—as the Inquisition, the elevation of Alexander
Borgia to the spiritual headship of Christendom, and
the fires of Smithfield. He also pointed out to her
what seemed to him one or two of the more glaring
contradictions between the spirit, and even letter, of
the Bible, and some of the tenets and practices of the
Church of Rome; and, while he assured her that there
were some members of that church, in whose saintliness
no one could believe more devoutly than he, declared
that all that was good in that, as well as in all the
other sects of the Christian church, was not what was
essentially sectarian, but what was essentially Christian.

Constance was too warm to generalize. "The
bishop," she exclaimed, "after being hard at work all
day among the poor, would jump up again cheerfully,

at the very beginning of the most interesting conversation with Aunt Cora and me, and hurry away to sooth the death-bed of some poor old ignorant negro cook."

"But that was his Christianity. So would any really Christian clergyman or physician, of any denomination."

"Oh, but he scourged himself dreadfully in secret, like any mediæval saint; and no one ever suspected it; until at last, early one morning, his valet put a new cassock in his room, and took away the old one while he was asleep; and there was the knotted scourge, all stiffened with blood, in the pocket."

"That might be his Romanism, I cannot deny," said Herman, with judicial solemnity.

Constance hurried on triumphantly: "And Sister Corona,—tender and gentle as Clara herself,—watching and weeping over the sick orphans as if they were her own,"—

"Her Christianity."—

"Once, just after she took the vows, she was ill, and was ordered to put her feet in warm water. The Sister Infirmarian brought it. Sister Corona tried it, and said that it was too hot; but the Infirmarian declared, that it was as it should be; and the dear soul was so meek and so firm, that she plunged her poor feet in directly without saying another word, and kept them there, as she was bidden, for twenty miserable minutes without so much as writhing; though when she took them out at last, and wiped them, all the skin came off on the towel."

"That was Romanism again, most indisputably;— slavish, cruel, unreasoning Romanism! Her feet were given her to trot about with, on errands of mercy. It was a great and barbarous mistake to boil them. There was a certain young quadruped whose *fortissimi* pedals she might have substituted as a sacrifice, if any such sacrifice was required of her, with the further advantage of providing a palatable jelly for her patients."

"Come, come, come! Stop laughing at what I say, or I will join the order of *La Trappe*. I will make a compromise with you, and own that no sect contains all truth or holiness, and that the Romish church may be no better than the protestant; but will you tell me, once for all, in sober earnest, how it is that she seems to you so bad?"

"Because, when I would have wooed her, she appeared to me in a vision, a glorified Lie!—a vampire of corrupt and mortal beauty, dead herself, and preying on the life of Christendom! Because she seems to me, like a heathen goddess, to delight in the needless tortures, bodily and spiritual, and the untimely death of the fair and young! Because,—but yesterday, Constance, for aught I know to this day,—in her stronghold, virtual licenses for every crime were freely sold! Because she seems to me, by her false miracles, to throw discredit on the true! Because she seems to me often to cheat the good, and·sometimes to make the good, cheats! Because she seems to me to have taken for her motto, where her own interests are concerned, the words of one of her most distinguished poets :

> 'Magnanima menzogna! or quando è il vero
> Si bello, che si possa a te preporre?'

Because,—the head and front of her offending just now, I confess, in my eyes,—she seems to me to have obtained possession by unfair management and artifice of my artless, true-hearted, unsuspecting lady-love!"

"'Licenses to crime!—Management and artifice!'—Herman, you shock and terrify me more than I can tell. Are not you prejudiced? Surely, Bishop Devereux!—But you do not know him; or you would know that he was above suspicion of cheating, or of being cheated."

"I have often heard of him. I believe he is, in most respects, a man of remarkable excellence."

"'In most respects!'—But you do not know him. Those who do, believe that he is, in all respects, a saint."

"I do not dispute,—I scarcely doubt,—that he may be so, according to his conscience. But he was educated at a Jesuits, college, was he not? May not his conscience and understanding have been early tampered with?"

"'*His* conscience tampered with!' Oh, Herman, you *are* prejudiced now, and against the bishop!—my dearest friend, against him whom I thought my truest!"

"Perhaps so."

"By whom?"

"Yourself, if by any one."

"By me!"

"Perhaps I cannot forget that the first time I met you, after years of separation, I found myself separated from you still,—at first, I feared, forever,—could not speak to you,—could not hear from you the only words which I then cared to hear from mortal lips,—could not tell you, when you thought me dying, that I died, as I had lived, your own!"

"Oh, Herman, it was terrible, was it not? But, indeed, he was not to blame. I told him, myself, that you were unworthy; and in pity to me he asked no more."

"But might he not,—ought he not,—in pity to you, to have asked more? On other points he did not spare you. It strikes me, that he should not have volunteered to take off your hands the management of your own affairs, unless he could manage them for you better than you could for yourself. When you followed his leading, with helplessness and trust which ought to have been so touching to him, and placed your youth and inexperience under his guardianship, might he not, with his knowledge of the world and insight into character, have ascertained whether my offences were of too grave a nature to be expiated by the amount of punishment which I had already undergone? Might he not have conjectured, that no one whom you were capable of loving so unchangeably, could be capable of disgracing himself so irretrievably? ·Might he not have tried to find out, whether the case was not one in which a reconciliation could be effected, by a little delicate paternal mediation on the part of your spiritual father? If he ever had the natural feelings of a man, and still retained any memory of his own youth, he might, knowing you, have guessed what I was suffering. Might he not, before shutting another door between us, have inquired whether natural earthly happiness was really impossible for you?"

"I do not know. I wish he had. I never thought of that before.—But, indeed, he meant to do all for the best. He did not approve of matrimony; and it was hardly to be expected, that he should take pains to lead me into it. Is that all?—What else have you heard, and from whom?—Speak out, and let me know the worst."

"The worst is nothing that need make you look so pale; and, I repeat, what I have heard against him, as I conceive, has been chiefly from yourself. The world says of him, that he is a good and upright man in all other respects, but a wily and unscrupulous propagandist. What you say, seems to me to confirm that view of him."

"It does not confirm my view of him, then. I did not mean to represent him so."

"No, dearest; you meant only, as you always do, to speak the truth; and the truth spoke for you. But all through your simple story I seemed to see, as if through a magic chant, the figure of a kind but crafty priest leading you blindfold, by a sort of spiritual magnetism, into the place which he really thought the best for you, or at least for the interests of his church, but all the while assuring you that your eyes were open, and that you were going where you pleased."

"These charges are very vague, Herman. Can you make none more specific?"

"Not of a single direct falsehood; but truths misapplied and exaggerated are often practically worse than falsehoods, because more plausible and effective. He exaggerated and perverted truths, I thought, in persuading you that your really very hard case was hopeless, in describing as he did the disadvantages under which learning and genius labor in women, and in endeavouring to convince you that you might, could, or should not prove yourself a woman of genius. Whether you are one or not, I do not know, or care unless you do; because no amount of genius could make you more dear and delightful to me than you are already,—or less;—but I do know that your having printed, in these days of universal printing, a few fugitive pieces anonymously without bringing down upon yourself a volley of criticism, is no proof at all, either way. If you had published a volume or two, which passed uncensured and unanalyzed, I grant that his test might have been more decisive. Professing to consider you a very extraordinary woman, he was in fact treating you as rather an ordinary woman. Almost every really intellectual person has some faculty or other which may be developed by a liberal education,—particularly with the facilities which you possessed in your wealth, leisure, and independence,—into a source of great and reasonable satisfaction. With your very uncommon eye for color, form, and expression, I am sure that you, at any rate, might have given yourself and your friends much pleasure by painting masterly portraits. Any such resource would be invaluable to a person in the condition in which you were, at that time; and if it requires perseverance to become an artist, so it does to become a saint."

"Yes, indeed," said Constance, blushing and sighing.

"It is much better, of course, to be a saint than a poet or artist, if one cannot be, as some persons have contrived to be, both; but it is not necessary, that one saint should trick another into sainthood by persuading her under false pretences,—no, I won't say that,—on doubtful evidence,—that she cannot be a poet or artist, and that therefore, *faute de* brush, chisel, or pen, she must take the palm as a *pis-aller.*—Oh, there was one thing more! I do wish I could know, how that copy of verses happened to come to you out of the casket."

"My dear Herman, do you *not* know?"

"I know how you think it did, I believe. Will you tell me once more?"

"The bishop thought of me when he was writing it, and in part described me and his wishes for me. By an odd coincidence, such as will happen sometimes, one cannot tell why, when Aunt Cora dealt the papers round at random, that one came to me."

"Precisely; that was what he meant you should think. I should like to know, how Mrs. Ronaldson came to give it to you."

"You shall know at once, from her, if the fact does not speak for itself. I shall be glad to be able to prove to you the groundlessness of one of your suspicions, dear Herman; and then I am sure you will dismiss all the rest, as unlike you and unworthy of you."

Constance walked out of the room with a firmer step and higher head than usual, and found Mrs. Ronaldson in her nursery. "Aunt Cora," whispered she, "you remember the night of the children's party?—when Annette was the Sybil?"—

"Oh, yes, love; how the little dears did enjoy it! We must have another."

"Yes, dear aunt. But do you remember how it was, that you came to give me that particular copy of verses,—that the bishop wrote,—out of the casket?"

"Why, he directed it to you, love, did he not?"

"No, Aunt Cora; it was in a blank envelope; it was not directed at all."

"Are you sure? I thought it was.—No; I can't positively recollect; it was so long ago. I'm almost sure the others were directed.—Oh, yes, I do remember! That was it. Each of the other young ladies there had one directed to her; and I gave you the blank one, because I knew there must have been some mistake. The bishop never would have meant to leave you out. Pretty, was it not?"

"Very pretty, indeed!" said Constance. The one half-proved prevarication served as a clue, by means of which her memory flashed back along a long series of more palpable manœuvres and stratagems. She hardly knew how she got out into the passage; but, when there, she put her hands to her bursting temples, and exclaimed, "tricked, cheated, flattered, beguiled, where I trusted most! He fooled me to the top of my bent! What a vain, weak idiot I have been! Thank Heaven, that I had already shown it to Herman, before I found it out myself!"

Minds of enthusiasm like hers are subject to tremendous revulsions of feeling. In proportion to her unbounded trust was now her unbounded distrust. Returning with averted eyes to her seat by Herman's side, she said, "Let us never mention that man's name again. All that he ever said to me of religion is, as it were, unsaid! You must guide and teach me, Herman. Your church shall be my church; and we will serve one God together."

Herman pressed her hand, but did not pursue the subject. He was sorry for her mortification,—not sorry to be, as every Christian householder ought to be, the bishop of the church in his own house. He said only, "We will study the Bible and the best religious books together; and I shall be most glad if we can think alike."

There were few difficulties in the way of it. Constance had become a Romanist from romance rather than from conviction. In one of her sweet confessions to her new director, she said, one day; "I need not blame—*another's* disingenuousness. I was not upright myself. I think, candidly, that it was with me much as it was with Henry of Navarre. I wanted the *cornichon*, just as he wanted the crown of France. I saw no way to reach it, except through the door of the church of Rome; and through the door of the church of Rome I went accordingly, as fast as I could. I listened to the arguments on one side only; and I knew nothing of those on the other; so that my conversion was a sure and speedy process. I cannot bear to think of it now; but indeed, at the time, I did not dream that I might be helping to tamper so dreadfully, as I now fear that I was, with the gospel of Christ. As I have often told you, I acted like an actress. Life did not seem to me, at all, the solemn and responsible reality that I have ever since been learning to consider it, but a sort of phantasmal tragic drama; and all that I thought of was, to make it as dramatic as possible, fill it with stage effects, play it out, and have it over."

"Perhaps," answered Herman, "when we are twenty years older and forty times wiser and more experienced, the young men and maidens in our neighbourhood who wish to escape from their empty, disappointed, or unsatisfied hearts, and take refuge in the service of Christ, will no longer need to serve an apprenticeship to Rome, but will come to Father Herman and Mother Constance to be taught how and where to work for a month, a season, or a year."

"To *me*, Herman!"

"Why should they not? Several of the best girls in our parish are beginning to come to Clara; and she is not forty, nor thirty. She gives them money to spend in alms for her,—buying, I think, a triple blessing to herself, them, and the receivers of their bounty. They render her a strict account of what they

2

spend, and how, and consult her in difficult cases about
the disposal of it.   They admire and love her, as it is
in the nature of fine girls to admire and love a woman
like Clara.   From time to time, she rewards them by
engaging some good master or mistress to give them
lessons with her, and at her expense, in some pleasant
accomplishment.   This makes them feel the better
acquainted with her, and the more at their ease in
seeking her counsel in their little perplexities.   Clara
has rare judgment, when she dares to exercise it, in
most matters of every-day life; and I believe that her
influence and example have done incalculable good
already."

"Clara! I can easily believe it.   But how could
you ever trust me to advise poor girls?"

"I appeal," said he, with his cordial smile, "from
Constance past to Constance future."

Herman would not let Constance fall into the bitterness of a renegade, as at first she seemed likely to
do from the vehemence of her natural temperament,
ever prone to extremes, and her special indignation at
her conviction, which grew stronger and stronger the
more she reviewed the past, that she had been unfairly
flattered and decoyed into the Romish communion.
He took pains to seek out as many as he could of
Bishop Devereux's good and beautiful deeds, which
were not far to seek, and laid the glowing list before
her, saying, "If he had but been frank and open, he
would have been perfect, Constance."   But frank and
open, his reverence's best friends, among his sincere
and discerning friends, could not say that he was.
Some shook their heads, some laughed, when that point
came up.

As regarded himself, the man was incorruptible.

He might have been intrusted for years with the richest benefices; and he would have lived penuriously, and died poor. He might have been, for life, the adored director of hundreds of inexperienced and confiding devotees; and no one of them would ever have needed to blush at the sound of his name. When Satan, as sometimes happened, presented himself before him with a cardinal's hat in his hand, and a brilliant little picture of the seven-hilled city, surmounted by the triple tiara, for a back-ground, and said, "All these will I give thee, and the glory of them, if thou wilt fall down and worship me," he always ejaculated his "*Vade retro*," with such promptness and energy that Satan executed a *retraite* which Cellarius might have envied; but, unhappily, he forgot the latter half of that omnipotent adjuration, and concluded it, by an awkward mistake, with, "It is written, 'Thou shalt worship,—*the Church of Rome*, and that only shalt thou serve.'"

Thereupon Satan, delighter in compromises, resumed his *poursuite* in a more masterly manner, showed him in a moment of time all the kingdoms of this world, and said, "All these will I give to the Church of Rome, if thou,—and the like of thee,—will only bow down to flatter a little, to hold thy tongue when thou shouldst speak, to speak when thou shouldst hold thy tongue, to compromise a little with the wrong, in order that the right may the more surely prevail, to be a little false to men, in order that thou mayst be the truer to God; and, in short, to crucify thy pride by stooping, as a Christian, to use means for the furtherance of the interests of thy church, which, as a gentleman, thou wouldst kick me, and justly, for proposing to thee to use for the furtherance of thine own."

Whereupon the bishop blushed, groaned in spirit, but bowed, put a cloak upon his conscience, and suffered the fiend to slip under it in the likeness of a fox. It tore him. He was too honest to be happy, though he was too strong and resolute to show his pain. He was a noble and a grand idolater. May heaven have mercy on his soul! Let us sinners beseech thee, good Lord, that all those whose consciences of his sin are accused, by Thy merciful pardon may be absolved!

What, my reader, do I hear you, instead of saying, Amen! thanking God that you are not as other men are, or even as this Romanist? Are you then, rare and happy human being, serving your pure God by pure means, in your trade, your profession, your politics, your church? Does your brave hand push aside everything which would come between your soul and Him,— your knee bow down to Him alone? Do you never stoop to bow down a very little to Satan, for the sake of the cotton-spinning of the North, or the cotton-growing of the South, or any other sort of money-making at the East or the West?—for the sake of the Whig party, or the Democratic party, or any other political party? Of course, we all know that the Union and the world would tumble to pieces if you did not, just as Bishop Devereux knew that this world and the other would tumble to pieces if he did not; but you know, besides, that there is such a thing as standing "serene amid a falling world;" and so you stand upright, and let the party, and the money, and the cotton, and the Union, and the universe too. if they must, take their chance, and trust God, as Bishop Devereux should have done, to manage His own affairs in His own way, without Satan's powerful assistance. I honor you, and acknowledge that you deserve praise such as few lips are worthy to utter.

" As the husband is, the wife is;" and therefore I need not catechise yours. I am sure that neither does she bow down to Satan at all, neither for interest's, nor fashion's sake. She loves her servants, her poor Irish neighbours, and even more, *mirabile dictu*, her *parvenue* neighbour, as herself, and persists in acting accordingly in all circles and situations. Her sweet voice has always its sweet word to say, to and for the oppressed, friendless, or slandered, in spite of the frowns or sneers of all wilful or prejudiced oppressors or slanderers, in *crinoline* or broadcloth.

But you, reverend Mr. Protestant, may I ask you one or two questions? Satan has devised for you a bribe as high and as subtle as, though less gorgeous than, that for which your Romish brother fell at his feet. Do you also prove stronger and wiser than he? It has been quite in vain, I am aware, for the tempter to represent to you that he is wealthy, and would, for a trifling consideration on your part, induce your parish to increase your salary, and, himself, make you very handsome presents. That was not the bribe I meant. You are not to be bought at that price; it is lower even than the cardinal's hat. But Satan is fascinating, and inclined to be fond of you. With all his faults, there is really something very striking and picturesque about him. Though you regret his delusion, you must own that he is evidently sincere in thinking that wrong is right; and if you do not, by telling him that it is not, imprudently shock his prejudices, he will find that out for himself, perhaps, by and by. He is fond of controversy, and very ready to believe any excellent doctrine you please, in the abstract, provided you will not call upon him to practise it before he is ready. He even enjoys hearing

you condemn your neighbours for any sins which he
is not, at present, in the mood for. He only begs you
to bend to him so far, as to put off to a more convenient season the discussion of one or two, which he
and his most particular friends are just now indulging
in, and to censure those of your brethren who are disposed to meddle with them prematurely. He is fashionable and influential; and if you can only keep him
in your sect, he will do a great deal to decoy other
members into it. It is very important that your sect
should increase. You look upon its increase as the
only means for the salvation of the world. Notwithstanding all which, when, in your secret, prayerful,
watchful soul, a voice deeper and purer than that of any
earthly policy bids you to speak, you do speak the truth
and shame the devil, and let him bounce from his seat,
bang his pew-door, stalk creaking down the aisle in the
face of your aghast congregation, and take refuge in
that of your rival, the Episcopalian, Baptist, Sweden-
borgian, or Unitarian. Very well. I was afraid that
there might be some Jesuits and devil-worshippers in
our days and churches, as well as in those of Pascal and
of Rome; but I see I was mistaken.

Herman made Constance introduce him to some of
her old friends in the Sisterhood. He found among them
much to admire and reverence, a little to smile at, and
some good hints for both imitation and warning, to be
carried out, perhaps, hereafter. He made her admire,
approve, and smile, with him, and exercise a little
calm discernment in winnowing the wheat from the
chaff.

"These good ladies," he would say, "are Christians
in their lives, as you who know them testify, if 'patience and abnegation of self and devotion to others'

can make them so; and in their creed they are so, too,
to the best of their ability. I, for one, will never condemn them for their faith, till I have excelled them in
their works. They were delicately bred, you say, and
some of them, I see, are delicately framed; yet they
devote themselves willingly, and even cheerily, year
after year, to the relief of squalid poverty, sickness, and
ignorance. For their sweet sakes may the sins of
Popes and Cardinals, yes, and of Protestants, too, be
forgiven; for these humble, saintly women belong,
evidently, to the Church of Christ, as well as to the
Church of Rome. Among their fervid and unceasing
prayers,—how many, it is sad to think, misdirected to
Saints and Virgin—some must yet reach the Father, in
the name of the Son, and—who knows?—may help the
souls of some nominally enlightened Christians, who
proud of their enlightenment forget to pray, and glo-
rying in their faith forget their works.—That dress?
I see no vanity or ostentation in it. I do not like it on
you; but I do on them. It is their defensive armour,
which they need to protect them;—the visible shield
of the church held over them,—when they must go forth
to relieve or rescue the wretched, it may be from the
very strongholds of Satan. It is the sorrowful and
sympathetic token, that they are ready to weep with
those who weep; for with those who rejoice, except in
their ministrations, I suppose they have little to do.
Constance, if a lonely life should ever again be the lot
of one of us, I should love to think that it was to be
spent in great part in works like theirs, adorning
what we hold to be a purer faith."

"'If!' oh, Herman, God forbid!—And we need not
wait for that! We each, in our several ways, enlisted
ourselves in the service of God in our sorrow. It would

be ungrateful,—unworthy,—base, to desert it in our joy, because he has blessed us with one another. No, let us lay our united hearts on His altar. Hand in hand and side by side, henceforth, let us walk in the narrow way. Strait as it is, it is broad enough for us two to tread together. Imitate our Lord; and let me imitate you!"

His beautiful dark eyes did not refuse, but met the ardor of her own with an answering shine that, through hers, showered down light into her heart; and the beautiful days passed on; and, as they went, she loved him only better and better, and understood him ever more and more perfectly. She grew up into his thoughts, as she grew into his affections. She learned more and more to "love God above all,"—but him,— "and every man as a brother." She ran, she rushed, she flew towards Heaven in those heavenly weeks beside him, and the last one before her wedding-day had come.

CHAPTER XVII.

NEMESIS.

"Who is the honest man?
  He that doth still and strongly good pursue,
  To God, his neighbour, and himself, most true;
    Whom neither force nor fawning can
  Unpinne or wrench from giving all his due.

' Who, when great trials come,
  Nor seeks nor shunnes them, but doth calmly stay,
  Till he the thing and the example weigh;
    All being brought into a summe,
  What place or person calls for he doth pay."
                            GEORGE HERBERT.

CLARA sat with Constance in her chamber. "Bring my—new white dress, Annette," said the latter, "and the gloves, and fan, and all the things with it from the wardrobe, and lay them out upon the bed, for Miss Arden to see."

Annette smirked, bustled, and did as she was bidden. Clara rose, went to the little French bed, examined, and admired. She was to be bride's-maid, of course, and had stipulated that she was to be allowed to assist at the nuptial *toilette.*

"Laws!" ejaculated Annette, "Whar dat splendiferous veil come from, like to know? Did'nt fetch dat out de *armo're* nohow!"

"Annette, hold your tongue!" said Clara, *sotto voce.* She had brought it in her pocket, and stealthily dropped it on the pillow.

2*

"Veil?" said Constance, taking her laced pocket-handkerchief from her *bureau*-drawer at the other end of the room, and catching only one word. "It will be sent home to-morrow. I ordered it this morning. It is to be *tulle*." She came to the bed, and took up the most beautiful point-lace veil in the world. "Where can this have come from!"

"Paris," said Clara.

Annette giggled. Clara was convicted, kissed, and thanked, and proceeded to rehearse the arrangement of the woven hoar-frost over the ringlets of the destined bride, that she might be at no loss on the next occasion. Very exquisite did Constance look in it, like a queen-rose gilt with silvery gossamer. Clara led her to a mirror, and bade her behold herself, telling her that the next time she had the honor of being her dressing-maid, she would either be in poor Uncle Ned's condition, and "hab no eyes for to see," or else she would probably have been injudicious enough to cry and *rouge* them, so that she would not be so well worth seeing. Constance looked timidly, and then forgot herself in looking, and even forgot that Clara was looking too. Why should not a beautiful young creature, who enjoys everything else that is beautiful, enjoy herself?

Constance Aspenwall was tall, lithe, buoyant, in the first freshest prime of her beauty. Her shoulders were sloping and not broad; and the natural tapering of her long slender waist gave them their just proportion. Her arms were long and slight, and as round, smooth, and white as those of a marble Venus. She had a well-formed and peculiarly well-set head, which she did not carry, as too many of us do, depending in front of her, like a desponding cow on the look-out for better pasturage, but reared it grandly, like a watch-tower from which a lofty soul would contemplate earth and heaven. Her complexion was of that finest lily-white and bright rose-colored kind, which is neither the *blonde* nor *brunette*, but has almost all the brilliancy of the one and the richness of the other. Her face was of a good oval shape. So much of her forehead as appeared, below and between the jetty tresses which clustered at the top and sides of it, was very smooth and white; but whether it was high or not, was not easy to say. She had too much intellect in the inside of her head, to be very solicitous about a phrenological display of it on the outside. Her temples were as delicate as those of a yearling child, and had sky-blue veins in them; as one saw when the wind blew back her hair. Her eyes were of a very uncommon, very dark, transparent steel-gray, of the hue precisely of the handsomest eyes in the best engravings. They were long, and rather large, at times splendidly though not sharply radiant, and had very expansive pupils, which, when she was a little excited, as often happened, almost overspread the irids. I hesitate to say that she had an aquiline nose, both because I am hardly orni-thological enough to know what sort of noses eagles have,—and do not believe that my readers are,—un-less, like those of most other birds, they consist chiefly of a couple of punctures just below the forehead, which, in a young lady, would be skull-like and not at all becoming, and because that expression is not uncom-monly profaned to signify a horrid parrot-like beak, like the arc of a circle, or a monstrous top-heavy dodo-like protuberance, which, however promotive of respiration it may be, and useful, especially when *mignonette* is in blossom, is anything but ornamental to the wearer.

But she had a nose of that rare kind, which, while it is as regular and delicate as the Grecian, is as much more expressive and spirited, as a Gothic cathedral is than a Doric temple. It looked quite straight in front, and was neither too blunt nor too sharp, too big nor too little, nor anything else that a nose has no right to be; but it was a two-story nose, and had, as any one saw, who was so fortunate as to see her turn her head sideways, a little aspiring prominence midway between the bridge and the tip, which was neither an angle nor quite an arc, but prettier than either. Her mouth was very eloquent. It always looked as if it had just said something so charming, that when one looked at it, one longed to say, "What?" Her lips were of the color and polish of ripe rose-berries. They were delicate, not full,—scarcely full enough perhaps for the taste of some persons,—but expressed the greatest innate refinement. The upper one turned up a little at the corners, and then down, and then up and then down again, to a little rounded point of coral in the middle. Her teeth were perfect in shape, hue and regularity. They resembled an even row of kernels of young white polished Indian corn, on the cob turned sideways. Her chin was worthy of the rest, and had a little depression in the middle of it, as if Nature, on finishing her most lovely work, had taken hold of her by it to take a survey of her, and the imprint of the grasp had not had time to die out. Her profile was as beautiful as—some, who preferred profiles, said more beautiful than—her full face; so that she seemed to have two beautiful faces instead of one. Artists and *connoisseurs* declared, that there were lines in her face that artists and *connoisseurs* only could appreciate; but there was something in it that everybody could appreciate, down to the little child in the railroad car, who once, when it smiled on him, broke away from his father, ran to her, and, laying one chubby hand on her knee, gazed up and revelled in it, with his wondering gaze, like a bee in a hollyhock. Thrown over it all, there was that inexplicable charm of expression and harmony, which sometimes by itself suffices to make countenances, otherwise plain and unmarked, bewitching.

Clara gazed on, glad of the opportunity. "One reads of such beauties," thought she; "but I did not expect ever to see one! I did not remember, that she was so lovely four years ago."

She had not been. She had then been too chiselled, too *cameo*-like, too sharp, and cold, and hard. Time, and sorrow, and joy, and love, had mellowed, and softened, and sweetened her now. As she gazed on, and mused, and appreciated her own matchless loveliness, it grew tenderer, sweeter, and more glowing, with some swelling inward feeling. Her cheek grew brighter; her liquid eyes, moist; and her gaze, more intense; and then, starting from the glass with a quick turn to Clara, and covering her face with her hands, she exclaimed, "Clara, whom do I look like?"

"Like no other earthly creature! Without flattery, I was just thinking so."

"Ah, yes, I do,—I hope I do,—sometimes, when I come the nearest to deserving it."

"Whose looks could you possibly find to like better than your own?"

"No wonder you ask, after seeing me play Narcissus for so absurd a length of time!—the looks of a better person, who deserves such—to look well—better than I."

"Sister Corona?—Let me see, darling. Put down your hands. What! Not another peep?"

The two pair of white hands resisted each other
softly, for an instant; and then Constance, with one of
the gleeful, girlish freaks in which she had lately sometimes indulged herself, darted away to the other end
of the room, threw off the veil, put on her riding-hat,
pushed back her hair under it till only the wavy ends
showed around her brow, fastened a plain, upright
linen collar around her throat, arranged a folded black
scarf, and small brooch, in a masculine fashion upon her
chest, and came forward with a bow.

"Herman!" cried Clara; "yes, you *do* look like
him! If the color of his eyes, or yours, could be
changed, and you were tanned, or he, bleached, you
would be as much like him as a most maidenly-looking
damsel can be, to a most manly-looking youth." Constance glanced timidly again at the glass, again turned
blushing away, put off her masculine equipments, came
back, sat down on a foot-stool at Clara's feet, took her
hand, laid her own warm cheek upon it on Clara's
knee, and hesitatingly and softly said:

" You cannot tell,—I never told any one before,—
what a comfort the resemblance was to me in those
blank days, when I thought that my waywardness had
deprived me of him forever. I was childish enough to
make a reward of it to myself; and when I had really
tried to do good in a good spirit,—when, for instance,
I had watched all day beside some desolate sick woman,
soothed her, and sincerely felt and prayed for her,—it
seemed to me that an expression of Herman's came into
my face, which made it truly like his; and then I would
steal away as soon as I could, alone, and look at myself
in a pail of water, or anything which would answer the
purpose of a mirror, and feel as if I had his picture. A
strange coincidence, was it not?—when he was at the

same time busy, without my knowing it, among the sick and poor? Mortifying enough it is, however, to think of my being so like him outwardly, while so unlike within!—It seems a kind of hypocrisy.—It is like fine clothes on a hunchback."—

"Hush, my lovely little sister! Herman would tell a different story. You are not to speak ill of the ladies of our family."

"Nor to be so egotistical any more; *am* I? It is a great temptation to talk too much of one's-self, to find congenial confidants after passing twenty-two years by one's-self, in this unsympathetic world. Let us talk of Herman's merits, instead of my demerits. You have have been a good deal with him among his poor patients, have not you?"

"Yes, and been delighted, as you will be, to see how some of them respect and love him. I dare say that his cordial, genial, gentlemanly visits, are almost the brightest gleams of sunshine in the lives of some of them. I believe there is often a particular appreciation of grace, cultivation, and refinement, among people who have no grace, cultivation, nor outward refinement of their own. Herman's presence often appears to me to change the whole expression of a squalid, bare room, as a fine picture might, hung upon the wall. Edward and I have often wished that he would take more pains to make himself known, in what is called society; but, after all, perhaps he does more good, and spreads round him more happiness, in houses and families where qualities like his are altogether *unique*, than he could among ladies and gentlemen."

"While I was a Sister," said Constance, "I began to suspect it might be a misfortune, that there was so great a gulf fixed, in general, between the families of the working and the *resting* classes. I suspected that neither their nor our heads, nor hearts, would be the worse for a little more mutual acquaintance. I cannot see how it is possible for us to love our neighbour, until we learn to know our neighbour, not merely as a useful, yet perhaps a very ugly and dirty, machine, but as a suffering, enjoying, hoping, fearing soul."

"Herman thinks so too," said Clara. "For two years past, he has given half an evening a week to studying over again certain matters, which he learned at college, with four young American mechanics,—poor public-school boys, who were obliged to leave their desks early to go to their trades, and might have betaken themselves to lower pleasures but for his sympathy, and encouragement, in their learning. One of them,—the most intelligent,—a young mason, when a boy of sixteen, was ill and under his care. He always had his Latin Grammar beside him on his bed. Herman offered to help him, and continued to do so, after he recovered, at our house; and he asked leave, very modestly, to have three of his friends come, too,—a baker, a carpenter, and a blacksmith. Herman says that, with the five or six hours a week, (besides those which they spend with him,) which they contrive to give to the valuable English reading he keeps them supplied with, they will be better educated men, in the course of time, than many merchants are; and I do not see how, at their age, they can enjoy, and try to deserve as they seem to do, the friendship of a man like him, without having a very fine standard of manhood fixed in their minds to act up to. Fine gentlemen, of course, it is not desirable that they should try to be; but they seem to be respectable and self-respecting men. I have seen them once or twice on their way to or from his office, with their hands and faces so clean, and their hair and plain clothes so neatly brushed, that they looked as little like boors as they did like fops. Their gratitude to him gives him an influence over them, which he uses in enlisting them to help him, in their spare moments and on Sundays, in his other benevolent undertakings."

"What are those?"

"Oh, I could hardly tell you a quarter; and I dare say I don't know half! Taking care of the sick, principally, of course. He has turned our old house-keeper, Sally,—don't you remember her?—out of one of her store-rooms in the *basement*, and fitted it up for what Edward calls an 'inquisitorial dungeon;' and he is there for an hour, three times a week, to receive any poor people who choose to come to him for medical advice. In difficult cases, he presses our good elder brother into the service, as consulting physician, which is a proceeding likely to be to the advantage of all par-ties concerned. Then he keeps an evening-school there, every Saturday night, for teaching some Irish-men reading, writing, and ciphering; and those classi-cal and mathematical pupils of his, that I told you of, take turns helping him in it. He often watches the coming in of the emigrant ships, I believe, and goes down to the wharves to give the poor friendless foreign-ers a welcome on shore, and tell them where to go and what to do. On Sunday, he sometimes visits the hos-pital or prison, and reads and talks with those who like it. In one way or another, his time seems all filled up."

"Does not he work too hard?—Oh, I hope he will not!"

"I have often been afraid of that; but he certainly

appears to thrive on what he does; and Dr. Brodie says, 'Bless your heart, my dear, do let him work! It's just as much his nature as it is a fish's, to swim; and, supposing we could put a stop to it, he'd be like a fish out of water. The fish won't drown; trust him for that. Inaction might be the death of a restless, high-strung young fellow, like Herman; but action never will, while he fences with my boys, and rides with you, and eats and sleeps as rationally as he does now.' Exertion for others does seem to be Herman's very life."

"Ah," said Constance, "Herman has no self; or if he has, it is all better self!"

"Just self enough to sacrifice, and no more. For example, he has the utmost aversion to surgery. But there was a poor old woman, whom we both knew, who had a tumour on her arm, which it was necessary for her to have removed. Ned would have performed the operation for her very nicely and kindly, and not cared; but our old woman had made up her mind, not only that it would kill her if performed at all, but that it would frighten her to death *besides*, if performed by any one except poor Herman. Her sister told me about it afterwards. She said, 'she heard the house-door open, and went out; and her heart was all up in her mouth, for there was the doctor a-takin off his gloves, half sittin and half standin,'—you know how, Constance, and so did I,—I could see him—in that pensive, stray Antinous way of his,-'agin the kitchen-table, lookin kind o' thoughtful an pitiful, so she knowed in a second what he'd come for; but the minute he see her, he perked his head right up, and stood up, not a-laughin, but all bright an ready, an give her a look, as much as to say, Well, if tain't jest the pleasantest

job in the world for any on us, Miss Thomas, I ain't a
bit afeared but what I'll make my way well through it,
and yourn, too; and then he stepped in and bid Miss
Todd good mornin, pleasant an hearty, and took her
hand a second in his so kind, she said from that minute
she wan't a mite afeared, of anythin such a kind
strengthenin young hand would do to her; an then
he had it all done and over in less than no time.'
Herman could not eat his dinner that day, and Ned
laughed him to scorn; but that the old woman did not
suspect. There he is, love; and I hear Edward's voice,
too. He has come for me; so we must both go down,
and I must bid you good night. Next week, next
week! *Constance*, and *Clara, Arden*, how natural it
sounds,—as if we had always belonged to each other!"

"Herman, I have something for you," said Constance. "You wanted to see some of my verses. I
have brought you a copy of the last, which I wrote
before I entered upon my noviciate, just after Sister
Corona's brother died."

Herman took the fair clear manuscript, and read its
contents aloud as few but he could read; while Constance's cheek grew brighter and brighter with one
gush of her sensitive blood after another, keeping time
to thrill after thrill of feeling in her happy heart; as
each flexile change and sympathetic intonation of the
voice, which to her, at least, was the most beautiful in
the world, surprised her at every turn and cadence of
the lines, by bringing out or throwing into them some
beauty, which she had never found nor dreamed of
there before :

"HAPPINESS, A TRUANT.

"When, with glances far and free,
My spirit stood at Childhood's knee,—
And gazed and smiled with careless glee,
To see the fateful spinsters three

Draw deftly out, from carded naught,
My first bright threads of life and thought,—
My play-mate true, delight and joy,
Was a tiny winged boy.
Nightly nestling in my breast,
His legends lulled me to my rest;
Thence his voice, awakening gay,
Trilled back the early linnet's lay;
On craggy rock, in greenwood tree,
Or by the purling rill sat he;
From wind-rocked blue-bells flashed his eye;
He floated round the butterfly;
He thrust a tawny-sandaled leg
Through the cygnet's bursting egg;
His little golden head rose up
In the water-lily's cup;
His saucy breath, with nectar fed,
Puffed at me from the violet's bed,
Half in sport, and half, caress;
Oh, dear, artless, Happiness!
    "Stately Womanhood me found,
And my brows with roses crowned;
In a naiad's glass I saw,
Pleased, my graces touched with awe;
And 'These royal flowers shall be
Fastest bonds, dear boy, for thee!'
So I said.   From morn till eve,
Through my haunts the shepherds grieve;
But the urchin bursts amain
Shouting, from my bloomy chain,—
Bursts and leaves me all forlorn,
Pricked and bleeding with a thorn.
'Why thus wrong my gentleness,
Light and fickle Happiness?'
    "All in tears, to bring me ease
Back he flew, and made his peace;
And my every art I tried
Still to keep him at my side,—
'April floods of tears and smiles,
Soft confessions, simple wiles;'
Then I seized my harp and sang;
Far and wide the chorus rang:
(Round me flocked the grave, the gay,

But the rover would not stay;)
' Pearless, wronged, thy votaress,
Cruel, fleeting Happiness!,
   "Oft and oftener still, his flight;
Longer still he shunned my sight;
Till I left my woodlands dim,
And set forth in quest of him,
To loud feast, and fair, and camp,
And halls where burns the midnight lamp,
And the blear-eyed schoolman delves
Slowly through the groaning shelves;
Where old minds, that erst were men,
Speak and teach mankind again,
Hollowly as from their tombs,
And, seen through ever-deepening glooms,
While creation's bounds they track,
Cast their endless shadows back.
Vainly still I sought to find
Him I sought, among mankind;
Still his semblance proved to be
Garish Mirth, or Vanity;
And still, of all, I sought in vain
True tidings of the lost to gain.
The scholar said, 'In poet's book;'
The poet, 'In a leafy nook;'
'Oh, which?' 'I know not yet,' he says,
'Go thou and look,—mid clustering bays;'—
The lawyer, 'In the judge's gown;'
The judge, 'In velvet's lordly down;'
The peer, 'He's in my liege's crown;'
The king, 'He rides the victor's glaive;'
The victor, 'In cool Lethe's wave,—
Or haply in the hermit's cell;'—
The hermit said, 'I know him well;
Seek him in the house of Prayer.'
'Nay, I know he can't be there.
Pride shall bravely fill thy place,
Treacherous, worthless Happiness!'
   "Prim sat Pride, then dropped asleep
Leaving me to wail and weep.
Round my dimpled shoulders clung
My dewy locks, at random flung;
Wildered strayed my fleecy band;

Dropped the crook my listless hand,—
Playing with the dreary rue
At my cavern's mouth that grew,—
And forgot its tuneful craft.
At my plight my shepherds laughed:
'She is sick at heart, you know;
She dotes; wise maidens do not so.
So are all idle fools, who chase
The slippery, coy sprite, Happiness!'

   " Dropped its silver balls from sight
The starry clepsydra of Night;
And the morn brought jocund glee
To the world and not to me:
'Would I ne'er had seen thy face,
Happiness, lost Happiness!'

   "Stung with swarms of wretchedness,
I plunged into the wilderness.
Towards the eastern lands of spells,
Me some secret power impels.
'There some wily witch' methought,
'In her toils the childe has caught.'
Through the shadows, through the sun
And surging sands, I journeyed on,
Till the day his gold lance set
In rest, to prick from Olivet.
Fairer light the morrow showed,
Nor to him its lustre owed;
Up the steep of Zion's hill
Rose a vision brighter still.
Silvery white, the garb she wore;
And a cross of flowers she bore;
Her modest countenance amid
A soft enshrining veil she hid,
Lighted up, like midnight skies,
By the splendor of her eyes;
Her dainty feet, with sandals shod,
Scarce touched the flinty road she trod;
O'er her brow a pearly shell
Gleamed, her pilgrim state to tell.

   "Dully, long I strove to see
What that which bore her train could be.
Now on this side,—now on that,—
Now it met a chiding pat,

For resting on her skirts to impede,
Impishly, her upward speed.
From stern crag or way-side stone
Flitting far, as bribes it won
Blossoms fair, and held before
As if her constancy to lure.
Graciously she marked its play;
Steadfastly she held her way.
Changed of mood, in tender gloom
It hung its garlands on a tomb
Full in view, thence reared its head,
Looked at me, and beckonèd,
Then, as if perforce, again
Fled and bore the lady's train.
Quick my heart's thick throbs confess,
'Surely that was Happiness!'

  "Panting, staring, faint I stood,
Then with foot and tongue pursued:
'Sorceress, fiend,—whate'er thou art—
Him from me no more shall part!
I defy the charms unblest,
That steal him from his true-love's breast!
I will rend thy veil away!
Show thine evil looks to Day!'—
My headlong race was won; and lo,
I tore it from her blushing brow,—
My foster-sister's, Holiness!
And her page was Happiness!

  "Oh, I owned her might too well!
Dazzled, in the dust I fell,
Then wondering heard a whisper low,
'Be my friend, my causeless foe!'
Doubtfully I raised my eyes;
Down she gazed with mild surprise;
Naught was there I saw to fear
But bounty, truth, and beauty clear;
As she raised me with a kiss,
Through her veil laughed Happiness.

  "When I slumber at her feet
His pinions scatter odors sweet.
While her step keeps pace with mine,
Round my neck soft fingers twine;
If I turn to seize, he's gone;

> But the rogue returns anon,
> Charged with heavenly fruit, to bless
> The handmaid meek of Holiness."

How well Herman might have liked the little allegory, if any other woman than Constance had written it, I cannot tell. Certain it is that, with all his knightly and hearty respect for the weaker sex, he had seldom been known to enter the lists against Edward, in defence of what the latter was pleased, very improperly, to denominate *petticoat poetry*. No other woman than Constance having written it, however, he read it twice through without finding any words in which to express his disapprobation; except, "Did you think yourself so beautiful, my love?"—words which were pronounced, as he raised his eyes from the paper to her glowing face, with a look in his own which implied that, on that point at least, he was not a little proud to agree with her.

Perhaps Constance forgave the words for the sake of the look. At any rate, her attempt to frown upon him was utterly unsuccessful, as she rejoined, "Did I think myself a shepherdess, my love? Can you make no allowance for poetical license? Come, you are unworthy of it, I see. Please to give it back." Whereupon he very ruthlessly and rigorously pocketed it, merely stating to her, in extenuation of his tyrannical proceeding, that, in the course of the next five days, the law would give him possession of all her worldly goods, and that it could not make much difference to her when he began to take possession.

"You will shake the head of an ascetic at some of my goods, and think them too worldly, I fear, when you see them. I meant to have a very simple dress for —Wednesday; but Aunt Cora has presented me with a white brocade, and Clara with a veil, which looks as if it had come from a queen's wardrobe. I was not taken into their counsels beforehand; and it would have been ungracious in me to refuse their gifts, after they were made. I liked them, too; was I wrong?"

"I think it prudent to withhold my judgment until I have seen them, and seen whether I can help liking them too."

"Uncle Henry told me that he should give me my ornaments, and bade me choose them. I chose orange-blossoms. Are you sorry?"

"Not I. They are the prettiest and sweetest things in the world."

"See what a trick he played me, notwithstanding," said she, unhooking a jewel-case, and putting it into Herman's hand. "Here they are, necklace, brooch, and ear-rings,—pearl flowers, and leaves of green enamel."

"Beautiful! and how becoming they will be to you! You must still have some real ones, though, in your hand and hair. I have always depended upon that. I shall get those for you, myself; and Clara will weave you a wreath."

"Ah, those will be the dearest, in one sense, of all my embellishments! As for the rest, at least they cost *me* less than the muslin and *tulle* I meant to buy. I am glad. It leaves me quite a sum of money,—five hundred dollars. I thought it would be more agreeable to the present feelings of both of us, Herman, to make a thank-offering to God, in some way, of what we each had to spare,—to sanctify our happiness,—than to spend it in any unnecessary expense."

"A novel idea for a young bride and beauty like you; but what a sweet and appropriate one! Let us do so. I can spare two hundred and fifty dollars, I think, with perfect prudence. Let us put that with half of your money; and then—how shall we dispose of it?"

"Oh, you must decide that for me."

"Perhaps Providence will decide it for us both, in some way. Suppose we were to "——

"Letter for you, Cozzy," said little Willy Ronaldson, running through the room; " and there's one for Dr. Arden; and here's one for mamma."

Herman was still deep in his, when he was startled by a moan,—actually a groan,—from Constance. Looking up, he was dreadfully alarmed to see her sitting, pale and rigid as death, with her starting eyes, wild with horror, fixed on a blotted paper which she held in her hand.

"What is it ? Oh, love, what is it ?"

Starting and drawing in her breath, she tore the paper instinctively from top to bottom; but, turning as abruptly towards him, "See; and spurn me !" cried she, gave him the two pieces, buried her face in her hands, and prayed, "Oh, my God, save me from the flash in his eyes!"

His eyes never flashed on her in anger. They rested an instant on the paper, whose contents, obscured by bad spelling and large and small, printing and writing letters used indiscriminately, ran as follows:

"Mis Constans, dr Mistis this is to nform u that I am oald gak. i kard u in my a rms an mi bak wen u ur a babe an i wus allwuz fa thfull to u an urz. i rit to let u no how i am getin along Mi wif wuz soald to a man to gorge i wuz soald to mistur Grand, North Carolina. she wuz sik the da they tuk her i kant here

how she is is getin alorng mi dawter Nans is here but i
dont hav no kum fut of hur kos of yung mastur mistis
sez its her folt an is cross to hur shee ses sheel hid
under the rivvur four long if tha wont let her b hur
swete hart wuz soald to mr clemunt for gods ak mis
konstuns rit an help us out of it u kan help us mi wifs
mt plas skars me wus than a goast u will pleas durrek
to gak hammil tun in kar ov Charles L. Grand, Esq.,
North Carolina [this direction to his master looked as
if shaped out of nail-rod, and had evidently been copied
or traced with the most anxious care from the back of
a letter], ur umbil servant gak hammiltun"

The blotted scrawl conveyed little meaning to
Herman's mind. He glanced at it, but could not wait
to make it out. "What *is* the matter, love? Tell me!"

"I sold him!" panted she hoarsely,—"I sold her!—
I sold them all!"

His face reflected the consternation of her own.
"My poor heart! You sold him!—'all?'—how many?"

"I don't know!—I never knew!—I dare not think!
—I did not know it was wrong, then—I thought it was
right;—I have never thought about it since—Herman,
help me!—I have done it! 'Forasmuch as ye have
done it unto the least of these my brethren, ye have
done it unto me!' I am undone!" She did not shed
a tear; but the veins hidden in her white forehead
started up into a dark network, and swelled almost to
bursting. "To all eternity!—that long eternity!—
undone! *undone!* undone!"

"Constance, it shall be undone,—not you!—I *will*
help you, God helping me! It is a bad business, but
not the hopeless one you think it;—I will take it on
my own hands.—Cry, if you can;—cannot you? Constance, my love. this will never do." He held her

back, with a strong hand, upon the sofa from which she was springing; and bathed her forehead plentifully with cold water, from a silver pitcher which fortunately stood just by, upon the table. "Constance, look at me!—no, not for the letter!—I shall not allow you to see that again, until you can control yourself. I know that you can do so, and you must, or you will be very seriously ill; and then I may be unnerved, and unmanned, and unable to do anything for you or for these poor people. You will summon up a little resolution, for my sake and theirs, I know, if not for your own.—There, that is right. Tears will relieve you.—Now, as soon as I can see you calm and collected enough, we will look the matter in the face, and settle our plans. The people are sold. Very well. The next thing to be done is, to buy them back again. I think I had better go at once to the South, myself, look them up, and bring them back with me."

"Oh, Herman, would you?—could you?"

"Would I—could I—not? Can a policeman track a criminal half the world over, in the name of justice, and for the sake of a reward, and shall not I, a slave, over half of one country, in the name of mercy and justice, and for your sake? Never did any of the knights of old set out on any quests enjoined upon them by their lady-loves, with higher heart and hope than I will, on this, to bring back your peace of mind. Constance, how often I have envied them in my secret heart, and thought how gladly I would even die for you!— How long is it since—this happened?"

"More than a year," sighed Constance, with a sob. "The bishop, when he knew me better, doubted my power of self-renunciation; and, to prove it, I wrote to my guardian the day I was twenty-one, and desired him to sell all my property, of all kinds, as I should never return to the South. He did so at once;— he was glad, I suppose, to rid himself of the care of it; and I put the money into the contribution at church. The bishop was troubled, when I told him what I had done. He asked me whether I had not slaves, and said that I had been hasty, and wrong in not asking his advice. He would have counselled me, by all means, if I gave them up for any reason, to see that they had Roman Catholic masters, that their souls might be cared for; but I did not think that that would have made much difference to them; for those who bought them might, at any time, sell them again; and I told him that they would probably be better off under any masters than they had been under only over-seers. He shook his head, and said he feared I was mistaken, but that, at all events, it could not be helped then, and bade me sit up from twelve to one, two nights in every week, for a month, saying prayers for the conversion of the world, and for all prisoners and captives. I did; and then I felt safe, and never thought whether or not the slaves were so, and dismissed the subject from my mind."

"'More than a year' ago;—it would have been an easier matter then, to trace them. I wish it had occurred to him that, at that juncture, he could best secure the welfare of your soul by setting you to see after other people's bodies."

"Oh, Herman, what if now it should be too late?"

"It shall not be, if they are above ground!"

"But, if any of them are not?—oh, Herman! Herman!"

"Constance, the mercy of Heaven is infinite and

unfailing. What we can do, we will; and God's forgiveness will supply the rest."

She burst into tears again. "'*We* will'?—*you* will; I can do nothing. Oh, if I could only sell myself to ransom them, and then die, how thankfully I would do it!"

"And leave me?—No, sell yourself to me;—and I will give you myself in exchange."—

"And pay you for them?—That would be the price I could not pay;—and yet it would be just. That poor, poor, girl has been a whole year, and more, and may still be for life, without her lover! And I have nothing else but you to buy him back with,—nothing but those few dollars out of which I was going to bear my paltry thank-offering so complacently to the altar, without even remembering. that those swarthy brothers and sisters of mine, so deeply sinned against, had aught against me! Herman, I *must* let you go, must I not?"

"Yes, and come back again, too, I hope, will you not?"

"If I did not hope and believe so, I *could* not let you go; and yet, I feel as if I were under a doom. Everything is perfectly dark to me; and where I shall find any comfort when you are gone, I cannot tell. The very Bible seems full of curses, all aimed against me: 'Whosoever shall offend one of these little ones!'" The words seemed to choke her; and she stopped, shuddering.

"Constance, you grieve and alarm me more than I can tell you, when you allow yourself to go on in this manner. If you did but know it, my dear love, one of your very worst faults, from first to last, has been nothing but this very unbridled vehemence, taking different forms, which is just now distracting you with remorse. If the Bible is full of curses for impenitent sin, it is full of blessings for penitent sinners. Despair is one of the very strongest of the spring-locks, which keep the strait gate fastened to us. You must not shut it against yourself. You will be ill! You will not be able to write to me, while I am gone. You will have a brain-fever. How can I possibly stay away, or start, even? I have a great mind to bleed you this moment!" Herman wiped his forehead. He had actually wrought himself up into giving her something like a scolding, the sedative effects of which he had perhaps witnessed before, in other cases less interesting to him.

"Oh, no, no,—you need not! I will be firm; I am now. I have been poor-spirited and weak, and given you trouble, Herman, when you were doing your very kindest and best for me. The fault is mine; the penance yours; the lamentation mine. That ought not to be. It shall not. But—will you tell me how I ought to feel?"

"By and by, perhaps, when the time for feeling comes, if you need to be told. Thought and action for you, in the first place, Constance.—If I am stern, dear, it is against your bosom foes."

"You are not. You are but kingly and strong; and I admire and love and trust you only the more. In your hands, I can fear nothing long."

His dark, deep eyes shone on her with their softest, tenderest pity. "'You admire and love and trust' me only the more, for my severity against the few faults that stand between you and perfection. You 'fear nothing long' in the hands of one but little stronger, and quite as mortal as yourself. Cannot you adore more heartily, and trust more implicitly, the One only really kingly and strong, and bear the discipline of the one only Wisdom and Mercy? Cannot we learn to fear nothing long in His hands, even if for a little while He sets us apart? High soul, will not you prove yourself worthy of your high Father? Fear Him reverently; but can *you* be afraid of Him abjectly?"

"God's will be done,—in mercy,—on *me!*"

"And on me, too. Say Amen!"

"I will——when you come back."

"Now."

"'A'——oh, Herman, indeed this is a matter of feeling! and you said, that I was to think and act now."

"True."

"I will act. Tell me what to do."

"Take this pen and ink, and write a few lines to old Jake, saying that you will send a person in a week or two, if possible, to buy him and his daughter.—Now, if writing does not increase your headache, I should be glad to have a letter of introduction to your guardian,— your cousin, Colonel Rochemaurice, is he not?—Tell him, that you wish me to buy back your slaves for you; and ask him to be so kind as to give me all the neces sary information in his power."—

"There,—it is done. But there may be forty or fifty of them, or more, even."

"The more, the merrier."

"But where shall you get the money?"

"Out of the bank."

"It may take the whole of your little fortune."—

"Then I shall have to make another."—

"And more."—

"Then Clara will lend me some more."—

"And be fined for my fault!"

"She will think it one of the best investments in the (other) world."

"And you are to keep yourself impoverished, in order to pay my debts!"

"'Parts and poverty' are as good a *recipe* for the making of a physician as of a lawyer."

Constance could not take this cheerful view of the pecuniary part of the business; and perhaps it was well for her that she could not; for her mortification and anxiety on this point served as a counter-irritant to pangs much more acute. When sensitiveness returns to a paralyzed part of the conscience, it is sometimes with intense anguish,—anguish proportioned both to the general constitutional sensitiveness of the patient, and likewise to the length of time that the numbness has lasted, allowing more or less numerous and grievous wounds to be unconsciously inflicted there.

We put an error into our lives carelessly and thought-lessly, as we sometimes do a poison into our bodies; and it works. Then, if we find it out in time, and are wise, we send for the physician, and he saves us; but it may be so as by fire. We take it for granted, that our fellow-beings are chattels; it follows naturally that, thinking no harm, we treat them as chattels; and then, sooner or later,—God grant that it may be soon, and not too late, for them or for us,—we hear in the cool,—chilling our blood,—of some awful day, the voice of God, saying unto us, "Where art thou? Where is thy brother?" and we know not what to answer!

Intentionally cruel, Constance had not been; but she was utterly ignorant of the black side of slavery; and, as we have heard her say with the characteristic candor in which no one could excel her, she had little or no sense of duty due from her to her fellow-beings,

3*

until taught it by Roman Catholic discipline. Roman Catholic discipline taught her many good lessons as regarded her outward life, and some as regarded her inner; but,—I cannot tell how far her experience in this respect was, or was not, peculiar,—she had, under that discipline, been exhorted to be good to others, more for her own good than theirs. Faults absolved were to her annulled and forgotten. Almost as soon as she had been actively employed as a Sister of Charity, in the service of others, to be sure, she had begun instinctively to feel for those she served, because she had a generous nature; but, ever since that time, her life had been crowded, at first with the duties, and of late with the pleasures of the day; and she had never reconsidered her rash deed. The subject of slavery, except in its political bearings, had never once taken strong hold of her mind. She had been learning, however, under Herman's influence and guidance, quite a new set of principles of universal justice, sympathy, and good will. She applied them to the simple summary of poor Jake's misery, when he presented it to her, saw her conduct, his situation, and that of his fellows, for the first time in their true light, and was utterly appalled.

Herman dared not let her sit down in quiet to brood over the past, and the possibilities of the case. He mercifully kept her as busy as he could, in dwelling upon and preparing the remedy. "You will think it best to send the poor things to Canada, Hayti, Jamaica, or Liberia, I suppose, Constance.—More shame for us, we can hardly shelter them now securely in Boston. Negro-hunters might come down upon them, some time when we were at Sea Farm or elsewhere out of the way, and make awkward mistakes under the law. The air of New England used to be like that of Old

England, which no man can breathe and be a slave ; but *nous avons changé tout cela.*—I have brought you here some pretty trustworthy reports of the condition of the negroes in all these places ; and, when you have decided which promises best, I will get you the addresses of some persons of color and condition, to whom you can write while I am away, in order, without loss of time, to concert some plans with them for your *protegés*. If I ever wished to be a rich man, it would be now, that I might take you with me, to see their poor black faces light up at the sound of your message. Part of your five hundred dollars will serve as a dowry, I hope, for poor, faithful Nance."

The wedding of Herman and Constance had to be put off, of course. No time was to be lost in righting the wronged ; and, besides, the means of the betrothed must be reduced, and their plans were unsettled. It was not impossible that the rent of even the tiny house in Pinckney Street, which they were on the point of hiring, might now be too high for them to pay. Their wedding was to be put off indefinitely.

To this, however, Clara demurred. "I have played the dog in the manger at your bidding, very obediently, Herman," she said, "and kept from you money which I could not spend myself, in my opinion quite long enough. It is time now for me to begin to have my own way. I have felt sadder than I chose to tell, at the prospect of losing you from our house ; and if I have said nothing about it hitherto, it has been only because I supposed that, if you could have a little independent establishment, it would be more agreeable to you and Constance both. If you give up that, you must come to us. There is more than room enough for us all. Edward says, that he should be particularly glad to have you. You know he always likes to be free, to go and come as he pleases; and I could not bear to be a *gêne* to him. He is afraid I should be lonely without you; and indeed I should. Think of that great house of ours half empty, and your dear, odd old room shut up. It would seem exactly as if you were dead. You must promise me that you will be married as soon as you come back, and let me make you a proper allowance, at least until you are able to stand on your own feet again. You must consider that I am getting on in life, Herman," continued Miss Clara, looking as elderly as she could, though not, with her best endeavours, quite equalling Joyce Heth in that respect; "and nothing does me so much good, or is so adapted to sooth my declining years, as having cheerful young people about me."

"Herman," said Constance, coming to him with a downcast look soon after, "have you any objection to my giving music-lessons, if I can obtain some pupils?"

He started and hesitated. Even those rare men, who can play their own sensible and spirited part in life, in the frowning faces of fashion and public prejudice, are often cowards for the women whom they love. Herman certainly had a very strong dislike to Constance's doing anything for hire. It was, notwithstanding, high-minded and spirited in her, to wish to do this; it would take up her time and thoughts; and he was not so sure as he would have been glad to be, that it was anything better than *snobbishness* in him, which made him object to her wishes. The proscribed, but unflinching patriot shrank from having his lady-love do anything, however fit in itself to be done, and desirable, which might make her lose *caste* in the eyes of the very silliest fop among her rejected suitors.

"I cannot say, that I prefer to have you give music-lessons, certainly, love," said he; "but I can admire and esteem you only the more for wishing to do so; and if I have any objection, I fear it is one which I ought to be ashamed to urge. It has become an obsolete notion among us,—thank Heaven!—that a man, in becoming a busy man, must cease to be a *gentle*man. Surely, being a busy woman, and working for yourself and me this year, as you worked last year for the poor, can make you none the less a gentlewoman."

"Would not you rather have me a useful woman *than* a gentlewoman, if I could not be both?—an honest woman, at any rate, working to pay, as far as it lies in her power, her own grievous debts to God and man?"

"You shall have my free consent to do anything that can in any degree relieve your mind, my dearest girl."

Again Clara interposed, however, when she heard of the plan. Perhaps she had some drawing-room prejudices, which she, not being a reformer by profession, did not think it incumbent upon her to try to overcome. If she had, she took an amiable way of showing them.

"I do not think that will do, at all," said she, "if you will excuse my saying so. Music in these days has to be taught as a science, almost as much as an art. You sing very beautifully yourself; but it must be a good while since you have taken any lessons, Constance; and, before you attempt to give them, I think you should have a few from Bendelari or Corelli. Besides, there are so many Germans and professional people always in want of pupils now, that you might not be able to get any, except beginners at five or six dollars a quarter; and Herman will be back again before you have had time to earn even that. Oh, give it up, dear! I know of something else which would be much more fit for you. An acquaintance of ours,—a maiden lady, not so young as she has been, but highly respectable and not so ill-tempered, I hope, as she might be, considering her desolate situation,—is very much in want of a companion,—'salary no object.'"

"Clara!" exclaimed Herman. He thought her beside herself.

Constance colored painfully. "I am afraid," said she, in a tone of somewhat proud humility, though evidently struggling for self-mastery, "that I am hardly equal to the duties of such a place. I am afraid that I should not suit her;—and yet Herman,"—

"Oh, as to that," resumed Clara, "the duties of the place are not so very hard! All that would be required of you would be, to sit with her, or in your own room when you preferred it, to chat, work, read, and drive with her, make yourself at home, and once in a while to write to her brother at the South; and there is one respect, at least, in which no one else could suit her so well as you; for she makes it an indispensable requisite that her companion shall be—Constance Aspenwall."

"Clara!" exclaimed Herman, again, but this time in a very different tone; and Constance sprang up and threw her arms about her neck.

"I will bring you back to Mrs. Ronaldson, in time to meet Herman here on his return. Will you come, and see his home, and make it cheerful while he is gone? I shall be disappointed, and grieved, and lonely, if you will not. It is the first favor I ever asked of you, Constance. Perhaps it will be the last, if you refuse."

Constance had no inclination to refuse, since the invitation was given with cordiality so unmistakable. The arrangement relieved Herman from great anxiety on her account, by placing her under Clara's cheerful, judicious, and watchful guardianship, gave both the young ladies sincere satisfaction, and supplied the grateful Constance with an additional motive, for her hostess's sake, to strive for hope, patience, and calmness. On the morning which was to have been that of their wedding-day, Herman and Constance took leave of one another, and went northward and southward on their several ways, she often taking from her pocket-book, in car or steamboat, and stealthily poring over, a little sheet of note-paper, which Herman had slipped into her hand when he pressed it for the last time. It bore but the following sentences in his hastiest hand-writing :

"The moment at which we first open our eyes, to the precipices over which we have been walking in our sleep, is not the beginning of our danger, but (unless we allow our terror to get the better of us, and go wild at the sight), of our safety.

"The moment at which we begin to say, 'I have sinned! God be merciful to me a sinner,' is not the moment at which He begins to be our Judge, but our Pardoner.

"The moment at which we begin to set our faces against the wrongs which we have done, is not that at which God begins to set His face against us, but at which He places Himself at our side to fight for us.

"So soon as we set ourselves to work, heart and hand, to slay and undo our sin, so soon, if not before, does He set Himself to work, not to undo us, but to spare and to save. As a surgeon he may wound us, but, if we are submissive and trustful, only to heal and to cure. He will pity, sustain, and comfort us, under our wholesome and needful sufferings, as a father.

"Of all the adversaries, which stand between us and heaven's gate, there is none more terrible than Remorse. The soul who can put him down before the Lord, can put down Satan. Wrestle with the dark angel when he comes upon you; and wrestle on, though the night about you be black as the grave, and as long as time. Let him not subdue you, nor yet let him go until he has left you the blessing of repentance unto salvation, not to be repented of. Then the morning, which dawns upon your weary soul, shall be as the morning of the resurrection."

CHAPTER XVIII.

THE KNIGHT'S QUEST.

"I know, this quest of yours, and free intent,
Was all in honor and devotion meant
To the great mistress of" * * *   Milton.

IN a very few days, a very handsome and graceful young horseman was trotting down a long, wide avenue between two rows of gigantic trees, with glossy dark-green, oval, myrtle-like leaves, and long, trailing, hoary beards of moss. As he supposed, they were live-oaks. No one of them need have feared to measure its dimensions with those of the Great Elm on Boston Common. Between their huge, brown, boled trunks and spreading boughs, he looked out to see the magnolias look in from beyond, sprinkled with blossoms like large snow-balls, as if Winter had come down from the pole, to cannonade Summer in her headquarters. These blossoms smelt as if each great porcelain cup held and hid a lemon and spices, stealthily filling the air with a sort of ethorial punch. Everything was on a large scale, as if Nature were showing herself to him through a magnifying-glass. On one side, the grounds seemed boundless. On the other, at a considerable distance, a faint pink line was drawn by a hedge of most *multi-flowering* multi-flora roses. Every copse, clump, and tree, seemed bursting and steaming with bloom, fragrance, and song,—strange to the stranger, yet luxuriantly and infinitely sweet and beautiful;—

and from one dark cloud of foliage to another, the red-birds flashed like lightning. The scene would have seemed Eden, if the little stray cherubs playing bo-peep and hide-and-seek, here and there and to and fro, from thicket to thicket, had been white instead of black; but perhaps they were dyed, to put them into mourning for Adam's fall. This paradise was Roche-maurice Park.

As Herman drew rein before a large, old-fashioned, and rather handsome house, a fine-looking and well-dressed negro man appeared at the door, came out with a bow, and took his horse as a matter of course. Another of similar appearance stood within the thresh-old, respectfully awaiting his pleasure, and, on his inquiring for Colonel Rochemaurice, led the way into a small, cool, dark parlour, set him a chair, took his letter of introduction and card, and noiselessly van-ished.

As the blindness of the sudden change from sunshine to shade left his dazzled and dust-dimmed eyes, he saw himself in a room carpeted with neat straw-matting, and tastefully fitted up with the lightest furniture,— Venetian chairs, a lacquered cane-bottomed Chinese settee, on which lay a guitar with a necklace of broad blue ribbon, and two or three small *tepoys*, on which were pretty little work-baskets, such as are braided by the slaves, and a glass of moss-roses. All the windows reached from the ceiling to the floor, and were hung with sky-blue, and wrought white muslin, curtains; all but one were darkened by closed blinds; that one was opened upon a piazza, through which came the sound of pleasant, well bred voices. Two of these,—those of a young lady and gentleman who passed and repassed, side by side, without seeing him,—were chatting together; two others,—those apparently of very young girls sitting or standing out of sight,—were warbling, half *sotto voce*, but in clear, sweet tones, a duet from *Semiramide*.

In a few moments, Colonel Rochemaurice entered the room,—a tall and handsome man of about fifty-five, whose presence might have been stately and imposing, if he had not taken too much, and too evident, care and pains to make it so, as if, through too much of his past life, his chief occupation had been to play the *grand seigneur*. He welcomed Herman courteously, if not so cordially as he might have done before he knew his business, or as he did other visiters in the course of the morning, begged that he would make his house his home for as long a time as he found it convenient to remain in the neighbourhood, insisted on sending for his baggage to the railroad station where he had left it, and had him shown at once to a pretty and commodious chamber, to make a hasty *toilette* before breakfast.

The party at breakfast consisted, besides the Colonel, of his wife, a dignified and courteous hostess, who had evidently been handsome in her time, and had still a striking, though a faded and rather languid, face, her two sons Harry and Temple, tall, unformed Nimrods of fifteen and sixteen, three daughters, apparently about fifteen, fourteen, and ten years old, and one more guest besides Herman, a young man near his own age, named Harrington.

The young ladies were, as well as their mother, well-grown, graceful, and gracious. The two oldest were not, however, beautiful; though all three had rich dark hair well-arranged, and fine black eyes. The eldest, Jane, was evidently much admired by Mr. Harrington, and somewhat monopolized by him. Alice, the second, was pensive, and looked ill. Rose, the youngest, had a round, glowing, laughing, gipsy face, with all the rich golden *morbidezza* and deep crimson of a Melancthon peach, a little saucy *nez retroussé*, that looked as if it was turned up at, and destined to upturn, every absurdity of every sort which came in her way through life, and leave it comic-side uppermost to the derision of all beholders, and, presiding over all, a broad, full, and rather high forehead, with the machinery lurking within it for a quick startling frown, which promised stormy weather for Miss Rose, if not for her neighbours, so soon as the little playful brains behind it should begin to work in earnest.

At present, her spirits were boundless. She chattered, ostensibly to her next neighbour, Alice. Herman, and her brother Temple, laughed. As natural consequences, she chattered more, and her mother chid her.

" Why, mamma, Dr. Arden told a very good story and made me, and all of us, laugh. Then, in common gratitude, it was necessary that some of us should make him laugh, in return. None of the rest of you undertook it; so that I was obliged to, for the honor of Rochemaurice. I succeeded, too; at least, thus much is certain, Dr. Arden laughed. Now, if he did not laugh at what I said, he must have laughed at what some of you did; for you must own, that none of you said anything at all diverting. I am sure he could not be so rude. I will put it to him. Dr. Arden, did you laugh at the boys, or at Jenny and Mr. Harrington, or papa and mamma, or at the little story I told my sister Alice, which nobody else needed to listen to, by the way, who did not like it ?"

" At your story, certainly, Miss Rose."

"There, mamma!—there, papa!—Now, don't you think it is desirable that I should go on,—until some of the rest of you become as entertaining as I,—for the honor of Rochemaurice Park?"

"No, Rose, hush!" said her father. "For the honor of Rochemaurice Park, I shall send you to the school-room, if you give us any more of your chattering. Good little girls should be seen, and not heard. Besides, good talkers know that when they have said a good thing, that is the best time for them to stop talking; for then people will take it for granted, that they could have said many more."

Rose frowned, pouted, and muttered, half playfully, half naughtily. She had broken the ice thoroughly, however, and stirred up all the grown-up members of the circle into mingling ingredients of one agreeable dish of chat, below which Herman, who chanced to sit next to her, could catch an under current of her murmurs, addressed to the silent Alice:

"And so I could have said a great many more good things, if they would only have let me. If it was quite respectful, I should like to say, How absurd! what nonsense! to put a stop to me, and compel me to waste the best years of my life in obscurity, while I have time, strength, and inclination, to make myself agreeable. In four or five years, all may be changed; I may have a lover, like Jenny, or a tooth-ache, like you, and be utterly engrossed by it. Nobody will ever know then how many droll and sensible things I might have said, if they had not been forever lost by my being nipped in the bud, by that nasty old rule, that people must never say anything at all till they are too old and stupid to say anything worth hearing. All my experience goes to prove, that persons spend the first years of their children's lives in teaching them *to* talk, and the next in teaching them not to. That is very unrational. It is putting the cart before the horse. It would be better not to teach them at all, until they are ready to hear them," &c.

By the time that the excellent coffee, rice-rolls, batter-cakes, broiled quails, cold venison-pasty, and orange-marmalade, were dispatched, Herman's social qualities had been so agreeably brought out, that there was a kind of amicable contest for the possession of him during the morning.

"Put him up at auction, papa, and sell him to the highest bidder," suggested Rose, forgetting her rebuff; "he's a *brunette*, and a Northerner come among us to see our institutions. Let's give him a chance to judge of them for himself."

"So be it," said her father, with whom she was evidently a great pet, and a privileged person; "Dr. Arden, if you will give me the pleasure of your company on a tour of inspection over my plantation, I have a saddle-horse to offer you, neither too tame for a young rider, nor too hard for a weary traveller."

"And I, Dr. Arden," said Mrs. Rochemaurice, with her engaging smile, "will offer for you a seat in my *barouche*, and a drive through the pine-woods; and if you were one of my sons, I should suggest to you, that you must have had fatigue and exposure enough already, under this burning sky, particularly as you are not accustomed to it."

"But if he was one of your sons, mamma," said good-humoured, merry Temple Rochemaurice, "he would undutifully laugh at such a suggestion, as I do now, and also, as I do now, say that he was going out into the woodland directly with one of my dogs, and a capital fowling-piece, Dr. Arden, that I got from New York only the day before yesterday." ·

"If you'll come with me down to the river," said Harry, gruffly, "you can have a fishing-pole, a skiff, and a nigger."

"Now, young ladies," said Colonel Rochemaurice, "Who bids more? Going,—going,—gone!"

"No, not gone, by any means, papa!" cried little Rose. "No fair; because I had to wait for my sisters to speak first, according to propriety and the rights of primogeniture. Since they say nothing, I will speak, first for them and then for myself. Dr. Arden, if you will go to ride with Jenny and Mr. Harrington, [who had just before left the room together,] you may have the satisfaction of much usefulness in finding their way for them; for they are strangely apt to lose it; [her mother very properly shook her head at her; and, afraid of being again stopped, she hurried on.] If you will sit on the piazza, and lounge, Alice will lend you a rocking-chair, a fan, and a smelling-bottle; and, if Miss Swayshon will let her leave the school-room window open, you may have the further pleasure and profit of hearing her repeat correctly all the dates from the Deluge down to the battle of New Orleans, and pouring her pensive soul out in mental arithmetic. If you will put yourself into my hands, I will take you to see my tame mocking-bird's nest, in the orange-tree under the Pride-of-China. You won't touch the eggs?"

"Among so many tempting proposals," said Herman, smiling, "I am really in the condition of the sailor, who was asked by Lady Hamilton whether he would take brandy and water, grog, or punch. I can hardly do better than follow his example, and try to secure as many good things as I can. The drive, and shooting, and fishing, I must deny myself, I fear; but, if there is time while your horses are saddling, Colonel Rochemaurice, I should be very glad to run down to the mocking-bird's nest with Miss Rose."

"Plenty of time, sir; time's a plentiful commodity with us, sad idle Southrons, planters and gentlemen. I will let one of my servants lead your horse down after you, and join you there myself."

"And after I have seen the mocking-bird, and the plantation, I should like very much to sit upon your piazza, Miss Alice, until I go, which ought to be very soon, I am sorry to say."

Little Rose was certainly not altogether an agreeable child. She might have been a very disagreeable one, if her over-shrewdness and forwardness of speech had not been recommended to mercy by a manner of great natural archness, and spontaneous glee and grace. Her peculiarities were, however, as amusing to strangers, as they were embarrassing to those whose business it was to keep her in order, and as they were likely to make trouble for herself; and Herman, always ready to be fond of children, was not sorry to have a further opportunity of making acquaintance with his droll little intended cousin. If he could have penetrated into the truly tragic future of those two little girls,—the tragic present, which was even now pent agonizing within the innocent breast of one of them,—that shining, singing, blooming morning's walk, would have had for him a deeper and a darker interest. Rose caught up, and tossed on, a broad-brimmed hat of yellow straw, which made a golden halo around her golden face, darted through the long window, and cleared the steps of the piazza at a bound.

"Will not Miss Alice come, too?" said Herman, looking back, as he followed her, at the pale, drooping young creature, who had sunk already into her little chair on the piazza, under the closing morning-glories, in what seemed to be a habitual attitude with her, with her elbow on the arm and her head upon her hand.

"To be sure! she must!—I forgot!—Come, Alice, darling. It's so cool this morning, it won't hurt you." Little fiery salamander! To Herman, the breeze of the yet early morning,—it was not yet nine o'clock,—seemed already like the panting from the open door of an oven. Rose snatched off the hat from her thick curls, (rich brown, with a twinkle like gold-dust in them,) more quickly than she had put it on, and, reaching up, clapped it on her passive sister's head with a sort of *tom-boyish*, but protecting kindliness, saying in explanation to Herman, "She got left by the boat over-night, last summer, with mammy, at our rice-plantation; and we think that the malaria must have affected her. She did not die at once, as most people would have; but she has been half dead ever since. It would never do to take her out in this sun without a hat."

"But you, Miss Rose!—surely it will not do for you either. Let us wait while you get another hat or a parasol."

"Not I. If the sun struck me, he's seen enough of me to know that I should strike back again.* We are not non-resistants down here in South Carolina." On she danced, looking like the sun's own daughter, while

---

*A late omnibus-driver, who had a peculiarly roseate disc of his own, was said by a wag to have probably owed his immunity from sun-strokes, during a long career of professional usefulness, to the sun's apprehensions of a retaliation on his part.

4

Herman, taking off his own hat, vainly tried to screen her with it. "Oh, Dr. Arden, you must not do that? It is very imprudent for a foreigner!—Oh, I know what I'll do! Here, Rafe, Rafe!"

Herman thought that she was calling a dog; but, at the word, out ran a fine boy of sixteen or seventeen, from one of the brick offices near which they were passing. He had light hazel eyes, straight hair and regular features, and was almost as well dressed as the young Rochemaurices. Glancing at his ruddy, animated, and intelligent face, Herman could hardly believe that he was a slave. He stood still when he came within a few paces of Rose, silent, but eying her with the same sort of half-respectful, half-affectionate, amused admiration, with which an Athenian stripling might have regarded the state of the little Titania.

"Rafe," cried Rose, with sharp good-humour, "come, be quick, now! Get me some branches of those rose-trees."

"A *bouquet*, miss?"

"Why, no. Don't be stupid. Don't you see? I want them for a hat."

The boy smiled, nodded, took out a jack-knife, and began to cut away to the right and left, among the trees;—as they might well be called, for they rose several feet above his head and Herman's, on each side of the path through which they were walking.

"Come; don't wait to cut down the whole arbour."

Rafe smiled again, and came forward with the best of the boughs which he had cut.

"Why, there are not half enough. I want at least a dozen."

He selected and handed more.

Rose grasped them, pricked herself, dashed them

down on the ground, pinched her finger, looked at it, and put it in her mouth, mumbling, "Hadn't you sense enough to know I would prick myself, if you didn't take the thorns off for me?" He immediately began to do so, without sparing his own hands, and looked very sorry. "Never mind, poor fellow," said Rose, relenting, smiling, and letting the wounded finger go, to take back the disgraced roses. "There! These will do beautifully."

Beautifully they *did*,—crimson roses with petals of mere translucent gauze,—very spirits of roses, looking as if the fiery light and heat had burnt all the earthy material part out of them, leaving nothing but form and color behind.

"You may carry them for me, while I weave." It was said, and received, as a favor granted. The boy, apparently quite comforted, walked assiduously, at Rose's side but just behind her, with the best specimens of his flowery burden carefully kept within reach of her little backward-seeking hand. In five minutes, she had deftly woven the green leafy branches into an oblong screen of basket-work, which she tied under her chin by the ends of two of the longer twigs; and on she skipped, warbling a little *impromptu* song:

> "Rose among the roses,
>   Rose without a thorn,
> Dancing with the posies,
>   In the merry morn."

The boy still lingered irresolutely, gazing wistfully after her, with the refuse of her flowers in his hands. Looking round and noticing his expression, the little despot said condescendingly, "Rafe, if you can leave your work, you may as well follow us. I may want something more." Then she sang and then she spoke again: "Does my cousin Constance wear a *bloomer?*"

"Why, no," said Herman, as well as he could, in fits of laughter at the question ; "What could make you think of that?"

"I thought all the women did at the North."

"Why, Rosebud!" expostulated the hitherto silent Alice, "don't you remember Mrs. Towdie and Miss Fybbes, who were here last winter from the North? Did not they dress like any other ladies?"

"I do not know, I'm sure. I was too much taken up with their hypocrisy to notice their clothes."

"Have you learned already how to tell hypocrites from other people, Miss Rose? How?"

"Oh," said she, shaking her curly head oracularly, "I know a way."

"Won't you teach it to me? Do."

"Why, papa says," said this *enfant terrible*, with the solemn and confidential air of one obligingly initiating a proselyte into a mystery, "that everybody north of Mason and Dixon's line is either a rank abolitionist or a hypocrite, and they'll come here,—if they are hypocrites, I mean,—and tell us that our institutions are all right and beautiful ; and then when they go back to the North, if they want to be sent to Congress or anything, they'll tell the ignorant common people that they hate slavery, and mean to put a stop to it if only they can get to Washington ; and when they get there, they let the Southern gentlemen twist them round their fingers, and do just as they like with them, till it's election-time again ; and then they go home and abuse us once more. Or if they go abroad, and want the English aristocracy to take notice of them and invite them about, they'll talk as eloquently against our institution as the father of lies himself, papa said ; but when they want us,—the aristocracy of *our* country,—to attend to them, they'll talk for it. Now, those Yankee ladies were all the time fawning, and wheedling, and mincing, to mamma, in their little pinched voices, from the first day they came, about our servants being so happy, and our being so good to them! So they are happy; and so we are good to 'them, to be sure; but what should strangers know about that? 'Tisn't very likely we would cuff them about in the parlour before people, at any rate, unless we wanted to have gladi—gladiatorious combats for the amusement of our guests; as they used to in my Roman history. So I know they were hypocrites,—*dough-faces*, Harry calls them;—and that's a great deal worse than being an abolitionist even ; and that's the reason we like you so much better than we did them."

The boy was still following close behind them like a dog, unnoticed and apparently forgotten, but not, Herman believed, unobservant; for at this time he began to remark, that he breathed quick and hard, though they were walking slowly.

"You are a natural enemy," continued the little speaker, her discourse taking a new turn; "and yet you see how generously we trust you and treat you. We receive you in a Christian spirit, and heap coals of fire on your head, as Roderick Dhu did King James. Papa even told me not to tell, that you were an abolitionist, for fear of your getting into some trouble,— like Mr. Hoar did,—while you were under our protection. But there would be no use in your asking our people to cut our throats; for they'd never think of such a thing for a moment; *would* you, Rafe?"

"I'd cut my own throat sooner than yours, Miss Rose," said the page.

"Rosy, Rosy!" cried Alice, her pale face growing paler and her wild eyes, wilder, "*don't* talk of such things!"

."No, no! pray do not! Never do!" said Herman; "and you are altogether mistaken in thinking me your enemy. I am your natural friend, if you will allow me to call myself so. Do not you know, that I am going to be your cousin?—And so you thought that all the women at the North wore *bloomers?*" continued he, eager to change the subject.

"Yes; Miss Swayshon don't to be sure; but then, she knew, when she had her clothes made, that she was coming down here among ladies and gentlemen,—I beg your pardon, Southern ladies and gentlemen, I mean.—I always wanted to ask her what she wore at home; but I was afraid it might hurt her feelings; and we are always taught to be very careful not to hurt the feelings of our inferiors."

"Is Miss Swayshon your inferior, Miss Rose?"

"Oh, yes!   Don't you know? She's the governess. A *bloomer* mightn't be a bad thing——to climb trees in.   Perhaps, when I am grown up, I will set the fashion of wearing them among ladies."

"Why, you will not wish to climb trees, *then;* shall you?"

"Oh, yes; all my life. I will go on as I've begun with perfect consistency. If I do break my neck when I get awkward and tall, I will have a short life and a merry one.—Papa said something about you to-day. Do you want to hear what it was?"

"No, thank you, Miss Rose; not from you. Listening to papa's talk from papa's little daughter, would be like listening to it through papa's little key-hole, would it not? Don't you know the old saying about listeners? I'm afraid to hear! I shall have to stop my ears."

"No, no! Pooh, pooh!" cried Rose, in a tone adapted to make any such precaution quite fruitless. "It was not anything bad. As if I would tell it, if it was! He only said you were 'gentlemanly enough to do credit to any part of the country.' He was 'glad, if Cousin Constance must marry a Northern man, that she had the good taste, at least, to pick out a gentle-man.' So there are really gentlemen at the North?"

"A few," said Herman, smiling. "Oh, yes, a good many."

"Well, but—you won't be offended?"

"Indeed, I hope not. I am sure you are too gen-erous to affront an unarmed man, at your mercy."

"Certainly," said she, solemnly; "but, oh!" and her whole countenance changed to a joyous sparkle, "I'll tell you what! You sha'n't be unarmed! You shall have a pop-gun! Oh, can you shoot with a pop-gun? Oh, what fun it will be! I can shoot with a pop-gun! Rafe, a pop-gun, directly, for Dr. Arden,— two pop-guns! and one for me. Oh, we'll fight a duel instantly,—how glorious!—and I will be the champion of the South; and you shall fight for the honor of the North; and the one that gets popped the first shall serve the other forever; and we'll settle the whole dif-ficulty on the spot, in five minutes."

Herman made a very long face. "I hope you will excuse me, and not consider me deficient in courage, Miss Rose," said he; "but in order to make the settlement final, it strikes me that we ought to get the whole South and the North to agree to the arrange-ment, before we peril our lives in such a conflict;—I should not wish to throw mine away in vain;—and,

the fact is, that my principles are altogether opposed
to duelling; and—and I think by the time we have
seen that mocking-bird's nest, Colonel Rochemaurice
will be waiting for me."

Rose pouted, and turned down another walk.
"We've gone the wrong way," said she, recovering
herself presently. "I forgot about the nest."

"Something else we have forgotten, too. What was
that you wished to say to me, about Northern gentlemen?"

"Oh, they can't be quite like the gentlemen here;
for they let the mean common people get affairs into
their own hands, and choose each other even to go to
Congress, papa says. Now *we*, I mean he, and my
brothers when they're old enough, and the other gentlemen, make them speeches and give them a treat at
election-time, and tell them whom to vote for; and
they have to mind and do it; because, if they didn't,
we would take our patronage right away, and then, in
a hard season, they couldn't get anything to eat sometimes,—much less to drink;—and so, in this district,
the Representative has always been an Aspenwall, or
a Rochemaurice, or a Clement, for a good many centuries, I believe. And then, you know, our working-
people here are almost all of them slaves; and we
never think of letting them vote, any more than our
cows and horses. Here's this Rafe, now, for instance,
he never can vote; though he's cleverer already than a
great many gentlemen, if that was all. Some grown-
up gentlemen can't even read; but he can write, and
cipher, and draw most beautifully; and the boys' tutor
is teaching him mathematics and chemistry,—though
it's a great secret, because it's against the law; so
please don't tell, will you?—and by and by, if he be-

haves well, papa will have him taught mechanics, and put him over our factories.—Does my Cousin Constance speak in conventions?"

Herman went off again in a second series of spasms, but managed in the midst of them to answer, that she had never done so as yet, and to ask whether public speaking was another Northern custom which Miss Rose Rochemaurice proposed to introduce among the ladies of Carolina.

"I have not made up my mind," returned she, contemplatively. "I am fond of it myself. You see that stump of a live-oak? I used formerly to hop up on that, and address the children of the plantation, and such of our grown-up servants as I thought proper, sometimes extempore, and sometimes out of the *Class-book* I found in the garret; and it was most exciting; but the overseer went spying round the quarters, and heard the negroes talking afterwards, and said that I told them too much about liberty. It was very impertinent in him to interfere; and, if I had permitted him to join the audience, he would have heard me always explain to them most emphatically, that the passages about men only meant white men; but the matter was misrepresented to papa;—I think Harry was at the bottom of it;—and I was too proud to explain. Thus my voice was silenced; and papa even went so far as to throw the nice old *Class-book* into the fire. He gave me a new one; but there was hardly anything about liberty in it; and I didn't like it half so well, and sat down and dogs'-eared all the leaves on purpose."

The child's tongue seemed bewitched; it was impossible to keep it from dangerous topics; and Herman was relieved when the mocking-bird's nest appeared, and effected a diversion. "Here we are! Hide be-

4*

hind those orange-trees, while I see if she is at home. Put me up, Rafe." The boy bent, and held his hand low, as if to lift her on horseback. Into the palm she sprang, as light as a shuttle-cock, and up into the Pride-of China tree, and from branch to branch, among the large light plumes of lilac blossoms. She peeped down through them into the orange-tree beneath, clapped her hands in dumb show, and came down. "Now, Dr. Arden," she whispered, "you may take your turn. There's her nest, just behind that twig of orange-blossoms. She sits and smells of it, all day long. I'll call her off to get some sugar; and then you can see the eggs." She stole to a little distance, on the side of the tree opposite to that on which the party were in ambush, took a handful of sugar from her pocket, and twittered with a wonderfully exact imitation of some of the notes of the bird, which instantly flew off towards her, and,—after she had thrown aside the picturesque green head-dress, which seemed to puzzle it at first,—ate, pecking the sugar eagerly from her hand and lips. Herman forgot the nest in watching her, but was glad, notwithstanding, when her father came up with the horses and, peremptorily resisting her entreaty, that she might send Rafe for her pony and ride with them, ordered him to attend her and her sister back to the school-room.

The sun, now, was sometimes obscured by a sultry haze, and sometimes broke through again with his accumulated heat. The ride was long and somewhat tedious. Colonel Rochemaurice, however, did what in him lay to enliven it by his conversation, showing a mind highly but only superficially cultivated,—whether from a natural shallowness, or for want of the sub-soil plough of a struggling manhood, set to make its own way in the world among its struggling equals, Herman could not determine. He could easily understand, from his own sensations in this short sojourn, how easily and soon one, born to be the master of others, might cease to be the master of himself, unnerved, mentally as well as physically, in the soft languor of that delicious land, where every sight, and sound, and scent, seemed wooing him to forget his inward in his outward life, in a community where the same influences which bore directly upon his own life and character, bore upon him indirectly also through the lives and characters of his neighbours, and where Nature and Fortune knelt together at his feet, to offer him every luxury that a selfish heart could desire, unearned at any adequate price of wholesome, bracing, counteracting toil. The Colonel was well versed in the history and politics of this country, and not ill in the light literature of England, France, Italy, and Spain. He even had on exhibition some evidently favorite, but hackneyed, scraps of Latin and Greek. But he appeared to have satisfied himself, for the most part, with retaining passive impressions of the thoughts of other men, instead of being stimulated by their thoughts to think for himself. Some shrewdness he had, but little sagacity; and there was something piteous, if not pitiful, in his utter inability to turn over any subject in his mind, and see any other side of it than that which came nearest to his own interests or prejudices. His intellect had been surfeited, rather than nourished, by what it had fed upon.

Whether it promotes one person's welfare to appropriate to himself, by force, all the leisure of ten persons, much further than it would for him to appropriate to himself, if he could, all the sleep and food of ten persons, we shall not now stop to consider. But Herman, in listening to his host's narrow, worn-out, and off-cast platitudes upon government and society, could not but doubt the advantage to either party of that sharp division—not of labor precisely, but rather—of labor and leisure, so highly recommended of late by certain sapient Southrons, which is to leave all of the labor on one side to a class of workers, and all of the leisure on the other, to a class of thinkers, speakers, and writers.

He doubted it still more when, leaving behind the fragrant shade of the pines, they came upon a cotton-field and the workers in it, women first,—a pack of women, working under the gentle rule of "the chivalry" of our country,—if to be plump is to be prosperous, very prosperous, if to be brutish is to be peaceful, very peaceful. They were clad in a uniform of gowns which seemed once to have been brown, but which were now grim with filth. These were restrained about their mon-strous Afrite figures by two bands, one passing round the middle of their thick waists, and another, just above the hips. Between these two bands, their skirts were pulled up, so as to make a circular pouch about their bodies, and to exhibit to the best advantage below their stumpy, elephantine legs, swathed in *bocking* or bagging, tied on with a string wound carelessly round and round in spiral lines. Very heavy, muddy shoes were upon their feet. On their heads they had handkerchiefs; and in their mouths, tobacco-pipes. Of their countenances, we will say no more than that they were in most perfect keeping with their attire, so that their *toilette* had one, at least, of the highest merits that the *toilette* can have.

Ditch-mud, for manure, had been cast upon the

ground among them in large heaps. Some of them were carrying this about in baskets upon their heads; and some, in their aprons. As they threw their loads down in smaller piles, their companions spread it upon the soil with their hoes; and one very untidy person, who had probably lost or broken hers, used her fingers for the purpose. Anything more disgusting, more hopelessly discouraging than these women altogether,—their employment, their condition, and their expression,—Herman had never imagined. Could nothing be done for them? What could be done? Yet Christ had died for them! What were his followers doing for them? Nothing but this? Could nothing better be found to do, than to cram their greedy bodies with coarse plenty, and starve their spirits?—to keep their heavy limbs safely at work, and their heavy brains safely idle?

But a good deal no doubt depends, after all, upon the view which one takes of things. Herman, looking upon these degraded beings as human beings, was mortified. Colonel Rochemaurice, on the other hand, looking upon them as prize-cattle, was gratified. After giving an order to the black driver, who was superintending them with much vigilance and efficiency, he turned to Herman for his approbation.

"They look well, do they not?"

"Very plump, indeed," said our *cornered* hero, just escaping the utterance of what, in his school-boy days, he might not improbably have termed a "plumper."

"I am always glad," returned the Colonel, flattered and complacent, "to have an opportunity of exhibiting my plantation, to any liberal and unprejudiced gentleman from your section of the country. A wise man takes nothing for granted. I require no one to approve of our institutions, before seeing how they work. You will excuse my saying even, that I doubt the sincerity of those who profess to do so. But the fact is, that servitude, though not abstractly the best condition in the world, is relatively the best for the blacks. You see for yourself how care-free and happy they are, according to their capacity for happiness."

He waited for an assent; but Herman's spur happened to tickle his very spirited horse just then; and he occupied himself wholly, for a minute or two, in subduing it.

"These field-hands are, by nature, utterly incapable of self-government. They will work only upon compulsion. [Unchristian souls! unwilling to 'do good, hoping for nothing again!'] They have no morals,—no gratitude. With all their wants generously supplied, they'll steal even from me, their natural protector!" Rapacious beasts!—to covet part of the lion's share and steal it from the lion!

Herman had an inquiring mind; and it asked him, just then, whether the balance of gratitude was, on the whole, due to Colonel Rochemaurice from the negroes, for his giving back to them a small proportion of their earnings, in the shape of a quantity of clothing, coffee, vegetables, bacon, and molasses, sufficient to keep them in a good condition to toil for him, or due from Colonel Rochemaurice to the negroes, for doing all his work for him without wages. He was not fond of harsh language, and was not inclined to call the Colonel a thief, especially as he did not believe that the Colonel's conscience called him one. In judging of the conduct of individuals, particularly in barbarous or semi-barbarous regions and times, great allowances should always be made for the moral standard held up to individuals by custom and legislation. A Spartan gentleman, under the laws of Laconia, might steal, and still be, in his own estimation and that of all his compeers, except those of them who had an experimental knowledge of the evils of his practices, a very honest fellow. Still, it is a bad rule, even of mercy or charity, that does not work both ways. If Herman did not convict the Colonel of robbery for taking the negroes' services without their leave, neither could he, the negroes for taking the Colonel's rice, chickens, or cotton, without his leave. If he thought that he had a right to help himself to everything that they had, perhaps they thought, that they had a right to help themselves to some things that he had. The human soul is subject to delusions of all sorts. Let us deal with them leniently, but impartially.

"A great deal is said," continued Colonel Rochemaurice in his studiously modulated voice, to which the first beginning of the tremulousness of age merely gave an added vibratory richness, "at the North, about the wanton cruelties practised upon the negroes in slavery. Such things, doubtless, may occur from time to time; but allow me to assure you, that they belong merely to the abuse of the system, not to the use nor necessity. [What a pity that all negroes under abusive masters could not be made aware of that fact, poor ignorant creatures! What a comfort it would be to them, when smarting under the lash, steel, or fire!] I dare say you know some masters and mistresses at the North, who would treat their servants with undue severity, if they had them completely at their mercy; as I do not attempt to deny that I know of some here, who do treat their servants with undue severity. [The Colonel appeared to lay great stress upon this argument; though what it went to prove, except that human nature was the same everywhere, and that servants could not safely be left completely at the mercy of masters and mistresses anywhere, Herman could not divine.] But undue severity defeats itself. Firmness—firmness is what is wanted. Like Lord Collingwood," said the Colonel, with a grand air of magnanimity, "I never forgive a first offence. [Again the inquiring mind was so impertinent as to inquire, on whose side *was* the first offence,—the slaves' or the master's.] My hands understand this, and act accordingly. I count them by the hundred; but sometimes as many as three or four weeks go by without a single whipping."

Herman's horse gave a great curvet and bound. The old Colonel turned his calm, elderly face upon him, saw him extremely pale, and apparently thought him frightened; for, with a little good-humoured contempt in his tone, he said, "Timour does seem restless this morning. My sons do not usually consider him vicious; though he is spirited; but the young gentlemen here are bred up in the saddle; and you, perhaps, are not accustomed to riding. We shall be at the quarters presently; and, if you wish, we will alight and wait there for a short time; while one of the boys will ride your horse home, and bring you down one of my little daughters' ponies. They are perfectly gentle and safe."

"I thank you. I like a high-mettled horse; and this appears to me as fine a one as I ever mounted, both as to blood and breaking."

"He is, and has a right to be;" and the Colonel rambled tranquilly off to a dissertation upon his pedigree and history, without the slightest suspicion of having said anything disgusting, or, indeed, otherwise than highly agreeable.

They passed the men and boys, at work in different fields, of whom it is sufficient to say that they looked,—except some of the drivers,—like worthy sires, sons, and husbands, of the females already described, brutish, gross, and innately soulless generally, Herman would have thought, if his zoological studies had not taught him, that there is an economical tendency in Nature to obliterate any unused and therefore useless organ, and so led him to suspect that even the soul, unfed and unexercised, may, for a time at least, appear to die out of a man.

They came to the cabins of the largest negro-quarters. One of these was the nursery; where a very good-humoured old jetty giantess was superintending the united babyhood of half of the plantation. Here, at last, was a gleam of hope and happy suggestion! Here, at last, was a woman, and she had been a field-hand, too, who looked and seemed somewhat womanly! She was engaged in a womanly occupation also; and was not that the secret, in part, of her kindly, intelligent look, her frank, unleering smile,—her ready speech and motion? She was trusted; she was busy, for hours every day, under her own direction. She had to think, as well as work, to rule as well as to obey. She loved the ebon babies, evidently; and they loved her.

They, too, looked human, as yet. How would it be with them thirty or forty years hence, when they had been in their turn for some time used as breathing ploughs and harrows or, at the best, as cattle? No matter. The suns and snows of this weary world are apt to fade the morning-glories of most of us, however sheltered, more or less, sooner or later. Why should not negroes be turned out to bear the brunt? When the common lot of humanity must, at any rate, be so hard, what use to try to soften theirs?

Herman, however, was young and Utopian; and he did think that he should like to try the harmless experiment of taking those little children, rolling in the dust or on the piazza in front of the cabin, or sitting placidly imbibing their thumbs in the pen, (a sort of human hen-coop, in which those that could not yet stand alone were kept from crawling into harm's way,) and distributing them among their cow-like mothers to let them taste freely of the wholesome sweetness of maternity, and kiss, and babble tender nonsense, and fondle, at their fill, and to see whether they could not learn of these yet unperverted creatures, fresh from the pure hands of the Creator, to smile innocently again, and hope, and love, and trust. He longed to let them become acquainted with their children, and fill for future days that domestic sweetmeat store-closet of dear little infantine sayings and doings, preserved in parental remembrance, which must be stocked for life in the season of those sayings and doings, or not at all. He longed to take away their hoes, put needle-books and scissors into their awkward paws, give them back the work which God gave wives and mothers to do,— the care of their own little ones, husbands and selves, —and see if, by the natural attempt to do it, some kind of a natural faculty, to enable them to do it, might not be developed in them. He longed, at least, to make some approach to setting the solitary again in families, to break up those monotonous assorted squads of men by themselves, boys by themselves, women by themselves, and girls by themselves, and to let daughters work beside their mothers, helping one another and cheering one another, and sons by their fathers. Still, undoubtedly, if father and mother, brothers, sisters, and babies, are allowed to assemble together only when their eyes are too sleepy to see one another, or on a holiday or at a dance, when there are a good many other things and people for them to see, they will be much the less likely to become dependant upon one another, or to form imprudent attachments to one another.

" On most large plantations, whether of rice or cotton, in Eastern Georgia and South Carolina," says Olmsted, " nearly all ordinary and regular work is performed *by tasks*. * * * These tasks certainly would not be considered excessively hard by a Northern laborer ; and, in point of fact, the more industrious and active hands finish them often by two o'clock. * * * In nearly all ordinary work, custom has settled the extent of the task, and it is difficult to increase it. * * * In fact, it is looked upon in this region as a proscriptive [prescriptive?] right of the negroes to have this incitement to diligence offered them. * * * Notwithstanding this, I have heard a man assert, boastingly, that he made his negroes habitually perform double the customary tasks."*

So much as this, Colonel Rochemaurice did not do. Higher motives apart, he was vain of his administrative and versatile powers. He was proud to show, how wonderfully it was possible for him to combine the accomplishments of the scholar, the gentleman, and the planter. He wished to raise the largest crops of any one in Carolina, to be sure ; but he also wished to display the finest stock of negroes. To see them look sickly, haggard, and over-worked, would have been a proof of bad management, and a mortification to him.

---

* " A Journey in the Seaboard Slave States," p. 436, *et ante.*

"But what would you have, sir?" said he, one day after dinner, to an old classmate, when reminiscences of boyhood and an extra glass of his rare *Sillery*,—he seldom took an extra glass of anything,—had made him genial and playful; "A negro is never happy but when he's sleeping or eating, and never out of mischief but when he's sleeping, eating, or working. Now I know to a nicety,—I've made a study of these things,—just how much he can work without injuring himself; and I make him work as much as he can; and then he has a fine appetite, and eats all the food he can get; and then he is drowsy, and sleeps all the time he can get." ·

In the meanwhile, while Herman was making the reflections which gave rise to our digression, the Colonel was surveying the children, with his critical *connoisseur* eye. He asked the old woman whether they were all well, and was informed that they were "All peart, 'ceptin jus dat dar, 'sleep in dat corner dar,—Ben's Bess' baby, mas'r. She powerful fractious wid her teeth. Got one a-comin now, mos' big as she head. Reckon she gettin she secon ones fus,—does so! Squeal mos' dis yer whole mornin wid it, poor little nigger!"

The Colonel dismounted, gave his horse's rein to the old woman, turned up his cuffs daintily, strode to the slumbering child, picked it up by a handful of the back of its frock, as some persons do kittens by the skin at the back of their necks, turned it over, and set it up in a sitting posture on the piazza, not violently, but with as business-like a disregard to its shrieks of fright and anger as if he had been a dog-fancier, and it, a little puppy. Holding the back of its head firmly between the thumb and fore-finger of one hand, he put one finger of the other into its screaming mouth, and ascertained that one of its gums was much swelled. He released it without a word of pity or consolation, fumbled in his pockets, produced a lancet, opened it, recaptured the baby, which was scrambling off on all-fours vociferously towards mammy, lanced the gum, let the patient go once more, washed his hands, and remounted. Not a particle of unnecessary suffering had been inflicted, if we except the shock, to the nerves of a feverish child, of being suddenly awakened to find itself in the gripe of a stern and silent stranger; but there was an indescribable absence of gentleness and consideration about the whole proceeding. The Colonel's air and expression had been anything but those of a compassionate man, ministering to suffering infancy; they were simply those of an economical proprietor of live-stock, taking care of his property. Herman hoped to hear an order given to the nurse, to keep the mother in from the field, that the child might sleep upon her knees instead of the floor, at least until it was well again; but no such order was given. No, the Colonel did not appear cruel,—that is, not wantonly so, from any abstract love of cruelty,—but dry, hard, and utterly unsympathizing.

Of this, Herman had another instance presently. They rode slowly through the little village of white-washed wooden cabins, the Colonel expatiating with much pride upon their superior construction, dryness, airiness, and so-forth, but still after that odd, cold, extraordinary fashion of his, as if he had been exhibiting his own model stables, or dog-kennels, or hencoops, or anything but the habitations of his fellow-men; when, in his thorough supervision, standing up in his stirrups and leaning upon his horse's neck, to peer round a corner not easily accessible from the street which ran between the cabins, he spied a fine climbing-rose carefully trained out of sight, by some sable florist, over the further wall and window of a hut. "Halloo!" cried he, "here, mammy!" Mammy came hurrying, with the gait and general aspect of a tortoise from Brobdignag, rampant. "That rascal Joe has been at his tricks again, training creepers over his cabin. Here, take my knife, and tumble over the fence, and cut them,—close to the root, do you hear?"

"Yes, mas'r."

"I have told them before," continued he in explanation, turning to Herman with an aggrieved air, "that I will not have it; and I will not. It rots the boards. They may have as many flowers in their gardens as they can get, and not be interfered with; but this is a specimen of their habitual conduct. As many of your directions as they think they can disregard without your knowledge, they will."

Herman said nothing. What was there to say, except that it was very hard if a grown man could not arrange and decorate his own home to suit himself, without so much as receiving any directions upon the subject from another man; and where would the use have been of saying that, to Colonel Rochemaurice?

Perhaps the latter began to notice, and weary of, his silence; for, after making a few inquiries about the public schools of the North, and asking whether it did not make "the democracy" turbulent, to give them a liberal education, to which Herman, considering the question only in the abstract, answered very innocently, that he did not think, that it had that effect upon a democracy more than it did upon an aristocracy, or an oligarchy, he also held his peace.

An elegant little luncheon of sandwiches, fruits, and

whips, was served as soon as they returned to the house; and Herman, in watching the Colonel's courtly and very engaging attentions to his wife and daughters, could scarcely believe that he was the cold-blooded and seemingly heartless despot of half an hour before; but so it is. The affections of some men are like wells, stony on the outside, narrow yet deep within, not flowing forth like a river, to seek thirsty souls far and near and gladden God's earth, nor gushing up and around like a fountain in the sun, for all who seek them, but useful notwithstanding, and very precious each to some one individual or household. It is not necessary to condemn such men *in toto*, because we can only *in parvo* commend them.

Luncheon over, the gentlemen at last got to business; and the business proved not so bad as Herman had feared; for, on examination of the records of the Colonel's guardianship, it appeared that, when Constance's majority began, there were but twenty slaves on her plantation. Of these, the Colonel had bought in ten, at the sale; and he immediately, and very handsomely, offered to resign them at the rather low price at which they had been sold. Seven others, he believed, had gone to Clement Grange, the plantation adjoining his, and would also probably be given up readily; as the owner was a hereditary friend of the Aspenwalls. Herman had already gone out of his way to buy Jake and Nance, who were left in safe hands at Savannah.

Thus only Jake's wife, and an individual called Sam, surname unknown, remained unaccounted for. Colonel Rochemaurice said that the whole lot had brought only about ten thousand dollars, at auction, and might very likely be repurchased for fifteen. He feared that they had been unavoidably neglected after young Captain Aspenwall's death; though he had taken much care to employ only the best overseers he could get; rascals they were, all of them! and only the worst, who knew they were good for nothing, would sell their lives to go on a rice-plantation; and there had been a good deal of sickness and death among the negroes. It was to be regretted that Miss Aspenwall had not, after she became old enough, returned to the South to look a little after her own property.

Herman thought so too, and feared that it must be a source of regret to her through life, that she had suffered a sentimental unwillingness to return to her brother's home without him, to interfere with the discharge of her duty to her dependants. He was somewhat relieved, however, by the Colonel's adding, "yet after all, she must have left the plantation to itself for a great part of the year, at any rate, or died; and it is doubtful, how strictly the overseers would have followed the directions of so young a lady behind her back, even supposing she had known what directions to give when she was on the spot. I will send down a list of the people directly, and have them brought up here, for you to see." He copied the list, and rang the bell. Rafe appeared.

"Drive a wagon down to the east cotton-field by the river. Read these names to old Jack; and tell him to send the boys and girls up here." Rafe took the paper quietly, but with a hasty furtive glance at it, and a flushing cheek, and withdrew. In about an hour he returned, and reported that the "boys and girls" were assembled before the piazza.

"Will you speak to them there, Dr. Arden; or

would you prefer to have them in here?" said the Colonel, condescending to the whims of his guest, but involuntarily casting a compassionate look at the beautiful inlaid woods and Persian rugs of his library-floor.—With the very most benevolent dispositions towards a herd of cattle, would St. Francis himself have cared to invite them to a *conference-meeting* in a parlour?——

"There, by all means, if you please."

"Very well, sir; you shall have the field quite to yourself; but, as you do not know these people, and I do, you will pardon my suggesting to you as a friend, that, before you say anything to make them discontented with their present condition, prudence would dictate to you to consider, for your own sake, how far they are fitted for any other. I honor your benevolence, and that of my young cousin; but I think you will find,—I trust not by painful experience,—that independence can be no boon to their unfortunate race. They are, as you will discover,—I hope not too late,—mere grown-up children, essentially thriftless and *shiftless.* Without the care of a master, they will not work, and must also be without clothes and food."

"Very likely!" thought Herman; "but let us see what the effect will be, of giving each of them a master in himself. It will be *himself's* interest then to make each of them work; and if he sees that, I should not wonder if he did it, and kept each of them supplied, besides, with food and clothes quite as good as they have now at the hands of Colonel Rochemaurice, who, on his part, cannot be said to be wholly disinterested in his exertions on their behalf."

He went out to them and stood upon the steps of the piazza, with the flowery garlands that grew on

5

each side and overhead making a frame for his form,
looking kindly down upon them with his spirited young
countenance all illuminated with glad and generous
feeling. It was one of those moments which light up
a lifetime. He had never addressed such an audience
before; nor had he ever seen such an effect produced
by his most studied and eloquent oration, as was now
by the few simple words in which he told them, that
their young Mistress Constance had sent him to see
them, and to ask them whether they were well and
contented as they were, or whether they would rather
go away and be free?

They did not speak, at first. They seemed to have
no words in their old vocabulary, to express their new
emotions. But their down-cast, side-long, shy, or sullen
looks were lifted together, as if by one impulse, to his
face; and, drawn by its bright benignity as if by magnetism, they pressed closer to one another and to the
steps, listening and looking, as if they could trust
neither their eyes nor ears; and in their stolid, stiff
visages, he could,—yes, he surely did,—see the first
workings of a soul,—a little glimmering hope, a little
gratitude, a little thought, beginning. Oh, that instant when a man perceives, that some bright word
or deed of his, has been a spark to kindle another's dim
mind! This was to Herman what it was to Howe,
the philanthropist, when first a flash of meaning over
Laura Bridgman's blind mute face, told him that his
fingered words had reached her soul at last through its
long, black, soundless solitude.

Herman went on, and explained to his hearers that
they would still have to work. This view of the subject was less alluring than the first; but, as they looked
round into each other's faces, the sense of the murmuring

meeting collected itself into the distinct answer, "Hab to work anyhow, mas'r."

"Yes; everybody, who is good for anything, does work in some way or other; but, when you are free, you will work for yourselves, your wives, your husbands, and children. You will have all your time for yourselves; and all that you earn in it will be your own."

"Dat good anyhow, mas'r."

"The more industrious and painstaking you are, the more you will earn; the more prudent and sober you are, the more you will save; and the more you can save, the richer you will be. But if you are idle and wasteful, I am afraid you will have to go hungry. I shall see that you all get into good places at first, where you can earn if you choose; but I shall have to give away a great deal of my money to pay for your freedom, and get you to the North; and, after that, I shall be poor, and have to work for my family, as you will for yours. If you want to be your own masters, you will have to feed and clothe yourselves, just as your master, Colonel Rochemaurice, has to clothe and feed you now."

"Ky, let dis chile 'lone for dat!"

"Don car for de ole man's nigger. Take good car o' dis chile's nigger!"

"People say that you cannot; but you must try to teach them better. It would be a shame if such strong able-bodied men and women could not shift for themselves!—You choose to be free, then?"

"Yes, mas'r, tank 'ou mas'r."

"Yes, mas'r."

"Yes, mas'r."

"If 'ou may be free, used to rather," said, *sotto voce*, the wag of the squad, attempting to quote St. Paul.

"Yes, mas'r, all but dis yer Sambo, mas'r."

"Sambo? doesn't he too? Why not?"

"He don want to leave widout Sue, mas'r."

"Couldn't 'ou buy Sue, mas'r?"

"No. I am sorry, but I cannot,—now, at any rate. I must get all your Mistress Constance's people first. If you go to the North, and are steady and work well, I dare say you can make money enough to buy her. You had better talk with her, and see what she thinks about it; and when you have all made up your minds, and bidden your friends good-bye, you can go down and wait at the landing. We must start when the steamboat passes, two hours hence."

All leave-takings were, however, forbidden by Colonel Rochemaurice, who had ordered the overseer to take care that no further communication took place between those who were to go and those who were not. He apologized for this to Herman, the next time he saw him, by saying, truly enough, that it was important to the subordination and contentment of the slaves, that they should have nothing whatsoever to do with free blacks. Poor Sambo went like a pendulum for half an hour, first towards the field and then towards the landing; but he could not make up his mind to forsake Sue, at all events without an explanation, and finally set his face manfully against freedom without her, marched off, and did not return. Education can do much; but nature is a stubborn thing, and will sometimes do more. In spite of all precautions, and under the best possible management, here really was a slave who had become fond of his wife.

As Herman turned to go in, he saw little Rose standing just behind him, with a wondering, earnest, puzzled face. "Why, Dr. Arden!" said she; "are you going to buy them? *Do* abolitionists buy negroes? I thought they only stole them, or sometimes, when they were very bad indeed, taught them to stab us all, and set our houses on fire, and then run away. But you seem so harmless, that we cannot help liking you very much. What are you going to do with them?"

" To take them to the North."

" How can you take care of them there? Have you a plantation?"

" No; I shall have to teach them to take care of themselves."

" Why, *can* negroes take care of themselves?"

" Some can,—so good care that they are richer than I am, or expect ever to be."

" Why! why! why!—What do you want them for? To work for you?"

" No; to work for themselves."

" Because you think they have a right to?"

He was silent; but the child's penetration spoke for him. "Do you mean to say, then, that we have no right to keep them working for us?" cried she, her face flushing with mortification quite as much as with anger.

" No, my dear little friend; I do not mean to say anything at all just now, except that I wish you could come to the North some time, after I go back, and see your Cousin Constance and me. Should you like it?"

" Oh! oh! oh! thank you! How much I would like it!—And Alice, too?"

" By all means."

" Alice! Alice!"

Alice's pale face and hands appeared between the draperies of the school-room window.

" *Wouldn't* we like to go to Boston, some time, and see Cousin Constance and Dr. Arden?"

Alice clasped her hands, and spoke low as if to herself; but it seemed to Herman that he caught the words, "Yes, indeed! Anywhere away from here!"

"Then will you ask papa and mamma?"

"I could not go to leave papa and mamma, and Temple," said Alice, sitting wearily down, her momentary animation passing away.

"Ah, yes, yes! You could for a little while. Oh, yes, do, do, do! They'll let us go in a minute, if she wants to. They always let her do just as she chooses; because she's ill. It must be fine fun to be ill," generalized Miss Rose; "I wonder if I couldn't be,—when the nuts are ripe,—or if I ate a great deal of sugar-candy. Oh, no; it isn't of the least use. Nothing ever did hurt me, nor ever will. Come, Alice, ah, now, *do don't* say you won't go! Do, do, do."

As she thus returned to the charge, Herman made his escape to his own room, and seated himself to report progress in a few cheering, affectionate lines to Constance. In five minutes he heard a low, hasty tap at the door; and, almost before he had time to say, "Come in," in came Rafe biting his lips, winking, and trying hard, but in vain, to keep his handsome, rosy face from working all over, in a sort of convulsion of hope and anxiety. Herman instantly suspected what was coming, and wished himself—in the library; but there was no help for it; and so, as the boy seemed waiting to consider where to have him, he lifted his pen from his paper, and said good-humouredly, "Well, Rafe, did you wish to speak to me?"

Rafe drew himself up, and bracing himself as it were, by a strong effort, from head to foot, came out with, "I did, sir. I wanted,—I hoped,—oh, Dr. Arden, sir, wouldn't you like to buy me?"

"If I could afford it, my boy, I should very much, if you wish it; but "——

"But, indeed, sir, I'd cost you nothing,—nothing at all, in the end. I'd be above that. I don't mean to ask alms; it's only a loan. I can write an elegant hand, they say. I can keep accounts. If you wanted a clerk or a secretary,"——

"But I could not keep one, if I did, my poor fellow. I must be my own clerk and secretary for many a long day. I left home not a very rich man; and when I get back, after buying Miss Aspenwall's people alone, I shall be poor."

"But, then, couldn't you hire me out, sir?—And I'd go where you please, and work like a galley-slave, and bring you every cent I earned, till I'd paid back my whole ransom, and only ask for enough of your cast-off clothes to cover me, and bread and water to keep me alive.—Or, if you liked, I'd be your body-servant, even, till my time was up. I've never blacked a boot yet, nor brushed anybody's hair, but my own," he continued, not conceitedly but with a little irrepressible pride, which sat not altogether ill upon him; "but I'd do those things for you respectfully and faithfully, and not be ashamed to make myself useful in any honest way I could, for my freedom; and when I'd paid you back all your money,—interest and compound interest, too, if you thought it right,—I'd still hold myself your debtor in gratitude all my life. They don't scarcely consider me a servant here. I only study, and read, and ride, like anybody else, and wait on the Colonel, my benefactor, and queenly little Miss Rose, just as the squires and pages used to in old times; and that's nothing." The boy had evidently picked up some romantic notions from the old novels in the library, and, from his white associates, some of the *Southern-gentlemanly* contempt for labor. It was natural, but, considering his prospects, unlucky.

"You have an easy time of it here, then; have you not?"

"Yes, sir, if ease was all a man wanted in life, I can enjoy that,—while they please to let me."

"Then why do you care so much to be free?" Herman's conscience pricked him as he asked the question; and it seemed to cut the boy to the quick.

"Oh, Dr. Arden! oh, sir!—why does anybody? Why do you?"

To be sure! Why does anybody care to be free? I am a fortune-teller, my reader; and, to prove to you that I am a true one, I will tell you now something about yourself. Whatsoever you are, or whosoever you are, I know that you like to be, or at least wish in the course of time to be, *something.* No matter what it is. No matter whether, in the opinion of other people, it is worth being or not. I think that to be that *something,* is in your opinion happiness; and if you are not, and think you can never be *it,* you are unhappy, whatever it is,—a soldier, a statesman, a sea-captain, a famous artist, a successful professional man, a gratified epicure, a rich man, a learned man, a travelled man, or a husband, father, wife, or mother, sure of having no gaps made in the circle round your hearth to fill the coffle, because at any rate, to fill the coffin, more loving faces and beloved forms must be carried off too soon, than you know how to spare.—Now, ask yourself what this something is, in your case; and then see how far your attainment, or *retainment,* of it is likely to be affected by your freedom or slavery. Ah, well! it is a little thing, after all, to. be. cut off from the ful-

filment of one's chief wish in life, as all of us know,—
but those who have tried it;—and if the slaves were as
saintly as they ought to be,—as saintly as we are,—
they would not mind it at all.

Poor Rafe turned, perhaps as much to hide his altered
face as to leave the room, and, with his whole form
drooping, laid his hand on the handle of the door-latch.
Glancing back irresolutely at Herman before he
turned it, he saw something in his looks which told him,
that it could have been no want of compassion which
prompted his inquiry; and, encouraged, he presently
set himself to work to answer it as well as he could.
Some of the simplest questions in the world are not
among the easiest to answer. Who can tell an en-
quiring five-year-old, why twice two makes four?

"Well, I don't know, sir. I'm afraid I'd take up
more of your time than I've any right to, before I
could begin to tell you all the reasons, or half. I
reckon it's partly the feeling that makes a cat waul, or
a child scream, if it gets shut in a pantry, or the birds
flap themselves to death if you put 'em in a cage, or
that made the Norsemen sail round the world,—a sort
of a pent-up, stifled, unnatural, raging kind of a feeling. Then,—I hope I an't conceited; and I don't
pretend I'm one of those you'd call geniuses, that can
do everything they please, first thing, right off-hand,
without trying ; but—there isn't hardly anything that's
come in my way to do, but I've always found that *by*
trying and trying, and trying again if necessary, I can
do it, just like any other man; and I'd like to *be* a
man, and my own man, and go off and see if I couldn't
make my own way up in the world, and be a great
man even, perhaps, if I could," he added timidly, with
another glance at Herman as if to see how far he

5*

might venture, "like Benjamin Franklin, or Daniel Webster, or any of the poor boys that made great men by trying hard, and doing their best. They didn't, half of 'em, I reckon, have as good an education to start with as the Colonel's given me, God bless him! When he's out, I just slip into the library, and put back the book I've had, and take another. He don't say anything about it; because my hands are as clean as his, and he knows it. Then I sit up in a big pine in the wood, and read about 'em all, and Howard in the prisons, too, and Washington, and Captain Cook, and feel as if I had all sorts of lives to choose between, and all sorts of countries; and then, when it gets dark and I have to shut up the book and come down, there's nothing round but the old plantation, year in and year out; and Master Temple will go to college, and Miss Rose, to school at the North, and then to see foreign parts; and here will I be till I'm dead—nothing but a slave tied to one place like an old stupid watchdog to a kennel."

Of course, this was not hard at all; for Rafe did not pretend to deny that he,—like any dog who happened for the time to have a kind master,—had plenty to eat, and was not whipped. But Herman was very bigoted and fanatical, as we have seen all along; and so he thought that it was.

"You must not imagine for an instant," said he, "that I do not feel for you. I see how hard it must be."

The boy clapped his hands together, exclaiming, "Oh, Dr. Arden, if you do, then I know you can't help taking me along with you! Won't you, sir?"

Pretty lady, now, as a fortune-teller, I will tell you something more. Do you happen to remember how the young lover, who has been your husband for more happy years than one would readily believe, (seeing your gentle beauty still so fair and fresh), looked, when he asked you for your hand? Or do you recollect how your son,—the lawyer, who is carrying all before him now in Court or Congress,—looked fewer years ago, when he was coaxing you to coax his father to let him go to college, instead of sending him into a counting-room? I have never looked upon the face of either; but yet I know,—and I defy you to gainsay me,—that, in your eyes at that time, it was a very handsome, or at least a very interesting and expressive face; and yet I know this also, that it was not much handsomer, nor at all more expressive, than the face of poor Rafe when he thought he saw a dawning of hope for him.

"I wish, with all my heart," said Herman, "that I could do it; but see how the case stands. There are many thousands of our fellow-countrymen in the same situation as yourself in some respects, and in all other respects in a much worse situation. I wish, with all my heart, that I could free them all; but I have only a few thousands of dollars."

"The niggers! Oh, but sir, how different that is! It's a shame to treat them ill, I know; but what are they good for, but slaves? What could they do with liberty, if they had it?"

"What, they pleased," was the answer which rose to Herman's lips; "pursue their own objects in their own way, which is all that I or you could do with it, how different soever our objects may be."——

He had no chance to say it, however; for the poor boy hurried on, flushed with a degree of mortification and distress which it was painful to witness. "Surely, sir!—oh, I hope, Dr. Arden, you wouldn't call me a nigger! Why, I an't colored hardly at all; and mammy says, when I was a baby I was lighter than Master Harry!" He held up one of his clean smooth hands, and stroked the blood down out of it. "See, sir, it's a little tanned, may be; but you wouldn't know there was a single drop of black blood there, hardly; would you, sir?—and here, if you'd please to excuse me;"—he turned up his coat-sleeve, and showed an arm of whose whiteness a girl might well have been proud. Poor, poor fellow!—with all the prejudices of a slaveholder, and the situation of a slave!—"And then, sir, I hoped I could convince you,—but all the while, perhaps, I've only been showing you how vain and foolish I was,—that I wa'n't as stupid as those field-niggers are, such as you've been buying. Oh, Dr. Arden!—surely, sir, you see there's *some* difference between them and me?"

"Indeed I do, Rafe! There is the greatest difference. You are not stupid. You are not ignorant. Unless your face and manners bely you very much, you are not vicious. You can forget the one great hardship of your lot for a time, at least, in reading, and studying, and preparing yourself for better days. Tell me now, frankly, would you, for the sake of being freed like them, change conditions in other respects with one of those degraded creatures?"

"Well,—why,—well, no, sir; I don't know as I would do that."

"Nor would I, in your place; because the better part of freedom is yours already. Hold fast by that, and the rest will come by and by, I hope, if you are true to yourself."

Rafe looked up, wistful and puzzled. "I wouldn't like to run away, if I had ever so good a chance; because I'm trusted, and everybody's good to me that's worth minding, except sometimes the Mistress and Master Harry, when I come in their way; and they daren't meddle with me when the Colonel's by. I wouldn't do anything shabby."

"But couldn't you work and save here, and buy yourself?"

"No, I couldn't, master, any way I see. The Colonel's very generous to me; he let's me have all the clothes the young masters have done with; and sometimes, at Christmas, he'll even let the tailor send me down a new suit with theirs; but he hardly ever gives me a cent in money; and I couldn't ask him for't. He'd think I was ungrateful. He isn't a man to take liberties with, and hasn't ever said a sharp word to me yet; and I don't mean ever to give him cause. He chooses to have me about here always, when he's at home, at his beck and call, and tells the tutor other times to see I mind my books; and, year after next, he means to make me his steward and engineer here, I believe. I don't see my way clear ever to get any wages."

"Then, Rafe, I must try to do something for you, I see; though I can't,—believe me, I wish I could,— do it at once. First of all, I must carry through the business I have in hand, and take care of some poor men and women who are not, I fear, half so well treated nor so able to help themselves as you are; but afterwards I will see what can be done, among benevolent persons at the North, about advancing the money for you, and write to Colonel Rochemaurice about it. [Herman did so as soon as he could, but was not surprised to receive an answer, in a sort of kicking and butting hand, signed by Henry J. Rochemaurice,

(Harry,) to the effect that, Colonel Rochemaurice
was not much in the habit of selling his servants, but
that, when he had any more to dispose of he would
inform the Anti-Slavery Society; and what became of
poor Rafe, Herman never heard.] In the meantime,
my dear boy, be true to yourself, your neighbour, and
your God, as best you may; pray, toil, and trust; and
here is a little keepsake to remind you of my advice
and me." He took from his trunk a spare copy of the
New Testament, an incendiary document which, as
we have seen, he was somewhat addicted to circu-
lating, and added, "Rafe, do you remember Essex and
Queen Elizabeth's ring?"

"Yes, sir."

"Very well. Let this be a token somewhat like
that between us, if you will." He wrote his address
on the fly-leaf. "Now, if you get into any bad trouble
hereafter that you cannot get yourself out of, send this
back to me, with a letter between the leaves telling me
where you are, and what the matter is; and, if I am
above-ground, and can help you, I mean to try to do
it." With less hope than that, it would have been
hard to leave the poor boy; and Herman hoped that,
to a person of Rafe's evidently romantic turn of mind,
the association of ideas would give the volume an
extrinsic importance and interest, which might lead
him to discover its intrinsic value. Rafe took it,
thanked him civilly, and, seeing that no room was left
for further solicitation, slowly and sadly quitted the
chamber.

Most of the Rochemaurices seemed sorry to have
Herman leave them; and Herman would have been
sorry to leave most of the Rochemaurices, but,—there
must always be a *but*,—for one thing. The grounds

were a paradise, the stable well-stocked, the house well enough without and very tasteful within, the host and hostess hospitable, Mr. Harry usually invisible, Temple clever, friendly, and merry, little Rose picturesque and diverting, and even poor pale Alice a curious and interesting enigma, and study in human nature. Truly there might have been many places less pleasant to waste one's time in than Rochemaurice, *but*, that one felt there continually a little like a receiver of other people's goods,—we do not say stolen, but—taken and not paid for. Herman could not tell, for the life of him, to whom he chiefly owed his good cheer and entertainment,—to Colonel Rochemaurice at the foot of the festive dinner-table, or Mrs. Rochemaurice at the head, or Bill behind his chair, or Phyll over the kitchen-fire, or Sambo, Sue, and Dick, down in the cotton-fields. It was "all a muddle," which he cleared for himself as best he might, by paying fees quite as large as his fast-dwindling purse could well spare, to the chambermaid, and footman, and groom, and every servant who did anything for him; and he felt as if a burden was taken from his mind, as well as from his lady-love's, when the last of his new purchases leaped from the shore on board the boat, and he sat with only freemen about him, enjoying the summer twilight as well as the mosquitoes would let him, and listening to so much as he could understand of the gibberish of his charges, as they chattered together like so many monkeys, in the joy of their hearts, but with their guttural tones lowered, out of respect.

"Ky! har de engine!" cried Lyd, catching hold of Sally with a giggle half of satisfaction and half of fright, as the boat began to move; "What make it keep such a whoof, whoof, whoofin?"

"Laws, chile! dat ar's its breff. Don't 'ou breave hard, when 'ou runs? All critters does."

"Mam," said a bright-eyed urchin of five or six, "Is 'ou free lady, now, like mistis?"

"Yes, chile."

"Why aint 'ou face white, den?"

"Bress de chile, dunno! Spec it's 'cause de color won't come out. Wish 'twas like mistis' mournin-muslin dat washed out. Wash it ebery day, den; would so! Yah, yah!"

"I know how de color got on," said the wag; "I h'arn de parson tell."

"How dat, den, anyhow?"

"When Adam fall, he upsot de blackin'-bottle. Little Cain, a rollin on de floor,—splash him all over. He so mad, he jump right up an kill Abel. Den he sold, an sent right off to de nigger country. All de niggers Cain's chilen, an so dey has to mind (de sugar-) cane."

"You shut up, Scip! Dat ar ain't pious."

"No," thought Herman, "it certainly is not; but is it any more impious, or even absurd, than some of the other so-called Biblical arguments, by which more learned men than Scip undertake to defend negro-slavery? How can they imagine that a negro, who has any mother-wit at all, will not see through such stuff, and turn it into a jest, or worse? How is it possible to preach lies in the name of religion, without making skeptics and scoffers?"

"Ise boun to get religion now, anyhow," continued the last speaker; "'cause now I dun foun out dar's a God A'mighty."

"Lawsy land, Tilly! how stupid 'ou is! Didn' 'ou allers know as much as dat ar?"

"No, I didn'. 'Pears like I couldn' b'lieve a word on it. But ebery day an night, eber since I come to Rochemaurice, I'se kep' a sayin', 'God A'mighty, if dar is a God A'mighty, do, do somethin noder for my chilens.' I gib Him His choice. I says: 'Le' me take care on 'em mesef, as I used to mos times at de ole place; or find 'em good mistises as 'll l'arn 'em, as my ole mistis Aspen'all done l'arned me; or if 'ou'd lievser put 'em right to sleep once for all under groun, whar dey won't neber cry no more arter dere mammy, nor neber hab no sich hard times like she done had, 'pears like I'd mos as lievs;' an at last it done git to a sort ob a tune in my head; an I'd chop to it all days long wid my hoe, 'If dar—is a—God A—mighty—do, do—somethin—for my—chilens!' T'ought He didn' h'ar den; but specs now he did, anyhow."

So then they sat and talked together, after their uncouth fashion, while the boat ran down the stream.

The boat stopped to take in wood at the next landing, giving Herman time to run up towards the house of Mr. Clement, Colonel Rochemaurice's next neighbour. As he approached, he heard music and merry voices, and saw lanterns, made almost superfluous by the light of the broad moon, gleaming among the pines. A black lady and gentleman, dressed in the height of the (negro) *ton*, encountered him in a sentimental *promenade;* and from them he heard that Mr. Clement was not within doors, but on a wide lawn, to which they led the way.

This was, for the time being, a ball-room. It was encircled by the illuminated pine-trees, which he had before noticed. On one side was a table, decked with flowers, and apparently well furnished with refreshments; on the other, a band of fiddlers and banjo-players. The company were, at the moment, executing a reel with much spirit. They were all black or yellow, and bedecked, not to say bedizened, in a high degree.

A little aloof from them, at the end which answered to the head of the dancing-hall, under a cluster of lanterns tied together to represent a chandelier, and held out on high over them by the projecting arm of a grand tree behind them, stood a wellbred-looking group, consisting of the proprietor of the place and people, with a few friends, and his wife and daughters in their tasteful simple muslin dresses, standing around him, looking on, and laughing as gaily and good-humouredly, if not as loudly, as any of the chief performers. It was altogether a pretty and picturesque scene;—one of those spectacles of benevolence, gratitude, and mutual good-will between owner and chattel, which would, if anything could, give a grace to the institution of slavery.

Herman was most courteously and cordially welcomed, upon the strength of Colonel Rochemaurice's rather guarded and diplomatic letter of introduction, pressed to stay and see the frolic through, and very sorry that he could not; but his host, on finding that his business was urgent, promised to show his hospitality in speeding the parting, rather than in welcoming the coming, guest; though he told Herman laughingly, that he had come at the wrong time, and that he did "not believe it would be in the power of Wilberforce and Clarkson themselves, with a select *posse* of Wendell Phillips, Garrison, and Company, to get the boys and girls away from their persecutors, while there was still any cake on hand, or capering on foot."

Stepping forward, he made a sign to the musicians.

The music stopped; and so did the dancers, with very long faces. Mr. Clement, in a loud voice, called out the names of those of them whom Herman wished to see. They came up timidly, and, as it seemed, unwillingly. The Clements, and their party, delicately withdrew to a little distance. The music struck up again; the dance recommenced; and things went on as before.

It proved as Mr. Clement had said. Herman's offer was heard by the negroes civilly, but coolly; his statement, that they might accept it or not as they liked, only, with relief and gratitude. They knew nothing about the North, except some dismal stories that they had heard, about the cold and the abolitionists. They were happy. They were gay. They were feasted and amused. They loved "maus an mistis." Clement Grange seemed an elysium to them, especially after the deserted home of the Aspenwalls. The present was too pleasant for these grown-up children to forsake. What did they care about the future? Herman thought it his duty to set it before them, and represented to them gently, that though their present master was evidently very kind to them, he might at any time die, and they fall into hands very different from his; but they reckoned "he lib;—he not ole;—he helfy nough, is so," and slipped away again to their partners, one after another, as fast as they could get a chance,—all but Nance's sweetheart; and even he cast more than one longing, lingering look behind as he manfully turned his back upon the whirling couples, and used his handkerchief a good deal as he bade his masters and mistresses good-bye.

An anti-slavery man may hardly travel with a retinue of negroes at the South, more prudently than a slavery man at the North. Herman feared that, through some indiscretion of his sable attendants, his peaceable and lawful business might get wind, and he himself be escorted from the State at the State's expense; as hath happened aforetime to a citizen of Massachusetts, engaged in peaceable and lawful business, in the law-abiding, loyal confederate realm of South Carolina. He lost no time, therefore, in shipping his charges under safe conduct at Savannah, with Nance, and went on, retaining only old Jake, whose wife, as he had ascertained from Colonel Rochemaurice's papers, had been bought for a Mr. Nardwell, of Georgia.

For Georgia, then, and old Betsey, they started. Old Jake was not an ungrateful companion; but he was a very gloomy one. He really seemed as if Jeremiah had got into him.

"Pears like we'se fine her dead, mas'r; but I jus like to go, and see whar dey put her, all de same; an tank 'ou for dat, mas'r. She done got used to libin wid ole Jake. She too ole to learn new ways. She not know how to lib all alone. I'se strong; and I reckoned 'twould kill me,—did so! I'd like to see her 'terred decent or comf'table anyhow, would so;—maybe mas'r 'd say a prayer."

"Say a prayer?—to be sure I will, Jake,—that we may find her well and hearty! Come, pluck up a good heart, old fellow! Don't borrow trouble."

"Reckon not. Allers had trouble enough of my own, widout borrowin on it,—allers did hab, allers will hab. Fus ole maus and mistis, dey die,—broke my heart a'most. Grand ole gemman he was, wid his rufflous shirt; and she rode out wid her coach an four,—not like dese yere mean common men;—and dey was mighty fine an mighty high; but dey was mighty good to dere people. High! dose was de times! 'Hallo, Jake!' de mas'r 'd sing out, so loud an cheery, when he'd jump off his hunter 'fore de door, an see me a-bowin to him, 'Brew me some punch; an don forget to taste on it, to see if it's good, you car'less ole fellow; an,—Jake!—arter dat, don you remember to gib me de same glass.' He'd allers hab his joke. An de mistis, she'd come a sailin down de walk,—when I was a gardenin in de garden,—in her white mornin-gown, jus like a white goose on de riber, an 'good mornin, good Jake,' she'd say, so nice an softly; 'you can gader me a *boquet* of dose vi'lets, if you tink you can spare 'em, an den go in an wash your hands, an ask de nus to gib you Maus George to fetch out here;' an de baby, bress his heart! when he'd see me he'd strike out wid his dannies an his toetoes, an chuckle an crow; an den de nus 'ud wait for to put on his cap an feaders; an den he'd kick and squall; an den I'd take him out; an his moder 'd kiss him an smile, an den walk on a little way and try to look at her flowers; and den she'd hab to come back to look at him, to see which was de purtiest. He war de purtiest ob all; an she knowed it; an he grow'd up such a splendiferous young gemman, tall an straight an likely. Nex to de ole mas'r, I lubbed him better nor anyting in de worl. An Miss Conny, den I used to ten' her, an sot more on her dan I did on Nance; an she'd cry arter me; an I said many a time, 'Reckon you'll allers be good to old Jake.'

"Den de old masr's hoss done tumbled wid him ober a fi-barred gate, an broke his neck;—so he die. Dat break ole mistis' heart; so she die, 'fore long. Den Maus George, he send off Miss Constance, an go off an get hesef shot! 'Peared like I done got shot mesef wen I h'ard on't. Wish't I had. Den we hab nobody to take car on us but de oberseer. Hard times, an bad times. De people all got cross an kind o' crazed. Dey was starbed, an dey was whipped when dey didn' desarbe it; so dey turned wicked an 'sarbed it all de time; cause dey didn' know what else to do. Reckoned 'twould rain fire an brimstone on de ole place, sometimes; did so. Reckon 'twould, if dey hadn used it all up 'fore, on Sodom an Gomorry. But I allers says to de ole woman, ' Betsey,' says I, ' Betsey, you jus hold on till Miss Constance she's twenty-one; an den you'll see.' An ebery summer, I'd get a white man to tell me if 'twas de fus ob June yet; an den I'd make a notch on a stick I kep; an I waited an waited; but at last I got fourteen ob 'em; and den I says, ' Now,' says I, ' we'll hab good news 'fore long, an a good purty mistis!' An I had a silber dollar dat Maus George he gib me not to cry, when he rode away de last time; an I done spent it at de steamboat, for de *bon-bons* an sweet tings she liked, to hab all ready for her when she comed; but de next ting was, Colonel Rochemaurice comed instead ob her; an we was all sole and gone 'fore we knowed it."

" Miss Constance had not the least idea of the trouble it would give you, Jake. When she got your letter, she was so sorry that I was afraid it would make her ill."

Jake looked conscience-stricken in his turn. " Didn' know no better. Was dar anyting wrong in it?"

" Oh, no, except the wrong that she had done you. But, Jake, who taught you to write?—old Mrs. Aspenwall?"

" No, I wouldn' l'arn den ou'y to spell; 'cause I

couldn' spare de time. Dey war so 'dulgent, de folks took advantage; tings 'ud get behinehand; an I had to be allers roun seein to 'em, an doin dis here, an dat dere.—Miss Clayry Grand, she l'arned me, de good little creatur! God in heaben bless her."

"What!—your last master's daughter?—Last year! Could you learn at your age?"

"Yes, de little six-year-ole gal, she l'arned me. Mighty proud she was on it, too. Hab to gib her a whole stewed pumpkin, not to tell her ma. Took good while; 'cause she's too young, an I'se too ole. Boun' to write to de young mistis long o' Betsey any-how, was so!"

Jake did not know his age, of course; but he could not have been less than seventy. Was Cato's learning Greek at the same period of life a greater achievement?

"Could not you get some one to write for you?"

"All strangers, mas'r. Don neber do to trust strange white men. Dar war Lingo Sam, now. He work extra, and get leabe to hire hesef out, and pay six hundred dollar to de oberseer to gib de Colonel to buy hesef; an de oberseer take it all, an go off when dey change him, an neber say a werd about it; so when we'se sold, Sam's sold too."

"What Sam was that?"

"Why, Miss Constance's Sam, mas'r knows."

"Oh, the very man I'm after! Colonel Rochemau-rice told me he was sold to a trader. Do you know where he is now?"

"No, mas'r. Spec he's a runnin away;—swored he would."

"Do you know whether he had any other name beside Sam?"

"Yes, mas'r, Sam Taliaferro."

A surname, and an uncommon name. Good luck so far.

The cars stopped; and Herman asked the way to Mr. Nardwell's house, took a wagon, and drove thither with Jake. The gate hung on one hinge; the house wanted paint; and a general aspect of thriftlessness pervaded the premises. The house-door was shut, for a wonder. Herman looked for a bell, but, not seeing any, knocked with the handle of his whip, once, twice, and thrice at due intervals, without any answer; until at last a sharp female voice was heard to ejaculate within, "Can't I ever get a sleep in peace, as feeble as I am? You, Lize, how dar you set thar a sulkin? Are you deef? I'll give you a rousin cuff on the ear, that'll make you, I reckon, if you don't learn to mind the door!"

A mutter was heard in reply; and the door was presently opened by an old negress, whose face struck Herman as the most sullen he had ever beheld. His next idea was, that she was trying to run away from her mistress; for with a cry, and a push that nearly threw him backwards down the steps, she rushed by him; and then there was, between her and old Jake, such a hugging and kissing match as Herman had never seen before in his life, but once, when Edward had gone off without leave to skate on the Back Bay, stayed out till dark, and come safe back after Clara had sobbed on the sofa for an hour, supposing him to be drowned. Evidently, "Lize" was Betsey, and had spied Jake over Herman's shoulder; that was all. When she had done with him, she dropped on her knees before Herman, blessing and thanking him with torrents of tears, and of guttural and unintelligible eloquence. While he vainly endeavoured to quiet her, and old Jake who joined her in full cry, and the noise brought her mistress to the window,—a slatternly, sallow woman with a sour face and yellow ribbons,—he heard a step on the path and, turning round, saw a pale lean man in a rusty coat, looking on with much astonishment. "Mr. Nardwell?" said Herman, lifting his hat.

"The same, sir. Will you walk in?"

Herman did so, through a dirty passage into a dirty parlour, and briefly inquired whether Betsey was for sale, saying that her former owner had a wish to buy her back again.

"Take a seat, sir. Do you reside at the South?"

"No; I have been here but a short time!"

"I inferred as much by your accent. At the West?"

"No; at the North."

"Ah, I inferred so from your method of speaking. Did I understand you to say, sir, that it was this girl's former owner who wished to repurchase? One of the issue of the late G. G. Aspenwall, senior, I presume. I understood that his only son was prematurely killed in the Mexican war?"

"You are right; but he left a sister," said Herman, jumping up and bidding Jake, through the open window, to mind the horse and wagon. He did not sit down again, but stood hat in hand, as a gentle reminder to his catechist that time was passing.

"Be seated, pray sir."

"Thank you; but I am somewhat in a hurry."

"Miss Aspenwall resides at the South, I presume."

"No; she is at the North at present"

"Was this a favorite servant?"

"I do not know. Not that I am aware of."

"Ah! I would have supposed hardly. Poor old Lizzy! We have net found her particularly well disposed. Did I understand you to say, that Miss Aspenwall entertained the idea of emancipating all her slaves?"

"She would be glad to do so, if it was in her power."

"Indeed! It is greatly to her credit. You, sir, are her man of business, I expect."

"Yes;—in *this* business."

"Oh! ah! I now comprehend fully the state of the case, and the motives which actuate you both, and honor you accordingly."

It was no great proof of penetration to see into the affair as far as Mr. Nardwell did. Poor boyish Herman's bloom, at the moment, might have enlightened a duller man.

"You are very kind; but I am really obliged to beg that we may proceed to business, as I have a long journey still before me. What should you think a fair offer for Betsey? You will not object to parting with her, I suppose, if she has not behaved herself well?"

"Far from it, sir, in such a cause as this. I consider, that every good man and true had ought to be ready to give you his God-speed at any sacrifice of personal convenience. I would it was in my power to enfranchise her myself; but the most as well as the least that I can do, is to facilitate you in doing so. I experienced religion five years ago the tenth of July next; and I purposed from that time, as our hereditary servant had just deceased, to employ free help exclusively. But they were aspiring and supercilious; and Mrs. Nardwell, being a Southern lady and inured to

Southern ways, couldn't progress with 'em harmoniously; and they kept deserting her at the most inconvenient times, and in the most ungrateful manner. She is a most excellent woman, and a church-member; but malady affects her nerves, which had always ought to be considered; and, as she is much too weakly to do her own work, there was a good deal of indignation against me excited in her paternal house. In fine, it ended in my father-in-law's presenting her with a mulatto girl; so that, manifestly, there was nothing left for me to say. Then the girl, being unaided, was overworked; wherefore I was, out of compassion for her, in a manner obligated to purchase another. You recollect, sir, of what we read in the sacred volume, 'If any man provide not for his own, and specially for those of his own house, he hath denied the faith, and is worse than an infiddle.'"

"Very true," replied Herman, mentally, "but it seems to me that I have also read, somewhere else, a true saying, that 'the devil can quote Scripture to his purpose.' The worse for you, poor, well-wishing, henpecked, white-feathered bantam that you look like. Since you do not make this brand of yours your boast and glory, as so many do,—since you have the sense to feel it as a shame and curse,—I will not point a scornful finger at it, even in thought. God pity and deliver you."

"I hope Mrs. Nardwell will have no objection to parting with Lize, for a reasonable consideration," continued this lord of creation, apprehensively; "though it must, I am fearful, much incommode her for the time. The girl's contrairiness while under my roof, which I ought not, perhaps, to have uncharitably mentioned, may, I reckon, be partially accounted for by regret at the separation from her husband, of which 1 was not previously made aware, to be easily remedied by a second marriage in this neighbourhood, and need not therefore necessarily depreciate her market-value."

"You bought her, I am informed, for two hundred and fifty dollars?"

"Well, perhaps I did; but it was a great bargain. 1 reckon I could get a handsome advance on it, any time when negroes were lively."

"Very good, I will give you three hundred."

"Thank you, sir; and if, in addition to that, you could offer six per cent interest from the period of purchase,"—

"Three hundred and fifteen." —

"Cost of carriage,"—

"Three hundred and twenty."—

"Thank you, sir; very handsome, I'm sure!—and if, in addition, you could assign something for board and clothing,—for really she has conducted herself in such a manner as hardly to compensate us for her salt,"—

"Three hundred and fifty."—

"I would be prepared to take your offer into consideration."

"No, I beg you won't! I shall miss the cars to a certainty. Once for all, for the sake of dispatch I'll give you three hundred and sixty dollars for her on the spot, if you will take it," cried Herman, almost out of patience.

"Three hundred and seventy?—not three hundred and seventy in such a good and worthy cause? Likely woman, sir."

"Yes, likely to die at any time on your hands and your conscience, at her age and in her state of mind, or else to fall ill and be a mere cross, sickly old burden, that you won't know what to do with. Good afternoon, sir." .

"Don't be in such a hurry, sir; stop to tea!" expostulated Mr. Nardwell, following him to the threshold.

"Thank you; it is not in my power. Bring round the wagon, Jake."

"Three hundred and sixty-five!"

"What are you about, Nat?" cried Mrs. Nardwell with her head, in green ribbons this time, popped out of her chamber-door, as Herman went down the steps, and he heard an eager colloquy going on:

"My! I never! what a fool!" Whether this epithet was applied to 'Nat' or himself, Herman could not determine. "Why, run right after him; go!—run!—put! Git shet of that cantankerous old huzzy, for goodness' sake, while you can! We'll never have such another chance."

"Well, if you've got your mind made up, Maria, I'm sure —— Ho, Mister!"

Herman jumped out of the wagon again, and settled the business then and there, which suited him much better than it would have done to be forced, as he expected, to break away again from poor old Betsey, and send back some more experienced trader to make a bargain for him. Business, and the fear of his gentle help-meet's disapprobation, over, Mr. Nardwell relapsed into sentiment, and congratulated Herman, with apparent sincerity, on his "being so circumstanced as to do so generous a deed."

Are there many sadder things in life than some of those upon which people congratulate us? This was not quite a case in point, perhaps; for Herman was glad, as the circumstances stood, to play the part which he was playing,—glad to give so much relief to

these poor negroes' hearts, and Constance's mind,—
very glad to be permitted to sacrifice himself for her.
But in almost every great and genuine sacrifice, there
must be suffering, must there not? By this which he
was making, all his and her prospects, lately so fair
and bright, were thrown into utter uncertainty and
confusion. They could hardly marry now, except upon
expectations dependant upon his health and popularity
in his profession, nor without living more or less, for a
time at least, upon Clara; and it had always been a
point of honor with both her brothers, to guard her
against her own unbounded liberality to them by their
own forbearance. This, Edward's wealth and Herman's economy had hitherto made easy to them; and
it was very painful to him to think of taking, or
seeming to take, any advantage of her, in order to
carry out his schemes or further his own interests.
If he should decide to receive any aid from her, he
could receive it only as a loan; and he hated the
thought of being in debt, never had been, and had
hoped and fully intended never to be. Besides, he
could not forget that the approbation of his conscience,
which might otherwise have cheered him upon this
occasion, was purchased by the reproaches of Constance's. She could not enjoy this triumph of his;
she felt it as her shame. Ah, for himself there was
more reason for rejoicing than regret; but for her it
might all have been so different if—if she had but been
better guided earlier!

However, his quest thus far had prospered beyond
his hopes. He had succeeded, in less than six weeks,
in finding and freeing all her slaves but one; and he

accepted it as a good omen in the remaining case of Mr. Sam Taliaferro. He shook off dull care with a shake of the reins, rattled down to the cars, to the merry music of the mutual felicitations of the dark old images of Philemon and Baucis on the back seat, saw them safe and joyous on board of a New Bedford vessel at Savannah, and set off on a tour of search through the neighbouring States, with much more confidence and cheerfulness than commonly attend the labors of an individual engaged in finding a needle in a hay-stack.

CHAPTER XIX.

THE OGRE'S DEN.

"Child Rowland to the dark tower came."
                                        SHAKESPEARE.

Days passed, and weeks; but Sam still appeared to be nowhere. Herman, at the outset, made it his business to find Mr. I. Neade Scurge, the trader who had bought Sam at the auction. He had the pleasure of an interview with Mr. Scurge at Tallahassee; and what he knew about Sam, he told with the utmost civility and good humour; but it was not much. He reported that, that chattel had proved as incorrigibly mutinous as any spiritual article of furniture, and that, as he "couldn't get along with him pleasant to Orleens," he had sold him again just as soon as he could, to "a right smart nigger-breaker, a planter up by Columbus."

Herman went thither, and made the acquaintance of this accomplished gentleman, but was informed by him, that the man had "had the devil in him right bad,"—to that degree, indeed, that his amiable owner had "almost worked himself up" in unavailing attempts to cast him out;—and that, "as it was the busy season then," and he "hadn't the time to give to him," he had sold him to a trader from Mobile, whose name he "disremembered."

To Mobile, accordingly, Herman posted; but nobody among the "Lots for sail to suet purchysirs" answered to the name of Sam Taliaferro; until the prepossessing aspect of the inquirer was perceived, when half a dozen did so, in the most obliging manner, but on cross-examination proved to recollect nothing about the former abode or history of their namesake.

Herman went on again through auction-room and jail and barracoon, in State after State, compelled to lift the veil through which the grim dark face of Slavery looks so fair and blithe, sometimes, to superficial eyes in pleasure-ground and drawing-room. He examined the records of sales, where any had been kept, and the memories of the sellers. Sams abounded; but they were for the most part, for anything that appeared, destitute of surname, or of any other token of identity with the Sam in question.

From considerations of various kinds, Herman had been very desirous, throughout, of keeping his business out of the newspapers; but, at length, he bethought himself of getting a certain well-known slave-trader to insert, in his own name, an advertisement in the "National Intelligencer," the "Picayune," and one or two other gazettes, offering a handsome reward to anybody who would make known the whereabouts of the "mulatto boy, Sam Taliaferro, raised on the plantation of the late George G. Aspenwall, South Carolina, thence purchased by I. Neade Scurge, Esq., of New Orleans, and by him sold", &c., &c., &c., with as minute a description of his person,—the scars, so important an item in the physiognomy of a runaway slave! not omitted,—as Herman had been able to pick up.

Contrary to his almost discouraged expectation, in the course of ten days this elicited an answer, almost as remarkable as Grammar itself for its treatment of

6*

"orthography, etymology, and syntax," which the trader made over to Herman.

It stated that the boy Sam Taliaferro, with one scarred lip and a hole in his ear, and without two front teeth, was now indubitably in the possession of "Antonie" St. Dominique, Esq., Blanc County, State of Bondage, but requested that, as the latter was "a excentrick man, and did not allwers take things plaesent," the name of the writer might not be divulged.

At the period which we now reach, Herman, having arrived at one o'clock the night before at a little inn in Blancville, was seated there at the breakfast-table, over his tea, toast, and poached eggs. "Can you direct me to Mr. St. Dominique's plantation?" said he to the landlord who, that music might not be wanting to the joy of the banquet, stood whistling on the threshold, with his back to his guest and his hands in his pockets.

The man stopped whistling, turned round, surveyed him somewhat curiously from head to foot, and then answered, "Reckon I can. What for? Want to go there?"

"Yes. How far off is it?"

"Some thirty mile. Friend o' yourn?"

"No; I have never seen him; but I wish to do so, on business. Can you let me have a wagon?"

"Well, I don' know. Purpose to be back afore night?"

"If I can, by all means; but it depends a good deal upon what time I can get off from here."

"All right; I'll go and tackle the horse right away; and I'll take a seat with ye as far as the next city."

The landlord's sister, a mild, sickly-visaged, middle-aged widow, who had been alternately knitting and supplying Herman's wants at the table, arose, followed her brother into the next room and, in a hesitating tone, gave him sundry domestic commissions: "We're in need of a bag of coffee, Isic,—the last was half beans, tell the grocer, I'll bet; and I'm ashamed to pour it out for gentlemen, that pays their full price handsome;—and a bar'l of flour, and some more o' that Peruv'an Syrup,—I kind o' thought it done me some benefit,—and some crash for floor-cloths,"——

"Well, want anythin more? 'Cause if you don't, I needn't be in no hurry about startin; and if you doos, I better just fetch the city back with me, and let you help yourself."

"Well, no, brother, nothin;—only you aint a-goin to let that nice, pretty-behaved young man go into evil communications, be you, without any warnin?"

"Oh, you go 'long, Liza Maria! You wait till next prayer-meetin, if you want to talk about warnins. Tell you what, you don't ketch a young feller with an eye like that chap's got in his head,—half on it black coal and the other half burnin,—that don't know enough to take car' of himself; an if he knows but don't choose, all the warnins in this world, and the other, won't make him. If he was so mighty pretty-behaved an all that, to commence with, I'd like to know what he'd be likely to want with St. Dominique."

"Well, but Isic,"——Herman coughed; but the dialogue proceeded.

"'Well, but,' 'well but!' Tell yer what: You mind your business; an I'll mind mine and let other folks mind theirn; and then we'll all be took car' on. Only wish I was sartain he'd be back in good time with the hoss; but I reckon I'll have to resk it."

The mild sandy woman brought her pale face and freckles back into the parlour, with an anxious and uncertain look two or three times meeting Herman's, and as often dropped on the sanded floor.

"Excuse me," said he, breaking the ice for her, " but the door was open; and I had heard most of what you said, before I suspected that you were speaking of anything which could concern me.   Was it I, that you were speaking of? and is it possible, that you wished me to be cautioned against going to see Mr. St. Dominique?"

She rose again hastily, closed the door, and returned to her seat all in a *flutter:* " Well, yes, sir; I think it is my duty, considerin you're a stranger an brother don't think best to speak. I hope you won't think I'm takin a liberty."

"Not at all, I assure you.   My business with this gentleman is a perfectly lawful and peaceable one; but perhaps it is as well that I should know, beforehand, what sort of a person I am to have to deal with."

" Well, sir, I'm fearful a pretty bad person.   I don't know him myself;—nor I don't wish to;—I declar' I'd be afraid;—but I've known them that did.   It ain't right to repeat all anybody hears about their neighbour; and brother is very fearful of getting his ill will, if I ain't careful; but you're young an inexper'enced; an,—if you wouldn't let it go no farther,"——

"Not for the sake of gossipping, believe me, nor in any way to compromise you, or your brother; but if this man is really one of desperately bad character, it may be your duty to expose him; and, as I am compelled to have some dealings with him, I shall take it very kindly, if you will tell me anything you know about him, that it may concern me to know."

"Well, sir, he aint much in society in this place. He keeps himself to himself a good deal; only, now and then, he goes down to Capet City when the Legislatur's a-settin, an launches out, they say, and gives elegant dinners and settin-down suppers; but, in the ten years he's lived in this State, he's had five fraycusses; and one day there was a gentleman stopped here over night,—he died shortly after;—he'd been up to his house a-peddlin tracts; an St. Dominique told him to go to—the bad place, you know, sir. An he told me he knew him, and all about him; if he wa'n't very much mistaken, he used to sail with him when he was a cabin-boy, afore he got converted; an then he called himself Captain Goat, 'cause Captain Kid wa'n't bad enough for him. His real name though, he reckoned, was St. Dominique, all the time. He remembered of seein it marked with a lady's hair on an old pocket-handkerchief in his locker, one day when 'twas left open; an the captain,—St. Dominique I would say,— come along behind, and give him a kick that chucked him right into the chest head-foremost, for peepin and spyin. He was raised on the West Injy islands. His father was a rich planter; an he had advantages an privileges; but when he was some sixteen years of age he had a misunderstanding with his own twin-brother, when they was out together a-takin a walk on the volcanoes; and I suppose he didn't think, or his brother's foot slipped, or somethin; for he come back alone that night; an the next mornin some hunters or shepherds or somethin, that was a mile or two off and see the fraycus, brought home the remains, all mashed and smashed, and said they found it at the foot of a precipice, as high as the moon. So then his payrints reproved him most awfully; for his brother was the favoright son; an he run away, like Cain, with his mother's curse upon him,—only think, sir, how awful!—an I s'pose then he felt under reprobation, poor young creatur'! and didn't think 'twas no kind o' consequence more·what he did; for he grew up a real awful young man; and he just first did one thing bad; and then, as soon as he got tired of that, he went on and did another. He was a Guinea slaver, when the colporter sailed with him; an before that he'd been a pirate an a highwayman an I don't know what all. He was so smart, he always made money, and never got caught, whatever he did; an, when they hanged the gamblers to Vicksburg, he was the wust of 'em all; but he got wind of the business somehow fust, and lay down his cards, and slipped into his state-room, and stuffed out his stomach, and put on a black coat an white cravat an gold spectacles, and shaved off his baird, an cropped and floured his head, and knocked out one of his front teeth, and made believe he was an old parson; and when the lynchers come aboard, he was a-readin the services in the ladies' cabin, an a-coughin an spittin blood now and then, and a-sayin it wouldn't harm him in the way of his sacred callin, as solemn as any saint. An when they strung up the other rascals on the trees, he went along, and prayed as impressive as could be; an he's got a chapel on his plantation now. Didn't you see it as you come along, about twenty miles after you passed St. Petersburg, half way between there an London,—a little temple on a mound, with four pillows in front and a cupolo, and not far from a high wooden mansion, in a clearin?— It's in sight, through a gap in the wood, from the cart-track you come over."——

"To be sure! So I did. So I have come thirty

miles out of my way! Well, I must only make the more haste now, then, and bid you good morning."

"What, sir! You'll go there in spite of the chapel!"

"'In spite of the chapel?' I beg your pardon; but really, I don't understand you."

"Why, sir, what do you suppose he does in the chapel?"

"Indeed I do not know," said Herman, hardly able to keep himself from laughing,—"has religious services there every Sunday, for his family and slaves, I hope."

"No, sir; he has no family; an I'm fearful his servants has few pious privileges. He uses it customarily, I've been told, for a store-house; but when his ill-looking friends comes up the river, from I don't know where, to see him, it's lighted up at night; an he has a table set out,—an altar, I s'pose he calls it, poor blasphemous skeptic!—an they all set round it on coffins, an feast, an drink, an gamble, an smoke, till you can't see your hand before your face, nor hear yourself think; an they sing, an has a service to mock the church people; an after that, you'll go there?"

"Why, I really have no choice; and, besides,—I thank you very heartily for telling me these stories, for there might have been something in them important to me to know; and you could not judge beforehand whether there was or not;—but do they not strike you, yourself, as a little improbable, or at least unproved?"

"Well, I don' know, sir. Isic says so; and I'd be sorry to think I'd been talkin scandal; but I'll tell you one thing, I may say I do know, that he aint good to his people; for, if ever they can get sent to this town on an errand, they'll come here to me, like mad, for something to put into their poor mouths; an many an many's the time I've filled their stomachs an hands, an a'most cried to see 'em eat; an anybody that'll starve a poor helpless nigger ain't no Christian, in my opinion, not if I was mocked, an buffeted, and spit upon for sayin so; an anybody round here that chose could tell you, that he'll cuss and sw'ar, an drink, an play for money; an, if you was a brother of mine, I'd a'most sooner see you on your way to the cemetery than to his place. You know best; but we can't never tell what we'll be left to do. I dar' say you mean well; but"— Herman took up his hat;—"anyhow," continued the sandy woman, coloring, and huddling and jangling the cups and saucers together, with an expression of annoyance and mortification, "I've said my say an cl'ared my conscience now; so 'tain't no business of mine; an I dar' say you think I'm a meddlin goose."

"Shall I tell you what I do think?—that it was most amiable and womanly in you, to take so sisterly an interest in the safety of a young stranger. I shall be on my guard, and thank you heartily for putting me upon my guard, against this man; but what you have now told me makes it only the more necessary, that I should see him; for my business with him is, to buy back from him a poor slave for a friend of mine, who sold him out of thoughtlessness, and was very sorry for it afterwards."

"You don't say so! Poor creatur'! Well, I hope to gracious you'll get him! But suppose St. Dominique wants to tempt you to drink and gamble?"

"I shall be obliged to disoblige him," said Herman, laughing; and out he hurried, and into the wagon. "So here goes," thought he, "for the ogre's den! Perhaps, out of this, I shall still get an adventure to tell the girls. It would hardly do, to end my quest without so much as one. Making all allowance for the tittle-tattle of Rumour, and a seaman's and a woman's credulity, the little stories, I have just been entertained with, are hardly of the kind most likely to attach themselves to the character of a Christian, a scholar, and a gentleman. If there are such things as thorough unmixed miscreants in this world, I should like to have just one come in my way, to see how he'd look. I am not satisfied that I have ever met with one yet; though I did see nearer approaches to it at some of the slave-pens than I supposed possible. I hope, though, poor Sam Taliaferro hasn't fared the worse for St. Dominique's eccentricities; but if he has, he'll be all the more pleased to see me.—How cold-blooded all this is! How calmly accustomed I've become already to human tyranny and human misery! Pleasing effect upon one's moral-sense, of a sojourn of a few weeks in our slave States! What must the effect be of a few years, or of many?"

Herman had not, perhaps, grown so callous as he believed; for, after his companion had left him, with the usual directions of "Turn to the right and then to the left," &c., to his own reflections, the idea of the possible situation of the poor captive returned again and again to him, and finally took so full possession of his mind, that his horse was all in foam when he drew rein at St. Dominique's gate.

As he alighted to open it, a huge gunpowder-and-sand-colored bull-dog-jawed mongrel, chained to a post a few yards within it, made a roaring rush at him head-fore-most, to the full length of his tether which, jerking back-wards as he rose for a spring, pulled him over, making him execute a sprawling somersault, and fall wrong-side up and hind-legs before, which performance he continued to repeat *da capo*, as if he could not have too much of it. The yelling bark of this faithful quadruped aroused sundry canine echoes in different directions, until the gamut terminated in the fine falsetto of a little, grisly, rough terrier, dancing on tiptoe on the door-steps, in an ecstacy of wounded feeling.

The house was square and high, with a piazza around the second story, and an observatory on the top. It might not be old; but it looked black and weather-beaten, from the absence of paint and from a recent shower. It stood at the meeting of four weedy private cross-roads or avenues, about a sixteenth of a mile from the gate, on the top of a rising ground dotted everywhere with burnt stumps like the dark grave-stones of an army of murdered trees. Not one had been left, within the enclosure, except in a little grove lately planted, apparently, around *the chapel;* but the wild-flowers, and the nature of such shrubs as still dared to lift their scrubby heads above the turf, seemed to show that the native forest had been but lately dispossessed. If the sun had shone, the aspect of the place in the wide light might have been cheerful, though solitary. In the shadow of the wet, lead-colored, pale-lipped thunder-cloud that now brooded with drooping wings over it, it looked neither cheerful nor hospitable, but sullen, ill-omened, black, blighted, and blasted.

The watch-dog continuing to bay and bray, until Herman began to fancy that showing himself to him was equivalent to blowing a magic horn for admission, an ill-looking negro came out of the house, advanced to reconnoitre, and, after a brief scrutiny and colloquy, took a key from his pocket, unlocked the gate, dragged

the yelling dog back by his chain, and kept hold of
him by it, while Herman, with some difficulty, led and
coaxed his horse past. The negro then let go and followed; and the alternate jumps and somersaults were
renewed behind them. As Herman drew near the
door, the terrier's exasperation increased; but the
negro, preceding him, seized it adroitly by its peg-like
tail,—" everything depends," as it has been very judiciously remarked, " upon taking hold of a thing by
the right handle,"—and steered it into the house; when
it indignantly, and in hot haste, scrambled up-stairs;
and he followed to the next story.

" Ho, mas'r!"

" Halloo!" answered a voice higher yet.

" Gen'l'man below."

" What gentleman, you — — rascal?" rejoined an
ore rotundo voice, evidently in good practice, with
much execution, beginning with a deep *voce di petto*
and ending with a rising inflection, in which Herman
imagined a whimsical resemblance to the canine
gamut aforementioned.

" Dunno, mas'r,—a strange young gen'l'man."

" Couldn't you say so, then, you — — villain?" resumed the sweet cherub that sat up aloft, to the same
chant as before, which, though certainly not Grego-
rian, was not without a certain rude, harsh, military
or naval music in it.—" Certain there's only one
coming?"

" No, mas'r, ain't but one, sure."

" I'll get up. Come up here; and give me my
things, and be —— to you!" In a moment the shutters of an upper room were unbarred and thrown open;
and Herman, who was still holding his horse, looking
up involuntarily at the sound, saw a rather stout

elderly man, in a dark green coat, looking down at them over the railing of the balcony. He instantly withdrew, and presently reappeared on the door-steps.

Herman, who had worked himself up into some degree of curiosity, was at first disappointed. There was nothing about Mr. St. Dominique that impressed him as either picturesque or grotesque, nor particularly ordinary nor extraordinary, except that he did appear to him, simply and instinctively, one of the most repulsive persons he had ever seen. A second look, however, showed that his jaw was strong and his head, intellectual. He looked weary, ill, and ill-tempered, but resolute. His eyes were stern and still, though not large, blood-shot, and disfigured with over-slept-looking chamois-leather-colored pouches underneath. His complexion was sallow and swarthy, over his coarse grizzled whiskers. He had now no need to stuff out his stomach, except, perhaps, from within; for it filled his commodious yellow waistcoat very sufficiently, though not excessively. His clothes, of no particular date, were yet of very good materials in good preservation; and his small, but disproportionately large-jointed hands, showed no marks of recent toil; so that it appeared, that his coarse dark nails and long hair were untended more from taste, or rather want of taste, than want of time or means. His manner had dropped on the stairs even the merits of frankness and spontaneousness, which it had seemed to possess in the above dialogue, and was now merely that forced civility which is muzzled surliness,—certainly among the very most odious styles of manner that man can assume towards man. His mouth was but a pantry-door,—a mere slit in his face. As he opened it to speak, Herman involuntarily looked for the gap in it; but, if it had ever been there, it had been refilled. The row of short, sound, yellow double-teeth was now unbroken.

"Pardon for keeping you waiting," said he. "Indisposed this morning. Come in. Down, Faust, down!" The terrier, which had returned with him and renewed its barking at his guest, instantly cringed at his feet.

"I am sorry to have disturbed you; but I need scarcely trespass on your time for five minutes. I wished only to ask whether you were disposed to sell a negro man, whom I understand you have,"——

"No hurry, sir. Come in! Come in! Take that horse, Abaddon."

"You are very kind; but there is so heavy a storm coming up,"——

"'Coming up'?—it's come," said he, with a snarling smile. A tremendous flash, instantaneously followed by as tremendous a crash, confirmed his words. "There! D'ye want to be struck by lightning? Because if ye do, I don't." He turned and reëntered the house, but so deliberately that Herman gave him little credit for cowardice, and the less, that the flaming air was at the moment quenched with a wide white deluge of rain.

Herman, springing from the wagon, followed perforce, throwing the reins to the negro. "He looked more like a *bad one* than a good one," thought he; "and I wish my gallant steed and war-chariot may be forthcoming again, when I want them. However, let us find an adventure if we can, and see the inside of this enchanted hall."

His courteous host led the way into a large unoccupied apartment, with a sanded floor, furnished with a billiard-table, two tin receptacles for tobacco-juice, and a long, hard sofa with a worn green morocco cover and tarnished brass-headed nails, and further decorated with a very large colored map of Africa, hung against the wall, every inlet and indentation of the western coast having its name put in by hand, in ink, where it was omitted in the engraving.

"Sit down," said he; "what'll you take to drink?"

"A glass of water, if you please, I shall be very glad of."

St. Dominique withdrew, and Herman heard him call again, in that peculiar measured cadence of his, as nearly as he could make out the words, "Ho, Hecate, Hecate, here; and be hanged to you!"

"A melancholy mad humourist, apparently," thought he. "If this is his taste in nomenclature, no wonder they tell queer stories about him." He supposed that Mr. St. Dominique was ordering the draught which he had asked for; but he presently heard one pair of boots and two, of pattering scratching paws go above stairs, and saw nothing more of him for three-quarters of an hour by his own watch; at the end of which time, he creaked to the threshold again, and said, laconically, "Come, get something to eat."

Herman followed into a long room, similar in size and shape to the one which he had just left. It looked like a ship's cabin. There was an oil-cloth on the floor, a large, long table, one end of which was laid for two persons, and two rows of heavy straight-backed mahogany chairs, set stiffly back against the bare berths which ran half-way along both sides of the room.

"Used to be a sea-faring man," said he, as he saw Herman look at them. "Bachelor's establishment. Like to have some place where I can put a friend or two, for a night or so. Nobody here now to stop with me these five months. Elderly man,—unwell,—alone, —dyspeptic,—can't talk till after dinner. Do you no harm to sit with me an hour, and tell the news, and take a bite."

This was rather pathetic; and Herman accordingly began to make himself as agreeable as he could in the circumstances; but there was one circumstance, in particular, which stood in the way of it; and that was, that he happened to be almost choking with thirst.

"Fill your glass," St. Dominique had said to him as soon as he sat down to the table, pushing towards him a well-crusted bottle with a cobweb *mantilla;* and he had obeyed, and swallowed one mouthful of the contents, and no more. The wine,—what wine there was there,—was a rich and costly foreign one, and almost as sweet as a cordial; but it tasted to him as if, not drugged precisely, but mixed, and one-half of it, at least, the strongest brandy, not to speak of a probable dash of pure alcohol. His head was not accustomed to such potations; and he did not intend that it should be. If he had done so, the present place, and time, six hours, full, since he had taken food, were certainly not those which he would have chosen to make a beginning. He looked round for water; there was none upon the table; and he addressed himself to his soup,—excellent, but high-seasoned and, unluckily, remarkably salt. "Will you give me some water?" said he to the waiter behind his chair.

The man removed his soup; and St. Dominique, whom the three applications, which he had made to the bottle, on his own account, appeared to have cheered and encouraged almost to the genial point, heaped his plate with French *pâté,*—still the same story,—good, but salt.

"May I ask for a glass of water, Mr. St. Dominique?"

"Water, sir?—oh, certainly, you shall have your water;—though I'm afraid you won't drink it, when you get it. The water round here, I'm sorry to say, is very strongly impregnated with lime. I have it boiled, which makes it rather more wholesome; but it's nasty stuff, after all. Apollyon, here." He spoke in a low tone to one of the waiters, who presently returned with an earthenware pitcher, and filled Herman's tumbler with water which was very strongly impregnated with lime, indeed, being nothing more nor less than genuine lime-water.

"You are a rascal, to be sure!" thought Herman, emphatically, all his professional sentiments rising up in arms at such a profanation of good physic; "but if you expect, by so shallow a trick as this, to make me drink what you please, you don't show much adaptation of means to ends. A fellow, who is capable of giving a well man medicine, may be equal to poisoning him at his own table for aught I know." But he caught St. Dominique contemplating him with a gratified expression out of the corner of his flinty eye, suppressed a wry face, continued to talk most agreeably, ate his bread, minced up his *pâté*, and shuffled it stealthily, from time to time, over the edge of his plate and of the table to Faust who, sitting under the latter, lay in wait for it, and with equal secrecy caught and obligingly gobbled it up.

St. Dominique seemed to appreciate the wariness and composure of his antagonist and, at first, rather to like them. "Perhaps this kind of wine's too sweet for you," said he; and he ordered up some of six or seven different sorts, and drank of them freely himself before

he grew morose again ; while Herman had leisure to
make his observations and reflections upon the table.

Besides the foreign delicacies already mentioned,
(the soup was evidently imported, as well as the *pâté*,
and kept on hand, probably, for occasional use and
chance comers,) there were the plantation luxu-
ries of broiled pigeons and *scrambled* eggs, sweet po-
tatoes and coarse hominy, followed by a dessert of
dried fruits and East and West India sweetmeats.
The utensils were as heterogeneous as the fare,—coarse
strong white boarding-house earthenware, and pressed
glass, being interspersed with single and beautiful specimens of Indian .and French china and Bohemian
"crystal," cracked and notched.   The spoons and forks
were, some of German silver, and some of pure Spanish stamped with coats-of-arms, and, in one or two
cases, with a French or Spanish name.   Again, "Liza
Maria"'s stories occurred to him ; and perhaps he
pondered longer than was quite polite ; for, when he
raised his eyes from St. Dominique's spoons to St.
Dominique's face, he saw St. Dominique's looks fixed
upon him with a gaze equally stern and sinister. He
colored consciously ; the gaze fell ; and St. Dominique
pushed back his chair and rose, saying, "Well, if you
can't find anything fit to eat or drink, we may as well
be moving, if you've done inspecting my silver."

"I beg your pardon," said Herman, thinking that
some apology was due, and anxious for the present to
keep on good terms with Sam's owner; "I am fond
of old plate ; and some of this is very curious."

"All right, sir ; no offence. Old tars are apt to
say whatever comes into their heads. I don't keep
more articles of that kind round than I want to use,
myself, commonly ; and, when a stranger drops in un-

7

expectedly, my black devils set out the table with any
odd things they can lay their hands on. Going round
and round the world, one who has a taste that way
picks up a good many of 'em, first and last. I bought
that spoon at an old curiosity-shop in Amsterdam.
Take it into the other room with you, if you like it;
and we'll play a game of billiards for it."

"Thank you; but I see the rain has held up; and,
as I have thirty miles to go before I sleep, I must run
between the drops."

"Oh, the —— ! 'Twill be down again within an
hour; and the thunder, too. Never saw such a place
for thunder! Lucky I don't mind it as some people
do;—should have been crazed before now;—I never
heard anything like it on the line, I'll swear. It
sounds, sir, as if the windows of heaven were opened
all of a sudden, to kick some new wild-oat-sowing angel
out neck-and-heels, and then banged down again, with
a crash that shivered them all into long cracks and
sharp splinters, rattling and ripping up the sky for
leagues over-head. When it wakes me, splitting my
head, in the night sometimes,—blast it!—I think it's
the day of doom come! Mighty hard, isn't it, when
you're all alone in the dark, and half-asleep or ill, to
get those d—d superstitious notions out of your head,
that the d—d nursery-jades and mammies put into it
when you're too young to know better?—Better by
half stop and stay the night. If folks knew you were
coming here, they won't drag the river for ye till to-
morrow. Your mother knows you're out, don't she?
Besides, your nice academic tongue has told me before
now, youngster, that your dear native home is too far
from here for you to reach to-night, or to-morrow."

"I thank you; but I am obliged to return. You
own a man named Sam Taliaferro, do you not?"

"Yes, I do own a man named Sam Taliaferro; and the very d—dest black devil he is, that ever I caught out of the pit."

"What may I offer you for him?"

"Well, I'm a law-and-order man, sir; and I don't know that there's any law against your offering me anything you please," said St. Dominique, laughing like a hyena; "but I don't make a practice of selling my negroes; 'tisn't considered respectable among the better class of planters here;—that, of course, as a stranger, you're not expected to know; so my feelings aren't so much wounded as they might be;—but if you'll stake a thousand dollars against him at billiards, I don't know but I'll play with you for that."

"It is utterly impossible. I even know nothing about the game," said Herman, who cared for none excepting active sports in the open air.

"Not know billiards, at your age! I'll teach you, then; and we'll play for small stakes at first. Come," said he, rolling the balls into the pockets with one hand, and with the other, poking a cue into Herman's, "I must have some amusement, I swear, or go moping mad in this solitary haunted old den."

"I will play a little for your entertainment," said Herman, really pitying him, "but,—excuse me,—not for money."

"Oh, the h—! What entertainment would there be in that?"

"About this business, then. You mentioned a thousand dollars. That seems a high price; but I will give it you outright for Sam Taliaferro, if he proves to be the man I think."

"Sam Taliaferro? Sam Taliaferro? What do you want of Sam Taliaferro? Got a spite against him, eh?"

"Not at all."

"Oh, indeed," said St. Dominique, mocking him malignantly, wine and disappointment having fairly got the better of him; "well, then, as I have, I suspect he'll be of more use to me than he would, to you." Herman turned red; and his eyes flashed; St. Dominique, pale; and *his* eyes flashed. York and Lancaster, understanding one another, proved hopelessly uncongenial.

"May I ask," said Herman, swallowing his choler, "of what use a man whom you hate, and who probably does not serve you satisfactorily, can possibly be to you in comparison with a good sum of money, which most men do not hate, and which serves them obediently, whether it loves them or not?"

"Most certainly you may, sir. Always pleased to gratify an enlightened curiosity. I'll satisfy yours, not myself, but by proxy. I'll place a highly intelligent negro oracle at your disposal, to answer any questions you please,—as I have my suspicions that you have an indiscriminate liking for that interesting race,—if you'll only be so good as to inform me, in return, if you're not the individual referred to here." He took a worn, dingy little newspaper from one of the pockets of the billiard-table, and pointed to a paragraph, adding, "One of my friends sent me up this, a while ago."

The paper was the "Chincapin Oriflamme, Nathaniel Nardwell, Editor." Herman took it and read, to his intense disgust:

"Abolitionism in High Life.

"One of the bright-eyed daughters of one of the most ancient and noble families of the sunny South, (Carolina,) who of late was driven, a weeping and brotherless orphan, by domestic bereavement, from her ancestral halls, to seek a hospitable asylum among the barren hills and icy snow-drifts of the North, selling her patronymic estates and stock, has adopted Abolition sentiments, and commissioned her favored and fortunate lover, Mr. Arden of Boston, to seek and re-purchase all her servants with a view to emancipation, making, as we understand, his success in this romantic but, whatever else we may predicate of it, amiable enterprise the condition of her ultimate acceptance of his hand."

So, Mr. Nardwell had had a professional reason for his interminable questions. Why could not Herman have parried them more adroitly? How vexatious and atrociously impertinent! His face was a sufficient answer to St. Dominique.

"I thought as much!" said he, with loathing emphasis. "A lad who can't drink or play! 'What were you made for?' as the catechism says. An abolition-ist! Oh, d—n it!" He spat emphatically and bel-lowed, "Ho, Abaddon! Fetch me something to rinse my mouth with, — Jamaica rum, you —— devil!— Thought you were going to take Sam right off to nig-ger's paradise, did you? Paradise's a hum—; can't get there; and 'twouldn't be worth getting to if you could. Oh, d—n the niggers, give 'em hell!—always ready, always real, always near!" Throughout this speech, he raised the deep bass of his voice only once, —and that was in calling to his servant.—One could scarcely say that there was any passion in it, or in his look, but only the bitter ashes of passions which had burned themselves out. His cool malignity was as much more hideous than the fury of a violent man, as a cold-blooded rattlesnake is, than a raging catamount.

"Will you allow me to see the man?" said

Herman, without the slightest expectation that he would.

"With the greatest pleasure, sir," said St. Dominique, turning upon him with a bow; "Ho, Abaddon, call Beelzebub."

"Is he going to take unto himself seven spirits worse than himself?" thought Herman. "Where will he go to find them?"

Beelzebub soon appeared; as is the custom of fiends when called for: "This gentleman wishes to have the pleasure of making Scapegoat's acquaintance. You will go down with him to the *quarter*, attend him while he stays, see him out of the gate, and then unchain Cerberus. Give him any profitable information that you can. He is no doubt engaged in writing a book upon our institutions. He will see them in perfection here; and perhaps he will have the goodness to make honorable mention of us." All this was evidently levelled at Herman, who could scarcely help knocking him down. "Take down a collar with you," continued St. Dominique; "and,"——the conclusion of the sentence was inaudible.

"An den take it off, mas'r?"

"Take it off when you're ordered, you —— jail-bird! Good-day, sir," said he, with another mock reverence to Herman. He turned and went upstairs; and Herman, turning himself after he left the house and looking back, to convince himself that he had really been in such a home of such a man, saw him lounging and swinging himself to and fro in nautical fashion,—with his hands in his pockets,—in his high balcony as if it had been a quarter-deck, and looking after Herman.

At the distance of nearly a sixteenth of a mile from

the house, with their doors open towards it, stood eight
cabins, or rather pens, built of horizontal poles fitted
loosely together, and kept in place by their sharpened
ends thrust into holes cut in an upright post in each
corner. They were low, about six or seven feet wide
and twelve or eighteen long, and had no chimneys.
Nearest, at the end of the row, was a much smaller
one resembling a kennel.

"Is that your *quarter?*" asked Herman. "Why,
you have not many hands, have you ?"

"No, mas'r. Nobbut seventy."

"You don't mean that you get seventy men into
those huts ?"

"No, mas'r; some on 'em's women an chilens.
Don take up so much room. Den dey has to put de
little ones in de corners, an pack close, an lay still ; an
if dey don't I jus takes de cow-hide, an cracks roun a
little, an pacifies 'em. Dar's room enough an to spare,
if dey ou'y lays right. Keep 'em warm to stow snug."

"Will wonders ever cease ?" thought Herman.
"Why, it must equal Dotheboy's Hall and ' sleeping
five in a bed, which no Christian should object to !'"

"You're the driver, are you ?"

"Yes, sar."

"What's that you have in your hand ?"

"What dey call de Lous'ana necklace, for Sam,
mas'r ?"

It was a ring of iron, with a padlock, and three
long prongs projecting at nearly equal distances.

"Why is he not at work with the rest ?"

"Laws, sar, he don't work much. He's de Scape-
goat, dese yer days."

"The what ?"

"De Scape-goat, sar,—what mas'r St. Dominique

call de precarious sacrifice. He keep de rest to work,
an one to chastify for a sample, allers. De ole Scape-
goat he die, just arter we got Sam ; an Sam, he de wus
nigger we ever cotched here ; so mas'r say he promote
him. He no good to work; so he de bes' one to
whip."

"Good God !" said Herman to himself; "this is no
conscious wilful blasphemy ! I cannot, will not think
it ! No soul ever fashioned by Thee could be capable
of it ! That wretch is mad, and knows not what he
does ! Deliver him from himself, and his victim from
him !" He looked at the negro. There was no malice
in his face, nor horror, nor remorse, but simple brutish-
ness. He was only obeying his lawful master, and
"doing his duty;" and that, as we all of us,—especially United States Marshals,—know, is the right and
unquestionable thing to be done on the whole, how
detestable soever it may be in the details. Herman
went on, "It seems to me your master trusts you a
good deal,—don't he ?—to have his cabins so close to
the fence, and the fence to the road."

"Laws, sar, he like to show how 'bedient an well-
broke de folks is, does so. He knows dey won't run
away ; 'cause when dey does, he pulls out deir toe-
nails."

"What ?"

"Wid pinchers, sar.* De fus time one, de nex
time two, and so on. Dey nebber needs it more dan
twice dough, sar ; make 'em keep roun steady as de
cows, widout no more looking after."

They reached the nearest cabin, and looked in.
Sam lay at his length on his side, on the earthen floor.

* See Olmsted's "Journey through Texas," p. 105.

He had about him nothing but a coarse, dirty, blue
shirt. He could hardly be said to wear it; for he had
stripped it off from his back,—which was red and raw,
—and covered himself with it elsewhere as well as he
could. It was difficult to tell how old he might be.
His cheeks were hollow, and of the peculiar dim, faded
hue of a sick negro; and his hair was gray. A crust
of hoe-cake, and a full dipper of water, stood beside
him.

"Halloo!" cried Beelzebub, "you bad nigger!
What! starvin you'se'f again! You better eat your
breakfast; 'cause dere's plenty more pepper-pods
a-growin whar de las' ones comed from."

The victim dipped the crust in the water, and
bolted it sullenly and silently, rolling his large wild
eyes as he did so, up to Herman's face with a sort of
hopeless expectancy and defiance, which gradually
changed to surprise and curiosity as he saw the expression there. Herman, in the meantime, studied his, with
equal surprise and interest, and perhaps with almost
equal gratification. Squalid, miserable, sick, as he was,
he looked like a man and an intelligent and undaunted
one,—St. Dominique's match perhaps in all but circumstances, and therefore the object of St. Dominique's
deadlier hate,—a sort of Prometheus cast by the Creator's hands in living bronze. Under Herman's gaze
his own grew still less defiant, more expectant.

Herman must speak to him, but how? He felt in
his pockets. Money?—yes, but it would be a suspicious act to request a private interview; and even if
Beelzebub was disposed to prove as corruptible as
Mammon, to pocket his bribe, and to withdraw, there
was St. Dominique with a spy-glass projecting from
his eye through the observatory window, inspecting
7*

the enemy's movements, and ready, no doubt, to inter-
rupt the colloquy, and promote Beelzebub himself to
the Scape-goat's place at a minute's warning. There
was something besides money, though,—a square
packet in the pocket of Herman's *aquæ scutum ;*—
what on earth ?—oh, yes, he remembered!—a paper of
luncheon, which 'Liza Maria had thrust up into his
hand just before he drove off,—hard gingerbread and
biscuit and cheese. He offered it to Sam.

He shook his head. He had finished eating his
task, and wanted only to lie still.

Herman sat down by him. " My poor fellow,"
said he, " I am sorry to find you in such a condition.
I have been looking for you this long time, for your
old mistress, Miss Aspenwall. She wanted to buy you
back again." Sam started into a sitting posture.
" But Mr. St. Dominique is unwilling to sell you."

Sam sank back again with a groan, then looked at
Herman, then all round the hut, and then at Beelzebub, who was looking for his part at the paper of provisions, and licking his lips. A thought seemed to
strike Sam. " Can he have some ?" said he, speaking
with a somewhat foreign accent.

" Certainly," said Herman, handing the paper to
Beelzebub, who instantly possessed himself of the largest
piece of gingerbread, and, carefully keeping his back
turned to the house, sank on the floor with it between
Herman and the door, his limbs seeming to be loosened
beneath him with excess of rapture. " But what can
I do for you ?" continued Dr. Arden.

" I would wish," said Sam, turning his shrewd,
watchful eye alternately on Herman and Beelzebub,
" a new vest, and some chocolate-comfits, and some"—
Beelzebub took a large mouthful, and gave a loud
craunch—" Parlez-vous Français ?"

" Yes ; *mais celui ?*" rejoined Herman, under cover of *craunch* the second.

" *Non ;* and some cigars, mas'r," added the Scape-goat, looking towards Beelzebub, whose progress through his gingerbread was for the moment arrested, apparently by the reflection that he could have relished a piece of the cheese with it.

Herman supplied him, and carefully selected for his benefit the most explosive of the biscuits. Then, placing himself so that he could watch him, he imitated Sam's *ruse*, speaking French at each bite and *craunch*, and relapsing into English as mastication advanced. " What sort of a waistcoat would you like ?"

" Yellow. *Voulez-vous m'aider ?*"

" *De tout mon cœur,—mais comment ?*"

" Good-bye, sare. *Quand il pluie,*——

" Yes, I must go."——

" *La prochaine fois,*"——

" Some more gingerbread ?" said Herman to Beelzebub, who did not refuse.

" *Venez-là, à minuit, à la* fence ;—*et sifflez comme un* quail. *Je viendrai.* Give me *a couteau, a pistolet chargé, un oignon,*"——

" *A quoi cela ?*"

" *Pour frotter les pieds.* My respects to mistis. *Dollar* now, for meat—*pour le chien.*"

" *Assurément. Est-ce que l'on ne vous écoutera pas, quand vous sortirez ?*"

" *Non ; je dors seul.*"

" Good-bye, Sam. I wish I could take you with me."

" Good-bye, sare ; *and you'll never see me again.*"

" Come, Beelzebub, get me my wagon." Beelzebub rose, locked the collar about Sam's neck, and preceded Herman, who dropped a gold dollar behind him just within the door, and waited before it, while Sam crawled to it and picked it up.

Never was conspiracy more speedily concocted. Herman had scarcely been ten minutes in the cabin. How often must poor mangled Sam, lying on his earthen floor, have rehearsed all the particulars of his escape in his hopeless day-dreams, in order to be able to make his requests so promptly and judiciously! How many times must he have longed in vain for that knife and pistol and onion and dollar!

St. Dominique's purpose, in permitting the interview, was probably only to harrow up the feelings of the young knight-errant, by the spectacle and story of the helpless misery of the person whom he wished to relieve. He had already become impatient and suspicious of the length of Herman's stay; but before Abaddon, whom he sent down to put an end to it, had time to reach the *quarter*, the conference was over; he saw Beelzebub bringing out the wagon; and Beelzebub was utterly unaware that anything of the least importance had been discussed in Sam's cabin, excepting the cheese, biscuit, and gingerbread.

Herman drove off from the gate feeling like one awaking, and scarcely awaking, from a wild weird dream, or as if, somehow, Memory and Fancy had been playing Puss-in-the-corner in his mind, and taken each other's places. "I must have been bewitched in this wild, strange country," said he, "or exchanged understandings with 'Liza Maria. I thought I had heard and seen the inconceivable worst of slavery before; but can I ever really have heard and seen such things as these? Can I be in the first stage of a delirium?" He put his hand mechanically to his pulse.

"Pshaw, it was all real enough, and too real; but I must set down a specimen of it in my note-book, or I shall scarcely take even my own word for it hereafter."

As soon as he reached the six houses of London (sneer not! Trans-Atlantic London was a hamlet once), he inquired for a lawyer, and was told that there was "a right smart one twenty miles off, to Nineveh." He rode thither early the next morning, hoping to be able to rescue poor Sam at once, without exposing him to the risks of a doubtful race or fight, with negro-hunters biped or quadruped.

Mr. Dunham, the lawyer, received him gladly, pricked up his ears at the idea of "a little business," promised secrecy, produced pens and paper, and was all civil attention. As Herman proceeded, however, in his brief account of his visit to St. Dominique, two perpendicular wrinkles began to stripe the bridge of his advocate's nose; he wrote slowly, and presently threw himself back in his chair with the inauspicious question, "Well, sir; and what did you propose to do in the affair?"

"To seek the remedy provided by the laws against the ill-treatment of slaves. I have been assured again and again, by Southern gentlemen, that, when applied for, it was ample."

"Indubitably, sir, indubitably; but in all cases we must have evidence."

"Have I not?—the evidence of my own eyes?"

"That the nigger had been chastised, you have, I suppose, sir; that the chastisement was excessive?"

"He was raw from his head to his hips."

"That is no proof at all that the chastisement was excessive. The nigger may have been very refractory; and the owner have corrected him just so far, and no farther, than was required to reduce him to needful submission. What would you do yourself, if you had a high-spirited colt, now? You would bear it no ill-will, very probably;—in your secret heart, you might even appreciate it all the more for its mettle;—but you'd have to beat it, till you'd broke it in, before you could make it of any service to you, wouldn't you?—and so you would a man."

"By how much, then," thought Herman, "is a man better than a horse?"

"The court couldn't manifestly," continued the advocate, "undertake to determine the precise number of blows required for the subjugation of the man, any more than the horse. Nobody, of course, would be prone wantonly to depreciate their own property, in the horse *or* in the man. In all these cases it is rationally to be presumed, that the master's interest is a sufficient safeguard for the safety of the slave."

"But if it proves not to be so?"

"We are arguing in a circle, sir. It can't *be* proved only by evidence; and what we have thus far elicited, don't commence to be the first commencement of evidence. The boy could talk and eat and drink and sit up, couldn't he? Did you, now, honestly, yourself consider that he was in the minutest danger of life or limb?"

"From anything which *had* been done to him, perhaps not very imminent danger, but,"——

"Oh, d—n it, sir, 'sufficient unto the day is the evil,' &c. If you undertake to right all the wrongs that may be hereafter, you'll have your hands fuller than I would wish to have.mine."

"But St. Dominique distinctly told me, he had a spite against the man."

"Did he? No? I opine you wouldn't like to swear to that."

"I should."

Dunham looked at him again, and set it down. "That comes nearer than anything we've had yet, to prove malice. Of itself, however, it don't amount to much. A man may have a spite deservedly against a servant, without the slightest intent to maim or kill. Anything more to that effect?"

"He keeps his negroes from running away, by pulling out their toe-nails for every unsuccessful attempt to escape. He keeps Sam less to work than to serve for what he calls a scape-goat, and tortures him as a warning to the rest."

"You don't mean to assert, now, that he told you these particulars!"

"No, but much the same thing. He checked himself, and called one of his drivers to answer any questions that I chose to ask."

"In his presence?"

"No."

"I expect not. Pretty smart customer, St. Dominique. You don't catch *him* napping. Now, don't you see? He can say the nigger lied; most likely he did, too. Anyhow, a nigger's word's no evidence. If you don't like to trust my opinion of the case, you may go around to every advocate in this State; and they'll one and all, singly and severally, corroborate you it's no go."

"Have you and Mr. St. Dominique's neighbours never suspected that he might be mad?"

"Not that I am aware of, sir. If he is, I must aver, there's a good deal of method in his madness. I heard him make a speech at a political caucus, of late. He is one of our most felicitous and scathing orators. Few of us, indeed, have a more severe or flowery elocution. The consideration of insanity, not-withstanding, if well founded, could not fail to be urged with great effect by his counsel, if appearances really went against him, and ought to plead, very powerfully, with any individual of common humanity to refrain from inculpating him."

"Well, suppose he should kill the man,—I don't say all at once, or by any extraordinary means,—but by inches of slow, ordinary, mental and physical torment,—by solitary confinement, blows, and irons, for instance?"

"Rather too rash a supposition for me to entertain, sir, on such trivial grounds. 'Charity thinketh no evil.'"

"Charity prevents evil where she can, sir, for the sake both of the sufferer and the doer. Excuse me if, as your client, I repeat my question."

"Well, I can only say what I've said till I'm weary, already. If you could prove it by legal evidence, he could be punished, of course, provided you could prove the correction to have been immoderate."

"What is immoderate correction?"

"That's as the court shall determine. Authorities conflict some, I expect. I would say, practically, correction that destroys life or limb, and that might have been expected to destroy life or limb."

"Then, until his 'correction' has ended in mutilation or murder, it is not immoderate, and he is to be left in the hands of his master?"

"Well, sir, you seem to have extra-ordinary difficulty in comprehending a perfectly clear case. Suppose, now, that you go into court, and find an advocate

to go with you, (I must take leave to decline, for obvi-
ous reasons), and state that you waited on St. Dominique at his mansion; he receives you hospitably;
you commence to ask questions presently, and to intercede on behalf of one of his servants; he calls another
of his servants, and enjoins him to afford you any information you demand of him, and to conduct you to
see the nigger in whom you take an interest; the one
servant tells you a cock-and-bull narrative, and you
discover that the other has had a flogging, cause unknown.

"Then uprises St. Dominique's advocate, and states
that you waited, as you allege, on his client, at his
mansion; he entertains you as a stranger, with open
arms, and makes you welcome with the best his resources can afford, but incontinently discovers that
you are a wolf in sheep's clothing,—in fine, an abolitionist; you commence to propound en-quirries about
his private affairs, which he don't like, nor would any
gentleman in the court, and to intercede on behalf of
one of his servants, who's a pretty bad subject. His
client won't take it upon him to deny, that he may
have said, he had a resentment or spite against boy
Sam,—had cause sufficient, boy Sam having repeat-
edly endeavoured to incite up the other servants to
insubordination, and caused him a good deal of inconvenience;—can't now recollect;—would regret to have
availed himself of such an expression, but may possibly
have thrown it out unguardedly in the heat of conversation, when inevitably exasperated by ungentlemanly
and unwarrantable prying into our domestic institutions; he doesn't opine, that it would be an example
of happy augury to make enfranchisement the boon of
mutiny; nor does he think your queries worth respond-

ing to in person; but, reluctant to pick a difficulty
with a guest, and anticipating a jest at the proverbial
credulity of your sect, he summarily consigns you to
the most mendacious liar on his plantation, who, according to anticipation, stuffs you to your repletion
with cock-and-bull narratives. Upon this, St. Dominique smiles benignantly, rubs his hands, and looks
in a jovial way around upon the auditors, who all
laugh likewise, and reflect, 'What a felicitous jest,
and what a genial man!' Counsel proceeds: 'A nigger, at his client's direction, attended you to visit boy
Sam; boy had been moderately flogged for insolent
and threatening demeanour,—could sit up, notwithstanding, talk, eat, and drink, as you don't undertake
to deny, and is now perfectly well;—didn't design to
make any secret of the chastisement, or wouldn't manifestly have sent you to see the boy.

"Counsel then summons witnesses to prove that St.
Dominique is a good master. Up step some of our
first men, from the nearest cities, to the stand, and testify that they have all been privileged to partake of
Esquire St. Dominique's elegant hospitality, at his residence or at Capet City, and that, though he is avow-
edly a gallant and highly-spirited gentleman among
his equals, they've rarely saw him lift a finger, nay,
nor so much even as a thumb, against any of his dependants.

"You summon witnesses to prove the contrary, if
you see suitable; but they won't come; for, in the first
place, they wouldn't wish to gain ill-will; and, in the
next, St. Dominique's nearest neighbour is domiciled out
of sight and sound of him; and, when gentlemen go
to trespass on the hospitality of another gentleman,
they don't customarily go prying and gossipping about

among his servants, to ascertain what scandal concerning him they can gather up upon his premises.

"Judge charges jury according to legal evidence forthcoming, instructing 'em that, as to any vague surmises and nigger-slandering without the court, they're to pass 'em by as the idle wind, which they regard not. Jury renders verdict accordingly. St. Dominique treats all around, and returns with three cheers to his mansion, to wallop Sam doubly if such be his pleasure, and you're rode out o' town on a rail.

"Take my advice, sir," concluded Mr. Dunham. "It don't do for us youngerly men,"—he might have been about forty himself,—"to attempt to mete out too rigorous vengeance to the infirmity of our elders. The charity which they now demand at our hands, we may ere long require for ourselves. I shall act honorable towards you, and retain the secrecy of our conference within my own bosom; but I would counsel you to expose yourself within the power of no other individual here, like you have done in mine. The fact is, we don't want any strangers coming here to look into our peculiar institution; and, should our community once be made aware that you were such, and so doing, you would find your own affairs quite sufficient for your management, without intermingling in those of other individuals."

This was significant enough.

CHAPTER XX.

THE RESCUE.

"These hands are spotless yet,—
Yea, white as when in infancy they strayed
Unconscious o'er my mother's face, or closed
With that small grasp which mothers love to feel.
No stain has come upon them since that time,—
They have done nothing violent,—
Of a calm will untroubled servants they,
And went about their offices　*　*　*
In peace.
But he they served,—he is not what he was."

PHILIP VAN ARTEVELDE.

WHAT was Herman to do? What he ought to have done, I leave to each of my readers to decide according to his or her strength of mind or strength of feeling, sex, associations, or knowledge of casuistry and moral philosophy. As it is a question which I find myself unable to answer, I am glad that my business is only to say what he did.

The legal consultation, recorded in the last chapter, was no sooner over than he was off again; and he went over the river which formed the nearest boundary-line of the State, to the log-house of a family of gallant backwoodsmen and women, whom he knew very well by name and reputation.

Ichabod Kuhn, the second son, a merry, broad-chested, sturdy man of twenty, eagerly undertook to show him an almost overgrown foot-path, little known and less travelled, which led by a trudge of seven or eight hours through the forest, to the highway, *alias* cart-track, which ran by St. Dominique's plantation. Further, he promised to be on the bank of the river opposite to the end of this path, at seven o'clock in the morning, the next time it had rained in the night, with a canoe, and to paddle across for our hero at the very first sound of a most discordant trumpet of his own manufacture, which was diverted from the use of his younger brother to Herman's, to the great relief of the former's mother.

The whole family agreed to be Sam's sureties, if he ever came among them. The good-wife packed up a goodly parcel of provisions for the young men to "camp out with;" and Ichabod at once took Herman through the path and back, that he might be perfectly familiar with it. His companion entered into the spirit of the thing so heartily, and enjoyed it so much, that Herman began almost to believe that running off with a negro, if not one of the most desirable, was one of the easiest undertakings in the world. An able and skilful ally won, is often half a victory.

Herman procured from the well-stocked farm-house a *revolver*, and suitable ammunition, two bowie-knives, an onion, and a paper of bi-carbonate of soda which he thought might have more effect in baffling the scent of the blood-hound, a pair of large, stout shoes,—upon which he rubbed the soda thoroughly, applying to them also snuff and red pepper,—and a pair of stout woollen socks, which he perfumed with camphor and lavender. All these things, and some *meaty* bones of tough but tempting quality, he locked into his *valise*, and, the next morning that promised foul weather, crossed the border again.

The greatest difficulty in the way of his plans

seemed to be, that the escape must be made on foot. The foot-path was impassable on horseback in many, and indeed most, places from the close, low, dense growth of the boughs which screened it. How was he to be upon the right spot at the right time, and still fresh and vigorous enough for the return-march? The Kuhns recommended that he should take the daily stage-coach, alight from it at dusk near a certain small village, about seven miles from St. Dominique's plantation, as if he intended to pass the night at the village, and then walk till he came within a quarter of a mile of the plantation, and lie down to rest himself within the cover of the woods until his time had come.

This, therefore, Herman did. He reached the opening of the foot-path at nine, as his watch told him. All was dark and still, except now and then the lightning and thunder, which seemed to belong to the place; the faint bark of some far-away dog, talking in dull, unintelligible accents with the Night; the whispering, mysterious voices of the wood; and the rain which fell heavily. He unlocked his *valise* softly,—for some one might be listening,—took out his pistol, and thrust it into his bosom with a strange and awful feeling. In whose cold breast might some of its six cold bullets be resting before the day? One sheathed knife he put into his pocket, and took one in his hand. Then, like a hunted felon, he threw himself down upon the dank, spongy leaves and earth, and, while the rain fell upon him, and the lightning and thunder flashed and crashed over him, had time to think and feel that he was an outlaw, out in that wild night upon a lawless errand,— a strange thought and feeling for him!

"God keep all His children from bloodshed this night!"

he said; but he no longer felt that it rested with himself, to keep himself from bloodshed. A dark destiny seemed to him to have seized upon him, and to be carrying him on whither it would!—whither God would? —or whither the devil would? He thought, he hoped, the former; but,—oh, misery!—he was bewildered now; and he could not tell. Oh, cruel, cruel Tyranny, to drive such souls into such straits as his!

By a strong effort he endeavoured to brace and calm his mind, while the dripping drops ticked out the moments on the leaves around him like the hurrying clock of Nature. There was time enough still for consideration. If on consideration, even now, what he was doing proved to be wrong, he must not, he would not, go on. It had hitherto been his care and his happiness, to avoid all questionable deeds; this deed was questionable; but was it a more questionable one than it would be to go on his way and leave poor Sam, even now panting and throbbing with expectation, no doubt, so near him, to die of hope deferred, or perhaps under the inflictions of his tormentor;—as has happened, it is said, before now, to one or more slaves, under the (happily) " peculiar institution "?

The latter appeared to him to be not questionable merely, but simply impossible. He had already, he said to himself, done all that in him lay to avoid the issue; he had offered almost *carte-blanche*, he had endured insult, he had appealed to the law, in vain. The case was a very singular one, and to him unprecedented. Common rules and customs did not cover it. It could be decided, if at all, only by a recurrence to *first principles*, generally, in new cases, of very uncertain application.

Justice, first: Constance owed Sam in strict equity,

for the wages of his lifetime, much more than would
have enabled him to buy himself his pistol, knife, and
onion. Then, whatever Herman might think about
taking the life of a fellow-creature, even in self-defence,
had he any right to impose his perhaps extravagant
theories harshly and rigorously upon another man, and
that other a man in such extremity? Besides, one of
his two reasons for accompanying Sam in his flight, instead of, as the latter expected, merely giving him what
he wanted and leaving him to shift for himself, was to
see that in his desperation he did no unnecessary violence to himself or his pursuers.

Secondly, human brotherhood: Could he have seen
Edward beset as Sam was, or pursued, as he was likely
to see him in a few hours, by blood-hounds and man-
hunters, and crying to him for help, without putting a
weapon into his hands? He could not. But the man-
hunters were his fellow-men, as well as Sam. Then
could he, even for the love he bore to Edward,—deep
and strong as brother ever felt,—have connived at his
brother's hunting a slave? He could not; but this he
said with less emphasis and satisfaction; for he could
not likewise assert, that he should have armed a fugitive slave against his brother. So he lay, wet more
with perspiration than with rain, and wrestled with
his thoughts; while the thunder struck the minutes,
and the rain-drops ticked the seconds, away.

Ten o'clock. There was still time left. He must
compose himself, and use it. If he could see that what
he was about to do was wrong, he must and would still
go back alone, and leave it undone. But what was he
about to do? To give a poor, oppressed, tormented
man, who had no friend on earth but himself, some
meat to keep the dogs from baying him, some shoes to

keep the dogs from tracking him, a knife to keep the dogs from tearing him, and safe guidance through the woods to the river. That seemed to him to be right. That was all that he would do, unless others forced him to do more; and, if they did so, must not their blood be upon their own heads? Should not he leave himself, then, to be guided by circumstances? But he who is guided by circumstances, may be guided into any crime.

But what evil motive in his heart could there be to prompt him to this undertaking? Hatred to St. Dominique? He wished him nothing worse than repentance. He had offered him money which he did not want, and which Herman could ill spare, to bribe him to a deed of simple justice. He was about to endeavour to save him from deeds for which injustice is a mild term;—a good end; but the means?—*were* they good, too?

Could self-interest be his motive? What profit, praise, or promotion, was to be won by his success? The Kuhns would be silent for their own sakes; and he, lest a procedure so doubtful, even in an exigency like this, should ever be adopted as a precedent. If he succeeded, a concealment,—hateful to ingenuous minds as the old cast-off cloak of the evil one which he left behind him when he went to his own place, to weigh many and many a noble soul down to him,— was henceforth to be his portion. If he failed, a bloody and untimely death was the best which he could promise himself; while for the fair name, and brilliant fame too, perhaps, which he had hoped to leave behind him at a ripe old age, he should leave only an ignominious example for those who hated his principles to point their moral with,

8

when they would attempt to prove the unrighteous tendency of attempting to be more righteous than the law.

But why should he fail? or why should he dishearten himself any longer by looking only on the dark side of the question? Three days before, Ichabod and he had trodden the path to and fro, and, at high noon, had met no living creature except the birds and woodchucks which shyly and slyly peeped out at them with their twinkling eyes, between the gleaming leaves, and heard no sound except twittering, and rustling, and their own whispers and footsteps. One more hour of waiting,—that was the worst of it,—and then seven or eight hours of steady, stealthy, marching through the friendly forest, night, rain, and fog, a stride over the few rods of bare upland and shore, a brisk *pull* over the early, lonely water, a merry breakfast at good Mistress Kuhn's, and Sam and he would be on their way rejoicing, within a few days' journey, the one of freedom, and the other of home; and his quest would be happily ended, and his Constance's heart at rest.

He waited for the next flash, and looked at his watch. A quarter past eleven. No more time for wavering, now. Be still, now, throbbing heart! Worn nerves, be firm! All concentrated now he lay, in one strong prayer that the rescue, *which was to be,* might be speedy, sure, and stainless. At a quarter before twelve, he arose and stole on. He must be in time, but not too early, and make Sam hear him, if possible, before the dogs.

Let us not condemn him; for he could not condemn himself. Let us not commend him; for he would not commend himself. Let us only pray to God that the time may come when, in our country, loyalty to our country's laws and humanity to our countrymen may no longer be so at strife in young and gallant breasts.

The grounds, which surrounded St. Dominique's house, were enclosed on the inside by a paling about five feet high; on the outside by a remaining belt of the virgin woods, five or six feet in depth. As Herman came in sight he was startled by seeing, in the observatory as he guessed, a lurid light, so intense that his first idea was that the apartment was on fire. All was still, however; and, stealing nearer and nearer, he perceived that the light, though very large, was steady and red. In a dry night it must probably have lighted the whole enclosure, from side to side and from end to end, so that St. Dominique and his spy-glass could have commanded it as well as by day. At present, though the rain had for the moment ceased, the moisture hung so thick in the air about it as to make, as it were, a ground-glass dome for it, and condense its reflection on the wet ground into an area of not very many yards. Unless a flash of lightning came just at the wrong time, the negro-huts could not now be seen from the house. Herman stole behind them, whistled once, and waited.

In five or six minutes he heard within, a rush, and a roar in which it seemed to him that he recognized the voice of the mongrel of the gate. It instantly sank into a series of low growls and chokes; as a dazzling flash gave him a moment's glimpse of a bronze group,—Cerberus holding Sam by the leg, and Sam holding Cerberus by the throat. Herman, half-blinded, hurled himself through the succeeding dark over the fence, passed his knife through the dog's throat from ear to ear, till it grated on the back-bone, with a second stroke, in the mouth, dislodged the jaw, caught Sam up, dropped him over the fence and himself after him, snatched him up again, and ran till he reached the curtain of wild-grape-vines, that fell over the entrance of the foot-path where he had left his *valise*, set him down, clapped the shoes on his feet, seized him by the hand, and ran again for about a mile.

Then they slackened their speed, listened, heard nothing, gasped, got their breath, and for the first time whispered to each other. Sam's teeth were chattering as if he was in an ague. Herman threw his own overcoat upon him and said, "Is your leg hurt badly?"

"Don know, sare,—never mind, sare,—runs good enough,— come, sare." Again they hurried on.

"Wouldn't the dog take your meat?" whispered Herman, after a pause.

"Hadn't none, sare. Bribed Billy to get it, and promised him half. Billy ate all. Saved ze dog some hoe-cake ;—he wouldn't touch it."

"Well, we've got off safe, at any rate; haven't we?"

"Hush, don speak so loud, sare. Excuse ; but it don do to holler till you gets out of ze woods. I sink so, sare,—I hope so ;—but it all depend on ze watch."

"So, St. Dominique keeps a watch, does he?"

"Yes, sare; two or three of ze house-servants takes watch an watch on ze gallery he call quarter-deck. When zeir feet stops a-walkin, he comes out an whips ; so zat zey cannot go to sleep. When it rain, zough, zey gets on ze lee-side. Lee-side, to-night opposite to ze quarter. When Cerbus yowls, ze watch has always to come to see what is ze affair. Often he yowls at nosing. Watch wishes not to come far out in ze wet for nosing; so if he see him lay down, an sinks he's asleep, he return an say, All right. If he come up close, and find he's deaded, he will call ze master, and ring ze bell, and get more dogs and men and neighbours. Got zat *pistolet*, sare?"

"Yes, I have it loaded and safe; and here, here's a knife for you. If the dogs come near you, use it; but we won't kill any men, if we can help it."

"I know one man zat's a dead man, sare, if zey gets round me again."

"Do you? Who?"

"Mesef." Sam paused, and began again in a pleading tone, "Won't you let me have that *pistolet*, sare?"

"I don't know that I can help it, tired as I am, if you choose to take it," thought Herman; "for, in this short hour of freedom, you move and speak already like a much stronger man than I thought you. What do you want it for, Sam?" said he.

"To die easy. I've lived hard."

"Oh, you're not going to die now, my poor fellow." —Herman ventured to sound his repeater.—"A quarter past one. If you push on at this rate, and I can keep up with you, we shall be on the bank of the river by six or seven; and a boat is coming to take us over. We shall hide you, feed you, disguise you, and get you to Canada. You'll like living free much better than dying a slave."

Sam went muttering on at his ease, through the dark, pursuing his own train of ideas:

"If zey owns my body, zey's welcome to take it off, an keep it; it never was no use to me, on'y to ache me, an starve me, an work for ozer people. If zey wants ze skin, liefser zan not zey'd take ze flesh an bones an all togezer. I'll be a ghost, an ha'nt 'em, may-be,—never a slave again. If zey whips a ghost, can't cut it ; if zey starves it, 'tisn't hungry ; if zey puts it into hell, I don believe hell under ground is worser zàn hell on ze ground, nor ze great evil devil, zan St. Dominique ; and I won't be ze worst punished zere ; 'cause he's got to come down hesef, too, an take it. Wants a change, anyhow. No use to run away in zis worl, and get cotched again. Tried zat twice afore. Las' time got on a log, an floated over ze river. Got clear to 'Hio, an said, ' Free now !'—Wented down on my knees, an kissed ze grass an flowers. Got a place in a hotel to wait and tend. Found out how to do everysing like I was used to it. Folks sought zere wasn't nosing like me. St. Dominique know, zough ; always knew everysing. He send two nigger-catchers. Zey comes, an puts up, an makes believe gen'l'men. I wait on 'em proper an nice an civil, wiz my white apron on. Zey says I steal zeir brooches ; so ze constable takes me up. Zen zey swears to me 'fore ze postmaster, zat zey'd knowed me six years at St. Dominique's. Wa'n't so ; never saw me in zeir lives ; but St. Dominique told 'em to swear all ze same ; he knowed 'twas I, anyhow ; an if zey brought ze wrong one, he could send him back fast enough ; so no harm done. So ze postmaster let 'em have me ; an zey tote me back in handcuffs. ' So,' says St. Dominique, when I come back, ' more toe-nails to spare, you — — villain ?' While he was a-tying me, an hauling 'em out, he whisper right over me, ' If you ascends into heaven, I am zere. If you makes your bed in hell, I am zere. If you takes ze wings of ze morning, an dwells in ze uttermost parts of ze sea, even zere I am wiz zee, and my right hand shall hold zee.' So, after zey'd done floggin me, an pepperin me, an all, when I was laying on ze floor I studied it, an sought it all out. Zat man ain't a man, sare. He's a real devil, come up from down zere, to show ze ozer masters how to do it. 'Oh, damn ze niggers, give 'em hell!' he says; an zen he does it. Zat's ze reason I know now I won't get away from him,—always hears everysing, always sees everysing, always knows everysing. God bless you, master, oh, give me zat *pistolet*, now; or shoot me yousef, an zen go off safe!"

"You have got these wild notions into your head, my poor fellow, merely from suffering and solitude, and the excitement of your escape. Leave off thinking about them, and they will leave you, when you have been safe and among kind friends for a time. There is a good God over us."

Sam pressed closer to him, and whispered hoarsely, "If zere is, why did He let my Georgy master pull me up from my knees and whip me, when I kneeled down to pray to Him? If zere is, why did He let St. Dominique crucify ze las' Scape-goat?"

"Sam! What do you mean? Good God! Will you drive yourself mad, and me too?"

"It was Good Friday night," continued the hoarse voice at his ear in the dark. "I peeped in t'rough ze window. Ze shutters was shut; but zere was a little knot-hole. Zere was ze master, wiz two men zat come up ze river ze day before. Zey was eatin, an drinkin, an laughin roun ze table. Ze lights all burned blue. Zere was ze Scape-goat, gagged, on ze great black cross. Nex mornin, when ze folks come out of zeir cabins, he was buried. Zey say he'd had a fit an died in ze night. So, after St. Dominique make me Scapegoat, I'se bound to get away, live or dead, 'fore Good Friday."

"Good heavens! I can't believe you! You were dreaming! You mean to pretend that you saw such a sight as that, and didn't inform against that fiend?"

"What use?—Never say nosing to nobody.—No use. He whip me to deas, and swear I lied."

"Sam," said Herman, after another pause, "I am trying to do you a great service, am I not?"

"Yes, indeed, mas'r! God forever bless you, mas'r!"

"Won't you do me one, then?"

"Oh, mas'r, *de tout mon cœur!*"

"*Don't* tell me any more of these stories, then."

"No, mas'r."

They pushed on steadily, speedily, and silently for several miles. The clouds lifted, and broke over the tree-tops. The pale stars came out. Sam's dark figure stood forth in stronger relief against the dark woods beside him; and Herman admired the activity and firmness of his stride, the strong desire so bravely bracing the worn frame and torn leg: "You are a powerful fellow. You ought to be able to serve yourself well in every way, when you come to be your own man. How quickly and cleverly you planned your escape! You chose a wet night, I suppose, that you might not be seen by the light of the great lamp; or is that burned only in wet weather?"

"Every night, sare, since a year. Ze master he like not ze dark in ze house. Abaddon, ze body-servant, he tell Beelzebub zat las' time zey wented to Capet City, ze master and he, zey wented to see some of zem witches zat raises spirits wiz tables. Ze wrong one come up to see ze master, an commence to talk sings zat he not wish to hear about. So he jump up out of ze circle, and come right away; but ze spirit come after, an knock in ze car, an come home wiz him an keep knockin all roun his bed's head every night; so he make Abaddon sleep on ze floor, an keep ze light burning. No use, zough. Ze spirit don mind;—it come every night, an knock on just ze same. Ze lamp keep ze master from seein when it lighten, zough; he never like zat, Abaddon say;—always sweared when it waked him up;—an zen, ze lamp good to scare ze niggers wiz. He tell zem it's a bewitched lamp, zat will show zem to him an burn zem up, if zey goes out of zeir cabins in ze night. Ze women believes it;— zey's always so ignorant;—I don, 'cause it never burn up ze watch; boun to try it, anyhow."

The chill of early dawn began to creep into their bones, in spite of their rapid motion. The first birds cleared their throats and tuned their little pipes discordantly. The day began to break,—day, whose approach is so infinite a relief to lonely watchers through a night of pain of body or of mind, if the pain be one which can be expected to be left behind with the night! The growing light brightened Herman's spirits; though his companion seemed to cower and shrink from it. He could not believe that their danger was now great enough to be appreciable. He took from his *valise* the bones originally intended as "a sop for Cerberus," but of which that fugitive slave-catcher's too "uncompromising discharge of the duties of his office" had forever deprived him, and urged Sam to keep up his strength with them. Sam would not stop to rest for a moment, and at first refused to eat, but, after his appetite had been aroused by the first few mouthfuls of generous food, devoured it with a famished voracity, which made Herman think it lucky for him that there was no more of it.

8*

Their feet jogged on ; and so did the hands of his watch : " Four o'clock !"—" Five !"—Half-past !" The path began to wind a good deal ; as Herman recollected that it had done near the river. "In half an hour more, or three quarters, now, if all goes well, Sam, we shall be in the boat, on the river,—able to sit down, lie down,—oh, delicious ! Aren't you tired almost to death ?"

" No, mas'r.   Oh !"——

A turn of the path had brought him directly upon a little encampment beside it, a smouldering fire, a smell of tobacco and whiskey, a small rude tent of two or three Indian blankets tied from branch to branch, and in front of it three rifles and a jug standing, and a feverish, bloated young man sitting, with his elbows on his knees, his head on one hand, and his eyes closed or nearly so, with sleep or headache. A dog growled. Sam, after one instant's stunned pause and stare, ran off. The young man looked up stupidly and wistfully at Herman, as if trying to collect his drunken thoughts. Herman coolly bade him good morning, passed him and moved on deliberately, to cover Sam's tell-tale flight, until he had doubled the next turn in the path, and then followed the latter as fast and noiselessly as his feet could carry him, followed himself by the other fellow's slow, thick speech still tingling in his ears, " Goo' morlin. Say ! Ho, mister ! Hain't I saw St. Dominique's Sam ?"

Strange to tell, Herman met Sam coming back. " The other way !" cried Herman.   " Run !   Why didn't you run ?"

" Wiz you, sare. Not wizout you, sare ! Ze nigger-catcher zat cotched me ! He seed me ! He'll shoot you ! Run, run !"

They ran. The path ran through the thick wood and coppice, in such a *zig-zag* that they could not tell whether they were pursued or not. Two parties ·might have followed without seeing each other in it, at a distance in a right line of a very few yards. It was possible that the negro-hunters, thoroughly roused, might be already stealing upon them by a short cut through the undergrowth; but it was not likely, Herman thought. The thicket was too thick; and the fugitives could have heard the crashing sound of any one tearing his way through it, even above the noise of their footsteps and panting breath.

A turn in the path showed them the end of the path, green upland, white light, and blue sky. The open ground, which ran upwards for about a quarter of a mile before them, ran down again more steeply on the other side, Herman remembered, for sixty or seventy feet; and then at its edge rushed the river. If the slave-hunters reached the crest of this rising ground before Ichabod and his passengers did the opposite bank, the slave-hunters could "scatter death" among them at their leisure with their rifles. If they did not, all was safe enough. But if they were now following them, before Herman and Sam could reach the river, or Ichabod have reached them, the slave-hunters might have reached the crest of the rising ground.

"Sam," gasped Herman as fast as he could speak, as they neared the opening, "take this trumpet; run straight on, up the bank, down to the river. Blow the trumpet. A boat will come. Jump in, go over, as soon as it touches the bank. I must stay here to see that nobody comes after you up the path. I'll come, if I can in time; if not, don't wait. Tell Ichabod to come for me after dark."

"Come, come too, for God's sake, mas'r!"

"No!—The dogs may track you;—I'm safe enough, if you go.—If you don't, we're lost, both.—Off, Sam, fly!"

In full faith and the instinct of obedience to a white man, Sam flew out into the sunshine,—up the green bank. Herman slipped back into the wood beside the opening of the shady pass, and looked and listened, pulling down a great branch of ash and holding it before him for a screen. He heard behind him Sam's receding footsteps,—before him a croak, a chirp, and then, he thought, a distant halloo. He saw a toad hop across the path, then a robin run up it, and then a man, *the* man, with his rifle. Should he fire? Not like an assassin,—not without warning. "Halloo!" cried he; "what are you after here?"

"St. Domilique's Sam. Who are you?"

"A friend, if you stand! A foe, if you come on. I am armed, and a good shot. Stand back, at your peril."

With a loud whoop and halloo, the man discharged his rifle towards the voice, making the bark fly about Herman's ears from the tree above him, and rushed on in a cloud of smoke.

As it cleared away, Herman fired. He seldom missed. The man went down on the turf with a ball in his knee, screaming at the top of his voice, "Murder, murder, murder! Help! Samson, Jeff, murder!" while in a breath the voice of the wood cried again, "Dastardly villain, to hunt a poor negro! Do you want to halloo all your other two-legged hounds upon him? Be silent. I meant to let you off easy, the first time, and did so. Don't make me fire again."

There was a pause. The man groaned and rolled

helplessly. The green turf grew crimson. Righteous indignation began to be tempered with mercy. "It seems to me, you are losing a good deal of blood. Haven't you a belt, or a handkerchief, or anything which you could strap or tie round your leg?—tight, close above the knee?"

The man mechanically fumbled in one of his pockets, half sat up, and rolled over again.

"Haven't you?—Take my cravat." Herman took it off, made into a ball, and threw it to him. He only griped his leg with both hands, writhing and moaning. He was faint, perhaps,—irresolute, at any rate. No one was in sight. It would not take a minute to do it for him. "Here, I'll do it for you." Herman ran out to aid him; when, quick as a catamount, the man sprang again into a sitting posture, and at his face and throat, with a bowie-knife, cutting, thrusting, and darting like lightning. "Down, down!" cried Herman, sternly, his moral and professional instincts alike outraged, as he knocked the knife and feeling together out of his patient's hand, with a dexterous tap on the elbow. "Don't you see your leg is spouting like a fire-engine?—There, that's right! I'm a surgeon. I won't hurt you." He hastily bound his rose-color-and-gray cravat, with Clara's little stitches in it, round the coarse, blue, bloody pantaloon, drew the charge of the man's rifle, thrust it through the bandage, gave it a twist or two, and put the muzzle into his hand. "There. Hold that. Don't let go." Back he ran to his covert.

Five minutes had scarcely passed since the rencounter. No one was yet in sight. Ichabod and Sam had had about time to join forces. If Herman ran now, he might be just in season to cross with them; while the man's comrades, if they soon came after him, would probably stop to attend to him. If Herman ran, and the man's comrades did not soon come after him, and attend to him judiciously when they did come, he must die! how unfit to die! Herman looked towards him. He was letting the bandage loosen itself. "No. Hold hard. Don't let go."

"Oh, d— it! I can't stand it. It's too goldurned tight."

"For comfort, I know it is; but it is not for safety. Hold steady, I tell you. Come, be a man! You would not lose your life rather than bear a little pain. You're a full-blooded fellow; but it won't do for you to bleed five minutes more as you did five minutes ago. Your friends were coming after you, weren't they?"

"Dang it, yes; but they was so all-fired sleepy. They was a-dousing of thar heads, to wake they-selves up. Bet they've snoozed off again! Oh, the h—, what'll I do?"

"When they come, send one of them for the nearest surgeon, as fast as he can go. Make the other loosen the bandage and hold your leg, with his fingers just, where you feel the pulse beat. Don't stir till it has been dressed. You understand?"

"Oh, dang it, strannger, whar'll they go for a doctor? Ain't none but you round, for miles an miles," said the man, beginning to cry.

"Let them put you carefully into the next boat that comes down the river, then, and take you to one."

"Won't no boat come by for a week, mebbe. Mebbe the boys won't come nohow. Oh, strannger, reckon I hain't hurt you, anyhow, half as bad as you've hurt me. Don't b'ar malice. You couldn't have the heart now to go off an leave a poor maimed feller here in the bush, to starve all alone by hisself, or be clawed and chawed up with wild-cats, could yer ?"

Could Herman ? He sprang out once more ;—for the man, in his piteous supplication, had raised his head and shoulders, supporting himself on both hands to look for him, let go the bandage, bled again, and again sunk, moaning and swooning.—He tightened the bandage, cut open the pantaloon with his pen-knife, and looked at the wound. If he could, he would dress it before anybody came, and watch the patient from his lurking-place until somebody came, or, if that should not happen before dark, get Ichabod to help him carry the man to the boat, and row him in it to some place where he could be properly tended. Would taking up the artery be enough ?—No, it would not, he saw. The young man must lose his leg or his life.

If all warriors were likewise compassionate surgeons compelled to heal the wounds they made, it is possible that mankind would be compelled to forego much of the advantage which, as some religious moralists inform us, they now derive from the wholesome exercise of shooting, and being shot by, one another. Even the overseer in the jail of New Orleans, who was forced to nurse the girl he had flogged, is said to have declared he would never treat another so; for he found, (blessed teaching of experience !) " it was too much for any one to bear."

As Herman bent over the man in the first misery of his discovery, he said, "Make yourself easy. I shall not leave you alone ;" and then he sat down with him, took his head upon his knee, fanned him with his hat, and waited patiently. He had not long to wait. A hairy muzzle was presently thrust between them ;

and a blood-hound licked the sufferer's face.   Herman looked over its shoulders down the path.   Three men were coming up.

"Hullo, Noble!   What have you been and done to yourself?" cried they.

"He has been shot by a person in the wood," said Herman.

"What's yer name, an what's yer business?"

"I am a physician."

"That's luck, anyhow!"

"Why, Noble!   Who shot yer?"

"Durn it!   How would I know?"

"Think 'twas the nigger?"

"I reckon."   Herman shook his head at him; and he corrected himself obediently: "No 'twan't.   I remember, now, of his not havin nothin but a knife."

"Bled a lot, ain't he?"

"Most to death.   Durn ye all!   I'd ha' died here for all you, if it hadn't been for the doctor."

"Bad hurt, strannger?"

"I fear so.   He will need to be put to bed presently, and have good nursing."

"Bones smashed?"

"Yes."

"Think ye can mend 'em?"

"No," said Herman, laying the patient's head gently down, rising, and taking his questioner aside.

"Reckon 't'll have to come off, then, won't it?"

"Yes.   Is there any place near here, where we could carry him, and put him to bed?"

"Reckon not.   We'll have, one or two on us, to stop an camp down with him har', till he's got over the wust on it."

"Have you either of you a saw of any kind?"

" No."

" A file?—We might make a saw, perhaps, out of one of your bowie-knives."—

" Wall, no; *I* hain't; Jeff, ha' you?"

" What?"

" Got a file? Doctor wants one to make a saw."

" No. Samson has, though; hain't ye?"

" A saw! What for?" cried Noble, catching the word; and, getting no answer, he rolled grovelling on his face, and sobbed and screamed like a child, while Herman, bidding Samson take the file out of hearing, and prepare the knives, vainly endeavoured to sooth and encourage him. The knives were brought back and handed to him, one with twelve small teeth notched in the edge, tolerably smooth and even, and the other whetted. Giving the leg for a moment into Samson's hands, he went into the bushes, and presently returned with his coat buttoned to his chin, and his linen torn in strips for bandages. By good luck, he had a roll of sticking-plaster and skein of sewing-silk, as usual, in his pocket.

" I suppose, of course, you none of you have a drop of ether?"

" ' Either '? I'll be durned if I know what 'tis."

" Gosh! It's that thar lullaby-water, that the man-carvers to the horspittles gives the niggers an Paddies, to snuff out of sponges afore they cuts 'em up. They goes off whole into a sweet snooze, an wakes up in so many pieces they can't find 'emselves, haw, haw! No, I reckon we hain't got much o' that in the bush h'ar,' strannger. You'll have to chop him with his eyes open, 'thout you sews 'em up. We'll hold onto him an keep him in order, soon as yer ready. Hold yer noise, Noble! I never see such a thunderin big coward!

Thar was my brother Elderkin, slashed his own hand off with one cut when the mad dog tasted on it, an made his nigger hold a red-hot axe to it till it stopped bleedin, an grinned all the time like a coon."

" For God's sake, don't talk so before him ! Have you no laudanum ?"

" Lod'num ? What would we care that round for ? Reckon he'll go to sleep without nothin soon, if yer don't git to work,—skeered to death, he's so skeery !"

Herman perceived that there was some sense in this suggestion, and that neither his patient's nerves, nor his own, were likely to be braced by waiting to hear more of this sort of conversation. He went up to the poor fellow, and said kindly, " I am very sorry to see you in so much trouble; but come, now, try to pluck up a good heart and behave like a man ; and I'll do my very best to relieve you as quickly as possible. See ! look at my watch ; see how fast it goes ! Before this second-hand has run round three times, 'twill be over, if you'll only keep still."

He had never before performed any considerable operation without the aid of ether, and of skilful assistants. The poor wretch's outcries under his knife harrowed his very soul, and made him feel a constant and almost irresistible impulse to throw down the instrument, and give up the business ; while Noble's struggles in the hands of the three who held him, for he was a naturally vigorous youth and still a little in liquor, added to his difficulties and distress.

The cries sank into gasps at length. The vessels had been secured. The sticking-plaster was applied successfully, and the last bandages were going on ; when the muffled sound of hoofs trotting on the turf was heard, and there was a start, an exclamation, and a burst of laughter from the attendants. Herman looked up, and saw a stag rudely harnessed with list and thongs of raw hide into a large red wheelbarrow, in which sat a little old negro woman, with a shrivelled, shiny, jetty face set in a golden rim of Bandanna, —a sight half-grotesque, half-picturesque,—an emblem of our wild, glorious South, driven and hampered by slavery.

"Hullo, mammy, who be you? an whar'd yer come from; an whar'd yer get so much team?"

She jumped out just in time to seize the head of the stag, which was bolting with starting eyes at sight of the dog rising and approaching curiously. She, herself, looked at the latter with much apprehension.

"Never mind, mammy. He won't touch yer, if yer out on lawful business. Here, Snuffy, down!"

"I'm Honor'ble Harrison T. Henson's nuss, gemmen," began she, in a high, shrill pipe, punctuating her sentences with a conciliatory jerking curtsy between each two clauses. "Been down to his mansion, gemmen, [curtsy], 'cause dey's had de measles;— allers wants me when dar's sickness; comin home now, 'cause got 'em all adolescent,—done so. Here's my pairss, gemmen, if you'd have de honor to rexamine it."

"Bad hand,—can't read it."

She looked anxiously round the group, and handed it to Herman. Turning it right-side up, a preliminary which had not occurred to the former inspector, he read, written in a pot-hook and trammel school-boy hand, the words,

"'Pass July Hennessy.

"'HARRISON T. HENSON, jun.'"

" Reckon 'twon't do for nobody to meddle wi' you.
Hensons is powerful grand folks, ain't they ?"

She strove for words in vain, appearing to be struck
dumb, alike by the impossibility of finding any adequate to express all the grandeur of the Hensons, and
by amazement at finding anybody in a state of uncertainty about it.

" Whar d'yer git so much hoss ?"

" Found him when he was a babe, mas'r. Raised
him, mas'r. Honor'ble Harrison T. Henson, he make
me a bonation of de ole wheelbarrow ; an young mas'r,
he done put on de stick an little wheels in front, to
make it run easy for his ole mammy and de beast."

" Where do you live, ma'am ?" said Herman.

" Well, I 'sides in de bush, mas'r, not far-off, on
Honor'ble Harrison T. Henson's ole place, mas'r.
When de ole mansion nigh here consumed, he move
down de river to his oder mansion ; but I didn't tink
I'd like de sitiwation ; and says I, ' Mas'r, I jus kind
o' lub my ole home de best; an if you'd 'low me to remain, I'll allers dissent to come to your resistance,
mas'r, wheneber you summonses me, will so.' Den he
apply, ' July, I ranticipate you'll be secluded ; and I
say, ' Well, mas'r, if I is, I'll foller arter ye pretty sur-
reptitiously.' So he 'lowed me to remain ; an nobody
ever interferes with me ; an I goes an makes dem a
visit now an den, when I wants society, to see if dey's
gettin along well, an don't want nothin ; and dey
comes now an den, an makes visits to me.—Dat ar
gemman indisposed ?"

" Yes. He has been very badly hurt. I wish that
we could get him to your cabin, and persuade you to
take him under your care." Herman looked in his
purse. " There's twenty dollars to help pay for the

expense and trouble. Do you think you can accommodate him?"

" Well, mas'r, if he'll be patient an spectable, don no but I might. De good Book say, Be not regretful to entertain strangers; for some on 'em is angels onawares. If you's de Good Samaritan, I'se be de host, will so, an purvide what is needful from de steamboat, can so. Steward bery nice colored gemman, friend o' mine. I has pou'try an wegetable at my residence, an eberyting very compatible. Dis way, gemmen, long de lawn."

She led her stag, and led the way. The other men, by Herman's direction, laid the longest of their blankets upon the ground, and his patient upon it; and he helped them to carry it smoothly and evenly over the smooth, short grass. They soon came where the woods were parted by an old half choked avenue, and then, in a cultivated clearing a few rods from it, to a little log-cabin, mantled and almost hidden by wild grape-vines. The little old negress tethered her stag without, and seemed almost swallowed up in the darkness within, but bustled about, produced, with a hospitable flourish, hard biscuit and cheese from a cupboard, and promised eggs and chicken, so soon as she should have bestowed her patient comfortably in her rude but tidy bed.

His safety was now, evidently, next to that of her stag, which was still scarcely reconciled to the neighbourhood of the dog, her chief idea: she was animated by that joy of nursing in which half the genius of nursing consists; and Herman, as he directed and assisted her, was greatly relieved as he noticed her zeal and skill. Noble was adjusted properly, with an extempore stump-pillow and *cradle* of Herman's de vising, and asleep instantly. The men went out for fire-wood. The old woman took up her frying-pan. Herman gave her his last orders, and took his leave in spite of her hospitable entreaties, promising to give or send further assistance, if he could. Free at last! He would go his ways, and take to the bush again while the men were at their dinner.

They were not getting fire-wood. They were loitering and whispering together, rifle in hand, before the only door. As he appeared within it, they closed side by side into a row, and faced him, stirring each other up with their elbows.

"Say, doctor! stop with us an take a bite."

"Thank you, I'm not hungry."

"Well, but, doctor, don't be in a hurry. *What d'yer say yer name was?*"

"Excuse me, I am in a hurry,—fatigued and un-well."

"Well, then, doctor, jest you set down an rest awhile, an take a drop o' whiskey."

"I shall come back and see your companion again, or send him another surgeon, if I can, in a few days. Now I have business elsewhere."

"Well, but ain't yer name Ard'n? 'Cause if 'tis, reckon yer'll have to stop."

"Have tur stop yer now anyhow,—'cause I'm a constable,—an take ye up to St. Dominique's, tur see if his pesky Sam ain't got away again. Noble thought he see him, jest afore we see you; an St. Dominique told me, if they war any abolition capers cut up around here jes' now, to have an eye arter a Yankee o' that name, that had been up to his place insultin on him. Make everythin pleasant to ye, along o' your attentions to Noble; an if Sam ain't got away, nor none o' the niggers around here, you'll be discharged in a day or two, an none the wus."

So Noble went to bed; Sam, to Canada; and Herman, to jail. Perhaps, even there, he did not wish himself back again in that night in the wood. However flinty the way before him might be, it was now at least straight and plain. The voice of Duty, no more confused and unintelligible, clearly called upon him to suffer; and to his suffering, accordingly, as best he might, he patiently and manfully addressed himself.

CHAPTER XXI.

THE KNIGHT IN BONDAGE.

"Oh, no! Believe, in yonder tower,
It will not sooth my captive hour
To know, in fruitless brawl begun
For me, that mother wails her son,
For me, that widow's mate expires,
For me, that orphans wail their sires,
That patriots mourn insulted laws,
And curse the Douglas for the cause."
THE LADY OF THE LAKE.

"ILL tidings," says the proverb, "fly fast." In ancient times they were carried by mysterious Rumor, outstripping in speed hoof of horse, sail of ship, or tongue of man. In modern days they are transmitted by newspapers, not unfrequently bearing paragraphs ominously and roughly bordered with ink, not printer's, and obligingly directed by unknown hands. One of these papers, "The Lone Star of Beddleham," came about this time to Edward, bearing one of these paragraphs, to the effect that: "A vile Yankee named Herbert Hardon, an emissary of the Abolition Society, has recently been arrested in the act of alluring away one of the servants of our public-spirited and esteemed fellow-citizen, Antoine St. Dominique. He had previously commenced by waiting upon and grossly insulting him at his residence, and, on being hospitably suffered to escape without merited chastisement, took advantage in this further manner of the generous but scarce politic forbearance of his host. The nigger has not yet been recovered. The kidnapper, narrowly escaping condign and immediate justice at the hands of our fellow-citizens, has been placed into Tadmor Jail, to await the tardier vengeance of the law."

This communication, as was no doubt intended, gently broke the shock to his brother when, three days after receiving it, he took from the post-office a letter which Herman had found means, after some difficulty and delay, to write and send to him.

Edward rushed about town, procured letters of introduction from everybody to everybody, told Clara and Constance, that Herman had got himself into a little scrape out in Bondage, where nobody knew who he was; but that he was going to set matters straight directly, get him off, and bring him back with flying colors; and that all they had to do was to make themselves easy and happy, and see to Sally's getting the young prodigal's rooms in order for him in the course of the next week. He then threw himself into the cars, and travelled day and night till he found himself at the door of Tadmor Jail.

It was a barbaric fortress, of what may be called a new composite order of architecture. The walls were about four feet thick, and made of four layers,— the outer one brick, the next of hewn logs, the next stone, and the inner one again of logs. A guard stood at the door with his musket.

"Can I see Mr. Arden?" said Edward.

"I reckon, if you go around to that third winder on the right hand. When thar ain't no gentlemen or ladies thar a-lookin in at him, he's mostly close to it, a-lookin out. If he ain't in sight, yer jest holler at him; an tell him to stir his stumps an let yer see him.

9

Most that comes is disapp'inted, though;—he ain't so much of a ruffian to look at."

"Drunken rascal!" muttered Edward; "what is he talking about?—Tell the jailer that a gentleman wishes to speak to him."

The jailer appeared.

"Mr. Arden is confined here, is he not?"

"He is so."

"I have come to see him."

"Walk in, sir; this way, if you please. Universal curiosity is generally exper'enced to see that young man."

He accompanied Edward into the building, and unlocked a cell where two villanous-looking fellows crouched on the bare stone-floor. A single chain, fifteen or sixteen feet long, came from the wall; and they were fettered to it about a yard apart from one another. It was towards dusk; and the window was small; but what little light there was, fell upon them. They glowered up doggedly from under their matted locks, but did not speak. Edward turned impatiently: "Here is some mistake."

"Edward!" exclaimed a well-known voice from a dark corner; the chain, clanking and jangling, writhed like a snake; and Herman was in his arms.

"What's all this? How dared you!" cried Edward, turning, in a perfect tornado of rage, upon the jailer; but he was just locking the door upon them, confiding in the *espionage* of the other rascals who would, he knew, be only too happy to turn state's evidence if there should be any treason talked.

"Good heavens, Herman! What is all this! Had you no acquaintance?—no money to bribe them into treating you like a gentleman, till I could have time to get at you ?"

"I did not try. I chose rather to stand on my rights as a citizen. I was willing to know how poor men fare under the laws which we help to make."

Edward actually stamped with his feet: "Quixotic nonsense! I'll have no more of it. Halloo, here! Where in Tophet are you all! Guard!" shouted he, battering on the door till it shook on its hinges, and the guard came trooping and gallopping through the passages, followed hard by the jailer. While the door was unlocking, however, Edward recollected himself, though he shook from head to foot in an ague-fit of suppressed passion, as he said, in the low, deep tone of thunder that mutters before it bellows, " How dared you chain this gentleman to those fellows ?"

" Which gentleman, sir ?" asked the jailer, confounded.

" ' *Which* gentleman, sir ?'—*The* gentleman, sir,— Mr. Arden !"

" They are kidnappers, sir ; he's a kidnapper, sir, ain't he?"

" He is a young gentleman of fortune and the very highest respectability, taken up through mistake, by some blackguards who did not know him, for a mere thoughtless boyish frolic; and, in serving him in this manner, you have probably done the worst piece of work for yourself that ever you did in your life. I have come to bail him out, with letters to everybody of any consequence in your State, from the Governor down. If you do not know how to treat a gentleman decently for a day or two, I presume that some of them do, and will have the goodness to teach you. Oh, you have some sense, I see !"—the jailer was giving, in an undertone, an order to send the blacksmith, with his hammer and chisel, to strike the fetter from Herman's ankle. "Now, show him into the best room you have; and give him something to sit on and sleep on, and something to eat and drink, too, if you've been starving him into the bargain," added he; for, as the light of the smith's lantern fell upon his brother's face, he was startled by its ghastliness; "and there's something to buy medicine for you, if you fall sick with the fright you've had."

"May I ask your name, sir?"

"Yes,—of a magistrate, when you see him here with me to-morrow. It is one you will be likely to remember to the last day of your life, unless you take better care for the future."

Herman was taken to another room, also upon the ground-floor, accommodated with a chair, bed, lamp, and table, and left alone with his brother. "This won't do, Ned," said he, faintly smiling, but shaking his head.

"'Won't do'! I should think not! Who but you would ever have supposed it would? My poor boy, can it be actual famine that has changed you so, in these few days?"

"Oh, no; I believe they have always offered us something or other, two or three times a day."

"What sort of something or other?"

"Really I don't remember. I haven't noticed. I dare say it is all very good. My chief hardship has been my companions, Ned. They are kidnappers, as the jailer told you,—wretches, part of whose regular business it is, to decoy slaves away by promises of freedom, and to sell them again;—and, conceive of it!—the gentry here have wrought up their notions of right

and wrong into such inextricable confusion worse confounded, that they really can see no difference between
my offence and that of my fellow-prisoners," (he sighed
deeply,) " or, if any, it is in their favor, not in mine.
The State-Attorney did me the honor to look in upon
me the other day, and said, in words I shall never forget,—they bore such internal evidence of truth,—' Had
you done what you did out of rascality, I would have
felt for you ; but you had no personal interest in view;
and such meddling I despise. Or, if it had been some
poor, ignorant, foolish fellow, I could have sympathy ;
but you are a sensible man, and I have no sympathy
for you.' Candid,—wasn't it ?—and showed self-
knowledge. But seriously now, my dearest fellow,
you must change your tone. You cannot, with all
your weight of presence and respectability, bear down
the higher powers as you did this stupid jailer and his
underlings. You have made them think you the
Vice-President, at least, or General Totten. 'Twas a
notable feat ; and I hope you'll be satisfied with it. The
magistrates and influential people here suppose themselves, at least, to be republican noblemen, as well as
you ; and whether, on acquaintance, you agree with
them upon that point or not, they will expect all observance. Your position, as well as mine, is an
exceedingly delicate one. I shall not be easy about
you for one single instant, till you are gone."

"How so? I've done nothing. The law can't
touch me."

" If the laws cannot, the lawless may. You are a
Northern man, and my brother ; and that's enough.
The State has no law that can touch you, to be sure ;
but neither, I believe, has it any strong enough to protect you against the mob if it rises, whether it takes it
into its hundred heads to hang, flog, or only tar and

feather you. Indeed, you must be careful. It sounds ungrateful to say so, but I do wish, from my heart, that you would be contented to provide counsel for me, and go back at once. If you stay here, you must make up your mind to have to do with a pack of born and bred moral maniacs, to be provoked every day as you never were before in the whole course of your life, and still to keep your temper."

"I shall stay, and take you back with me."

"Hush! Hark!" The clapping sound of bare feet, hurrying over the ground without, had just been interrupted by the hoarse challenge of the guard: "Hullo, stop! Who goes thar?"

"Jerry," presently answered a hesitating voice.

"What's Jerry arter, this time o' night?"

"Goin to fotch de doctor for missis."

"Whar's yer pairss?"

"Oh, mas'r, mas'r said, 'Neber mind de pairss, 'cause missis she powerful bad!'"

"Pull off your shirt."

"What's all that?" said Edward.

Herman ground his teeth, and made no other answer. The dialogue went on without:

"Oh, mas'r, couldn't stop to be flogged now, nohow; 'cause missis die if she don't get de doctor. Mas'r said,"——

"Pull off your shirt!"

"Oh, mas'r, couldn't do it, nohow,—so damp;— cotch death o' cold,—got de rheumatis' drefful!"

"Blisters between the shoulders is good for the rheumatis'. Jest yer strip an hold still, an we'll put some on yer in less nor no time."

"Oh, mas'r, le' go! Mas'r 'll come to-morrow an settle it. Take so long! Shirt come off drefful hard!"

"Come, the sooner it's off, the sooner 't'll be on again. We'll help yer. Say! You here, Samson, Washington, jest you lend a hand a minute, an help me skin this here slippery squirming eel of a rascal." Then was heard a trampling, and struggling.

"Thar! Didn't I tell yer? Come off jest as easy. Now, who's got the strap?"

"It's in the office, I reckon. Go get it, Wash. Put! Colored gemman says he's in a hurry.—Come, that won't do. Hold still, or I'll give yer my club in yer wool."

"Ho, Wash! Hold on. I've got one here in my pocket."

"Give it him, then; an cut him up well, for makin such a d—d fuss about it aforehand." Then were heard outcries like those of a person in violent pain, and the sound, strange to civilized ears, of the strokes of raw ox-hide falling on presently raw human flesh. The guard laughed. "Thar, go long off home! Yer won't cotch cold arter cuttin them capers, I'll warrant! —Hullo! he's gone the wrong way!—he's gone arter the doctor, arter all!"

"Well, let him. He's 'arned it."

"Does this happen often?" said Edward, hardly knowing how to trust his own ears after all that they had heard of the Arcadian happiness of slaves.

"This is the third time since I have been here," said Herman quietly, wiping the perspiration from his forehead.

Edward looked at his white, sharp features, whitened and sharpened perceptibly by the suppressed indignation and agony of even those few minutes, and was at no further loss to account for the change in his general appearance. There are some souls, uncomfortably,— we will not say unfortunately,—for themselves, so

finely strung, so bound by a thousand delicate cords
of sympathy with the great heart of Humanity, that,
to them, to know of cruelty is to undergo it.   Unfortunately for Humanity, they are few.

"Now, dear Edward, *do* let me persuade you to go
back."

"Now, dear Herman, do let me persuade you that
you mention such a thing to me at your peril."

"It is most kind, most noble in you; but I shall
never get over it, if you get into any trouble on my
account."

"Trust me to take the best care of myself and you,
too."

"It is a new thing, I know, for me to be the one to
lecture on prudence and policy, and for you to be lec-
tured; and, if you *can* keep up your usual calmness
and composure in this land of Bedlam, I own that I think
you will save yourself,—and serve me, if mortal can.
But, Edward, there is one thing in which I must have
my own way.   If I can get away by fair means, I will,
—not otherwise.   I cannot consent to sneak off like a
thief, who dares not take the consequences of his own
acts, nor with other men's death or perjury to answer
for.   There has been violence enough already.   I was
forced to my share of it.   I do not repent of it.   I am
sick of it, notwithstanding.   It is a sorry sight, trust
me, to see a poor ignorant ruffian struck down by your
hand, and to all appearance about as fit for death as
the devil is for baptism, sinking to perdition in a pool
of his own blood.   I have always said and thought,
that if a good citizen found it impossible, on any occasion, to keep the laws of his country, he should break
them only so far as he must, and certainly not in his
own quarrel, and yield to them so far as he could.

The laws of this part of my country I have certainly broken, whether, acccording to them, it can be proved or not; and I can resist the penalty by no unlawful means. The position and property and influence of our family give me, in themselves, an advantage against these laws over poor and obscure men, in obtaining bail, counsel, mediation, and so-forth, which I might well hesitate to avail myself of, on such an occasion as this, if it were not for—*poor* Constance!"

" Clara and I are very much obliged to you!" said Edward, with some pique.

" Clara and you and I," rejoined Herman firmly, " have always loved one another too well to leave any room for doubt of one another's affection; but you two will have one another, if,—at any rate; and Constance has only me."

" Quite as much as she deserves to have, too, it strikes me, in the circumstances!" broke from Edward. "I wish to my soul, Herman, you could have been contented when you were well off, and never had had anything to do with the South or Southern people."

" Oh, Edward! Edward!"

" There, I ought to have bitten my tongue off before I said that! 'I didn't mean to; I won't again,' as Bessy says."

" Nor think it, either, *will* you?"

" No; at least, not after you are out of this scrape."

" Nor before. Poor, inexperienced, unguided orphan, she did not know what she was doing. How should she?—brought up, so far as she was brought up at all, to consider slavery a branch of patriotism; with most of the ' respectability ' of the North around her, as well as that of the South, practically upholding it; and some of the clergy of the nation, even, declaring

9*

that it was right, and some more, openly or tacitly, that it was wrong to say it was wrong! If,—if anything goes ill, she will blame herself enough; I dare not trust myself to think how much.—Well, there is no use in bragging of what one might or might not do, in other circumstances. Freedom *is* pleasanter than confinement; fresh air, than the smell of that pig-sty beside the window; home, than a jail; and your company and sweet Clara's, than that of any of the men and women, (so-called by an abuse of speech,) whom I have seen under this roof. I hope I shall get out."

"'Hope' you shall! To be sure you shall, in a day or two at the furthest, my dear boy, God bless you!"

"If He pleases. Edward,—how do they do?"

"The girls? Oh, very well,—bravely, when I left them. I burned your letter, and gave them my own version of the story. Just at first, of course, Constance was a good deal cut up, if you must know,"——

"Yes, all."——

"She looked like Lot's wife, and went off into a sort of pale, rigid agony,—not fainting, but worse,"——

"I know. I have seen her."

"I actually started forward to catch her, and thought she would be on the floor; but Clara got her into her arms and down on her knee, and fondled her as she does Bessy; and first she made her cry; and then she made her smile, and argued very judiciously that she was only romantic, and that nothing very bad ever happened in our times, to people like us, and was so busy in comforting her, that I think she quite forgot that she needed to be comforted herself."

"What an angel she is!"

"She is! I declare, she looks so like one sometimes, when I'm plaguing her and she's trying to put me up to some troublesome piece of goodness or other, that I'm afraid I shall see the wings sprout from her white shoulders, and carry her straight up away from me."

"Or with you."

"If I ever get up there, I believe it will be in that way.   She is very fond of Constance; and so am I."

"What have you not, both of you, always been, that was kind and generous to me?   If,—if things do not turn out as we wish, I know I can depend on your doing all that the most delicate and affectionate sympathy can do, to sooth her and support her."

"Rely upon it, rely upon it, my dearest fellow!— Pshaw, what nonsense we are talking!—And, if the sky falls, rely upon our helping her to catch larks. You are a little nervous, I see.   You want a little more travelling and exercise, to set you up.   We must be at home, if possible, by the end of next week. I left the girls full of business, fitting up your room for you with new curtains and carpet, and seeing that Sally, and Paul's man, didn't break any of your rattle-traps.   There, it was to have been a surprise for you, and I've let it out!"

Herman's head sank into his hands, upon the table. When he raised it, he talked of other matters.

"If you can believe it, nobody but my man himself knows yet, apparently, that it was his surgeon who shot him; and he is doing very well, I hear."

"Lucky for us."

"For him, too, I hope."

"Why, aren't you afraid, reverend sir, of his adding by his lengthened probation to his list of transgressions?"

"I am afraid that he had less room left upon it for *addenda* than for *corrigenda.* I left him in the hands of a good old, Virginia-'*raised,*' Methodist slave-woman, who knew half the Bible by heart; and I charged her to ply him well with it, as well as with chicken-broth, as soon as he should have reached a proper stage of his convalescence, hoping that the one might make the other go down!"

"You did, did you? You're an image of a regular old Puritan, cast out of a fusion of the sword of the flesh and the sword of the spirit,—the same materials, only in rather different proportions. In your case, it is not exactly six of one and half a dozen of the other."

The tramp of feet, and banging of doors, was now heard, drawing nearer all along the passage; the jailer came with his heavy double-handful of jingling keys; and Herman was locked in; and Edward, out.

CHAPTER XXII.

THE KNIGHT'S CHAMPION.

"Pour toute vertu, on ne lui enseigna que l'honneur."
LAMARTINE.

"There are men in the slave States, slaveholders, who feel the ineffable degradation of this position. Not only conscientious men, who abhor the injustice, but spirited men, who cannot brook the shame, are chafing impatiently under the yoke they wear, felt by them to be heavier and more dishonorable than that which they impose. They see their case themselves, and how ludicrously it belies that large prating in the * * vocabulary of *honor*, in which they have been wont to indulge." PAPERS ON THE SLAVE POWER.

RESTED, shaved, and most correctly dressed the next morning, Edward was himself again. At the earliest hour admissible, he waited upon Judge Sharper, and offered his bail. The judge hesitated, thought it would be necessary to put the bail " pretty high,—as high as,"—he eyed Edward keenly from head to foot,— "well, ten or twenty thousand dollars."

"If you will have the goodness to bid your clerk make out the bond, I will sign it."

" Well, that is, supposing I conclude to allow of bail. I am not as yet prepared to decide, without further consideration and consultation. I would, at any rate, require some prominent citizen of this State to be bound together with you."

"I will call on your neighbour Mr. Trimmer, then. He was an acquaintance and friend of my father formerly, I understand, at Washington. Will that do?"

"Well; yes, sir,—perfectly well." The judge's brown leather lips pursed themselves firmly up in the middle, and drew themselves down at the corners; but, —Edward could not guess why,—his eyes lighted up through his spectacles, like those of a wicked little terrier with his nose at a rat-hole. "If Hiram Trimmer agrees to offer bail, I think I can, without farther demur, engage to accept of it."

And Edward accordingly, in his most urbane and courtly manner, straightway presented himself, and a letter of introduction which he had brought with him, to the Honorable Hiram Trimmer, a magistrate high in office. He found him bearing his honors meekly, a bland fatherly man with obtrusive false teeth, who received him very civilly. After a little easy and agreeable conversation on general topics, sufficient, as he rightly judged, to make a most favorable impression, Edward opened his business, offering the best securities in Boston.

"Hum, ha,—very sorry. I would be very happy. Any service within my power. Was in Congress with your late lamented payrent. Most enlightened and patriotic merchant! We gentlemen of the South always knew where to go, when we wanted a vote for the rights of our whole glorious 'Union, however bounded.' Did much, indeed, to establish our mutual interests. Most statesmanlike mind! Saw through the intricate science of political economy, to use a bold hyperbowl, like a lynx through a stone wall! He ever protecting the property of our section of the country; we did the like, as often as we saw occasion, and found it compatible, for his. Then, again, secondly, the revenues of the property of his section enabled the holders thereof, at election-time, to disburse such sums as were requisite to elect men like him anew, anew to protect our interests. *E pluribus unum.* United we stand; divided we fall.—Most to be regretted that boys should lose their fathers! Get into bad company and misguided. Regretful for it when it's too late!— Unfortunate and embarrassing occurrence. Public mind's a good deal excited. Ironical in Sharper." [For this reason, perhaps: Mr. Trimmer had for some years held an office within the State, to the mutual satisfaction of himself and of a majority of the citizens. They paid him his salary; and he let them alone. Judge Sharper's brother, a more "earnest man," had, however, just been put up against him by a large minority, as a rival candidate at the next election.] " Brother'd be safest just now in jail, I opine, wouldn't he?"

" How so, sir?"

" Well, the mind of the public's exasperated,—much to be deplored!—a good deal exasperated. Two most alarming attacks on the jail already. Didn't he inform you?"

" No, sir."

" Yes, sir. Extra guard ordered out; and, night before last, I was fearful they'd have had him in spite of it."

" Am I to understand," cried Edward, struggling to keep up his courtesy and keep his seat, " that, in this part of the country, prisoners are at the mercy of the mob?"

" Far from it, sir! The furthest possible from it, I assure you. Never when it can be obviated. That was the object of ordering out the guard, sir."

" Could not he leave the State on bail?"

" Well, I'm fearful that could not be suffered in the present attitude of the public mind."

"Is there no safe place of confinement to which he could be sent?"

"There'd still remain the peril of effecting his transfer. Public would be liable to be very apprehensive of a rescue. Wouldn't hardly like to dare to venture to assume the responsibility.—Brother calm, when you left him?"

"I believe so; I have hardly seen him otherwise; except once, indeed, when a poor man was flogged for going in the evening, by his master's orders, to call a physician for his mistress." It was very impolitic; but, somehow, Edward could not help saying it.

"Oh, ah! Unfortunately caught without a pairss, I presume."

"But if he was sent off in a hurry, and could not get one?"—

"Very culpable negligence on the part of his owners, in that case, I should infer. But the patrol having their stated orders, can't deviate."

"Should they not be ordered, in such cases, to flog the owners?"

"Ha, ha! Poetical justice. Pleasant vein of humour!—Owners make the laws. Fearful you couldn't induce 'em to coincide. Furthermore, your proposition wouldn't affect only them. Present system affects both parties."

"Does it? I am no lawyer; perhaps you would be so good as to explain to me how."

"Why, humane masters do not like their servants to be whipped, and therefore sedulously retain them in;—not quite such cruel fellows as you make us out to be, up North, ha, ha! Regulation operates beneficially, upon the whole. Ruin servants to sanction their running around at night."

"But would humane slaves like to have their owners whipped?"

"Ha, ha! Well, I wouldn't hardly like to venture to express an opinion. Can't expect much sensibility on the part of the inferior races." Edward was about to receive a reward for his resolute imitation of complaisance, such as it had been. "You have no conception, sir, if I may be permitted to mention it, how you recall to my remembrance your dear mother. Your lineaments, and—there—your smile! Ah! what a fine lady she was! You do not see such ladies at this day, sir."

"At home, I think I do; one to whom I should be very happy to present you, if you should ever come into our neighbourhood. I have a sister, who is said to be very like our mother; though she seldom has the rosy cheeks of the West."

"Ah! I would like to meet her! I would like to meet her! Your dear mother, sir, was, similarly to you I perceive, partially tinctured with the prejudices of your section of the country; but, oh, what a sprightly and engaging method she had of expressing them! Your deceased father, I inferred, was always apprehensive of her getting him into hot water, as the vulgar expression is; but, dear me! we were all of us wholly too rejoiced to get a few words with such a heavenly beauty, to regard anything that she said in any offensive way; and as for me, I never was very bigoted or sectional; and I've become less and less so, as I've advanced in years and seen more of the world. I often observe, to Hangfellow and the chivalrous high-souled young fellows who ride in his troop, 'Toleration, my dear boys, toleration! A man's opinions are his own; and so long as he don't undertake to arrogate to himself a claim to act upon 'em, there's no occasion for you to break the peace.' I was remarking?—oh, your mother! She exerted a great influence in her sphere ; and she sedulously kept within it. I was young and thoughtless then ; but for years I never lifted my hand against a servant, without imagining to hear her say,—as she did once, when I hit my boy Jim a clip on the side of the head, for pushing by her into the hotel with my baggage, and tearing her gown all to remnants with a nail that protruded out, out of my trunk,—'Ah! don't, Mr. Trimmer! be merciful! what would become of us, if our Master were to punish us for every inconsiderate thing we did?' We were fearful, sometimes, that she might use her influence with your late father, to tamper with his vote ; but that, I believe, she was rarely ever guilty of. The fanatics used to endeavour to poison her mind, and, being feminine, I dare say they biassed her a considerable ; but she ever had the sagacity to observe, that ' women could not expect to comprehend politics.' "

How those few words had seemed to raise, before Edward's mind, the double image of his mother and his sister,—the good, brave heart, the good, yet timid mind! If, before yet the North had so rashly tampered with the hell-forged chain of slavery,—before, like a magical clue, it had entangled those who dared to touch it to bind it faster on their brothers, and wound around and bound them all together, black and white, in one inextricable coil of struggling, writhing, strangling bondage, misery, remorse, and crime,—Mrs. Arden, that one gentle Christian woman, had rallied self-reliance enough to use her benign influence with her husband, and through him upon his colleagues, would his two sons have been in these straits this day? Edward asked himself the question; but he could not answer it. Many such questions may have to be asked and answered on the Day of Judgment. Well for her sex if all of them, who then stand in need of mercy for inconsiderate errors, have known like Alice Arden how to show it!

Her sweet memory was even now pleading for her son, with the miserable old sycophant and time-server before him. Greatly disappointed, but softened, Edward rose to take his leave.

"Brother her son?"

"No; my father married again."

"Ah, didn't perceive how an offspring of hers could be concerned in,——ahem. Step-mothers ever wont to spoil their own children, and tyrannize their husbands'. Anything that *is* in my power, sir, for her sake,—as well as your own, I would say,—advice, any little indulgence in my power, you will command at all hours. Think brother'd like to eat some apples? I have some very fine. Just as well not to state where they came from. Might prejudice my influence, and impair the success of my exertions on his behalf. Hope to meet you here as frequently as you can consistently call. *In the evening*, sir, I am more especially wont to be at home. Any middle given name, sir? 'Edward *C.* Arden,' I observed on your card."

"Yes; Charles."

"Ah; Charles not easily mistaken for a surname. It just occurred to me that, if you preferred to designate yourself by any other appellation while you stopped in this State, the public might the less readily recognize your relation to the culprit."

"Thank you," said Edward, rather haughtily; "but those of our name have been accustomed, as far

back as we know anything about them, to regard it as
a title to respect rather than otherwise; and I have
yet to learn, that any culprit has ever borne it."

"Oh, ah! *prisoner* I should have said. Young yet.
Feeling for brother very generous. Didn't purpose to
injure your feelings. No offence, I hope. Any service in my power, at any time."

He said it so kindly, that Edward shook the hand
which he held out to him, and exclaimed as he did so,
"Oh! by the way, there *is* one thing in your power,
which I almost forgot to ask. Will you be so kind as
to write me an order to the jailer, to prevent the pop-
ulace from peeping and prying about my brother's
room, as it seems they have been allowed to do?"

The old man's countenance fell again. "Very
sorry. I would be very happy. Fearful I could not."

"In the name of Job, why?" cried Edward, losing
all his patience. N. B. He did not find it again.

"Public would be very apt to apprehend his eva-
sion. Be liable to exasperate 'em, too, wouldn't it?
Ah, feel for you! Very hard. Very sad." He bowed
him out.

So any one who chose came to the grated window
of Herman's cell, much as loungers through a *mena-
gerie* hang about the lion's cage and stir him up, coax
him, or simply stare at him, according to their humour.
Even the little boys from the streets would suddenly
reach up, and draw a clattering stick along the bars,
and cry, "Heh, nigger-thief!—goin to steal any more
of our niggers? heh!" Some of the spectators spoke
brutally; some few, with tasteless and galling commis-
eration; some, with mere passionless curiosity. They
discussed before him his probable fate. Some talked
of whipping; some, of hanging. Edward's indigna-

tion, at all this, almost boiled over; but Herman seemed to look above and beyond most of these mere annoyances of his situation; as the moon looks over the dogs that bay at her. His heart and mind were too full of other thoughts and feelings to leave much room for anger. At times, indeed, the absurdity of his tormentors would recall in him some faint gleam of his boyish archness.

"How do you feel?" asked one of those inquiring minds, on one of those occasions, with his chin on the window-sill, breaking into the midst of an important conversation between the brothers.

"Very well, I thank you, sir," said Herman, turning round upon him with great cheerfulness; "how are you?"

He was put in spirits for a day by the account of a visit which Ichabod Kuhn, who could not have talked with him at the jail without compromising both parties, paid to Edward at his lodgings. According to Ichabod's deposition, Sam was no doubt already far gone on the under-ground railroad, on his way to Canada. He had not appeared wild at all, after rest and food; but his grief had been really overwhelming when, at night, Ichabod came back from his second trip, without Herman; and, after they heard of his arrest, Sam actually could be kept from returning to give himself up only by the most positive assurances, from all the Kuhns, that he would vex Herman very much if he did, and very likely make his case the worse instead of the better, and by their equally positive refusal to let him have the paper of rat's-bane, which he wished to carry back with him secretly, as an antidote against cow-hide and collar. Noble was doing well in body, and in spirit as well as could reasonably be expected.

Ichabod visited him frequently with comforts of his mother's providing, and was, at his urgent request, to come for him with his boat as soon as he was fit to be moved, and hide him before the trial, that he might not be forced to testify against Herman.

For the most part however, Herman, still, silent, and braced, appeared like an athlete straining every nerve to bear up against a weight thrown upon his shoulders, which must crush him if for an instant he gives way beneath it,—firm, collected, but too self-concentrated to be fully conscious of anything but the burden and the bearing,—well-nigh speechless and breathless.

In the novel circumstances in which both were placed, it was remarkable to see how much more at a loss the man of the world found himself, than the man of the other world. Few men, probably, have ever led a life of self-indulgence in modes more innocent, or with fewer distinct stains on their consciences, than Edward Arden; but a life of mere self-indulgence, in modes how innocent soever, is a bad training for a season of trial. He was driven almost beside himself in the course of the first three or four days, angry with everybody and everything about him, and angry with himself for being angry. The "public readily recognized his relationship to the culprit;" and he was once or twice hooted in the streets. The lawyers, on whom he called to defend his brother, were civilly "too much occupied already by stress of business to do justice to the case," or insolently "little disposed to mingle up their names in any such transaction;" and he succeeded in retaining only an inferior practitioner at an exorbitant fee. Through him, he made almost unlimited offers of compromise-money "for the sake of saving time," to Squire St. Dominique; but Shylock preferred his pound of flesh, and seemed not altogether unlikely to be able to help himself to it in simple earnest, if he chose, in person or by proxy.

On the third night, Edward dreamed at his hotel, that he was presiding in the midst of a frog-*caucus*. He woke; but the croaking and clamor sounded still in his ears, louder and louder. He sprang to his window, threw it up, and heard the peculiar sound of a crowd of men's clamoring voices echoing from a still, midnight sky. They were attacking the jail. He tossed on a few clothes, armed himself, muffled up his face, found the bar-keeper, and told him that if he would proclaim a " free treat," and draw off the crowd to carouse till morning before his door, he would pay for all that they could eat and drink. The man agreed.

Edward rushed on before him, and mingled with the mob, shouting and feigning to join them in their attack, and worked his way through towards the foremost rank, meaning, if the doors should be forced, to reach Herman, and cut a passage for him, or die with him. But how should he let him know that one heart was beating in unison with his, in all that fiendish uproar? There was a peculiar whistle, by which they had been used to make signals to one another in their earlier days,—a free imitation of the call of the whippoor-will. Throwing up a shower of stones, Edward gave it now; and in a moment it rang back, soft but clear, through the grim wall between them,—how strangely!—seeming to conjure up about them the green Common, the brown Malls, the Frog-pond, the comrades, the old boyish gaiety and security,—and the freedom which, they learned every day at school, was the proud privilege and birthright of every American of the United States. Could they be in the same country,—their own country,—still? or with Huger at Olmutz?

In his utter helplessness, Edward had recourse the next day, again, even to Mr. Trimmer, told him his difficulty in obtaining counsel, and asked his advice:

"Ah! Share brother's unpopularity at first; natural;—unfortunate!—Prejudice dissipated. on further acquaintance. Invite some prominent members of our bar to dine, suppose. Couldn't attend myself;—dyspepsy;—but loan my cook with pleasure."

Edward gave the very best dinner the place could afford. He succeeded in getting together a number of middle-aged and elderly men, who ate and drank his good things with encouraging avidity. He told his best stories with the best humour that he could, and propitiated them so far that, by the time the cloth was removed and the cigars lighted, they appeared to concur in the opinion, " I doubt not that your brother was infatuated, and acted under the most amiable motives."

" You are very kind, and very right, I believe, in not doubting that he always acts from the most amiable motives; but what proof you have of his being infatuated, I have yet to learn."

"How! Did he not purloin Esquire St. Dominique's Sam ?"

" Excuse me. In my opinion, he never purloined anything in his life; but that is a question not for me, but for a judge and jury. As I am a stranger here, could not you recommend to me some good senior counsel, gentlemen, if you can none of you undertake the case yourself?"

"I much regret not to find it in my power."

"Most unfortunate that it occurs thus!"

"At any other period, I would rejoice to do so."

"There's Broadstone, down to Capet City, Mr. Provant. Wouldn't he? He has never an undue amount of engagements."

"A sagacious suggestion. Provant's hit it, I conjecture. Mr. Broadstone is a very talented man by nature, Dr. Arden. He might be very high at the bar, were he not over-technical and otherwise fanatical."

Edward wrote to Mr. Broadstone, but received no answer. Mr. Trimmer informed him, in the meanwhile, that he had "disappointed his guests most favorably. Now, suppose you were to pursue it up," he continued, "and invite some of our young chivalry. Colonel Hangfellow's gone over into Kansas, for a few days, leading a party of them to vote at different precincts; but Judge Lynch's son, the captain, who has great influence with his father and with the public generally, is yet here, with many of his retainers, and does not purpose to leave prior to the day after to-morrow. Suppose you were to dine them to-morrow. Take your pencil, and I will dictate to you the names of some of them. No one need be made aware whence you obtained them."

Edward did so, and sent his invitations with such fortitude as he had. His messenger presently returned, saying that Captain Lynch, on reading his own note, had called him back, looked over the addresses of all the others, and taken them from him, promising that he would take care of them. The next day. dinner-time came and passed. Dinner was served, and stood an hour; at the end of which, shouts of toasts, speeches, and laughter, began to grow louder

10

and louder, from a public room over the way; and from the house a servant crossed the street, with a note in these terms:

"Captain Lynch and his Borderers present their compliments to Yankee Arden, senior, and have the honor to inform him that, when they want tall feed, they know where to get it. Further, that if he has come on hither, thinking to interfere with the execution of Law and Order in any confounded sneaking, insinuating method, they will feel themselves compelled, as patriotic and spirited Sons of the South, to supply him with something that he will not like to eat.

"(Signed for) Captain Lynch and Borderers,
"Robert A. Dill, *Sec'y.*
"P. S.—All right on the goose. N. B.—Likewise on the hemp."

In the afternoon, on his way to the jail, Edward was jostled on the pavement by a tall round-shouldered individual, with a swaggering air, and in a sort of half-military dress. Edward turned about abruptly and faced him. With a hiccough, he inquired, "Abolitionist, strannger?"

"I never have been," said Edward, with the mental reservation, "I believe you'll drive me to it among you!"

"Luck-lucky for you. Had you been-been one-one-one, I would-w-would have c-c-counselled you to abandon the S-St-State."

"Indeed! May I ask what would have entitled me to the benefit of your counsel?"

"Why, I—I—I and my friends have c-con-concluded to see justice executed on the k-k-kidnappers. If they ain't c-c-con-convicted, we will hang-hang-hang 'em."

"Indeed! Supposing you succeeded in carrying out your conclusions, are not you afraid of some little odium's attaching itself to such proceedings, in the eyes of the civilized world?"

"Oh, Lord, no!" said the man, with a drunken laugh. "W-what-what harm would that do us? We-we-we're pretty well used to that-that-that."

In the evening, Edward went yet once more to Mr. Trimmer's, and told him of the events of the day. The old man looked downcast and foreboding. "The individual stammered?"

"Excessively; but his condition might have accounted for that."

"Military air? Noble bearing?"

"Very likely; I'm no judge," said Edward, dryly; "but he wore a blue coat, with large gilt buttons."

"Ah! I'm fearful that was Draycoe!—very fearful! I would be very sorry to think so,—very sorry. Draycoe's a man of his word,—fine, generous, noble-hearted fellow, as ever lived,—but ardent and patriotic, almost to a fault. I expect he had just quitted Captain Lynch's table. Lynch gave an early banquet to his friends, to preclude them from desiring to attend yours. This very morning, on receiving intelligence that such was his design, I observed to him, 'Lynch,'—I spoke to him very plainly;—'Lynch,' said I, 'now, if you can restrain the public, and refrain from so doing, your conduct is culpable. You are all of you inclined to proceed too much upon the hypothesis, that the criminal,'—I ask pardon, your brother,—'will fail to be convicted in the regular course of unperverted justice. Why will you not be calm and neutral, and see what measures Judge Sharper and the jury will adopt ?' Now, the best and safest course, and most satisfactory eventually to all parties, in my candid judgment, would· be to let brother be sent to the penitentiary for a few years, and quietly pardoned out by the Governor, so soon as the public mind is soothed."

Edward was not struck so agreeably as his friend had hoped, by this proposal. The next morning, at the suggestion of Herman, who longed to have him out of harm's way if only for a few hours, he went down to Capet and applied, for aid in finding and engaging an advocate, to a clergyman whom they both knew indirectly through some common friends of his and theirs.

The little, neat, tasteful, quiet study, into which Edward was shown, looked like a transplanted bit of New England; and as Mr. Halifax raised his head, and came forward from his writing-table to receive him, he felt instinctively that he had come to the right place.

Mr. Halifax was a remarkable-looking man, and was the man he looked. He was, apparently, about forty years old. His frame was fine, a little above the middle height and full, but muscular rather than corpulent, and with a slight monastic stoop in the shoulders. He had glorious prophetic eyes, but a somewhat feeble mouth, and a whole countenance in keeping with these two hints; as if Nature had given him the power to see more than she had given him the power to utter. His forehead, grand in height and amplitude, was wrinkled as if with endless anxiety and perplexity. His face was somewhat pale and weary ; and his look and smile, bright with that sort of wistful, innocent, and half-mournful sweetness, which one might expect to see in some marvellous child, marked for an early death by its own brilliancy and unearthly loveliness. His voice was the perfect melody of melancholy. Further, there was that about him altogether, in the midst of so much that was fine and interesting, which might give to a physiognomist the idea that he had fallen short, by just a hair's breadth, of the stature of the perfect man in Christ. He was the image of a rare hero, marred by the absence of some small, but essential, hardening ingredient in the materials of which he was cast. The outlines,—I speak now of him as a spirit, he is a spirit now,—were symmetrical, *suggestive*, almost faultless, but a little wavering and uncertain ; a want of firmness and boldness spoiled half the effect. He clave to that which was good, but did not sufficiently abhor that which was evil. Thus, while he saved himself, others he could not save. His enemies called him cowardly. He was not,—not physically so, at least. He would have marched to the stake unflinchingly, if he had seen that his duty led him there ; but the mischief was that,—though he was rarely clear-sighted when he dared to trust his own remarkably fine eyes,—when they showed him things, as they often did, which his neighbours could not see, he suspected that they cheated him, shut them up, kept them shut as well as he could, and let his neighbours lead him. His cowardice, if he had any, was an almost purely intellectual defect,—an error of the judgment rather than of the will. For fear of self-conceit, he put from him self-knowledge.

Self-conceit is a bad thing ; let every man think of himself soberly ; but let him also think of himself as he ought to think. And woe to that nation whose spiritual leaders turn followers, throw down their

batoons, and fall from the van into the rear of public
opinion for want of a right self-confidence or, to speak
more truly, for want of confidence in their in-dwelling
God !

Peace to his pure memory ! May he be as peaceful in the world to which he has gone, as he was
peaceable in this ! If he was not, in the manlier and
more heroic attributes of holiness, the holiest man our
hearts can imagine and pray for, in the present ex-
igencies of our church and state, he was at least,—in
tender gratitude for all that was tender and reverent
and beautiful in him, let us say it,—one of the holiest
men that our eyes have ever seen !

But we are putting on our mourning for him a little too soon. He was alive at the time of which we
are speaking ; and it was fortunate for Edward that he
was. His smile grew dim, and his face a shade more
pale and careworn, as Edward told his story ; but he took
up his hat and gloves at once, and said, " I have a
parishioner, a good man and lawyer, who would undertake the case unless I am much mistaken ; and, as you
are in haste, we had better at once go to his house, and
see. I ought to let you know beforehand, however,
that he is a humourist, though the very soul of honour,
and that he has a particular aversion in general to
abolitionists, some of whom he thinks, and I think,
have used him ill ; but I am sure that you will not
force your principles upon his notice, unnecessarily."

" My principles ?" thought Edward ; " what are
they ?—Depend upon it," continued he, aloud,
" I brought no abolitionist principles with me, when
I left Massachusetts. If I take any back with me
when I go, they must have grown here in Bondage."

The clergyman made no reply. As he presented

Edward to "Mr. Broadstone," the former started. "I should have told you before, Mr. Halifax," said he, "if I had heard the name of your friend, that Mr. Broadstone has already been applied to, to defend my brother."

"And refused?" asked Mr. Halifax, colouring slightly.

"Never!" exclaimed Mr. Broadstone abruptly, to him. "What do you mean, sir?" cried he, turning to Edward, with a choleric jerk, upon his office-stool as if upon a pivot, lifting his feet from the floor in order to do so, and setting them down again at the distance, from their starting-point, of an arc of the circle of which his long legs were the *radii*.

"I put a letter directed to you into the post-office, myself, six days ago."

"I took out none from you."

"Some irregularity in the mails, I presume," mildly suggested Mr. Halifax.

"You are very presuming, indeed, sir, if you presume anything of the sort," returned the lawyer with a bitter laugh and frown, rising as he did so, and stalking like pendulums, back and forth, from one end of the little office to the other, as if he wanted to get out. "It was read and stopped in the office, *I* presume; as my letters, and other people's, have been before and will be again!" He paused an instant, as if for redress, before Mr. Halifax. "Creditable impression we must make upon strangers!" continued he, resuming his strides, and measuring off the sanded floor with his long legs like a pair of compasses. "Abolitionist, sir?" asked he with another pause, this time before Edward.

"I vow I don't know what I am!" cried Edward,

starting up in his turn, and smiting his forehead in utter desperation. "A maniac, by all rights, I ought to be. All I can answer for is, that twenty days ago, at any rate, I was neither a lunatic, nor a fanatic, nor anything else but a peaceable, respectable citizen in Boston, sitting in my own parlour and poking my own fire. In came a letter, to say that my younger brother, —positively the finest and most honourable young fellow I ever saw in my life,—who was travelling hereabouts, had been taken up on suspicion of having stolen a negro, by a man who had lost one. The poor youngster might have got himself out of harm's way as well as not, but was taken up in the very act of stopping to save the life of one of the party who arrested him, who was bleeding to death by himself in the woods. Of course, then, I came to do what I could for him; as anybody would have done in my place; but I expected to behave and be treated like a gentleman, as usual, meddle with nobody and have nobody meddle with me, pay any sum that was wanted, and get my brother and myself out of the State again as fast as I could; and judges won't take bail except from natives of the State; and natives won't give it; and lawyers won't plead; and magistrates won't put down riots; and young men won't eat my dinners, and insult me for inviting them; and people I don't know speak to me in the street, and the very children hoot at my heels; and now postmasters won't send letters; and, by Jupiter, if this sort of thing is to go on much longer, I'm in a very fair way to wish the South, and the Union, and the whole world abolished, and myself into the bargain!"

Edward had no sooner finished than he felt that he had been betrayed into rather a plaintive, undignified, and ludicrous exposition of his piteous plight; and the discordant, mocking laugh, which Mr. Broadstone repeated upon hearing it, increased his wrath. With a hasty bow to Mr. Halifax, he caught up his hat; but Broadstone thrust himself between Edward and the door, seized his hand, and ground his knuckles within his own sinewy palm with such a grip, that he was forced to squeeze back again in self-defence with such another, that, having shaken hands collectively, they were each fain to do so singly and severally.

"Say no more! I'm your man. I would have had to do your business, at all events, for the honor of the State; but I couldn't have done it much to my own, if you'd been an abolitionist of the common sort; for I hate 'em to that degree that the sight of one actually affects my reason. As to thinking, though, 'twould be a blessing to have everything and everybody abolished,—except Mr. Halifax here,—I go with you from my heart, under the circumstances, whenever I sit down and think about them, which I venture to do just as often as I can't help it, and no oftener. Where's the honor of the South? Where's the good fellowship? Where's the hospitality? Where's the,— by Jove, sir, within the last few years, when I look about me, I don't know my country; and I don't know my neighbours; and I don't know myself! The earth must have settled, I believe; and hell's come through to the top. I don't wonder you're astonished, a Northerner coming here for the first time, though as to that,—you'll have to allow me to speak my mind, as you did, yours,—the North's just as much to blame in the matter as the South. If we have built up Pandemonium, with our cotton and sugar and pounded human flesh and bones, you brought your confounded

10*

cash to the work, for the mortar that stuck it together. It was so close to our eyes, that we couldn't see quite how ugly and horrible it was; but you were further off and might have known better, if the gold spectacles you looked through hadn't been blinders. As for the doings around here now, they are bad enough to mortify Lucifer and disgrace Gomorrah; and if we can't have slavery without 'em, why, then I'm perfectly prepared to say, with you or anybody that has the soul of a gentleman, Slavery be "—— He saw the clergyman wince, and, turning upon him in his peculiar way, ejaculated triumphantly, and with tremendous emphasis, "CONDEMNED!—*that's* unexceptionable, I believe. Oh, hang it all! It's enough to make St. Paul swear! He'd rip out with his ' Anathema Maranatha!' quick enough, if he was here; and I wish, for my part, he was, though he swore at me. Anyhow, I whould know right from wrong, then; and, now, I don't."

The clergyman sighed deeply and, after begging both of the gentlemen to give him their company at dinner, went home to finish his sermon. "' Keep slavery confined to your blacks, gentlemen,'" then continued Mr. Broadstone, resuming his discourse and his seat, "I say to my neighbours, sometimes, when they dare to interfere with me, and to come telling me what I may do, and what I mayn't,—' and I won't say it's a bad thing, if you treat 'em well, which, by the way, you know you don't; but don't try to make white men slaves; or, if you do, be warned in time, and don't commence with trying it on to me!' But I declare, I'm beginning to think it's just like the leprosy, sir. Let your fellow-creatures at your side be afflicted with it, and, before you think, it's commencing to

spread over you." He jumped up again and, again
striding away as if he had a thousand miles to walk in
a thousand hours, was continuing his harangue; when
a hammering sound was heard on the other side of the
door, and a tiny voice cried, "*Bopa! Bopa!*"
A softening change instantly passed over the whole
man. He stopped, smiled, unlatched the door, hid behind it, and cried, "*Coop*, Nelly."

A beautiful little child *toddled* in and, with shrieks
of laughter and pretended fright, was caught in his
arms. Handling her as if she had been made of blown
egg-shells, he set her up, upon the top of the high
stool, and stood holding her, quite absorbed in her and
in the soothing occupation of tickling, but taking care
not to scratch, her apple-cheeks with his rough whiskers. Edward then, quietly but heartily, made his
acknowledgments and, rather as a matter of form than
of fact, hoped at the close, that coming to Tadmor to
manage the case would put Mr. Broadstone to no inconvenience or trouble.

"As to inconvenience or trouble, I can't answer for
its causing or not causing any; but whether, if it does,
the inconvenience is like to be confined to myself, you
shall be the judge," said he; "I go warmly dressed
sometimes, on such occasions." He gently placed the
child on the floor, told her to run to her mother, and
took from a clothes'-press a heavy great-coat, which he
buttoned up to his chin. In front, it had six pockets
on each side. Beginning with the upper one on the
left hand, he took from it a pistol, and tried the bar-
rels. "Loaded," said he. Replacing it, he took out
another from the opposite pocket on the right-hand
side, examined, approved, and replaced it in like manner, and so on through the whole dozen, repeating,

" Loaded !—loaded !—loaded !—loaded !—loaded ! Revolvers," added he, restoring the last to its place ; "six bullets in each, equivalent in my hands to six men's lives. Upon occasion, I can manage two at a time, one in each hand. I am ambidexter, see ;" and lifting both hands together to the back of his neck, he drew a bowie-knife from its sheath with each, and, with the *leger-de-main* of a juggler, made lightning passes with both, so quick and dazzling and so close to Edward's face, that he started back involuntarily in some fear of losing his very handsome nose.

His host gave his bitter laugh again, as his only apology, and put his weapons up, or rather down his back, like snakes running into their holes, with a shake of the head that looked as if he meant mischief. "To-morrow," said he, slowly, holding back the words as if he relished them too much to let them leave his mouth, before they must, " I shall see your brother, if I meet as many devils in my way as I do fellow-citizens, one in each man ; or those about me will see a corpse, and probably more than one. I shall plead his cause if he likes, whether his pleasant neighbours like it or not. They know me, and my *coat-of-arms*. Since it appears that they don't like the looks of it among them, let them paint it crimson, if they can. If they do, some of them will only have to be in uniform with me. I know my duty, sir ;—at least, as an advocate and fellow-countryman, I do. You told me just now, very handsomely, to name my fee. I will. When you go back to something like civilization, you will, in consideration of the best services which I can render you, forbear to say that Honor and Hospitality have quite abandoned their old home, the South."

True to his word, he rode up to the jail the next day, and met Mr. Halifax, who had driven over also to call on Herman. After half an hour's general conversation, and a promise to send the latter some curious books from his library, and to make interest for him that he might be allowed to have them, Mr. Halifax took his leave. When he was gone, Herman,—partly because he perceived that his new lawyer was a man of honesty and good faith, and partly because it was so natural to him, when he spoke at all to speak the truth, the whole truth, and nothing but the truth, that he could only have bungled very badly if he had attempted to do otherwise,—told Mr. Broadstone simply the whole story of his dealings and doings in the matter of poor Sam. He said nothing, however, of Constance ; but Edward, in terror of the effect which his communication might have upon the anti-abolitionist, hinted his brother's motive, himself, to him.

That impulsive gentleman sprang from his seat, crushed both of Herman's slender hands in his vise-like grasp, and flung away again with his usual mocking laugh, which seemed to set at naught all the world and, above all, himself; but his eyes, as he did so, had a moist sparkle in them. Seeming to feel as if Herman's confession required a counter-confession on his own part, he presently began, with his usual action and mode of delivery which, as we have observed, were those of the peripatetic school :

"I'm a slaveholder myself; and I suppose you think I ought to be ashamed of it. And so do I ; and so I am, as things go now. I didn't use to be, when my sainted father and mother were slaveholders, and blessings to strangers and neighbours, white and black, and couldn't have got their servants to leave 'em, if they'd tried; but slaveholder has come to signify rowdy and bully, eavesdropper and letter-opener; and I *am* ashamed of the name, and of those who bear it with me,—so ashamed that it's more than I can stand, without going beside myself, to have it slapped in my face by fellows from the free States, who wouldn't have done any better in my place than I have; though that's bad enough, Beelzebub knows. It makes me mad, mad perfectly, so ashamed and so enraged, with myself for bearing the title, and with my neighbours for disgracing it, that I can't get myself, twice in a twelvemonth, into a fit frame of mind for going to a certain holy table, where the good man who left us just now tries to draw me every month. When I first went to it, my parents walked with me. My mother leaned upon my arm. The cup passed from her to me. She has since drunk it new in the kingdom of God; but now, when the day comes round, it kills me to think, that if, when Christ comes down to meet the two or three gathered in his name, she accompanies in hopes of meeting me, she must either see my old place empty, or profaned by the presence of a soul soiled by deeds which, where she lives, are called by their right names." His wild hypochondriac eyes were up-raised, and really suffused with tears. " Oh, God help all poor souls struggling blindfold with Satan! I didn't walk into his black net of slavery of my own free choice; as many do. I grew up under it; and it entangled and darkened me of itself; and I can't see my way out. It's bondage to the souls of the masters, as much as to the bodies of the slaves. Death frees them; will it us ?" He turned on Herman, and bent towards him with his haggard, hungry look, as if to hear his doom.

Herman said something, soothingly; he knew not what; nor, perhaps, did his hearer; but the expression of sympathy in his face and voice seemed to appease and tranquillize poor Broadstone; and, recollecting himself, he went on : " I very seldom speak on this subject; and thus I get so much trouble and wrong accumulated within myself that, when I begin to let it out, I don't know where to stop. You'll think I must be crazed, to talk so freely to you ; as your brother thought you were just now, to tell the truth to me; but I'm not, or, if I am, it's only with remorse and perplexity upon this single point. Now, don't say you didn't think he was, sir !" exclaimed he irascibly, to Edward who had looked a polite disclaimer ; "because I saw you did; and don't think it necessary to apologize for thinking so, neither, after what you've seen of us here. It's for us to apologize to you ; and, since you don't taunt me with my misfortune and curse, I'm ready enough, for one, to do so. But as for those other abolition fellows, that come down upon you like *lynchers*, and first string you up, and then cut you down to ask if you're guilty, my temperament's peculiar, and they don't get many excuses out of me.

" Our slaves are mostly my wife's ;—her whole inheritance was in them ; and she won't hear a word about setting them free, because we have a hard struggle, at the best, to bring up and educate our children properly ; and I couldn't see my way clear to do it against her will; because I think women have their rights, that it's a very dishonorable and unmanly thing to interfere with,—as long as they stay at home, and behave themselves, and don't make a commotion about them ;—if she took to racing about, haranguing at conventions, and so on, I would claim the privilege the old law allows me, of taking a stick to her no bigger than my thumb, and be glad that my thumb was no smaller.— As to the rest, as I'm known for a soft-hearted fool when not in a passion, any poor black boy or girl, that has a hard or insolvent master, will come to me and say, ' Mas'r starves me,' or ' beats me,' or ' I'm gwine be sold,' and beg me to buy them. Well, what in the world can I do? I'd be glad enough to put my hand in my pocket and say, ' Here's your price; pay for yourself, and take yourself off;' and sorry enough to say, ' I can't help you.' But I'm unpopular and poor, and have a perfect checker-board of black and white mouths to feed already; so all that I can do is to answer, sometimes, ' Here you, Sam,' or ' Suky, I don't want you; but I'll buy you, on condition that you'll work hard for me and mine, and do as much as you can. I'm used to negroes, and can judge how much that is; and if we strike a bargain, I will expect you to keep to it; and if you don't, *I* will keep you to it.' Then they drawl out, ' Yes, mas'r,' of course; and as soon as they're paid for and feel themselves out of danger, they turn careless, and lazy, and wasteful, may-be, while, I'm at my wit's end to make both ends meet; and then,—I treat them accordingly,—some-times,—not because I'm a fiend by nature; but merely because I'm a poor, fallible, frail human being, forced into a position that only an angel is equal to.

" Those that come into my possession in this way are pretty apt to be unprofitable, unless I'm more cruel to 'em than I know how to be in cold blood; but I had a pair of brothers, once, who were first-rate hands,—a carpenter and a blacksmith. I took them at the request of their master, a friend of mine, who had just failed in business. They were favorites of his; and he thought I would treat them well. I thought so, too. But you can never know what's in you, till temptation comes to bring it to light. Put the cheese before the empty-looking hole, if you want to know whether a rat's nose is in there. They were as capable and industrious as any white mechanic you ever saw. I hired them out; and they brought me their wages,—high wages, too,—as honestly as possible, never a cent missing but what they were allowed, for extra work. I never saw such fellows. The times grew very hard; I was offered more than I'd paid for them, two or three times; but I hoped we would all manage to struggle along through together; when an abolitionist got hold of Tom, the carpenter. He told him, I was informed afterwards, that a promise made under such circumstances as his was, to be faithful to me, wasn't binding. Tom hung back at first; but the fellow clinched the business by saying that I had been talking with a man from Red River about selling him. (So I had, and refusing to part with him.) He ran away.

"I was in a tearing fury. My wife cried. She had just been packing our oldest son's trunk, to send him to college; and, after such a heavy loss, I didn't know which way to look to raise the money to pay for his first term, or travelling expenses, even. The boy was half beside himself. The lads here are mostly high-tempered; and he took after me. His mother pleaded for him, and urged me, and said that if he could only get his education, and make his way in the world, nobody could calculate how much good he might do; and, at any rate, we could buy Blacksmith Bill back again, if I'd only consent to sell him for a few years till the times were better; and, if I wouldn't, he'd be very sure to run after his brother. Another high offer had just been made us for him; and, in short, I gave her leave to sell him.

"I went out of the way for a day. I was pretty angry; but my rage is wont to be more loud than lasting; and I couldn't trust myself to see him taken off. In two or three weeks, his wife came to me in terrible trouble. A servant, who had been down the river with his master, had seen Bill, and he was poorly, and ill-used. He had been laying up his money for some time, and was to have been allowed to buy himself when he had enough, if his master hadn't smashed up. Nine hundred dollars of his went in that crash; and ever since he came to me, he'd been laying up to try it again. I never promised him; but I wouldn't have denied him. He had one hundred dollars with him when he was sold; and his new owner had taken it all away. What went to my heart most, though, was to hear from her, that the same representations which prevailed with his brother had been made to him, but that he had said he would trust me, and I might trust him. I had no ready money; but I rushed out into the streets after it, like a beggar; and Mr. Halifax lent me some. He sold some of his books to do it, I found out afterwards. I would have, if I'd had any that would sell. I took it, and went down in the first boat. I found them just shovelling in his grave."

"And she?"

"His wife? Oh, she went mad, sir, just as if she'd been quite a human being, very much so indeed! She was luckier than some human beings I could name, who haven't that resource. She came down to the pier to meet us, and stood; and when she saw me alone, and my news in my face, I suppose, she just went down into the river, head-foremost, like a pearl-diver. I ducked in after her, and clutched her clothes on the bottom; and they fished us out together; and we brought her to. But she had a fever after that, and never was quite right again, nor will be. I bought her with part of what was to have been his purchase-money; and I keep her, and will keep her to my dying day, if I starve to feed her. But I can't let her see me as often as she'd like; because she always goes down on her knees to me, as she did that day, and wrings her hands, and asks me to buy back her husband,—a sort of living 'skeleton in my house,'—ha! ha!"

"How had he died?"

"Of a fever,—the place was new and unhealthy,—not otherwise murdered, thank God! so far as we could learn—only broken-hearted. No one watched over his death-bed much; but I hope he went to heaven from it. Mine will be haunted, perhaps; and from it I shall go—where? No matter. He who dares serve the devil, should at least be brave enough to face the devil, and receive his wages." His whole swarthy, strongly-marked face assumed an expression of hard and haggard resolution. "Where I am, my sons must follow. What I am, they will be; and even my darling little innocent daughters can find no husbands to cherish and protect them, after I have gone to my own place, but such as have grown up under the influences which have made me what I am. Now, gentlemen," concluded he, bringing himself up short, "as quite enough of your time has been taken up with the consideration of my affairs, we will, if you please, turn our attention to yours."

They did so, and were agreeably surprised, after

the display of his peculiarities which he had made before them, to find how much professional knowledge, shrewd sense, and practical sagacity, he had. If his mind was disordered, it was so, certainly, only on one side.

After the specimens we have had of his manners and conversation, it is hardly necessary to say that he was, however, a person of a most excitable temperament, and of more sentiment and sensibility than clear and steady moral insight. Too true-hearted to swim with the tide, too fitful and unstable to stem it, his life had been spent like that of a *water-skipper*, in now jumping spasmodically a little way up the stream, and then being borne passively a little way down by it. Nature never meant him for a spiritual leader; but he was a most intelligent and generous, and might in ordinary circumstances have been a much happier and, outwardly at least, a better man.

He spent from this day much time with Herman, interested apparently in himself as well as in his cause, and attracted to him doubly, perhaps, by finding in him both the frankness, fairness, courage, and generosity which he himself had, and the calmness and elevation of mind which he had not. United by the free-masonry of large and patriotic hearts, they soon found themselves discussing "sectional" matters and things more freely with each other, than either could have done with many of the citizens of his respective State. In one of these conversations, Herman even ventured at last to repeat to Mr. Broadstone, Sam Taliaferro's singular communication in the wood. To his astonishment and almost horror, Mr. Broadstone rubbed his working forehead, apparently as much with perplexity as with anger, and at first made no reply.

"Why!" cried Herman, "do you think it possible? Would such things be suffered, even here?"

"'Suffered,' sir!" cried he, springing up. "Do you know what you are talking about? Do you take us for fiends, sir, 'even here'? If such a thing was known, do you suppose that devil's house wouldn't be pulled about his ears, 'even here,' just as quick as it would in Massachusetts?"

"I should think so, certainly."

Broadstone, mollified, sank down again into his seat and his cogitation, rubbing his forehead, and muttering slowly between the rubs, "If 'twas known,— there's the point. If 'twas true, who could know it? And who could make it known? Not you, not I; for we don't know it, and we can't afford lightly to run the risk of painting even the devil blacker than he is; and should we, 'twould only be taken for abolition slander. Not the actors in it, for their own sake. He lives out of sight and hearing of his nearest neighbours. It seems that, of the negroes even, this fellow was the sole spectator belonging to the place; and probably he never dared to speak of it until, in the excitement of your common flight, he let it out to you. Did not you think he lied?"

"No. I was convinced, I mean, that he was speaking from a very vivid impression left upon his mind; but, whether by fact or frenzy, I could not, from my brief acquaintance with him, judge."

"Well," continued Broadstone, in the same dejected, conjecturing tone, "I don't know that it makes so much difference, after all. I didn't think that anybody was bold enough for that;—I won't say bad enough; for if our Father has the heart of a father,— such a heart as mine, even,—and He knows I'm no model,—He'd, beyond all reckoning, rather men would abuse and insult Him,—Who can defend Himself, and will, when He gets ready,—than hurt His helpless children; and so I don't know that blasphemy's really any worse than cruelty?" He paused for an answer; but Herman was posed by the, to him, novel metaphysical or moral question brought up, and had none to give. "And so, as I was saying, I don't, after all, know that it makes much difference whether this St. Dominique actually crucified one slave, or merely got another one, by other barbarities, into such a state of torture, terror, and mental unsoundness, as to make him capable of fancying such a thing. Would any marks be left upon the skeleton, if that was taken up, —if it could be found?"

"Probably not. Indeed, now that I've shocked you and myself by repeating this story, I'm sorry that I've done so,—and half glad, too, though; it sounds to me, by day-light, so utterly impossible."

"Because it's so atrocious? Well; keep that standard of judgment as a test, while you can, young man. It shows how little you know of the devil, and is so far satisfactory, if no further. Some people, who know him better than you do, or ever will, I hope, would tell you that,—if it isn't quite true of him, as we are told it is of God, that 'with him all things are possible,'—there's only a pretty narrow rim of things that aren't possible with him. Queer things come to lawyers' ears, sooner or later. St. Dominique's not a native of this State, though, remember!"

"Nor even a countryman of ours, I have been glad to hear."

"No; nor long a resident, nor really well known here; so much I'll say for my neighbours. He can behave himself like a gentleman, usually does so when he's on his guard, and takes pains to make himself popular. Before you, a New Englander and an abolitionist, he wouldn't think it so necessary to mind his p's and q's; because he knew that, if you tried to get him into hot water, you'd only find yourself over head and ears in it. The raw back and iron collar you saw proved him no angel; but in all* that, our equitable laws protect him explicitly, and do so, virtually, in any other little eccentricities that he may choose to practise out of sight,—or out of *white* sight. As to this particular anecdote, I advise you, for the credit of our country and humanity, never to repeat it again. If true, it must have been the drunken bravado of some delirious orgy,—only a frantic and unparalleled exception, even in his bad life. You'll never know the truth or falsehood of it. It could be known only through a proper legal investigation; and a proper legal investigation can't be had. It never can be known by any one—unless, in some foreign hospital may-be, leagues away, or slave-ship sweltering along the line, one of the miscreants who assisted, pants it out with his last breath into the ear of some priest sworn to secrecy,—until the day when these remote plantations shall give up their dead, and their dead secrets; and then, depend upon it, strange stories will be told about others beside me, and *by* others besides poor Bill!" concluded this unfortunate man, whose remorse seemed to underlie his every other thought and feeling, and to make him regard, hate, and scorn himself almost as a sort of representative and incarnation of the iniquitous system which had so fatally overthrown his peace and happiness on earth.

------

* See Note A at the end of the volume.

In spite of all the real kindness which, in the midst of his impetuosity, he showed to Herman, there was often something in his manner towards him, which tended to depress his young client. He could not at first tell why. It was not unlike the compassionate gentleness of a physician towards a desperately sick patient. He found out why, one of the first times he was left alone with Mr. Broadstone; when he seized the opportunity to ask him what he thought of his case. He put the question with the mild gravity of an invalid who would gladly live, but is prepared to die; not that he thought, however, of the possibility of the loss of life, but of life's better half, liberty.

Mr. Broadstone started, looked at him, paused in his walk, and then came up to him and took a seat by his side. "My son," said he in a low tone,—"you'll excuse my calling you so; for I have a poor boy who must be about your age, and might have been more like you, if he'd been brought up where you were;—you surprise me. Tell me exactly what you mean."

"I meant," said Herman, colouring with the effort, "to ask how good a chance you thought there was of my acquittal?"

A very dark shadow, like the shadow of coming Fate, fell on Broadstone's face.

The poor young man saw it, and was sufficiently answered; but turning very pale, he urged, "They can have scarcely any satisfactory evidence against me, —scarcely any evidence at all except, perhaps, that of St. Dominique's driver; and he is a black. They cannot legally receive his testimony."

"They cannot receive it in court; nor can they, according to man's law, act upon it; but man's law does less than nothing, in such a case as this, to keep it from acting upon them. That blackguard,—good, appropriate, generic term for us slaveholders, by the way, ha, ha!—St. Dominique, was in this town this evening. He was giving a treat in the public square as I rode by, and set his negro up on a stump, and made him take turns with himself making speeches. I stopped and heard one of them. 'Twas getting so dark he didn't notice me. He had taught the fellow his lesson; and he recited it trippingly enough,—an account of the whole affair, but of your first visit to Sam principally. I must say it didn't tally remarkably with that you gave me;—no plagiarism there,—perfectly original. Great Jupiter, sir, could we have that sooty liar into court for cross-examination, I would in five minutes take the curl out of his very wool! But there it is; St. Dominique was telling them, from time to time, that he was a pious negro whose word they might take as soon as his own; and they were swallowing it all for gospel. From that audience your jurymen will probably be taken; and if not, from persons who have communicated with it. I will do my best to have your term the shortest possible; but pray God, my poor boy, you may be sentenced to imprisonment; if you are not," said he, in a still lower tone, "you must hold yourself prepared to render up your soul to Him through the hands of a mob! You are man enough to face the worst; and therefore you have a right to know it; and therefore I tell it you. Could I have supposed you in ignorance of it, I would have told you before, and given you a little more time to make up your mind. Life looks bright at your age; but those don't suffer the most, I believe, who part with it earliest; and a brave man holds it in his hands, at all times."

He spoke with a kind of feeling firmness unusual

11

in him. Herman pressed his hand gratefully, walked
to the grated window, stood gazing wistfully out into
the darkening night a few moments, at the few stars
beginning to prick through the sky over the north-east,
returned, and talked of other things.

He spent the afternoon of the day before his trial
in writing long letters to Constance and Clara; and in
this occupation his brother, stealthily glancing at him
over his newspaper, could see that, from time to time,
he was a good deal moved. This over, however, he
was so collected and cheerful in conversation through
the evening, and seemed so well content that, at any
rate, their suspense was so soon to be at an end, that Edward could not believe he shared his own agonizing
apprehensions of violence on the morrow. He was
surprised, therefore, and unable to account for it when,
on parting with him for the night, Herman, as if by
a sudden and uncontrollable impulse, threw his arms
around his neck and kissed him.

CHAPTER XXIII.

THE KNIGHT'S TRIAL.

"He hath resisted law;
And therefore law shall scorn him further trial
Than the severity of public power."
SHAKESPEARE.

THE trial came on. The jurors were called.
Eleven of them, under oath, confessed themselves prejudiced, but thought, notwithstanding, that they could
decide according to evidence. They were challenged;
but the objection to them was set aside, because, as it
was forcibly argued, other people were prejudiced, too.
In a shed not far from the court-house, twenty men,
with blacked faces, ropes, and materials for putting up
an *impromptu* gallows, awaited the result of the process.

Edward stood at Herman's side. Mr. Broadstone,
in his *coat-of-arms*, had ridden over on a hired horse,
—his own having been found mysteriously lamed in
his stall,—and interposed every possible obstacle at
every stage of the proceedings. From time to time,
the spectators hissed him; and he foamed at the
mouth. Tobacco and its consequences abounded.
The jostling crowd, of the species that most doth con-
gregate at a horse-race or a cock-fight, eddied to and
fro, and alternately pushed and fought for places nearest to the noble young forms in the dock; as the Roman *vulgus* used to do, no doubt, some centuries ago,

for posts of observation nearest to the edge of the
arena, when certain eccentric religionists, patricians
and others, were about to be thrown to wild beasts.
(What is the precise difference between these " Christians " and those Pagans ?)

Messrs. Broadstone and Hartgon, opposing counsel, pitted against each other successively all the he-
roes of antiquity whom they could catch in their memories.   Mr. Hartgon's chief dependence was upon
Leonidas, Herman being viewed in the light of an
invading Persian, coming with an army at his heels to
take away the rights and liberties of Bondage ; (woe
to those whose " rights " are but wrongs against their
fellows !)   Mr. Broadstone's, upon Aristides; because
he was fond of justice, and that was what Herman
wanted.   " The public," meanwhile, officiated as a
Greek chorus.   They cheered Leonidas uproariously ;
but Aristides found little favor with them.

Having first in a manner exhausted literature and
eloquence, the legal gentlemen had, lastly, recourse to
law and logic.   They had *paired off* upon the facts
immediately connected with Herman's capture.   Noble
had vanished, leaving word with old July that he was
going to one of the free States, to try to learn an honest
trade, and be an honest man.   In the absence of his
evidence, the lawyers had therefore made this compromise : Hartgon agreed not to accuse Herman of shooting the slave-catcher, on condition that Broadstone
should not " put to the jury the intrinsic improbabil-
ity of a slave-stealer's tarrying in the very jaws of
danger, to nurse a slave-catcher."

However, Mr. Broadstone proved conclusively, to his
clients and himself, that there was no existing statute
under which Herman could be legally convicted upon

such evidence, or rather utter absence of evidence, as the case presented ; and that, if such statute was wanted for the preservation of their property,—he " would recommend first trying a little more corn-cake and a little less cow-hide,"—as he made this suggestion, he chanced to catch the cold sardonic eye of Squire St. Dominique, shook his fist at him by an involuntary variation of his violent and incessant gesticulation, and was called to order by the judge,—they " must wait for the next Legislature to pass it, and in the meantime, of course, discharge the prisoner."

But it was ruled by the court, Sharper, J., on the bench, that it could make no manner of difference to the criminal, if he be convicted, whether the statute according to which he be convicted was made before his sentence or after.

Mr. Hartgon then demonstrated, to the perfect satisfaction of the majority present, that, as to anybody's treatment of his servants, that was nobody's business. A merciful man was merciful to his beast; as we learned from a Book which we could none of us peruse too frequently.*　Now, it was notoriously manifest that it was as much for the interests of the owner to treat his negro well as his ox, and self-evident that slaves were almost universally kindly used, and happier far than their masters.　[Disinterested fellows! Why

---

* Query: did the learned counsel mean, that the Book referred to was one which we *did* none of us, then and there. peruse too frequently, or which we [more literally] *could* not, most of us, from the fact of our never having learned how?　The latter interpretation would seem to be confirmed by the following statistics,—I am sorry that I have not at hand the means of making them fuller,—of the comparative cultivation of letters, in our *enslaved* and our free States: In 1840, the proportion of free white inhabitants who could not read, to those who could, was, of New Hampshire, as 1 fraction of a person to 300; Connecticut, 1 to 590; South Carolina and Georgia, about as 1 to 13; and of North Carolina, 1 person and a fraction to 9.

[*See " Papers on the Slave Power."*

don't they make them change places ?] In those rare
and exceptional cases where they were not so, it was
palpably merely because severity had been rendered
imperative by the gratuitous interference of the abolitionists, to prevent said severity ; wherefore humanity
to the slave peremptorily enjoined severity towards the
abolitionist.

Doubtful cases left undecided by the letter of the
law, it was obligatory to decide in accordance with the
spirit of the law. Now, larceny was an indictable
offence. Sheep were property. If a man, by exhibiting salt to so much as a tottling lambkin, lured him
away from the fostering shelter of his master's fold, he
was guilty of a larceny, and punishable accordingly.
Negroes were property,—very similar, indeed, to
sheep in regard to their wool, though less so in respect
to their innocence, (yet perhaps more resembling hogs
with regard to their habits and appetites,) and,—
though slow and sluggish too frequently, partly, no
doubt, in consequence of the too lavish feeding which
they enjoyed among us,—not inappropriately to be
compared to the fleet coursers of the race, by reason of
their market value. Just as an individual, by tender-
ing the tempting saline particles to the silly sheep, and
enticing him away from his lawful protectors to misery, want, or death, stole said sheep, so had the individual before them, shrinking before the universal eye
of public ignominy riveted upon his unblushing front,
by holding out to the silly slave the delusive prospects of the freedom for which he was most utterly unfit,
stolen said slave from the patriarchal and paternal
sway of his venerable master ; and the latter offence
exceeded the former in its heinousness, even as far as
the value of even a bondman exceeded the value of a
sheep.

Nay, the offence was one whose heinousness was a theme for feeling rather than for argument. The moral sense of man,—man in a state of nature, noble, chivalrous, unperverted by fanatical sophistry or the malignity of sectional prejudice,—branded it with one harmonious voice as a crime of a deeper and darker dye than any mere material theft! It was the theft of a soul,—from the slave's master in this world, from the slave himself in the other!—For the sake or the hope of a little delusive, transitory, earthly bliss, the besotted wretch was induced to fling from him forever the heavenly glory of those faithful servants who,—" like many, I trust, whom I see around me to day,--obey the blessed Apostle, who declared, 'Servants, obey your masters.'" For a like offence, laid under the ban alike of all the more enlightened States and citizens of our Confederacy, had Dillingham perished in his unrepentant sins in the penitentiary of Tennessee. For a like offence had the felonious hand of Jonathan Walker smoked and sputtered under the branding-iron of Florida, laid on by a marshal of these United States, a patriotic, loyal son of Maine. For a like offence had Thompson, Work, and Burr, languished in the prison of Mizzourah, and for years Sayres and Drayton, in the jail of Washington under the shadow of the national ægis, until the latter came forth only to drag a wretched existence and to die by his own hand, overwhelmed by a guilt too heavy for a weak intellect to bear, accursed of God and man!

As for the evidence which had been offered, [that of St. Dominique, and Noble's two compeers, given discreetly enough under the sharp eye and ear of Broadstone,] Mr. Hartgon was free to leave it without one glozing word to the candid consideration of the enlightened jury. It mattered little how the prisoner had accomplished his evil purpose ; for an evil purpose can convert to evil instruments the simplest acts. For the credit of the humanity which he disgraced, we would hope that he had not endeavoured, (as from the artless but too tardy statements of a servant, whose incorruptible fidelity had yet suffered him to suppress his account of the interview until too late, from a sentiment of weak and mistaken tenderness for his fellow, there was too much cause to fear that he had,) to incite the miserable but cowardly fugitive to compass his design through conflagration and murder. It was to be regretted, that while our law,—from a kind consideration for the natural feelings of slaves, analogous to that which excuses wives from giving testimony against their husbands,—refused to receive their testimony against their masters, it did not consent to receive their testimony on behalf of their masters. It was to be hoped that our code might be perfected by an amendment in this regard. But in the meanwhile, after all, —whether the criminal had indeed poured his evil suggestions forth in a full free flood as great as his baseness, or dropped a few insidious hints as covert as his crime, or only, in a silence deep as his perfidy and dark as his doom, had, with sinister glances riveted askance, malignly pointed to the fell North Star,— what mattered it how he did the deed, so that the deed was done ? If for any reason whatsoever, conclusive to their own minds, the jury was satisfied that he was guilty, they would of course find accordingly, unbiassed by any of the artful sophisms of the opposing counsel. Routine and technicality were innocuous in their place ; but they must never be suffered to interfere with the execution of justice ; or we would have anarchy at once.

Mr. Broadstone arose from his seat like a roasted chestnut from a hot stove, and desired to know, Whither loyalty to the Union, and good-fellowship and hospitality between the States, were flown, if a countryman and a stranger couldn't travel among us, and ask a gentleman to sell him a slave that he had a fancy for, for any private reason, and offer to pay a good round price for him, too, fairly and honestly as a gentleman should, and then go to look at him by his master's permission, and perhaps even speak a kind word to the poor, smarting, beaten wretch in his iron collar,—though, as to that, there wasn't a penumbra of legal evidence of the prisoner's having done so,—and then go about his business in a quiet, gentlemanly way, without being exposed to all sorts of ignominy, to be taken up and sentenced without law to nobody knew what, "and all on the circumstantial evidence of an abused servant's running away between two floggings, the hearsay evidence of two topers deposing that, while snoozing between their cups, they heard another toper, (whose condition was palpably enough to account for his seeing double,) say he had seen two men half a mile off from where they found only one, and the word of a sooty black liar of a driver, who had to make up some sort of an acceptable story, in order to get his ' venerable master ' not to crucify him for not keeping a better look-out."

St. Dominique took a pinch of snuff, and appeared to relish it.

Mr. Hartgon rejoined, amid much applause and merriment, that, " as to inter-State relations, if the slave States lost a nigger, and the free States an abolitionist, ' held to labor and service,' " he reckoned the

11*

loss and gain of both would be " about mutual ;" and
that, " as to domestic discipline,

> ' Folks, that live in houses of glairss,
> Better not throw stones at they who pairss.' "

His opponent was popularly reported to have a crazy
yellow girl in his residence. He " would just like to propound the en-quirry, what caused her hallucination ?"

Broadstone writhed ; and the perspiration started
on his furrowed forehead ; but he made no answer.
The crowd laughed again ; and so did the judge. As
in duty bound, however, he impartially reprimanded
all parties, and then charged the jury, who went out.

Almost immediately, with only so much delay as
was required to inform the mind of the unprejudiced
twelfth, who was doubtful, (having just come over the
border from a little public business in Kansas, and
having been sleeping off the fatigues of his journey
during the greater part of the trial,) they returned, and
announced their verdict,—" Guilty ;" and sentence
was pronounced, " Five years in the penitentiary !"

Edward started and clenched his fist, not knowing
what he did, but feeling strong enough and wild
enough at the instant to knock down everybody and
everything, and carry Herman off in spite of them all ;
but before he betrayed himself, Herman had caught
his hand in his own death-like fingers, turned upon
him a countenance as solemnly bright as that of a
young St. Stephen, and murmured almost imploringly,
with his dry lips cleaving to his teeth, " Let us only
think how much worse it might have been !" In his
high, yet fluttering, young heart he felt what he did not
say, " How much worse, if not for me, still for you,
and for all who love me, it may be yet !"

There was no riot, however. It was dinner-time; and some of the crowd were hungry. Some were appeased, if not fully satisfied, with the measure of vengeance which they had obtained. Some, perhaps, already regretted it, from one of those revulsions of feeling to which mobs are prone; and,—that better side of the distinctive Southern character coming uppermost, which some persons think is so much better than the best side of the distinctive Northern character, as more than to equalize the two,—perhaps they were moved even to pain by the sight of the two brothers, so young, so gallant-looking, so attached, and so unfortunate.

Be that as it may, Herman was detained in the court-house but a few moments, before it was sufficiently cleared for him and his attendants to reach the jail-cart without difficulty; and he returned to his cell with no molestation, except from the eyes of the lingerers; and even those he could not see, for the sunlight of that dazzling day was black to him; and his sight was turned inward upon himself, and his own and his Constance's great appalling misery. It seemed to crowd and fill his whole being, heart and soul, so utterly with its swelling and spreading darkness, that no room was left within him for anything else, except for Him Who is in mercy everywhere.

In this stunned condition, he remained at Tadmor a week or ten days more. In the course of that time, the excitement against him was partially renewed by a false report which got abroad, no one knew how, that the lenity of his sentence had been procured by a bribe. Edward, who had written to the Governor before the trial, did so again upon its conclusion, and received a second answer, courteously worded like

the first, but little more than a repetition of it, renewing his Excellency's assurance that, at the fitting
time, Dr. Arden's father's services to the South would
no doubt be remembered, his assertion that the fitting
time had not yet come, and an invitation to his house.
He promised, however, a very strong and "reliable"
guard to convey Herman to the penitentiary; and with
this Edward had to be satisfied. That the time could
ever have come when the offer of a strong guard, to
take Herman to prison, should seem a boon to his
brother!

Herman's chain was put on again. Letters of recommendation to one of the wardens of the penitentiary were given him, not only by Mr. Broadstone, but
by Judge Sharper and his jailer. It rained hard; but
a crowd assembled to see his departure. Edward was
allowed to enter the stage-coach with him, in company
with the sheriff. The savage-looking guard rode on
horseback on each side of the windows, armed with
dirks and pistols. The brothers said little, but sat for
the most part tongue-tied, under that cruel and mysterious spell which makes us often most dumb when
we have the most to say, and the shortest time to say
it in. Herman had given to Edward very long letters
to his betrothed and his sister, containing much that it
might have been more difficult for him to utter than
to write, even if there had been no third person present. He seemed now to be racking his brains to recall
the names, haunts, and wants, of all the sick and poor
who had learned to depend upon him, that he might
leave them as a legacy of love to his brother. At least,
when he did speak, it was chiefly of them.

The journey was brief and blank. As the dismal
walls, which awaited the young captive, stood up in the

distance and came forth, with their whited-sepulchre front of blackened and mildewed stucco, to receive him, one of the guard suddenly thrust his shaggy head in at the window, and said, in language rather above his station, "You may be happy in another world; but you will see no more happiness in this one. You've spent your last pleasant day here below; and all that's at an end."

He then withdrew, and rode on as before. It was not easy to judge whether he had spoken from cruelty, or from a sort of rude impulsive sympathy; but it was as if an ill Omen had spoken.

Herman shivered slightly as if a cold wind, from within the mouldy-looking tomb of living men before them, had breathed upon him; but instantly rallying himself, he turned to his brother and said, "One would think he was a student of Dante,—

'*Lasciate ogni speranza, voi che entrate.*'

Oh, no! There is but one prison, if any, in the universe, over whose door those words belong. The fellow is mistaken, Ned; as I shall show you five years hence."

The news of their coming had preceded them; and a throng had gathered to witness their arrival. They alighted, and entered the office. It was at once crowded with strangers. The guard, armed with muskets, kept the door. The overseer, with his bowie-knife and pistols, stood over Herman. His name was written in the prison-record. The harlequin, parti-colored prison-uniform was brought forward. One would have thought that it was for Edward; his face flushed, and his lip trembled,—a sight which Herman had hardly ever witnessed before. He tore out his purse, and showed a couple of gold eagles to the guard. "Put all this rabble out!" said he, in a hoarse whisper which choked in spite of him. The men, half cowed by his expression and manner, obeyed instinctively, almost as much for fear as fee.

Herman pushed the clothes aside. "Wait a moment," said he, gently, but in a tone which scarcely admitted of denial; and his hand passed on and clasped his brother's in its vigorous, manly grasp. He took out his watch, and gave it to him ;—"*Aspenwall*," said he ; Edward nodded ; his gold pencil,—" *Clare ;*—God bless you ! God bless you ! Now, Ned, go."

And it was over,—that bloody wrenching apart of two hearts which had grown together! Edward, at the door, gave one glance over his shoulder, and saw his brother standing erect and stately as he had ever seen him, looking very pale but undaunted, with cow-hides and handcuffs hanging on the wall over his head, and the slouching, ruffianly-looking turnkeys busy all about him. It was enough. He fled from the spot and the State, as if chased or led by the Furies.

CHAPTER XXIV.

THE PENITENTIARY.

" Lo svegliarsi la prima notte in carcere è cosa orrenda."
SILVIO PELLICO.

" Who, when he is to treat
With sick folks, women, those whom passions sway,
Allows for that and keeps his constant way,
Whom others' faults do not defeat,
But, though men fail him, yet his part doth play."
HERBERT.

IT was twilight without. Within, everything was dark and still. Herman was taken to his cell. He was thankful for its sheltering shade and solitude. It was about twelve feet by eight, arched over the top, built of brick and plastered, as he saw by the glimmer of the turnkey's lantern, unwarmed, and very damp and chill, like a vault in a cellar. This was to be his home, then, for the next five years,—perhaps for all the remainder of his life on earth! In one corner, near the ceiling and too high to be looked out at, was an open window guarded by two iron bars, with no glass, but a wooden shutter on hinges, to close it. The door was about four feet by two, and double, the inner leaf being of iron, and the outer one of thick wood. There were two beds, one *double* and one *single*.

On the last of these he seated himself, the instant the officer had locked him in, bowed himself, covered his face, and let the black Niagara of his long-pent grief sweep over him. He hoped that if he suffered it thus, once for all, to have its free course, it would pass on and off; but it did not; and how long he sat there, stupifying and drowned in agony, he never knew.

At length he was startled by a distant jangling sound, like that of "many pairs of oxen walking over a wooden bridge, with chains" dangling from their yokes, mingled with the grating of bolts, the clang of iron doors, and the banging of wooden ones. They were just locking up for the night, then! Could it be, that the whole, endless night was yet to come? The tramping, banging, grating, and jingling drew nearer, and reached his door. It burst open; and two dark forms came crouching and stumbling in, dragging their chains behind them; as was plain more from the noise than by the wandering gleam of the jailer's lamp. One was a horse-stealer; and the other, a murderer. It struck upon Herman as an aggravation of his misery, to find that he was to have companions in it; but perhaps it saved his reason. It turned his thoughts, and forced him to rouse and control himself.

Before long, he was brought before a synod consisting of the two wardens and two or three of their friends, the overseer, and a turnkey, in the guard-room. One of the two former officers, Captain Robespierre (commonly called Robby Spear) Rodrick, who appeared to be somewhat in liquor, and on the verge of *delirium tremens* or spontaneous combustion, took the word. He questioned his prisoner about the "underground railroad" and the principles of the abolitionists, proposed to "seize him up, and give him fifty lashes" unless he would "confess his guilt," and at the same time went through an alarming sort of single-stick exercise with his hickory cane, which he flourished in Herman's very face.

To all this Herman, folding his arms, quietly and decorously replied, taking up the heads of his interlocutor's discourse in their order, so far as they had any, that he knew scarcely anything about the "underground railroad;" that there was almost as great a variety of opinions and principles to be found among the different classes of persons called abolitionists, as among those opposed to them; that he did not consider himself guilty of any crime; and that, even if he had been, he could not legally be required to criminate himself.

"You lie!" said Captain Rodrick.

Herman said nothing. Mr. Royal Log, the senior warden, to whom Herman's letters of recommendation had been directed, fidgeted, and whispered to his colleague, who presently proceeded in a somewhat lower tone, though none of the lowest, and with his whisking cane slightly lowered to correspond.

"We don't have no gentlemen here! We won't have no gentlemen here! We don't have no misters here, but Tom, Dick, and Harries. We're dimocratic here, *we* are. It's fare and share alike here with our black niggers without, and our Yankee white jail-birds within, when we cotch 'em,—eat hog and hoe-cake or starve,—work or be hided. Needn't go to va'ntin to us, through friends or otherwise, about none o' your advantages to home."

Herman stood patiently, waiting for more if there was more to come.

"How? Why don't you speak when you're spoken to?" roared the official.

"I thought what you said unanswerable, sir; but I should consider the advantages you alluded to disadvantages, if they had pampered me into being lazy or dainty. I believe you may find me equal to quite as as much labor, and endurance of all kinds, as the average of healthy men."

"We will see, sir; we will soon see. We will make you toe the mark here, and no mistake. If you wanted a lesson to learn you to stop home and mind your own business, you've got to the 'cademy now. Such canting traitors, like you, is always a-preaching about the laws of God. We go by the laws of Bondage here. You better acquaint yourself with them, I reckon, now you've got a little lezzure and retirement for reflection. I will now purceed to communicate the regulations of this here penal institution; and you will comply rigorously, or wish yourself in Tophet and find it a pleasant change when you git there.

"You will converse with no other convict, in your cell or out; nor with any visiter; nor look up from your work at them, if they come in, without permission,—not if it's your own brother;—if you do, as sure as you live you shall see the black cell in lieu of him; and the first time I have lezzure, I'll give you the strap. Twa'n't by no invitation of our'n you come here a-disturbin of our peace and tranquillity; and now you've saw fit to come, you'll be subservient to our ordinances.

"You will receive and send no letter to friends, only after inspection of warden or wardens,—penalty, complete interdict of correspondence.

"You will always pull off your cap before you speak to any officer, or when any officer speaks to you, on pain of having the head shaved.

"Git out, and carry yourself straight."

After Herman had been again locked into his cell, the overseer came to him, and addressed him with sincere though rough kindness, encouraging him especially with the assurance that, if he "behaved in future, the past would be overlooked;" for that he, himself, treated "every man, not accordin to his reputation, but his conduct." He further exhorted him to wink his eyes up, and go right along off to sleep, 'cause the fust night o' comin was allers the wust on it; an 'twould make the mornin come in a jiffy; an then he'd git into the work-shop with plenty of company, and everythin would look so kind o' cheerfuller, and home-like to him; and he'd feel like another man, and never think o' carin for it no more, arter he'd got somethin or nuther to do; and the five years would go a-slidin off just like the half of no time. What 'ud he ha' done, had he been oncarcerated for life? He followed up his remarks by stirring up Kane the murderer, who had in the meanwhile ensconced himself in the single bed, and driving him off to share that of Spurr the horse-stealer, who was already fast asleep.

Herman obediently threw himself, in his prison-uniform, on the miserable little deserted pallet, wrapped its one coverlet (a thin and much too short Indian blanket) corner-wise about him as well as he could, and strove for rest. In vain. The nearest approach which he could make to it was one of those dismal trances, in which the two lobes of the brain appear to work together for double wretchedness, in harmony though not in unison, the one being occupied in keeping up a constant consciousness of present misery, and the other, in getting up a busy panorama of misery, absent, yet scarcely less real. He never for an instant forgot where he was, his cell, his bed, the darkness, the iron bars and doors that pent him in, the cold fetter that clutched him fast by the ankle like a claw of steel, and the prison-roof which brooded over him. He never ceased to hear the loud and heavy breathing of his companion criminals. Yet, all the while, he was almost equally conscious of his brother's solitary and desolate journey, bearing on with him evil tidings to agonize, perhaps to kill, his love. He heard the steam-engine's bell and whistle and clamor, redoubled as often as the train of cars passed over one of the rivers which ran between him and his home. He *felt* Edward in the darkness, sitting and slumbering muffled in his cloak; then saw him, when the cars emerged from the covered way, stirring, looking wearily and drearily out into the night, and then trying to forget himself in sleep again. He saw his arrival, the eager home-like faces springing to doors and windows, to welcome him, and *him*,—old Sally, Patrick, Clara, Constance—no! her he would *not* see! As often as the distracting vision reached this point, he started up, threw it off, and cried to God with his moving voiceless lips to save her and him, over and over, many times, before he could lie down again; and then it all began again at the beginning, and went on again towards the same consummation as steadily as the march of Doom; and still, through all, and keeping time to all like the ticking of a metronome, his hard-throbbing heart beat on, and seemed to say two words, " Five—years! Five—years!"

Those five years!—waking or sleeping, he could not get rid of them. The present was to him just five years long. Time seemed to stand still before him, continually facing him with them, and insisting on forcing them upon him in one huge, bitter, choking, solid ball, which was to be swallowed whole, not part at a time. The sense of the whole period appeared to pervade every instant of it, just as the complete magnetic polarity does every particle of the magnet. Every instant that he lived, he seemed to live five years.

In the midst of this state, he was suddenly startled by the sound of terrible cries, groans, and prayers for mercy, as he thought close to his ear. He once more sprang up in bed, and strained his starting eyes to see. He saw only "darkness thickest on that side." He put out his hand, and felt the wall; but the cries grew louder; and his first idea was, that his reason had given way under the weight of his sorrows, and that he was the subject of auricular illusions. This notion was, however, quickly dispelled by the mutterings which he heard between his waking room-mates.

"The devil!" said Spurr; "old Rodrick's at it again, strap and paddle, paddle and strap!"

Herman remembered, then, that the way was not long from the guard-room to the cell, and rightly conjectured that they were on opposite sides of the same partition.

"Hush!" whispered Kane. "Keep still, and make believe sleep, and may-be he won't think of us." ·

The cries, intermingled with the noise of blows and struggles, continued with short intervals for about half an hour; after which they yielded to the night-mare stillness of a prison at night. But Herman had been thoroughly roused, and dreamed and slept no more.

It was yet dark, when the door was opened, and something was apparently thrust through it; after which it was shut again with a jarring clang. There was an immediate bustle and scrambling over the other bed; and Spurr in a moment came to Herman's side, saying, in a practiced *sotto voce* undertaker's murmur of his own, which always contrasted oddly with his very unstudied language, " Here, look sharp, younker; grab your grub, and gobble. They'll be arter yer in less nor a quarter of a second, to set yer to slavin."

Herman thanked him in a whisper, sat up, put out his hands, and received in them something that smelt like meat, upon something else that felt like rough biscuit. " I can eat here, at least, if I cannot sleep," said he to himself; " and I must, or I cannot live five years. Fortunately, this is a matter which my will has some control over."

He bit off a morsel of the slippery fat pork, which slid away out of his fingers when he tried to tear it, broke off a corner of what proved to be a crust of cold corn-bread, and was glad enough to find himself able to relish his coarse food. He stood in great need of it after his vigils of the night, and his unconscious fast of the day before. " I am strong; and, at this rate, I shall keep up my strength," thought he; " and I can trust Clara for taking care of Constance. Five years are not forever; we are both healthy and young, and probably have many more after those in store for us."

As the words passed through his mind, while he ate on mechanically, his teeth suddenly came together through the tough rind of what was like a round mouthful of pork; and his mouth was filled with a cool, disgusting, tasteless jelly. It was the eye of a hog.* In his exhausted state, the discovery almost nauseated him; but he hastily and resolutely took another mouthful, selecting it with greater care, as well

---

* See " Prison Life and Reflections," by George Thompson, p. 124.

as he could in the dark. It proved to be gall; and he was instantly seized with violent sickness. The sleepy, careless negro cook, as sometimes happened afterwards, had by mistake mixed the offal with the rations.

Spurr's stifled merriment knew no bounds. Perhaps the mischance was of his contriving; for he was, though less from malice than from sheer coarseness, a most unfeeling and brutal wag. Kane, however, at once chid him, came to Herman, assisted him, threw his breakfast out of the window, and begged him to share his own. Herman could not swallow an atom of it; but grateful for the kindness which pressed it upon him, and somewhat recovered, though still faint and giddy, he left his cell.

In the passage murky with the morning twilight, he, for the first time, saw assembled the drove of his fellow-prisoners, from eighty to a hundred in number, —a ragged, squalid, evil-looking crew enough. The greater part of them were in chains, some with one passing from one ankle to the waist, others with three,— one on each leg riveted to another passing round their middles,—and others ironed in the same manner, but more heavily, with larger chains fastened to clumsy fetters, which made them walk like bears. Clanking, tramping, jingling, and jangling, they sullenly and slowly formed into distinct packs, and went their several ways, followed or led by their respective drivers; some, to the different work-shops and yards attached to the main building; others, marched in double file with one guard in front and two behind, all three gun in hand, to the neighbouring city, to work in the open air, as carpenters, masons, or pavers; and some again, in like manner, to a quarry for stone. The overseer, meanwhile, made prize of Herman, and appeared much at a loss to know what to do with him; while the latter was in a state of as great uncertainty about what trade he was to follow, as he had formerly been about, what profession. The only difference was, that this time he was to be spared the trouble of choosing.

They passed through a brick-yard. Mr. Bush, Herman's present possessor, looked at him, and probably decided that he was of too different a kind of clay from that commonly used there; at any rate, he went on to the stone-cutting yard, where the work was cleaner, but hard, jarring, and noisy. He took him to the rope-walk, wagon-shop, and carpenter's shop, but, rather to his regret, left him in neither of them, and finally set him down in the hot, close, weaving-room, to a loom, showed him how to weave coarse bagging, and told him that thirty yards a day would be expected of him, after he had had the remainder of the week to practise himself in the craft. He meant kindly; but he would have done better by Herman, if he had put him to sawing wood, if not stone.

Yet this occupation, monotonous and mechanical as it soon afterwards became, at first required and absorbed his whole attention, and was so far a relief. Twelve o'clock speedily came, and with it pork and bread-time the second, *alias* dinner-time. The prisoners began to move towards their cells. Just as Herman was congratulating himself on his approaching escape from the close heat and oily smells of the shop, and the prospect of a little rest to his weary brain, dazzled eyes, and aching arms, the overseer stopped him: "Say Arden, you've been a medicle man, hain't yer?"

Herman took off his cap as in duty bound, and replied, with a momentary surprise at the fact recalled to him, that he had. It appeared to him that, if true at all, it must have been so in some state of pre-existence,—that for one mortal life he had been a prisoner, and for one half of that, a weaver.

"Then," continued Mr. Bush, "I want yer jest to step this way a second, and look at a feller's back. Our doctor wa'n't on here last week; an I'm keen to sw'ar he won't come this, nuther."

Herman did go to the hospital accordingly, and did look at a fellow's back. It was such a sight as he had never seen before, and such as it is very disgusting and shocking in anybody to describe. Whether it is disgusting and shocking or not to the patient to present such an appearance, is, we are constantly assured,—provided he is a negro,—no business of ours. Notwithstanding, as "*humanum nihil a me alienum puto*," I proceed to state that this fellow's back was mortifying and putrescent in the middle, and on the edges, variegated, and sprinkled with a few dark raised spots like kernels of burnt coffee.

"What has happened to him?" said Herman, turning from it somewhat confounded in spite of all his previous experience.

"Wall," said the overseer, putting a quid in his mouth, and his hands in his pockets, "nothin; on'y he's been paddled, I reckon, and hain't got over it quite as well as war to be expected."

The sufferer was but a youth. He had blue eyes and straight fair hair. He appeared to Herman to be white; but in slave States, distinctions of color exist less to the eye than to the mind, and it is difficult to discriminate. He might have only been an *invisible-black*. It did not occur to Herman to inquire; be-

12

cause, as a physiologist, he had not ascertained that the nerves of negroes were less sensitive than those of men properly so called, and because, as a psychologist, he would have supposed that the sufferings of a negro slave in the circumstances might be, at least in one respect, even more severe than those of a *man* in durance merely for a limited term of years, since the latter might reasonably expect in the course of his mortal life to get beyond the power of his tormentors.

In enforced silence Herman bent over the groaning· victim, who writhed and shrank from the lightest touch of even his delicate and practised fingers, as he dressed his wounds with his utmost tenderness and skill. Afterwards, having no other mode of communication at hand, and himself feeling the need of the consolation which he longed to impart, he ventured to take from his bosom his little pocket copy of the New Testament, and read a few verses in his soft and modulated tones. The poor boy, meantime, in some degree eased and comforted, gazed wonderingly up at the refined and noble countenance, and slender, gentleman-like, blue-veined hands, contrasted strangely with the parti-colored ignominious dress of his singular visitant ; and the overseer, starting and turning round from the window to which he had lounged, leaned against the side of it, and listened without interrupting, as the sweet words, old but ever new, broke the silence, instead of the moans which alone had been heard before: "Come unto me, all ye that labor and are heavy laden, and I will give you rest. Take my yoke upon you, and learn of me ; for I am meek and lowly in heart, and you shall find rest unto your souls." " Blessed are they that mourn, for they shall be comforted."

Having satisfied his curiosity, and perhaps some better feeling, by hearing Herman out, Mr. Bush satisfied his official conscience by telling him that he had broken the rules, and that it must not happen again, but that as he hadn't hardly got into the traces yet, he wouldn't report him this time. But when Herman was forced to follow him, and leave the sufferer to his unknown fate, he felt, in the midst of all his indignation, grief, and gloom, a solemn thankfulness beginning to spring up and grow within him, to find that God had not as, in the despondency of his weariness and exhaustion, he was at first ready to imagine, set him aside from His service in the service of His creatures, but, in his lowest estate, had still placed him where he could carry comfort to those more miserable than himself. He returned to spend the afternoon at his loom, and, in spite of cold and home-sickness, fell asleep at night the moment that his head touched his pillow, utterly wearied out.

Thus Herman's convict's life began; and thus, for a considerable time, it went on, with little variety. As the first excitement of his coming passed off, perhaps the load settled down upon him more heavily,—the instinctive shame of a man of honor, at finding himself in a felon's position even without a felon's guilt, the disgust of a man of great delicacy of mind and manners at continual association with men of brutal habits and characters, the pain of monotonous inactivity to a most active youth and of intellectual famine to a student, the bitter home-sickness of a sympathizing and home-loving person whose absence, he knows, is making day by day a sweet home desolate, and still more, if anything can be more grievous, the frequent knowledge of cruelty, which he cannot prevent, to a generous and high-spirited lover of his kind.

As my reader may have already suspected, Herman was not fortunate in either of the wardens. Log was an old man, and little more than a cipher in the jail. He was Rodrick's father-in-law, and had been associated with him in his office, with the idea, probably, that the weak and silly good-humour of the one might temper advantageously the violence of the other. It had, on the whole, the contrary effect.

There was one thing which Log loved better than mercy, and even than money, and that was his ease. Rodrick agreed with him in nothing but avarice. He was a schemer, more ambitious and enterprising than able, a speculator, and a small politician. In order to get time for his operations without the penitentiary, he insisted upon handing over the entire management of it, on alternate weeks, to the senior warden. During Log's nominal reign, the reins of government were slackened, and the lawless crew he should have ruled grew more disorderly. When Rodrick resumed the command, not being able to beat his father-in-law for his remissness, he beat his prisoners for it and their own irregularities, too. His exasperation exasperated them; and now and then they would mutiny. Suffering much from nervous dyspepsia, and being an economist of time in his way, he frequently flogged them at night; when he was unable to sleep and they were unable to work. It was said that he " experienced religion " more than once, but usually experienced irreligion again soon after. Finding himself, after a few spasmodic days of first horror and then rapture, not yet quite a new man, he was plunged into a gloomy despair which made him reckless. In this state he happened to be upon Herman's arrival; and, while it lasted, he was cruel even beyond the wont of his bitter, bilious nature.

Not only blacks, visible or invisible, were beaten frequently in Herman's hearing, but, as he soon found, undeniable whites, besides. One case of this kind, which came to his eyes and ears, appeared to him particularly barbarous. There was a laboring man, named Wellbeloved, confined in the penitentiary on a charge similar to that against himself. He had borne an excellent character, was much respected even in the jail, and was, after his fashion, a zealous Christian. His fashion was not Herman's fashion, to be sure, and appeared to him, indeed, rather a fantastic fashion, consisting as it did, in part, of noisy and violent bodily exercises which, Herman suspected, profited little. Herman clung fast and most affectionately to the doctrine of the Holy Spirit, as the inward breathing of God upon the imperfect and degenerate soul of man, quickening and hallowing it by degrees, when sought and welcomed, into a Christ-like purity, benignity, and holiness, quite above and beyond the reach of mere unaided humanity. But he had seen no evidence to satisfy him of any miraculous manifestation of this spirit later than the apostolic age; and mere physical excitement did not seem to him any conclusive proof of its presence. It was very disagreeable to him to see, as he sometimes did, a man wrought up, by exhortation or otherwise, to jump and scream as if possessed by a spirit of doubtful origin. He took little part or pleasure in the *inquiry-meetings, experience-meetings*, and so-forth, to which the worthy Mr. Wellbeloved invited him at his own cell, every Sunday when leave could be had to hold them, and went to them with some unwillingness; though he did not think proper to refuse, in the dialect of his Christian brother, "to fellowship with" him. On the other hand, Mr. Wellbeloved doubted his "assurance," and was "fearful he laid too great stress upon his morality." Herman certainly did lay very great stress upon his and everybody's morality,—for the plain reason that his conscience and, as he thought, his Bible did ;—but he had as little idea as any man that, as a matter of strict justice, buying and selling, he could pay for an eternity of happiness by half a century or so of reasonably good behaviour. It is so difficult for men, of natures, educations, and original positions so different as theirs, to judge fairly of each other in matters of faith and doctrine, that they can hardly attempt to do so without running some risk of playing the Pharisee.

Herman endeavoured, notwithstanding, to have patience with what he esteemed the vagaries of Mr. Wellbeloved, and in the meanwhile esteemed him on the whole highly,—more highly still a few months later, when he stood by his death-bed, and saw how nobly and manfully his faith and trust supported him, under more than the common agonies of death,—admired the courage and enterprise with which, in circumstances so depressing, he attacked the strongholds of sin in the hearts of the sneering and scoffing criminals about him,—and believed that he did a great deal of good among rough spirits upon whom his own refined and retiring piety was powerless. Perhaps he undervalued himself in this respect; for genuine superiority of character, however unobtrusive, can scarcely fail, sooner or later, to *tell* upon those closely associated with its possessor, in most cases; and, in Herman's, it is certain that, shy as his fellow-prisoners might be, in their more careless and reckless moments, of one whose life was a constant, though modest and generally silent, reproof to theirs, he had not been in the penitentiary half a year, before, " I want to speak to Arden,"—" Oh, for pity's sake get Arden here !"— began to be the cry of those in any physical or mental straits. Still, there is room for, and need of, all sorts of good people in this naughty world ; and the Well-beloveds have their place and use.

One Sunday morning, Herman was enjoying one of his seasons of comparative luxury. (All things are comparative and relative.) He had had his weekly shaving the night before. Clara's favorite, his *moustache*, had long ago fallen a victim to the ruthless razor of the jail-barber ; and cheek and lip were left in a most inelegant and stubbly state six days in the week. Fondling his unusually smooth chin with much approbation and comfort, with the long slender fingers of one hand, he was lying, for warmth, in his mean cot-bed. Spurr, to his secret and perhaps unjustifiable satisfaction, had been detailed for extra service at a brick-kiln. Kane, who in his shrinking way was become very fond of him, had by permission drawn the other bed up to his side, and, in it, was listening eagerly while Herman read aloud, and explained to him, a part of Locke's paraphrase of the Epistles, which Mr. Halifax had lent to the former. Kane could not read easily, even if he had had any books ; and Herman, rather than neglect him or lose his few opportunities for continuing his own studies, often contrived, in this manner, to share them with him. This poor man had a two-fold interest for his mind and heart. He could never forget Kane's kindness to him on the miserable morning after his arrival ; and, on the other hand, it was a moral riddle to him, which he longed to read, that a creature so timid and mild could ever have wilfully,—as Kane, he understood, did not deny that he had done,—taken the life of a fellow-creature.

Their quiet was, before long, interrupted by Rodrick's voice, raised in loud threats. The answers to these, Herman could not distinguish; but his patron, the overseer, soon came along; and he asked him what the matter was.

"Wall, Wellbeloved says it's a sin to carry around the mush on the Sabbath."

Herman smiled. In his judgment the fourth commandment, in its strict and literal sense, was a rule to regulate the observance of Saturday among the Jews, not that of Sunday among Christians. He thought that Saturday was the Sabbath,—not Sunday. He had found no scriptural precedent for calling the latter two days by the same name. This was one of the chief points at issue between him and his worthy friend. He had never looked into it as far as he now wished that he had done; but he had a strong impression that the Jewish observance of the seventh day,— the Sabbath of the Old Testament,—had been as a schoolmaster to lead men to the Christian observance of the "first day of the week,"—the "Lord's day" of the New,—not so much as a period of rigorous physical inaction as of spiritual progress.

Notwithstanding, he looked with great dislike and distrust upon all approaches towards making it a mere holiday, in the modern sense of the word. He believed that if this change was effected, even our annual "Fast-day" would soon cease to be the *fastest* day in the year. To his thinking, what Christendom needed, at the present stage of its developement, was less to secularize Sunday, than to spiritualize Monday, Tuesday, Wednesday, Thursday, Friday, and Saturday. By the very instinct of his poetical temperament and reverent nature, he was prompted to have a ready and affectionate respect to all times and places consecrated by the time-honored habit of the church ; and, to the celebration of this day in particular, he had been accustomed at home to make a free-will offering of more deference than is usual in men of his, or perhaps of any, class. The noise of old Bayard's hoofs was never, except in case of absolute necessity, allowed to break the holy weekly stillness of the streets of Boston, nor to clatter rudely in among the chimes of the church-going bells ; nor were opera-airs pealed out from Herman's chamber on that day, as on others, to drive out of the ears or hearts of passers-by the lingering echoes of the hymns, from church or chapel. It was to him a season of especial convenience and leisure for prayer, religious study, self-examination, and preparation for duty. As such, he observed it at home ; and, as such, he observed it away from home. But,—so that the less important was not suffered to encroach upon the more, in himself or his neighbours,—he saw no harm, after the soul's due refreshment had been secured, in refreshing the body likewise, with a little gentle and decorous motion. And as to walking through the wards of a Sunday, with a kettle of smoking-hot mush and a pitcher of molasses, to give his fellow-prisoners the chief treat they had during one quarter of the year, he thought it rather a benevolent and praiseworthy exercise of one's arms, legs, and social qualities, and saw little more sin in it than in the apostles' rubbing the

12*

ears of corn in their hands, as they walked through the fields of a Saturday.

But he soon found that the case was serious. Luncheon, which was allowed only on this one day of the week, was always carried about to the different cells by a few of the more trustworthy convicts in rotation, the number of the turnkeys being diminished by leaves of absence, and only enough of them kept on duty to guard the penitentiary. Captain Rodrick was very angry at Wellbeloved's refusal to serve this extra meal, from quite a complex mixture of causes. First, because he had intended it as an indulgence, to put the prisoners in a good humour, and was disappointed to find it ill received in any quarter. Secondly, because he himself suspected it to be a sinful indulgence, and did not like to have his suspicions confirmed by one of his subjects. Thirdly, because he owed Wellbeloved a grudge, for not thinking well of his, Rodrick's, spiritual condition. Fourthly, because he envied Wellbeloved his own spiritual condition.

"It seems to me that Wellbeloved is mistaken," said Herman; "I hope he won't get himself into a scrape. Can I speak to him?"

"Wall, I reckon not. He's in the dark cell, a-keepin his Sabbath."

Herman saw him the next morning, heavily ironed and with one side of his head shaved. He found an opportunity to speak to him; but, as he had feared, he was unable to shake his convictions; and he therefore, of course, made no attempt to shake his determination. He could not, indeed, help admiring the latter as much as he regretted the former. Still, he was so anxious about the consequences, that he took the liberty of begging Mr. Bush to let him take Wellbeloved's turn, as often as it came round, with the mush, and of asking the overseer, further, to suggest to the captain that, after all that Wellbeloved had already suffered, going without his share of the Sunday luncheon would be a sufficient chastisement for his continued contumacy. Herman did not think of sending his proposal in the form of a message to the captain; but Mr. Bush managed badly.

Captain Rodrick presently sent his compliments, and desired that if "Esquire Arden was perfectly at lezzure, he would give him the pleasure of his company in the guard-room." Herman went. The captain made him a very low bow, walked up to him with his little red eyes flashing fire, seized him by the collar, and marched him up to the wall, till his own eyes were close to a stained, dark, leather strap, which hung there. It was thick, about one inch wide, and two feet long.

"D'yer see that?"

Herman saw.

"Look a little nearer, if yer don't," said the captain, pushing his face against it two or three times. "D'yer know what it's for?"

Herman knew.

"Then don't yer have the impidence to send me no more of yer messages. How?—Here! seems to me, I have got as much time to break you in this mornin as any day; and I have sor I would have to do so from the first day you come. You go right down on your knees, an ask my pardon; or I'll let you feel of this here now, on your bare back."

Herman did not kneel,—nor strike him. He only looked at him, thinking the while instinctively of a certain gripe and trip that he knew, which, if he thought fit to put them in practice, would probably throw the captain's own back over that of the heavy chair behind him, and into no condition for bruising the backs of his fellow-men for an indefinite period. But from that look, the captain jumped a yard, as if it had been a blow. "Ho! here! mutiny! murder! help,—guard!"

Herman folded his arms, as he usually did when he found it hardest to keep his hands off his superior, and stood very still, with his dangerous eyes on the ground. The guard came; but after them, by good luck, in hobbled the other warden, who had his own reasons for befriending Herman.

"Why, I thought yer was murdered! What's the matter here, sonny?"

"Messages! Mutiny! Chain him up, guard! To the dark cell with him!" ejaculated the captain, prancing in a war-dance.

"Pooh, pooh. Don't you always be so nervous. He didn't mean nothin, I'm keen to sw'ar. Arden, don't you be aggravatin. What have you been up to?"

"I made a suggestion to one of the sub-officers, sir, which the captain understood as a message to himself, it appears. I am sorry for the mistake."

"Well, mind you don't never make no more mistakes, then; an seein you're free to say you're sorry for the past, I reckon we'll be easy with you.—Captain, I guess your lady wants to speak to you about the new uniforms.—Never mind about another chain, guard; that thar is big enough. Arden, you'll have to go along to the dark cell awhile, just to pacify him. Lay down, and take a nap; an I'll come myself, an see you're let out, an hour by sun."

On the following Sunday morning, Herman, coming from the cook-shop with his kettle, heard, as he passed the open door of the guard-room, the strokes of the strap. Looking in, he saw Captain Rodrick standing, and swinging it, over the body of a silent, writhing man, who lay, without his shirt, bent together on his side, his hands being tied together, slipped over his knees, and made fast over them by the captain's hickory-cane, passed between them and his wrists. It was Wellbeloved.

Herman had a curiosity to examine the paddle with which, or a similar one, his first patient in that place had been mangled. One Sunday afternoon, when the wardens had cast up their accounts and gone out, the overseer took him into the guard-room, and showed it to him. It was a board about twenty-four inches long, and six inches wide, one end being narrowed and rounded to a handle, and the other bored full of holes, each of which, when it was applied with skill, was said to raise a crimson blister at every stroke. Among the curiosities of the place, Mr. Bush gratified Herman with a sight also of the " ducking-apparatus." This consisted of a large arm-chair into which an offender might be securely tied, hand and foot, and of a wooden box fitting pretty snugly round his neck at the bottom, but at the top open to receive water, poured from a jug or pail into his face at discretion. Until such water had had time to trickle, ooze, and run, up his nose and down his throat, back, breast, and shoulders, without and within, it seemed likely to embarrass and impede his respiration not a little. Herman heard a poor fellow gasping, gurgling, and struggling in this one day. His offence was said to have been, that he was troublesome upon the point of his letters to his wife. These were sometimes longer than Captain Rodrick liked to take the trouble to read, or than the poor husband liked to wait till he found time to read.

But what use is there in my detailing any more of the trying scenes which took place, day after day, within the sight, hearing, or knowledge of our young hero? We can bear, some of us, to read those in "Never Too Late to Mend." We know that, in the course of the book, poetical justice is to be done by the author. Poetical justice is not to be done by me, either in my book or in my country.

From time to time I read in the newspapers,—and you may, if you choose,—accounts of one after another of our young men, our middle-aged, or our old men, (and to which of these such a doom comes the hardest, it might be hard to say,) sentenced to imprisonment for years, upon an accusation similar to that against the youth, Herman Arden. Read for yourselves, if you will, such accounts of such imprisonments as are to be had. ✔ Make all moderate allowances, —it is just and right that you should,—for the exaggerations of suffering prisoners, for the inaccuracies of uneducated prisoners, and for the falsehoods, even, of unprincipled prisoners; and yet, when all is done, see for yourselves whether a penitentiary in a slave State, or indeed in any State, can be a pleasant place for any man,—a fit place for a guiltless man,—to spend the best years that may remain to him of life in.

I think even that you may know, if you choose to find out about it, and that I know already, that, within a few days' journey from these pines of New England, which sigh, weep, and shiver around me in the sullen storm as I write, there is a jail, or jails,— "let x equal their unknown quantity,"—at which men, and women, if not children too, guilty, or even not guilty, of skins not colored like our own, may be lashed and lacerated, time after time, at the request of their possessors, upon no other accusation than that of their being slaves. (Suppose they are. Whose fault is that?—Of the slaves, or of those who made or who keep them so?) What Southern Howard have we among us, to put a stop to that?

It is enough. Why should we know more! "Where ignorance is bliss," &c. We cannot help this state of things, nor can we help its spreading year by year over shrinking Kansas and all of our free soil; or, at any rate, we say we cannot help it. Therefore, what is the use of our talking about it? Let us shrug shoulders too well-bred to tingle with any fanatical sympathy for those of Christ's unnurtured, uncouth, black lambs. Let us dress and dance, and think of something more polite and pleasing. Let us eat and drink, for to-morrow we die; and after death comes the judgment, when we shall see black sheep among the white ones on the right hand of the Throne, and hear it said, " Forasmuch as ye have done it unto the least of these my brethren, ye have done it unto me;" and after that, perhaps, we shall have but little appetite.

But unmingled misery was probably never yet the lot of any being upon God's earth. Before many weeks had dragged themselves over him, Herman, seeing a shadow fall across his loom and supposing it to be that of the overseer, looked up into the working features of his emotional friend, Mr. Broadstone. Mr. Bush granted Herman a half-holiday, and permission to go at once to his cell with his guest. As soon as Herman could succeed in calming Mr. Broadstone's first transports of rage at his occupation, dress, lodgings, and accommodations or want of any, he found that he had smuggled in a goodly packet of letters from home, of contents too sacred to be subjected, like all directed immediately to Herman, to the scrutiny and sometime suppression of his jailers. Forgetting himself and everything else in his eagerness, Herman seized and tore them open, and read and re-read them as fast as he could, that he might know them by heart before the coming steps of any officer warned him to destroy them.

They were letters such as any one might account himself happy in a dungeon, or on a scaffold, to receive,—such letters as few women could write, such as few men could call forth,—sweet as the consolations of angels, fervid as the adorations of saints! The poor girls who wrote them were, as well as Edward, leaving no stone unturned, far or near, to obtain his freedom. *That*, he did not need to be told. They were kept from coming to him only by his command and entreaty. They spent hours on their knees, daily and nightly, with their arms around each other's necks, in prayer for him. They drove; they walked. They *would be* strong and cheerful, for his sake.

How touchingly sad those letters of theirs were, like his own to them, in their vigilant suppression of all sadness! How much more than any speech their silence told! Five years!—five years before he or any one could comfort them! It was fortunate for him, though he felt it hard, that in common gratitude he was forced to restrain and compose himself, in order to pay the attentions due to his visiter.

Broadstone was admirably considerate, however. He had been apparently employing his leisure, while Herman read, in investigating the deficiencies of his apartment. He exacted only time enough to tell him, that he had received the first quarterly remittance of his income, which, by a previous arrangement of Edward's suggestion, was to be sent him regularly to supply Herman's needs so far as might be, and that he should insist on providing him at once with sheets and blankets, to begin with. He then drew paper, a portable inkstand, and a pen, from his pocket, bade Herman write his answers as fast as he pleased, and promised to guard the door, and give seasonable warning of the approach of any intruder.

This was a rare privilege. Herman was allowed to write by the post four times a year; but every manuscript in his cell was at all times liable to the inspection of any of the officers who could read; and he could not bear to have the dear, sacred, household names of Constance and Clara in mouths like theirs, or his pure and reverent affection their jest. Therefore he had told Edward to ask the girls to let him copy all their letters in his unmistakably masculine hand, and to set to them only the manly signatures of " *Clare* " and "*Aspenwall*" respectively; and Herman, himself, had written to them as if they were men, the only time that he had yet been allowed to write. He poured out his full heart now, in a few unconstrained, unstudied pages overflowing with love, gratitude, and anxiety for them, and with resignation and trust for himself, so far as he spoke of himself.

In the first year of his imprisonment, however, he seldom did speak to them of himself,—except to say that he was well;—and, for the most part, when he did so it was indirectly and briefly, in sentences which, having the air of abstract quotations, would give out their meaning to those readers only for whom it was intended, and pass unnoticed by those who had no right to it.

"Better souls than mine," he would then say, "have looked through iron bars, before me, and seen the better for it.—Clear and open windows are the best for getting views of this world through; grated and darkened ones, often, for getting clear views of the other.—The unjust reproaches of men, if we can learn to attune our hearts so that the echo which they awaken within us is forgiveness, and not resentment, may be but the prelude to the congratulations of angels.—The imprisonment of the body may be the enfranchisement of the soul."

Sometimes, too, his meditations accumulated in the form of verses, which he sent to his betrothed and his sister. These spoke on the surface only of hope, courage, and trust; but it was easy to. see, that it could be only a very deep and heavy sorrow in him, which could draw him so near to the Source of consolation.

In the meanwhile, through all and in all,—he knew not how,—his life became by slow degrees sublimed into a prayer,—one long intensity of answered prayer! He soon began to prove again as he had done before, by his own experience, the solemn and inexplicable mystery, that it is by the hands of the deepest earthly sorrows that the highest heavenly blessings are sent down to man. He entered gradually, slowly, surely, into the awful blessedness of the thorn-crowned Son of Man and God. Thus, day by day and night by night, in loneliness that yet was the highest companionship, in fastings that fed and vigils that refreshed his soul, and in profitless and sordid toil that helped to furnish royally his heavenly mansion,— the highest joy and deepest grief fought within him for the mastery, and wore invisibly within upon the frail clay sheath of his unresisting spirit.

Broadstone, henceforth, came to see him every few weeks. He brought him not only letters, but books from Mr. Halifax's excellent little library, and clothing. Of the latter he stood in great need.

The penitentiary had been sold,—so at least it was generally understood by its inmates,—for ten years, profits, prisoners, and all, to the highest bidders. It was conducted on an economical plan. The care of providing clothing for the convicts devolved chiefly upon the gentle ladies of the wardens, Mrs. Rodrick and her step-mother, Mrs. Log, who did not love one another tenderly, or, in short, "not to put too fine a point upon it," hated each other as hard as they could.

According to the judicious system of the division of labor which prevailed among these two kings and queens of Brentford, the royal house of Rodrick were to provide shoes and pantaloons for their subjects; and the house of Log, caps and shirts; so much was agreed; but which was to provide jackets, and which stockings, for winter, was a long-mooted question, pending the settlement of which many of the prisoners went without both, in some of the coldest weather which ever visited the fire-fed State of Bondage; until some of them managed by hook or by crook, (words which admirably picture forth the appearance of their knitting-needles before they had done with them,) to knit some *loop-holy* and hoof-like or banana-footed socks for themselves, at odd minutes.

Herman did not give away quite all his stockings; but as to his blankets he was incorrigible. The region was one of fever and ague. Many men were

sent out to work in a costume more picturesque than
salubrious. The rogues soon found out what physician it was best to send for at night, when they were
shuddering in their " shakes ;" and Dr. Arden would
roll his patients up snugly, in their dank, chilly cells,
with his own good bed-clothes around them, and never
have the heart to ask for them again. His friend almost always found him *minus*, scolded, but re-supplied
him ; and " Broadstone's bundle of bedding" became
a standing joke in the prison. The wardens kindly
winked at an innovation which, as they justly observed, did nobody any harm. They found Herman
profitable ; and even Captain Rodrick began to treat
him accordingly, when he was sober, which not infre-
quently happened.

He treated him still more *accordingly*, after the
end of the first year. Rodrick's chief redeeming point
was his love of his little girl. Little May, (from
hereditary predisposition, she labored under the bap-
tismal name of Mariamne ; but in her case the judgment had been mercifully commuted, in common par-
lance,) little May was always fluttering to and fro, like
a stray butterfly, through the close dusty work-shops
or shadowy passages of the prison. In spite of her
pale cheeks and languid eyes she was pretty, and, in
spite of much spoiling, gentle and loving. Her parents pronounced her " not long for this world," and
therefore, as if in order to make their prophecy work
out its own fulfilment, usually allowed her to do exactly as she pleased. She pleased, among other things
more pleasing, to partake of all sorts of sweet things
at all sorts of hours, of course to the utter neglect of
her regular meals. Herman, foreseeing the consequences to a constitution so frail as hers, often per-

suaded her to give away her sticks of candy, or greasy *doughnuts*, to some hard-working, hungry fellow in whose ostrich stomach they could do no harm, and rewarded her with some of his thousand-and-one beautiful stories of all times and climes. She soon grew very fond of perching on a table by his loom; and when she came crying to him with a broken-legged kitten, which some boys had worried, and he mended it, he bound her to him for life; while the poor worshipper of grace and beauty, surrounded with all ugliness and brutality, himself became attached, more than he knew, to this one choice little morsel of the loveliness and innocence of infancy.

When she fell sick and came no more, he really pined for her. The whooping-cough, with which she began, was succeeded by lung-fever. She sank under it day by day. One morning when her mother, after long watching and a short exhausted sleep, sprang up to look at her, she found her in a torpor, from which she could in no way rouse her. She sent for her physician. He was gone to visit a patient twenty miles off. She remembered how, in the first days of her child's illness, the little voice which she might never hear again had pleaded, that May might be allowed to go and see her " good prison-doctor." Catching at a straw, Mrs. Rodrick sent for him.

Herman came out and crossed the street to her house, in his chain and prison-uniform. How strange it was to be without the walls! He had hoped that he never should be in that guise; but all that was forgotten now.

He stood by the little bed. The prisoner and the jailer's wife trembled with one fear. He spoke his little favorite's name. He kissed her tiny hand.

There was no motion,—no answer. She looked like death. She breathed; and that was all. The subtle soul might be even now sliding through the thin white casket; and who could hold it in? Her mother stared him in the face with her horror-struck hopeless eyes; and he looked back in hers. He had already heard all that had been done for the child. It had been well done. Medicine could do no more. A sudden thought struck him. He had somewhere read of the powerful effects of sunlight in certain cases. Turning again from the child, he asked whether there was any room in the house into which the sun was then shining. There was.

"Is there a fire there?"

"No; there could be."

"Let one be made."

As soon as the chamber could be prepared, he gathered the drooping snow-drop gently up in his arms, carried her out of her darkened room with careful gliding steps, and held her in the warm blessed light, speaking encouragement to her breathless mother. At the end of half an hour, she opened her little heavy eyes, like a human flower as she was, and feebly pushed her hand up through her wrappings to fondle his cheek. It was one of those delicious moments which repay a physician for years of toil and struggles, often unsuccessful, with Disease and Death.

Mrs. Rodrick was a woman of words to the purpose, if not few. In fact, it was rumored that the captain, by being more than ordinarily tyrannical abroad, merely brought up the average of manly wilfulness, being more than ordinarily submissive at home. However that may be, his energetic love waited only to see their little one sip a wine-glass-full of hot broth administered by Herman, and go off comfortably to sleep, before she waited on her spouse, who, giving up all for lost, was taking an extra glass to drive away care. She informed him of what had happened, adding with a flashing eye and trembling lip, that "that young man should never put his healing hands to a shuttle again, nor go clinking a chain about his heels, like an angel of mercy, into sick folks' rooms; or she'd know why."

The captain thereupon consulted with his colleague; and Herman was forthwith unchained and appointed steward of the hospital, to the great benefit of all parties concerned; namely, of the wardens, for they saved by it the salary which they were otherwise bound to pay to a physician for the penitentiary; of the sick, for they were no longer locked up in their cells over night to live or die, as the case might be, by themselves in the dark; and of Herman, for he was raised by it, according to his notions, to the very summit of possible *penitential* prosperity.

His loom was become very irksome to him. A burdensome system of task-work had lately been introduced into the work-shops. A reward was first offered to any workmen who, at their different crafts, would accomplish within a given time larger amounts than usual. As soon as any one, by accomplishing a larger amount than usual, had proved it possible to do so, the same amount, within the same time, was adopted as the regular task for all his fellow-workmen of the same craft, and, on pain of punishment, exacted of them; and another reward was offered again to any one who could exceed it. Herman's *stint* had thus lengthened to hundreds of yards of bagging a week. -

He did not spare himself, when his promotion made him in a manner his own master again; and perhaps his new work, as he did it, was little lighter than his old; but it was in itself more profitable, and to him most interesting. It was, besides, accompanied with perquisites and privileges. If he was up in the night, as he had often been before as a volunteer watcher in one cell or another, he could now often sleep in the day, and could, at all events, have the satisfaction of gathering together all who needed his attention, and taking care of them at once. He had a comparatively comfortable cell on the south side of the building, opening into the hospital and out of the way of the midnight cries of the guard-room, to himself. He was also allowed to burn a lamp and read in the evening, if he would; but he could not, much; this indulgence came too late.

He had been unable, in his first months of monotony and vacuity, to resist the temptation which assailed him, to read a few pages every night when the moon shone in upon the wall of his cell, "*sub luce maligna*," standing on tiptoe on his bed and holding his book up, often at arm's length, to catch the straggling rays. He promised himself that he would abandon the practice, the moment he perceived that it injured his naturally very strong eyes; and he did so; but they never recovered from the strain. His bodily constitution was now in all respects of that deceptive and treacherous kind, which does its utmost without flagging, and, like a generous steed, gives little signs of suffering until all its strength is spent; and unwholesome food and air, a sudden and great change of climate and habits, and all the influences of a sedentary and afflicted life, had been imperceptibly wearing upon him, in the course of the last twelvemonth, in all sorts of ways. Perhaps it was unlucky for him in the circumstances, that his health, from his childhood up to the period of his arrest, had been so perfect as to require no direct attention; so that he was almost utterly out of the habit of paying attention to it. His conscientious observance of the Archangel Michael's "rule of *Not too Much;*" the sort of religious, self-denying, but not self-murdering, simplicity which ran through all his life, showing itself even in his early hours and plain and temperate meals; and the manly out-of-door sports, with all of which he had preserved, and hoped to preserve up to four-score, his "body's health and hardiness, to render lightsome, clear, and not lumpish obedience to the mind, to the cause of religion, and our country's liberty, when it shall require firm hearts in sound bodies to stand and cover their stations," had long kept him so well that perhaps he almost forgot that he could be otherwise. At any rate, it was time for him to have a release from his weaving. It came none too soon.

In the midst of his zealous and almost gleeful entering into the duties of his new office,—going about to the cells of all the sick and cheering them with the news, examining into the very deficient pharmacopœia and surgical apparatus of the hospital, and making out a list of articles wanted, to be supplied at his own expense if not otherwise,—one of the first uses which he made of his emancipation was, to write a hasty account of his good fortune to send home. He quoted in it, with "confirmation strong," the overseer's distich,

"The fast
'S the wust;"

and just as he was about to close it, as, school-boy-like, he did all his homeward epistles at this time, with a calculation of the lessening number of months, weeks,

13

and days before he should return, Mr. Broadstone was announced.

Mr. Broadstone came, after an unusually short interval, on purpose to tell him that the Governor had commuted his remaining four years to one! If joy could kill a man, he would have died. What was one year? He had lived through as much as that already. Then those five, that had frightened him so, were after all nothing but a bugbear,—a mere humbug! Mr. Broadstone further brought letters from Constance, Clara, and Edward. They had written in hope, but not in certainty. They did not know the news. He was to tell it them.

Edward had been at Washington. Clara had written to Mr. Trimmer, and sent him a *photograph* of her mother's beautiful picture, praying him to let its dead lips plead with him for her brother. Constance, probably, had clinched the business; for she had gone to Carolina, looked up her relations and the influential connections of her family, near and distant, and bewitched them all with her gracious beauty, eloquence, and lovely melancholy. In midnight confidences, she had won the hearts of more than one of the romantic daughters of the South. In rides, drives, and drawing-rooms, she appealed not tamely to the chivalrous championship of more than one young man, who had plenty of it at the service of so beautiful a girl, declaring herself his first, second, or third cousin, and suspected neither of a drop of black blood nor of aggressive abolitionism. Colonel Rochemaurice held a little aloof. But that was no matter; for nothing could exceed the kindness and sympathy shown her by Mr. and Mrs. Clement. Constance had paid them a visit of some days; in the course of which she told her hostess what Herman would not, that all which her gallant young lover had done, had been done on her account; and Mr. Clement was, in that day and generation, taking his family's turn in Congress, as a member of the House of Representatives.

Soon after, it began to be buzzed about, in the anterooms of Washington and elsewhere, that young Arden's conduct had been very much misrepresented. He was a very gentlemanly fellow for a Northerner, and had not gone into Bondage to steal negroes at all, but merely to get back, by fair means if he could, an old family-servant, whom his lady-love had sold in a girlish freak, and very properly wished to have back again; and as for St. Dominique, he was a detestable scoundrel, who merited to be tarred and feathered as a disgrace to the South. So, all the wires had been pulled all over the Union,—wire-pullers only know how;—and here was the result.

Herman's postscript was not soon finished. In the course of it, he found room to beg Edward to take the girls to Europe. They had all worked hard enough to earn a little vacation, he said; it would make the remainder of his absence seem shorter to them; reading their descriptions of what they saw would almost enable him to see it with them; and he should feel less restless, when he knew no longer that they were so near, and yet apart. He was sure that their health must have been shaken by their suffering, and wished to see no trace of it when he saw them. His will was law at home now; and perhaps Edward was glad, by obeying him in this instance, to find means to divert some of his thoughts before they distracted him. He soon embarked with his charges, and left Herman with a quiet mind to devote himself to tending the diseased bodies, and souls in many cases far more grievously diseased, of the outcasts of society about him. He presently found himself admitted to a field of usefulness so very great and blessed, that he thought he could almost have been contented to pass his whole life in it, if it had not been for Constance. It must be acknowledged that, that was a very great *if.*

His former life for some years had been a remarkably apt preparation for his present; a *singularly* apt one, I do not say; for I suppose that, if we were more in the habit than we are of looking at life religiously, we should more often see that it is God's wont, busily and steadily, though little by little, to train His few obedient sons and daughters for uses higher and broader than they know or think of, even in this world.

Herman believed that it is almost as difficult for a man, living among men, to have and keep heresy or infidelity as to have and keep the small-pox, to himself. He had striven hard therefore, as a good citizen of the commonwealth of Christ, to reach the knowledge and practice of a pure and genuine Christianity. Though he did not expect to be able, in the spare hours left to him by his own very engrossing profession, to explore for himself the whole field of the all-engrossing profession of theology, he was not contented to be in religious matters an ignorant, or passively instructed, layman. He was happy in the friendship of a clergyman of natural critical ability, as he believed, much greater than his own, and of integrity and piety inferior to that of no man. This gentleman, after the researches and experience of his own diligent and studious fifty years of manhood, was better able than himself to judge from what religious writers he would be likely to gain trustworthy guidance, and from what ones he would not. So at least thought his modest young disciple. Was he very servile and weak-minded? Herman read, and marked and inwardly digested, too, for the benefit of his unlearned and unintellectual neighbours as well as himself. In his opinion, no one could be a perfect physician to the body, who was not also a physician of the soul; for in this mortal life the body and soul are kneaded so inextricably together, that anything which hurts the one very much, is very apt to make the other sick. He strongly disapproved of proselytism, in general; because he thought that it was often much easier to take a man's creed away than to give him another instead of it, and that any *tolerably* Christian creed, honestly and earnestly held, was a great deal better than none; and Constance was the only convert, from a creed happily held, whom he had ever tried to make. But when he found any of his Boston patients suffering from Calvinism, skepticism, or any other form of religious melancholy, he had made it his business to go to the bottom of their difficulty as if it had been his own, studied, thought, and cheered them out of it, and had thus added to his faith, knowledge which now stood him in good stead. He had made his mind a conduit, through which he poured the ideas of those better-informed than himself in religion, into the minds of those worse-informed than himself, filtering through his own clear soul and eloquent speech the muddy flow of many a wholesome, but heavy, sermon and obscure treatise.

Dignified without distance, kindly without familiarity, and sympathizing without mawkishness, he at once commanded, sustained, and soothed those placed under his care; and any account of the influence which, from the beginning of his stewardship, he exerted in the prison, would seem fabulous to any one who has yet to see the feats of that almost omnipotent person, the right man or woman in the right place.

"Be done sw'arin!" said a pretty bad subject, soon after this time, to his fellow in the workshop, on hearing a coming step.

"What for? 'Taint nobody only Arden."

"He don't like it."

"How d'yer know?"

"He told me so, the night he got me out o' that thar quinsy that had me by the throat a stranglin on me, jest like a rat with cheese in its mouth an its neck in a trap, 'fore he come along and heared me."

"Wall, s'pose he don't like it?"

"Wall, I'll only jest break my fist on yer nose, if yer do it afore *us*."

All sorts of strange stories were told of him. It soon began to be rumored in the prison for instance, half in jest, but half in earnest, that one night passed under his care, by the hardiest offender, gave Herman henceforth strange power over him, like that obtained in a private interview by some persons over animals; and a prisoner, who before his imprisonment had been by profession a "horse-whisperer," gave the young steward the title of "the rascal-tamer." His dignified pathetic patience among the querulous and fretful fellow-sufferers about him,—the spotless sanctity of his life, in that harassed and crowded life, where every man could know and see what his neighbour's life was,—his half-melancholy and half-prophetic look, as he passed them pacing up and down, in silence and thought, the long shady passages, or as he hung over their sleepless sick-beds, in the still watches of the night, with a tenderness to which many of them had been strangers since their childhood or, it mgiht be, even in their infancy,—and his varied powers and accomplishments, all combined to invest him with a kind of supernatural awe and mystery in the fancies of these ignorant and superstitious men.

He could tell them about "every country on the face of the earth, and the moon, too, jest as if he'd been there," till it almost seemed to them as if they had been there too. Yet more, he talked to them about the other world beyond the grave till, under the spell of his deep, solemn, and silence - surrounded speech, it appeared more real than this. He spoke of God even, as if he had seen him. Perhaps he had; that blessing is promised to the pure in heart. A poor maniac, named Transe, who had once or twice stolen in after him and heard him pray over a dying criminal, declared that he cured little May with only a prayer and a sunbeam; and that he had had power to do so much more for her even than for them, because she was as innocent and holy as himself.

The feats of his fine and well-trained tenor were marvels to them. He sang them wonderfully beautiful songs, in unknown tongues,—the finest compositions of the German and Italian masters. Though there was much severity in the penitentiary, there was little strictness; and Herman had long ago found out that, when Captain Rodrick was not near or not out of humour, he might sing as much as he pleased, like a caged nightingale. The wakeful liked to hear him; the sleeping did not hear him. The guards, when they found their watch tedious, would often condescend to "knock up Arden," and graciously bid him to give them a "Sarahnade;" and he did his best for them, glad to have it in his power to afford them a taste of a pleasure so innocent and elevating. The fault of Herman's singing, in his drawing-room days, was that,—

quite unlike his reading,—it was too careful,—too little spontaneous. It seemed now the very upward breathing of a sad, sweet captive soul, home-sick for heaven, and justified the wild fancy of poor Transe, who always, when he could, crept to the door to hear it and said, that when Arden sang hymns to a dying man, his voice called angels down to bear the soul away, that stayed to sing with him before they went.

Mr. Halifax would have come to visit Herman; but he, with many and kind acknowledgments of his kindness in proposing it, never encouraged his carrying out his proposal. With all his merits, Herman could not help being human. He was still very young, and too simple and free from self-consciousness to perceive how his character ennobled his situation. He shrank instinctively from being seen and remembered as he was now, by any one whom he was likely to meet hereafter. He chid himself for this feeling and would not, perhaps, have yielded to it, but for a better reason that he had for his refusal; and this was, that he thought Mr. Halifax a timid man, who not only probably disapproved of the conduct which had placed him there, but who would be likely and sorry, by coming to see him, to get himself into trouble with his parish.

Mr. Broadstone continued to come frequently, and was heartily welcomed. He had broken the ice long ago; and Herman was not likely to see him again after he left Bondage. Besides, they had a topic to discuss together, of much common interest. Herman had, as his friend thought, more than repaid all his past or future good offices to him, by a suggestion to him to allow his *charity-slaves* to repay to him the price which he, at their entreaty, had paid for them, and then to go free.

This was managed according to the plan devised.

and carried out, by the wealthy Mr. McDonough of New Orleans.* Strange to tell, Mr. Broadstone had never heard of it before. How many slaveholders have ?

The slaves were accustomed to have a half-holiday on Saturday. As they were also excused from work on Sunday, this left them only five days and a half, or eleven half-days, a week, to work for their master. He told them that when they should have earned, by extra-work on Saturday afternoon, one eleventh part of the sum for which he had bought them, he should consider them to have bought another half-day of their time, or Saturday morning. Having now a whole working-day a week, to themselves, they could of course earn Friday afternoon in half the time which Saturday morning cost them; and so on, with a speed in inverse proportion to the number of remaining days. When, in this manner, they had bought all their time, they were to be free and to go, with a suitable outfit, under the care of trustworthy persons, to Liberia, Canada, or New England, as they pleased. (For the tyranny under which their master lived, permitted him to enjoy only their extorted service. Under it, he might compel them to serve him as unpaid, unwilling, or servile slaves. He might not keep his grateful, zealous, intelligent freedmen about him.) Lest Broadstone should die before the arrangement was consummated, they were ostensibly bequeathed to Mr. Halifax, with the private agreement that they were to be allowed to hire themselves out for the remainder of their terms of service, and that the legatee, receiving their wages, should pay the proportion due, to the estate of their master.

---

* See a "Cincinnati Gazette" of March, 1834, for interesting details for which I am sorry to have no room.

13*

A copy of his sealed and attested will, containing a clause to this effect, was placed in the safe hands of the clergyman; for sad experience is said to have proved that the families of testators are not always to be trusted to fulfil such documents. To Mr. Halifax were given also copies of the receipts for the sums paid in, from time to time, by the slaves.

In the meanwhile, to Mr. Broadstone's great surprise, —(these human creatures had so much human nature in them!)—most of them worked twice as fast and well, for themselves and him, as they did before for him alone. From being provokingly lazy and stupid, they grew busy as beavers, and shrewd as Yankees. They learned to think. Their master was turning his beasts into men and women. He had honestly feared what others,—some of them less honestly,—said, that these biped cattle were too incurably idle and helpless to do anything but steal or starve, if they were let go; but he soon found them devising a hundred ways, which he would never have dreamed of, to turn a penny, and so bent on labor that he was sometimes obliged to check them, for fear of their over-working themselves. His neighbours saw the change, wondered, envied, and offered him fancy-prices for his human negroes as if they had been natural (or unnatural) curiosities,—like rational and spiritual monkeys;—but I need not say that they did not get them. Broadstone laughed his bitter laugh, kept his secret, which it might not have been safe to tell, and came to his young friend to report progress.

So Herman's days went by, though lonely, too useful and too fully occupied to be unhappy now, except when "the sorrow of others flung its shadow over him."

CHAPTER XXV.

THE KNIGHT AND THE PESTILENCE.

"The Cross, if freely borne, shall be
No burden, but support to thee!
So, moved of old time for our sake,
The holy man of Kempen spake.
Thou brave and true one, upon whom
Was laid the Cross of Martyrdom,
How didst thou, in thy faithful youth,
Bear witness to this blessed truth!
Thy cross of suffering and of shame,
A staff within thy hands became;
In paths, where Faith alone could see
The Master's steps upholding thee."

WHITTIER.

A MONTH passed,—two, three, four. The season went on without. Within, Herman's cell grew hot, and so full of mosquitoes that the spiders, instead of being as heretofore disagreeable intruders, became welcome guests. Little May brought him in wild-flowers and apple-blossoms, then strawberries, and then peaches. A quarter of his last year was gone; and every day was happier than the one before. The shorter and darker it grew, the brighter it seemed to him. Only two-thirds of autumn now to come; and then winter; and then,—oh, what a spring! He wrote monthly to say that he was well, contented, and happy in the thought of a reunion with his correspondents,— perhaps, on the whole, as happy where he was as he could have been anywhere away from them. Every steamship brought him back good news. Edward constantly reported to him that the girls were well, and recovering their spirits more and more as the time of their and his return drew nearer; and as Herman read Constance's brilliant and charming descriptions of every brilliant and charming scene she saw,—written as if the very *genii* of Art, Nature, and Love, had possessed themselves of her as their proper medium,—he enjoyed it all, and felt it all with her and in her.

When we open the first letter from any friend to us, we are about to learn something about that friend besides what he, or she, is conscious of telling us. As Byron said in substance, though in words which I do not now recollect, The being that writes, is something apart from the being that *is*. One of the most gentlemanly men that I ever saw in a drawing-room, was boorish upon paper. Two or three of the most unhappy women I ever knew, were playful when they wrote. Easy people may be stiff, and simple ones affected, and, on the other hand, ugly and awkward ones beautiful and graceful, in their epistles. When one's nature is very complete and harmonious throughout, the person, pen, tongue, and act, may all breathe the same language; but most of us are chaotic more or less, and act in one style, look in another, speak in another, and write in still another.

Now, if Constance had let all her paragraphs run together, like portions of molasses-candy in a warm cupboard, or, worse still, had begun them at the very edge of her pages,—if she had underscored half her words, and even mis-spelt one of them now and then,— if she had characterized (!) all the women whom she met and liked as "sweet," and all the men as "pleasant,"—and if she had furnished only geographical statements of the names and situations of the places which she visited, or described them in stereotyped and constantly-recurring guide-book phrases, interspersed at random with the merest babblings of sincere affection, I believe that Herman would have shut up his brain, read them with his heart, found them enchanting for the sake of her who wrote them, and asked no better. Wherefore, I think that he deserved to receive just such letters as he did. I am sorry that I cannot show you any of them; but I will tell you a little about them.

Constance's letters were, in all respects, of a piece with the rest of Constance,—very intelligent, very spirited, very graceful, and very lady-like. The hand in which she wrote was almost as beautiful as the hand *with* which she wrote. As elegant and finished as her *toilette*, it adorned and set off her words, and seemed, instead of obscuring her pages, to illuminate them with its gleaming, flowing lines. The cadence of her written, was as musical as that of her spoken sentences. Her language was transparent and spontaneous, refined yet racy, and witty, tender, sublime, or bewitchingly pretty, in turn, according to her subject. She always expressed exactly the thing she meant, and always meant the right thing. Whenever Herman had read one of these letters of hers, he felt as if he had seen her, and as if he could hardly wait a single day to see her again. He had just read one of them,—in which she informed him that Edward was having her picture taken,—for the third or fourth time, one Saturday morning, when the overseer called him :

"Say, Arden, jest you step here, will yer?—an see to Bludgeon. I've found him all doubled up neck and heels in his cell, with the lock-jaw or suthin."

Herman hastened to the cell. He had passed its occupant in one of the passages the night before, on his return from the woods, where he had had leave to go for the afternoon to gather wild grapes. He had come back in high spirits, and apparently high health, refreshed by a taste of freedom and fresh air.

It is a very sad thing to see a person in the lock-jaw; but the sight prepared for the young prisoner was one more frightful still to see, where life is crowded, and flight from the impending death impossible. The man was violet-colored. He lay on his back, with his knees drawn up to his chin, and his lips drawn back from his teeth with the grin of agony. His voice whistled and puffed as he tried to speak. His breath was as chill as that of his tomb would be presently. His features were sharpened and sunken like those of a corpse. His skin was wrinkled already,—he was not above thirty years old,—and as cold and clammy as that of a toad. Old Age, Death, and Decay, seemed let loose together upon him, to make him at once their prey and their sport. His eyeballs were distorted, rimmed with purple, and patched with red; and the black pigment of the inner coat was beginning to show through the transparent and shrivelling whites. In a word, he was in an advanced stage of Asiatic Cholera.

Herman wrung his hands behind his own back as he first looked at him, but kept a calm face, and gave the disorder no name but cramp. He did what he could to relieve him, worked over him hard all day, heard his last groans, at eleven o'clock at night, mingled with cries of pain from the neighbouring guard-room, covered up his body, sent for the wardens, and told them what had happened. He wished to give them time, before they saw the other prisoners again, to get over their first consternation at the news, and to concert such measures as they could to prevent the spread of the malady, and especially that of a panic, which would be very likely to act as a predisposing cause. Then he went to his cell; and it was like a new Gethsemane.

To die!—not merely to die so young! not merely to die alone! not merely to die in a jail! not merely to be dragged down to corruption in a day, by the ugliest of deaths! but—to die with home and *her* so near! Might not some recantation, some submission, now avail him, and obtain his freedom, and flight to safety, joy, and length of days? He knew that it might. Again and again already, he had been visited by members of the Legislature and magistracy,—pitying his youth, ashamed of the oppression under which he suffered, or fearing the effects of the sympathy which he excited,—with offers of an immediate discharge, if he would but declare himself a convert to slavery, or would only own that his action against it, among them, had been an error. Those who tempted him well knew the value of such an apostacy.

Had he not already suffered enough, for what was no fault of his? Had he not already served his country enough, against her will? Had he not already done and endured enough, for a class of despised men, to whom a majority of his countrymen, by their laws, had solemnly declared that little or nothing was due? Was he, indeed, so much wiser than they? Or was it merely his own headstrong, inexperienced self-conceit, which was about to draw down death on him, and lifelong despair upon his beloved? Might he not have been wrong,—could he not conscientiously say that he had been,—at least in some part of the proceedings which brought him there, even if the motives from which they proceeded were right？ Ah！ we may think our principles much stronger than his, and wonder at his wavering; but until our principles have stood one such dreary, weary, lonely, midnight wrenching as that, following hard on such a day, we must not be so ready to condemn him as he was, shortly after, to condemn himself.

His pulses throbbed, his brain burned; and, as for one dreadful instant he entertained these questions, the light of his little lamp, on the plastered wall of his cell, was as the glare of the pit. Then, with one tremendous thrust, he put these questions from him: "When I was calm and fearless," he said, "I settled all these points in my own mind, as I thought, well. I shall hardly settle them better, or more wisely, in a spasm of selfish and unmanly terror like this; and therefore I leave them where they are. There is appointed unto all men a time once to die. When it has come, what can it matter whether the time which preceded it has been long or short？ When it comes to me, let it only find me at my post, as becometh a true soldier of Christ; and, Father, into Thy hands I commend my spirit！"

Humbled, but calmed, he threw himself on his knees and, unable to sleep, continued all night in prayer to God, not so much for himself,—he had put himself aside for the time,—as for two or three who were dearer to him, and for one who was dearest of all. Every hour, he glided softly through the still, dark corridors, listening to make sure that there were, as yet, no new sufferers agonizing in their cells. At day-break, another man was seized and, crawling on his hands and knees to the door of his cell, cried to him for.help, as the light of his little lantern danced through the crack on the wall. By breakfast-time, their room-mates reported two more as ailing. Bad air, bad diet, bad clothing, and bad constitutions, welcomed the destroyer with open arms and began to install him, and carry him through the establishment, with awful rapidity.

The secret was out, and could not be got in again. The prisoners were almost frantic. Log ran away. Rodrick remained, but was half stupified by consternation, and the other half by something stronger. The overseer came to Herman for instructions. The imprisoned abolitionist, by the simple force of character, ability, and knowledge, was become the virtual ruler of the prison.

It was Sunday morning. The chaplain did not come. Herman appeared at the door of the hospital, and desired the overseer to assemble the men as usual, for religious exercises, in the long narrow hall, or large main passage of the prison. He also sent for Mrs. Rodrick. She was on the spot with only so much delay as was necessary, to enable her to pack up her pretty little daughter and her clothes, and consign them to the care of an aunt, who lived in a neighbouring town. Hard-featured, crabbed, wiry woman of forty-five as she was, she was softened and humanized by the sight of so much suffering, and elevated by the presence of so much danger. Herman, as he had hoped, found in her a most valuable assistant. His manners towards every woman with whom he had to do, by seeming to take for granted in her everything that is most delicate, dignified, and womanly, seldom failed to call forth all the delicacy, dignity, and womanliness that happened to be in her. Besides, Mrs. Rodrick believed that she owed to him the life of little May; and she loved him like a son. She wished to transfer him at once to her own house; but it had become clear to him,—how strangely things do clear themselves up after earnest prayer, sometimes!—that it was his duty to cast in his lot with his fellow-prisoners', placed as he had been by Providence over them, in a post of great trust which no one else could fill; and she the more readily agreed, for his sake, to· every measure which he proposed for the common safety. He gave her his directions, left the hospital under her care for a little while, and went to administer a few ounces of moral prevention to his quaking congregation.

They sat on stools in the shady hall, each at the door of his own cell,—a strange and motley audience. Some of them had their caps on; some, blankets wrapped around them; some, merely their pantaloons and shirts. Many were in chains. A man with a musket stood on guard over them. A low murmur ran through their double line, as Herman, with his firm, light step, and young, calm, gravely bright look, came forth among them, like the conqueror that he was, from the chamber of Death, and for the first time took the preacher's place.

Speaking as a brave man to brave men, he quietly told them that a refuge had been offered him without the walls, but that he had determined to stand by them, and expected that they would, by him and by one another. They looked at one another, and at him again. He said that an immediate change for the better was to be made in their diet and clothing; that he thought, that the epidemic had come too late in the season, in all probability to last long; and that he was glad to see them so orderly and composed, because cowardice, besides being selfish, slavish, and contemptible, was of all things one of the most likely to bring on the disorder, in men situated as they were. Sweeping the ranks with his imperial eyes, he saw, in the abashed countenances around him, that the reproof of his words and his example had struck home. He added, that by and by he should choose out from among them a few, whom he believed to be courageous, firm, and kind-hearted, and ask them to help him, if he needed any further help, in taking care of their sick comrades ; but he advised any who were afraid, to ask, see, and hear as little of the sickness as possible, but to work and pray, that they might be fit for both life and death, now or hereafter.

Passing on as if the subject was disposed of, he made them unite in singing " The Lord is my Shepherd," the words and air of which, many of them had learned from him. He wished, by the music, and especially by giving a degree of regularity and even formality to their services, still further to tranquillize them, and to avail himself of the interval to see how his patients were going on.

Returning as they finished the last line, he gave out for his text the words, " Under the shadow of Thy wings will I make my refuge, until all these calamities shall be overpast." Then, in the few minutes which he still dared to spare to them, he poured out to them as it were, in one rich gush, the very essence of his whole past inward life,—of many a yearning supplication, stifled sigh, mournful vigil, and secret triumph. Homeless, he spoke to those homeless ones around him of the heavenly home that was waiting and longing to take them all in,—large enough, pitying enough, joyous enough, to receive and to forgive and to enrapture them all,—drawing even now, perhaps, very near to some of them. With a look brighter than any smile, he bade those who were now heartily endeavouring to walk with God to remember always, that over them Death had no power, except to remove them into His nearer and dearer presence. For those who knew themselves to have been hitherto ungrateful and undutiful towards Him, he repeated the stories of the malefactor on the cross and of the Prodigal Son, and entreated them to offer up to Him all their remaining time, in a pure and faithful service. Like a brother, he talked to them of the infinite tenderness and compassion of their common Father, and entreated them to believe, that, though He did not choose to be served by slaves, and suffered those who wilfully preferred destruction to follow their choice, yet He would be more eager to receive and welcome them, if they turned to Him with sincere repentance even at the eleventh hour, than they were to seek Him. Rising with the theme, and raising his hearers with him, his sermon imperceptibly soared into a prayer, and lifted them,—so one of them afterwards said,—"almost to the gates of Paradise," as he implored in the name of them all, that the sorrows of their present life might be turned to the blessedness of their future.

When he ceased, the men crowded about him, some of them in quiet tears. They pressed his hands. They begged him in the same breath, not to expose himself and not to forsake them. They promised, in humble, broken words, to obey him to the death, if he would but stay among them and direct them. The bolder ones contended with each other for the privilege of assisting him. He accepted the services of four, on whose nerve and strength he could rely, and promised to allow others to serve in turn with them, if it should be necessary. He lent all the books he had, to the rest, and asked leave for them to assemble in the work-shops, that those who could, might read aloud, and those who could not, might listen, for the remainder of the day. On the morrow, of course, they would return to their work. They went submissively where they were bidden. The panic was at an end.

Thenceforward, all went on in the penitentiary with a kind of grim and ghastly regularity. The disease was kept as much as possible out of sight. After the prisoners were locked up for the night, the guard went the rounds every half-hour; for "this is a pestilence that walketh in darkness;" and most of the seizures occurred between sunset and sunrise. The moment a man was found to be attacked, either in cell or work-shop, he was carried off to the hospital, where he went through the dismal routine of symptoms within closed doors. The night after he died, if he did die, he was taken away privately and placed, with a large hand-bell at his side, in an unused shed in a field apart from any other building, for two days and nights; after which he was buried. (This arrangement Herman insisted upon, though to guard against his patients' fears of being interred alive, quite as much as their danger of it.) If he mended, he was put, as soon as might be, into a large store-room adjoining the hospi-tal, under the joint care of the overseer and Mrs. Rodrick.

Except to look in on the convalescents, or to speak to some one in the passage, Herman scarcely crossed the threshold of the hospital for two whole weeks. It was not that he would not, but that he could not. The dying eyes there, were fastened upon him. They held him fast, and would not let him go; or if he went, they drew him back. The poor, cowardly, time-hardened criminals about him clung to that fresh, fearless, unsullied manhood of his, as the last spar which might buoy them up over the fiery waves of Gehenna. When Death the reaper was sounding his harvest-home in their ears, and calling them to gather in the evil harvest they had sown, no long-hidden memory of guilt seemed to them too hideous to leave behind, a loathsome legacy, to the shrinking soul of their young physician; and he listened patiently, mastering his own horror that, if possible, he might minister relief to theirs, and change it into a hallowing contrition. In vain he threw himself, when quite worn out, upon his pallet, to try to catch a few hours' rest even among them. They shouted his name. They clutched at his bed-clothes. They were in torment,—death,—hell!—and he must come and help them out, and sleep afterwards! And he would arise and go, with his gentle weary smile only a little wearier and more languid day after day, and night after night, sooth them, give them their medicines, and pray beside them. His place was one which no one else could fill; though he allowed his assistants to spare him all the physical fatigue that they could, in moving, chafing, and bathing the sick.

The chaplain came twice,—a worthy, common-place, formal man, ossified with his own diffidence;—but the prisoners knew him little, and cared for him less. He preached to the well, but had to leave the sick to Herman.

Mrs. Rodrick watched over the latter like a mother; but she scolded and coaxed alike in vain. She could not obtain repose for him. All she could do was, to confront him resolutely three times a day, like grim Destiny at every turn, with cups and plates full of things which he did not want, but which she compelled him to swallow before she had done with him; and this she faithfully and regularly did.

On the third Sunday, Herman was told that Mr. Broadstone and another gentleman wished to see him. Hoping for letters, he went to them as soon as he could. At sight of him, Broadstone started, exclaiming, "Good heavens, boy, what! You've had it?"

Herman walked and spoke as if in his sleep, and looked like the ghost of himself. His complexion was naturally so brilliant, that the paleness of fatigue made a very great difference in his appearance. "No," answered he; "so many other people have, though, that I believe I've hardly had time to take my turn."

"You sha'n't, then. We've come to take you out. Mr. Whittles of the Legislature, Dr. Arden. Dr. Arden, Mr.——why, what's got into you? Sit down; sit down here, my dear boy!"

Herman had waked up. The blood gushed into his cheeks; but he staggered, and was glad to drop into Broadstone's offered chair, as he looked from one to another for explanation.

"Am I to understand that I am pardoned? I have promised the poor fellows here to see them through the cholera,"——

"The deuce you have!" growled Broadstone, in parenthesis.

"But it appears to be diminishing. Then "——

"Ahem!" remarked Mr. Whittles, ascending an internal rostrum with a rumbling sound. "There is every disposition on the part of the legislative body, which I have the honor unworthily to represent, to

make each and every allowances for sectional prejudice,
sir, and educational fanaticism, and the obliquities of
youth. If your offences, sir, against the laws and
peace of this glorious Union however bounded, and the
rights and property of your neighbour, has been
grievious, so has your chastisement been sore *and*
heavy and, it is to be hoped, efficacious for to turn your
mind and effect your present and everlasting well-
being. Amen. [He was a deacon, and had just come
from church.] I hold a pardon for you, from our
excellent chief-magistrate, signed and sealed; but,
before I tender it to you, it devolves upon my duty to
propound to you one or two en-quirries, on which I
doubt not you will be able to afford satisfactory re-
joinders."

Poor Herman! What a revulsion of feeling!
Already, in imagination, he had stood at Constance's
side in St. Peter's, and seen her start of delight. So
it was only to be the same old story over again! It
was lucky for him, that he had fought through his
inward battle beforehand. Having conquered Satan
within, he had little more to fear from Satan without.
Turning paler than before, he arose from his seat and,
wishing to cut short the interview, said, " I must ask
your pardon, sir, for begging that they may be made
as short as possible; as I am wanted in the hospital."

" Ahem," repeated Mr. Whittles, putting on his
spectacles and fumbling over a note-book. "It has
been represented, sir, that, in spite of one unhappy and
exceptional error on your part, you have been falsely
accused of being in sympathy with the abolitionists?"

Herman looked at Broadstone; Broadstone walked
to the window. "I sympathize with no man's bad
judgment, bad taste, or bad temper. I know of no

party or sect, all whose members are free from bad judgment, bad taste, and bad temper; but with the abolitionists, in what properly constitutes them abolitionists,—their desire for the abolition of all institutions which degrade the black race and disgrace the white, —I am 'in sympathy,' and shall continue so, I hope, till death and after."

Herman spoke in his usual, rather low, tone. The worthy legislator was somewhat deaf, somewhat blind, and somewhat stupid; and, taking it for granted that all was right, occupied himself, after hearing the first words, in puzzling out and preparing to " propound " his next " en-quirry:" " You will promise,—promise that you will never more return to this State, nor interfere with our domestic institutions, directly nor indirectly ?"

" No. When I leave this State, if ever I do, it shall be with a soul as free as my body. It is my right as a citizen, to go, in a peaceable manner, where I will in my native country. It is my duty as a citizen, to maintain my rights. My duty to God and my neighbour may call me here again; and where it calls me, I must go. My duty to God and my country may bid me hereafter to speak against your institutions; and what it bids me, I must say."

" Hey? How? What?"

Herman spoke a little louder, and very rapidly. " Briefly this: you have come to a place of peril, as you thought on a humane errand; and for that I thank you,—thank you both,—[and he glanced at Broadstone, who still looked doggedly out of the window, and did not turn his head,] most cordially. I am a prisoner in your power, and the power of those who sent you here; and I know my place. I should not

14

have thought it well to force my sentiments upon you; but, since you have inquired into them, you shall know them too distinctly for any chance of misunderstanding. I have just come from the death-beds of others. I am just going back, very likely to my own. Grave-damps clear the eyes, I find. The blindest men can sometimes see their sins when they are pushed to the edge of the tomb. I see mine. Many things which I ought to have done are yet undone; and I have done some that I ought not; but as for that which you call my crime,—if it is, saving one of my fellow-countrymen from torture, and another perhaps from murder, —I am ready to let all my other actions go, and take that single one with me to lay before the judgment-seat, and stake my salvation upon all heaven's verdict that it was none. The dying have their privileges; and, as a probably dying man, I tell you, that when you die,—and God grant that Death may not even now stand nearer to you than Repentance,—all the piteous dusky faces of your human brothers and sisters, cut off by you, as a legislator or master, from all which makes it life to live, will loom up through the darkness of your past and future, and lower upon you, and crowd, like those of accusing demons, between you and the mercy-seat."

Whittles opened his mouth mutely, as if to let his amazement out. He had got his *quietus*.

Herman had said his say, and felt that his constancy was unlikely to be endangered by any future importunities. Renewing his acknowledgments for the favor intended, he turned to go, but went to Broadstone first, and looked into his face. There was no anger in it, but much grief.

"Good-bye, my son," said he, in a husky whisper.

"If I could, I would have saved your life, and lost your honor, wouldn't I? I meant well."

"I knew you did."

"God help us all! Lads like you, die. Lads like mine, live. I don't know whether your death or his life will stab me nearest to the heart. He had a fit of *delirium tremens* last week, poor fellow! or I would have been here before."

Herman wrung his hand in silence, and they parted. On his way back, through the damp, still passages, he opened some letters which Broadstone had brought him, and glanced at them as he passed the windows, but folded them up again and put them into his bosom. They were too full of fond hope to be read just now; and he had, by this time, become a personage of too much importance and consideration to have much more to fear from the personal inspection of the officers.

As he passed a door which stood ajar, Wellbeloved, who was evidently on the watch for him, opened it noiselessly, and beckoned him in. The sight which was prepared for him, there, suggested to his mind, in an instant, a more vivid picture of that first Last Supper in the upper chamber at Jerusalem than, with his best endeavours,—constitutionally fond though he was of ceremonial beauty and solemn pomp of worship,— he had ever succeeded in calling up before it hitherto, in any stately church, in the midst of scientific music, richly-clad worshippers, and silver plate.

He had, some months before, joined Wellbeloved and a few other Christians, of different sects, in the prison, in a request to the chaplain that he would administer to them the Communion. He had doubted the propriety of admitting convicted criminals, one of them (*i. e.*, Herman) "confessedly impenitent," to such a privilege, procrastinated, conferred with some of his clerical brethren, who shared his scruples; and there the matter rested. In the confusion and dismay of the present time, it had not again been brought up.

Wellbeloved and his friends, in the meanwhile, had consulted together and, after much deliberation, determined to carry out their Master's parting request, if not as they would, as they could. The little bare cell, with its stone floor and plastered walls, had been swept and set in order with the most scrupulous care. A small deal table had been borrowed, cleaned, and placed in the middle of the room. The two beds were drawn forward, and ranged one on each side of it, for seats. Upon it were put a squared piece of biscuit, saved for the purpose from their dinner, and one of their tin cups, polished and brightened, full of water. The poor men, five or six in number, were assembled waiting for Herman, silent, awed, devout, and reverent. He sat down with them, with the tears in his eyes. Wellbeloved prayed. They ate, drank, and sang together a simple hymn which one of them had composed for the occasion, touching from its appropriateness, trust, resignation, and gratitude; and Herman left them, presently, feeling as if Christ had been as truly present there, as in any chapel or cathedral all that day.

As he hurried past an angle of the wall, he saw, with a start, the haggard yellow face of Kane, who also was evidently lying in wait for him, though in an irresolute, timorous way. Putting out his hand to him, he cried cheerily, "Ah, Kane, how are you? It is a good while since I have had a chance to ask you."

"I thought you'd forgot all about me," replied Kane, querulously.

"Not I. There's nobody here whom I shall remember longer, or more kindly. We shall have some more good talks and readings together soon, I hope; but My patients first, then my friends, must be the rule for the doctor, mustn't it? You don't feel unwell?"

Kane shook his head. Herman pressed on. "I wish I was sick," muttered Kane; "and then, may-be, you'd take pity on me."

Herman caught the words only imperfectly; but, looking over his shoulder at the sound, he was struck by the haggard misery of the man's face. The sardonic grin of his room-mate, Spurr, had now been for some days under-ground; and it instantly occurred to Herman, that the solitude of his cell and the loss of his old comrade, taken together, might have been too much for the poor fellow's morbid temperament and affectionate disposition. It was his nature to cling to something; and Spurr, though a ribald and blasphemer, had pitied him, and treated him with a sort of coarse kindliness. Taking him by the arm, Herman led him at once into one of the emptied cells and, sitting down with him, said soothingly, "The sick in soul must be taken care of, as well as the sick in body, Kane. If there is anything on your mind that you want to say to me, out with it at once, my poor fellow."

"You'll despise and hate me," said Kane, hanging his head and looking to the right and left, out of the corners of his eyes, as if for a hiding-place.

"If I hated any man, I should be hateful myself. I despise no one, who has courage enough to look his or her sins in the face, own them, and conquer them."

"If you knew I was a murderer!" He caught his breath, and hid his face in his hands.

"I have known that, my poor friend, almost as long as I have known you."

"And been so kind!" exclaimed Kane, looking up with a flash of astonished gratitude. "But you'll say there's no help for me." He burst into tears.

"I shall not. If Satan himself, the father of murders, stood before me, grieving for his horrible past and desiring to do right for the future, I should not tell him that there was no help for him. I should see, that *all* the angel in him had not been quite dashed out by his fall. I should tell him that God's goodness was greater than even his wickedness, and that, since he could repent, I believed that even he need not despair."

"But I can't repent," said Kane; "that's just it."

A message came from the hospital to hasten Herman. He rose, as poor Kane thought, to abandon him.

"Going away to leave me? There! I told you so."

"I must go, I am afraid; but I will not leave you, if you would like to come with me, Kane. Come with me, in Christ's name, and help to tend the sick and do His work. Those who are called into the vineyard at the eleventh hour, you know, are offered the same wages as the earlier workers; but, in common gratitude, they should work the harder. Let us forget ourselves and serve our neighbours now, while God is calling upon us to do so through the cries of their suffering; and we will talk further together by and by."

Herman did not wish to lose sight of Kane, and rightly guessed, that his was one of those cases of religious melancholy which need for their relief outward, quite as much as inward, Christian working. He did work hard and heartily, night and day, and grew less moody and more cheerful, as he thought more about doing, and less exclusively about feeling, right; but he was evidently still anxious for a further confession; and, as soon as he could, Herman found an opportunity for him to make it.

It was midnight. The sickest men lay half-stupified with laudanum. Herman and Kane went from bed to bed, as they were wanted, and whispered together in the intervals of their attendance:

" You see, sir," whispered Kane, "this was why I shot George Bowie. George and me was both sparking after Sue Marigorownd; and first she'd be sweet on him and tart on me; and then, if I commenced to run after somebody else, she'd just take a sort of a twirl, and be sweet on me and·tart on him; as the young ladies will, just because they'd rather, of course, have two *beaux* than one as long as they can. It's the natur of 'em; and we hadn't ought to mind it. I didn't car a pistareen; for I knowed, all the while, she purposed to settle down on me when she'd had her swing; but George, when he commenced to see how the wind sot, he got as mad as any dog. He swore he'd shoot me, and so have it out of both on us, seein there wasn't no other way a gentleman could chastise a lady. Sue, she heared on it, and commenced to feel almighty bad. She sent for him to come and call, and writ him, and stopped and spoke to him when she met him a-walkin; but he wouldn't hear to a word. You've remarked, I dessay, sir, a pretty young miss o' that description, among the young men, is just like a poker; she can stir up a powerful great fire, but she ain't no great account for puttin it out. George was a mighty ugly feller, always, when he was in liquor; and, arter he found Sue purposed to jilt him, he was tightish or so most all the while. Well, up to that time you see, sir, I hadn't been what you'd call every-day wicked, but only Sabbath-day wicked. D'ye see?"

"No; do you mean that you did not spend your Sundays well?

" Well, no; I only mean that I was under the wrath o' God. I hadn't done nothin; but I was impenitent, you know."

" You mean that you were not a religious man?"

" Well, yes. I always went to meetin reg'lar, and read my Bible, and kep the commandments, said my prayers mornin an evenin, an all that, and went to revivals, too, time after time; but somehow or other I couldn't seem to get converted; and so I knew, if George did shoot me, he'd shoot me right into hell-fire; for he was a plaguey good marksman, drunk or sober; and I couldn't abide the thoughts on it; and it h'anted me day an night. I couldn't eat; nor I couldn't sleep; and I got as lean as a rail and as yeller as I be now; and I thought, even if I did repent, under such circumstances, I couldn't be sure 'twas genuine, nor anythin but fear o' the consequences of transgression; so I just got behind the bush on the road to the tavern, with my shot-gun, an shot him to give myself time."

" But surely you are sorry for it now?"

" Well, I don't know, sir; that's what I never could settle rightly to the satisfaction o' my own mind. I have it over and over sixty times in an hour, this way and that way, sometimes, for days and days; and just as soon as I think, I've got it put down, up it jumps again, like the stick that was so crooked it couldn't lay still; and I can't get it out of my head, till it seems as if my very skull would split. I'm sorry; and I ain't. I'm sorry for George. I don't owe him no grudge; nor I didn't at the time. If I could pull him up out of the fire and brimstone without gettin in myself, I'd do it in less nor no time; but if one of us has got to be in there forever, I'd sooner 'twould be him than me; and I can't help it. His was the fault. He didn't ought to act so. I'd ha' let him be, and glad to, if he hadn't threatened me. If 'twas to do over again, I'm fearful I would do just so; and that ain't repentance; and them that don't repent can't hope to be saved."

"'Assolver non si può, chi non si pente;
Nè pentere e volere insieme puossi,'"

thought Herman. "Kane and 'il nero cherubino' have arrived at the same conclusion, in their separate inferni; and no doubt it is a true one."

"When I want to repent, it's because that I want to keep out of hell-fire; and I can't want to keep out, and wish at the same time I'd let him pop me in, can I? And it's just like a snarly skein of silk in my brain; and the more I try to get it untangled, the more it snarls up." The poor half-distracted creature actually squinted, in the intensity of his introspection.

Herman laid his hand upon his shoulder: "Let it alone, Kane; don't try any longer just now. Let me see if I can't disentangle it for you. You must have been very young when all this happened?"

"Nineteen."

"You think, then, that if you had died at that time,—a well-meaning and inoffensive, though very likely a very imperfect and thoughtless boy,—God would have punished you with an eternity of torment, and that if you should die now, after committing a murder,—since you, and the judge and jury who convicted and sentenced you, it seems, are agreed in calling

14*

it one,—you would have just the same punishment to fear, neither more nor less?"

"Well, yes, sir; just so."

Kane had acted consistently enough with his premises; but Herman did not see how such premises could possibly be correct. "I don't," said he.

"Why, sir, don't the Scriptures say we must be born again, or we shall not see the Kingdom of God?"

"Born again, or from above, they do; Christ himself says it; and God forbid that I should gainsay it. We are, I fear, only too apt to forget it. But I don't remember that we are anywhere told, that this is to be in all cases an instantaneous process. I think that you may have made a good beginning, even at that time; though I suppose you are quite right in believing that you were not so good a boy as you might have been, and that if you had been living as near to God, and as truly in charity with your neighbour, as you ought, you would not have fallen into this snare. You are sorry at least, aren't you, that you were not in such a state as to dare to die?"

"Ain't I? I reckon I am. I'd have wished myself dead many a time, if it hadn't been for the anguish and gnashing of teeth."

"And if I can show you a better and happier way, which you might have taken, shall you not repent that you took the one you did?"

"Bless your heart, sir, so I could! Show me, for pity's sake, now. Show me!"

"I think you seem to have been somewhat in the situation of the young man whom our Lord loved, when he ran to him to ask him what he should do to inherit eternal life. You kept the commandments, you say? Honored your parents?"

"I did. They sot a store by me. I was mother's cosset. She died after they put me in here." The tears rolled down his cheeks.

"That was good; but it was not enough. You were not perfect. At least one thing more was required of you. God seems to have called upon you, if you had only understood it so, to run the risk of a possible evil to yourself rather than do a certain mischief to your neighbour; just as Christ called on the young Jew to leave all his great possessions and follow him. If he promised that young man treasures in heaven in return for the sacrifice of his wealth, I think that he would have given you treasure there, too, for the sacrifice of your young life laid down in his spirit, however imperfect your life may have been. And so all these miserable years, which you have spent in prison and in despair, might have been passed blessedly with him in paradise, while your murderer, it may be, touched by your example, was repenting in this world. Kane, you can repent of that rash action now?"

"I can! I do! Hallelujah! I've got dug out! Hurray! I've got deliverance! Salvation! Oh!"—

"Hush, my dearest fellow, hush! You'll disturb the other men!—Now I advise you to think henceforward as little as you can about the past. Mental troubles like yours are apt to return, by force of habit and association, if one looks back to their causes. Take care of the present. Serve God cheerfully and diligently with work and worship; and don't scare other people away from His service with your gloomy face. As soon as this sickness is over, I must give you a little medicine. Men don't get the clearest or brightest views, of this life or the other, with the whites of their eyes as yellow as yours are. Now lie down, and get

a little sleep, while I watch; and, when you wake up,
I'll follow your example."

The third week passed. The bottles and bathing-
tubs were cleared away. The sick were recovering;
the dead, buried. Within the penitentiary, many
" places were empty,"—Wellbeloved's among them,—
or " filled already by strangers," never long wanting
there. Without, St. Dominique had died.

A neighbour on the plantation nearest to his, a man
also of desperate character, had several times had his
poultry-yard trespassed upon by the terrier Faust. His
negroes reported that the dog came every night, stole
a cock or hen from the roost, and then ran away. The
neighbour watched for it with his gun, and shot it.
Wounded, but not killed, it started for home. He
pursued, without getting a fair chance to take aim at
it again, meaning to despatch it, if necessary, in its
master's presence. It ran through St. Dominique's
quarter. This was still, and seemed empty. The
cabin-doors hung open. The broad moon shone on
two or three black corpses, putrefying on the ground.
A living skeleton of a blood-hound, chained to a kennel, dragged itself up to its feet on its thread-like
quivering legs, and strove to bay at him with the very
ghost of a howl. The wounded dog limped on, now
but a few yards before him; but he no longer cared to
shoot, and followed it, as if through a bad dream,
unhindered and alone even to the open door of the
chamber of St. Dominique, where the bleeding dog,—
the only thing that loved him, the only thing that he
ever seemed to love,—with one last effort sprang upon
his bed and, staining it with its gore, licked the blue,
fixed, hideous features of his corpse, and died.

It was supposed, though never clearly known, that,

he and his *driver* having been among the first seized by the cholera, the other slaves had run away, and left them to their fate; and that even his favorite, in its starvation, feared his savage temper too much to help itself to anything of his for food; though it loved him too well to forsake him. Poor dog! Poor man! If he was not fallen too low for one creature still to love him, let us hope that his Creator may have mercy on him, if only for that miserable loving creature's sake.

Edward and his charges returned to Boston on the first news of the danger, determined to see Herman again, at all hazards, if he still lived. They were met at the dock by the faithful Patrick, with a face and letters which told them that the danger was over. Herman wrote in a spirit of thankfulness almost too deep to be otherwise than solemn; though in a post-script, with playfulness intended completely to reassure them, he said that he was too much ashamed to acknow-ledge what a coward he had found himself; but that he believed his terrors must have been, more than half, owing to the melancholy influence exerted upon his mind by a certain Sister of Charity.

He had still before him some laborious weeks, though infinitely less so than those which were behind. The chief physician of the town had died; and there was still a good deal of sickness in it. Herman had much ability in his profession for so young a practitioner, and, having had more than ordinary success there in the treatment of the cholera, was reputed to have even more skill than he had. The aid of the Eastern fanatic was eagerly sought, in their extremity, by many who had been among the first to vilify him in their prosper-ity. It was never refused. Worn as he was, he went

from house to house as willingly as wearily, in his
prison dress, with a guard at his heels; shared the
anxieties, and did his best to relieve the sufferings, of
his enemies, and very often turned them into friends.
True to a rule which he had long ago laid down for
himself, he never forced his views of slavery upon
them; but, when they showed their growing interest
in him, by trying to make him a convert to theirs, he
was always ready to discuss the matter with them as
temperately as firmly; and frequently, after half an
hour of his eminently agreeable conversation, they
would find new ideas in their heads which they could
never afterwards get out again. They paid him liberal
fees. These, the wardens of course pocketed. He was
not very sorry for this, for two or three reasons, one
of which was, that it enabled him the better to enter
into the feelings of an intelligent slave, at being obliged
to give into the hands of others all the wages of his
lifetime. Presents of delicacies, also, were lavished
upon him. These were left at his disposal, and were
most welcome for his convict patients' sake; for since
Mrs. Rodrick had fallen ill, exhausted by her exertions, the hospital-table was but ill supplied with wholesome and tempting food.

Towards the end of the autumn he wrote to the
girls that, finding himself a little *run down*, which was
not very extraordinary in the circumstances, he was
going to take care of himself, and avail himself of a
permission that he had obtained, to take a walk into
the country every day on *parole*, with no other guard
than his little May, who marched him out with comical
gravity, with a wooden gun which he had made for
her. He soon took a heavy cold, however, that,
together with the unusually wet and stormy weather,

kept him much of the time within-doors; and he passed a very quiet winter without much variety in it of any kind, excepting the agreeable novelty of being able to make up his sleep.

Even Broadstone came to see him but once, and sent him his letters through the hands of the jailer's wife. He and his were in a great deal of trouble. His oldest son, a young man of about Herman's age, and the very one to whose "education" poor Bill the blacksmith had been sacrificed, could be kept from bar-rooms and their effects only by his father's constant personal oversight.

States rich in slaves are wont to be poor in colleges; or, if they have them, the colleges are wont to be poor in intellect and learning. Young citizens of slave States, therefore, if they are to have a chance of a liberal education, must frequently be sent into free States for it.

Young Broadstone had been sent hundreds of miles from home, at the very age when good domestic influences are most important to a man. Through the weakness of his mother, and the ignorance of both his parents as to the actual needs of his situation, he was kept supplied with twice as much money as would have been thought a sufficient allowance for a Northern youth of his expectations, and with nearly as much as was spent at the same time by all the rest of his family. He had excellent parts by nature, and was ambitious of distinction, but was, for want of good preliminary training, utterly incapable of signalizing himself by anything but "good fellowship" and *fastness*. In these, accordingly, he took one part and degree after another and was, at the end of his academical course, returned upon his father's hands a confirmed sot.

This was a grief to poor Broadstone the elder, for which even Herman could find no consolation, and which, therefore, he could hardly bear to see ; so that he was in a manner resigned to his old friend's absence ; while so much kindness and personal attachment was shown him by his new friends throughout the town, that he ventured in the spring to write to Edward, that he would graciously permit him to come to Bondage for him, if he had no other engagement, and give him the pleasure of his company on the way home.

CHAPTER XXVI.

THE KNIGHT'S RETURN.

"Wings flutter, voices hover clear:
'O just and faithful knight of God!
Ride on! The prize is near.'" TENNYSON.

EDWARD found Herman looking out for him in the same guard-room with the handcuffs and cowhides hanging over his head, and in the same clothes,—old-fashioned now,—in which he had left him more than two years before, looking so sad and strong. There was one change, however, which struck him like a blow. Herman now looked so happy, but so weak! His body and limbs seemed wasted; and, though the loss of flesh was less perceptible about his face, it was full of that kind of languid animation and excited debility, which appear only, like the last flare of a dying lamp, to foretell their own extinction.

He was in the spirits of a school-boy on the first morning of a vacation. When he could speak, which was not the first nor the second instant after Edward's hands were clasped in his, it was after the following fashion: "'Altered'? To be sure I am! I'm two years older. Other people are, too. Isn't that a wrinkle, I see, over somebody else's nose? Oh, it is gone now! It was only a scowl. Avoid scowling in future, Ned; or that furrow will become chronic, to the great detriment of your beauty."

"You did not tell me that you had been sick."

"Homesick? I thought that would be no news; everybody is, more or less, in a jail; did you need to be told that, O student of human nature? I wrote you word, I'm certain, that I was rather *seedy* after we had the cholera;—after I didn't have it, that is, but most other people did;—and after that, in almost every letter, I took pains to inform you that I had taken a cold; till I thought I must have sufficiently impressed the fact upon you, and that you would think I was repeating myself for want of topics. I took another last week, and feel a little *springy* to-day. That's the whole story."

"You walk like an old man!"

"I *am* a little stiff, I believe, just now. It's half of it laziness; and the other half, want of exercise. A gallop or two on old Bay will set all that to rights, and bring back my appetite; and then I shall do well enough. The people here say there never was such a spring before. For the last month, it has done nothing but pour. I couldn't get out very well, and felt the worse for it when I did; so at last I gave up the point, and made up my mind a change of air was what I wanted; and now, with your good leave, I'm going to try it, the very moment after I've said good-bye to a few of my acquaintances here."

"You look as if you'd lain awake all night long, every night for a week."

"May-be I have; it was such a terrible disturbance to me to think of going home! Home will cure me! —home! If I be sick with joy, I shall recover without physic! Come, come, sir! I'm the physician of this establishment. Don't poach on my manor. If I'm not quite as well-conditioned as some people I

could name, I'm not so ill as I was once before, when
Sea Farm and Clara cured me; and now I shall have
Constance, too.—Who's there? Oh, walk in, Mrs.
Rodrick. I was not going without taking leave of
you. I was coming to see you, as soon as I had been
through the workshops and yards to speak to a few of
the men."

"Well, sir, the convicts felt so powerful bad about ·
your leaving, that I just interceded with husband and
father to let 'em quit work a quarter-hour, and come
into the hall to see you when you'd pass through."
Herman was not the only person who was changed, by
the two years spent by him in the penitentiary. Two
years before, how much would that woman have
known, or cared, about how the prisoners felt? "Can
I help you put up your things, Arden?—*Dr.* Arden, I
would say."

"No, thank you. I shall leave most of them; and
I've written upon them the names of the men whom I
should like to have keep them. This copy of the
Psalms, I hoped that you would do me the favor to
accept."

"Well, I'm sure! What grand, great letters! It
seems as if they'd read 'emselves out loud, without
specs. If you'd just write my name in it, sir, and who
it's from. Here, May, come. Why, you know you
wanted to tell your good prison-doctor good-bye."

Poor little May had been hitherto, it appeared,
lurking behind her mother somewhere in the scant
folds of her gown, and stopping her eyes and mouth
with it, *à la* Bessy Flint. On being extracted from
her hiding-place, and lifted in Herman's arms, she
burst into a passion of very genuine grief, and scarcely
feigned anger: "Oh, dear, dear, dear! I can*not* let

you go. You must not. I thought you was good. You're naughty and cruel to leave little May. I'll get a great big chain, and hammer it all round your hands and feet. I'll get pa to hold you. Oh, oh, oh!"

"Oh, fie, fie!" said Herman, kissing her, "don't you remember the day you cried before, because you could not get your father to let me go to see my little niece, Bessy? The week after next, when I get home, I must give Bessy two dollars in her little purse, and send her out to a toy-shop to buy two beautiful dolls, with eyes that will open and shut, one for her and one for you; and I must have yours put in a box, and send it by a carrier, directed to Miss May Rodrick; and you must unpack it yourself, after the nails have been taken out of the box for you; and what color do you think its eyes had better be?"

He went out, leading the child by the hand. Edward followed him. As he passed, the turnkeys touched their hats. In the hall, the men thronged about him, many of them with their rough, squalid features working painfully. It was a brief, but agitated interview.

"Good-bye, good-bye. Riggor, you'll find a blanket labelled with your name, in my cell; the overseer will give it to you. Holt, I've left you my chair. O'Gee, you'll be out next, you know. Mind you don't get in again, there's a good fellow. You're older now than you were when you came in; and you've seen the folly of—never mind what. Vylepig, don't forget your promise, will you? Remember, it's 'never too late to mend.' Ah! Quackleben, I've put up a large packet of your medicines for you, with full directions; don't take too much. Good-bye. Romer, I've written your name in my 'Two Years Before the Mast.' Why,

Kane!—why, pluck up a good heart, man. I've left you half my books for keepsakes. You must write to me. Penn will write for you."

"A gentleman would be ashamed to get a letter from such a place," said Kane, dolefully.

"If he was *no* gentleman. I'll answer it directly, and tell you about Boston; and if you don't make haste, I shall write first. Let by-gones be by-gones, my poor fellow; but do the duty of each moment as it comes. Men of consciences as delicate as yours, must take care how they ever trifle with them, if they want to be at peace. But remember, that there is an un-regulated repentance, which eats up the fruits that repentance should offer to God and man. Good-bye, good-bye. God bless you all!"

He hurried through them, and bowed in silence to the wardens, who stood loitering together with rather mortified aspects in the yard; but in the gate he turned and paused, gazing for an instant at the grim walls in which he had left two years of his youth. He then sprang into the carriage, threw himself back in it, and slouched his hat over his eyes. Some joys are so akin to grief, if not so mingled with it, that their oppressive weight is only to be wept away.

Edward was as eager as he, to get him over the border into a free State, but, after that was done, greatly doubted the feasibility of his going on, until he should have spent some days in recruiting himself at the best hotel, and under the care of the best physician, attainable. But, though Herman endeavoured to relieve his anxiety, unfounded as he considered it, by a cheerful acquiescence in this arrangement, his disappointment showed itself so clearly through his transparent face, that his brother had not the heart to enforce it and feared, besides, that it might injure him in his enfeebled state, even more than fatigue. He set out with him anew, therefore, meaning to induce him at least to travel slowly, and only by day ; but Herman, with his most submissive efforts, was unable,—from eagerness and nervous excitement,—to sleep without the use of opiates, which his condition in other respects imperatively forbade ; and Edward soon made up his mind, that the only thing to be done was to get him home first, and let him rest afterwards, which it seemed that he could do only in his own bed, or in his grave.

As the scenery began to wear a more and more home-like aspect, full of farms and frequent houses, towns, churches, and schools, instead of the late huge half-dead, and a-quarter-inhabited, plantations, his spirits rose higher and higher, but his pulse's rate with them. "If he could only be kept from being so happy!" thought Edward as he looked at him.

As they reached Springfield, he had one of the long heavy swoons of his childhood ; but he rallied quickly after finding out where he was, which he did from Edward's proposing to stay at Warrener's, and telegraph for Clara to join them there with Constance ; and they soon set off again. And next, he saw little crowded, clean, red-and-slaty Boston butting the clear sky with its familiar chimneys, and then,—he was on the sofa in the dear old drawing-room ; and Clara's arms were round him ; and his hand was wet with Constance's tears ; and old Sally, more toothless than ever, held his nose from force of habit, as she administered to him some hartshorn and water ; while the cheery fire-light and gas-light shone again on the warm bright crimson walls and furniture and the old pictures and, through the open door, on the rich dinner-table ready-set; and then they all talked and laughed and cried together; and Patrick brought him his slippers, as if he had not been gone a day, except that they were well-warmed this time,—the girls had seen to that,—and Bondage was all gone from him, hundreds of miles away in the dim distance, as if it had never been! Sweet voices, graceful movements, luxury and beauty, were all around him;—how strangely sweet, graceful, and beautiful they were!—and it seemed as if home *had* cured him, after all; for he arose, took his old place, made a good meal with a good appetite, chatted and frolicked away the first consternation of the girls at his shadowy looks, and *kept it up* until the bronze Time, over the clock on the mantelpiece, was heard to strike reprovingly as many strokes as he could with his scythe on his hour-glass; and Edward ordered his patient to bed, saying, in his capacity of master of the house, that he was going to turn off all the gas.

"Twelve? Can it be? Well, I suppose I may as well go to my *cell*," answered Herman; and when he laughed at himself, for his odd mistake, it was with the tears in his eyes, as he thought of the misery which he had left behind, and of the many whom he had left behind in it, who had not merely no such comfort and luxury as this, but no such affection, honor, and happiness to return to, when their prison-walls should give them up. On his way to the door he stopped, riveted by the sudden sight of Constance's picture.

I have seen it. It is worthy of its theme,—a worthy mate to that portrait of himself which I have mentioned before, and painted by the same artist. It is a magnificent battle-piece, turbid with smoke and flashing with cannon, as the other was, with cloud and lightning. A battery is apparently changing its position and, across plunging and falling horses and fighting and fallen men, the slight Valkyriur-like form of the young Sister of Charity, in her sable robes, darts to the aid of a crawling soldier, who lies struggling just before and half under a wheel. She stretches one slender hand towards him, and with the other, half-buried in the mane of the huge dapple-gray horse, pushes its rearing neck aside, with courage more than strength. Her white hood has fallen to her neck; and her beautiful dark hair clusters around her temples. Her head is thrown back; her eyes are lifted to the face of the driver; and her lips, parted as if with a cry of warning and horror. Her attitude and expression are full of an extraordinary mingling of command and entreaty. Her face, lighted and brought out into strong relief by the glare of the artillery, might well be taken for that of a Joan of Arc. It is perhaps the most beautiful and spirited female one that I have ever seen on canvas; but Herman did not think it so beautiful as hers, and called her to stand by it that he might compare the two. "How kind it was in you, to be taken in this costume! The very thing I should have wished! (and could not have asked," he added mentally.)

"I hoped so," answered she; "I consented to it as some little recompense to Edward, a pleasure to you, and a penance to myself." She added something that Clara did not hear; but she supposed that,—in spite of Constance's previous resolutions, that her sorrow for the past should not sadden her lover's enjoyment of the present,—some irrepressible expression of self-reproach, for the mistaken sacrifice on her part which had been the cause of his sufferings, must have burst from her; for Herman stopped her by bending quickly over her hand and kissing it, and saying low, in his most soothing, most heartfelt tones, "Settle that with God, sweet soul! I can find nothing but blessings to lay to your charge."

Edward gave him his arm, and led him to his chamber; and there the same affection which had welcomed him below had been before him. This apartment, too, was bright and warm and seemed to say, "Walk in!" Flowers were on the dressing-table, and flowers in the carpet and window-curtains,—the only new things there, except a handsome dressing-gown on the chair by the hearth.—Everything else was familiar, and in its familiar trim and place. The beautiful wood-fire glittered and flickered as of old, on the *bas-reliefs*, carvings, and *significant andirons*, and on the worn gilding of the ancient tablets gleaming from the wall with the Creed and the Ten Commandments; and I account him happy who, returning to his early fireside and altars after an absence of years in the flush of his manhood, however worn in spirit and broken in body, can look upon such solemn symbols of Faith and Law, and remember that he has neither broken the one nor made shipwreck of the other.

Herman sank down on the side of his bed with a deep sigh.

"There! you're ready to acknowledge now, perhaps, that you feel the least in the world queerish?"

"Yes;—like a humming-bird drowning in honey. Pull off my stockings, and put on my night-cap;—I never mean to do anything for myself any more; it's a folly;—and when you have put me to bed, you can send Clara Arden up here to read me to sleep. Oh, Ned, Ned, go to jail, if you want to know what it is to come home, and to such a home as this! Be a slave once, if you want to know what it is to be a freeman!"

15

"Hold your tongue, sir; and go to sleep like a Christian, if you want to know what it is to be a live man!" And Edward, having *tucked him up* with most thorough and comic energy, sent the obedient Clara, bidding her to read as little as possible and talk not at all; and Clara came again, and sat in the light of the lamp, and read him to sleep, as she had done six years before: " This poor man cried; and the Lord heard him, and delivered him out of all his troubles."

And by a singular coincidence,—arising, perhaps, out of the similarity of the circumstances,—he had a repetition of the dream of heaven which he dreamed then; and, besides the chorus which he had recollected on that occasion, sung by the angels, he remembered when he awoke another verse of Herbert's song:

> "Lo, he ascendeth,
>   And not he alone!
>   Of those Thou hast given him,
>   Hath he lost none!"

He remembered, too, when he awoke, that he was not on the morrow to go away again far from those he loved best, but that they were all under the same roof with him, and perhaps made wakeful like him by joy at his return,—and Constance among them, waiting only for the day to bless and cherish him.

A long and wide career of public and social usefulness, and of domestic honor, peace, and bliss, seemed to be opening before him and luring him on. "But first," thought he, "I must regain my strength;" and so he ruthlessly denied his eyes the pleasure of searching, through the fading fire-light and the shadows, for glimpses of the old, familiar, long-unaccustomed things, shut them close, and slept once more; when once more he dreamed of the crucifixion.

But as he toiled, bearing his galling and crushing
cross, up the steep of Golgotha, and Constance followed at a little distance, wearing his crown of thorns,
a hand of light flashed suddenly out of the black
clouds above, caught up his burden from him, and
presently let down instead a flowery rood of asphodels,
on which it gently laid him. A wonderful feeling of
peace, comfort, ease, and rest, spread through his every
pulse and fibre; but he looked to see how it fared
with Constance. Orange-blossoms were mingled
with the thorns around her brows; she appeared, in
her white beauty, like one on whom Sorrow had done
all its work and gone away and threatened nothing
more, leaving the sufferer in the healing hands of Resignation and Hope. She looked not down on his
prostrate form, but up into heaven, and sang; and on
the golden tones of her mounting *soprano*, as on a
golden stair, his soul seemed to mount step by step,
and climb and leap up to the Infinite, and lose itself
in a blaze of light, love, harmony, and joy unspeakable.

When he awoke, he was better. He was better; but
the next day was too much for him; and so was the
next week. He had been strong to bear the unkind-
ness of his old neighbours and fellow-townsmen; he
was too weak to bear their kindness now. Too many
people came to see him at home; too many people
were glad to see him when he went out,—not merely
poor or sick people whom he had befriended, though
these besieged his door and his walks as soon as they
heard of his return, but to his astonishment "respectable," fashionable, influential, political, and estranged
people, saw him again, bowed and spoke to him courteously again, smiled upon him again, and even took
the bold step of crossing the street to welcome him

back, or honoring him with their long-discontinued invitations to dine, or "drop in sociably of an evening."

The circumstances which had led to this reversal of the social verdict in Herman's case were numerous. Of these we will, in passing, notice a few, both public and private. First, the public: Demos, in broadcloth as well as in homespun, is a testy and fitful old fellow; and, like some other old fellows, he is somewhat given to contradict anything that you say to him, in the first place, and, in the second, to lay it up, forget where he got it, and to repeat and assert it most positively as quite his own. In this manner, some scraps of political sagacity which he had had originally, much against his will, from Herman, had now been for so many twelvemonths rusting in his wits, that he thought they grew there, and was almost ready to act upon them, and quite ready to thank anybody who would show him how. Moreover, he is fond of a frequent nap and, while he is trying to take one, will scold you if you disturb him, even in order to tell him that his stable-door is open. Then, if his horse runs away, he may scold everybody for not having told him that the door was open; and, if you venture to suggest that you did, he will reply that, then you did not modulate your voice agreeably, and trod most unnecessarily and exasperatingly upon his toes; but after that, he will very possibly forgive you, and beg you by all means to shut the door now and to lock it, taking great credit to himself for his condescension and candor. Demos had had his fill of napping for the time; for, as it happened, the saucy and wakeful Council of Three Hundred Thousand, emboldened by his lethargy, had been, as the stable-boy said, "kind o' 'ticing him with a pitchfork" labelled Kansas, Nicaragua, or Cuba, or something,—

never mind what; you will know, probably, before the year 1870;—and he was shaking with rage, both as to his head and as to his fists, and very eager to "have something done about it," until he forgot it again which, for a wonder, was for once not till after the next elections. This fellow-feeling made him wondrous kind to Herman. He was certain, to be sure, that Herman in past times must have been wrong somehow; else why had he not agreed with Herman all along? But, at any rate, he was very happy to be able to agree with Herman now, and would charitably let by-gones be by-gones.

Secondly, the private circumstances: Mr. Flint had been led,—we can guess how,—to identify the interests of his growing family with those of the Ardens. He shook his head at first, indeed, at Herman's enterprise as " a pootty silly, fanaticle way of wasting a young feller's time and money," and, on the news of the disaster in which it terminated, was heard in the bosom of his family to ejaculate, " Sarved him right !" But that was too much for even the timid Catherine. Cat-like she bristled, astonished inwardly at her own temerity, and scrupled not to declare, that if he said " another such a word," " would go right along off up to Aunt's !" which alarming string of adverbs and prepositions, and unprecedented threat of desertion and travelling-expenses, coupled with the probable consequences of exposure, and disgrace with his sister-in-law, speedily brought him to a better mind. Personally, he had little to do with the first class of merchants. He had, however, a great deal to do with some *middling* merchants, who had more to do with the former. Glad of a good chance to boast of his wealthy and genteel connections, he expressed much more interest in the misfortunes of his young brother-in-law than he was capable of feeling, and spread the true version of his story on 'Change, day by day, in a prudent, clear, business-like manner.

Mr. Halifax, in a private letter to an influential brother-clergyman in Boston, had described Herman as in all respects a very remarkable young man, who had "done the work of a caged Howard in the penitentiary in Bondage."

Clara, instead of hiding general indifference under her faultless politeness, and dividing her real sympathies for the most part between only some half-dozen intimates, according to the custom of her earlier days, had, when Herman was put into prison, already been for some years on the watch to do, by look, word, and smile as well as purse, all the kindnesses that she could, among all who crossed her path in any way. Innumerable little graceful tokens of genuine, thoughtful interest in others, combined with all the *prestige* of beauty, wealth, and fashion, had made her irresistible; and many friends, both high and low, had gone to her to hear and share her troubles, and carried away the echo of her sweet, grieved, trembling voice in their hearts, to break forth in many a pathetic or indignant speech in their different circles.

Then in Edward a change had taken place, or rather was taking place,—it was not completed for some months yet,—the beginning of which struck his brother with astonishment. Summer lightnings are the sharpest. Men of his stamp, easy-tempered and inert while absorbed in their own enjoyments, are capable of becoming the most formidable antagonists when their enjoyments are interfered with. Pleasure-loving and pleasure-having, they can hardly believe in the objectionable qualities of political or social Evil, until political or social Evil breaks into their charmed circle to reveal itself to them experimentally. He had fallen into the common mistake of judging of a system by a few of the most favorable specimens of those born and bred to defend it. He had known and liked some Southerners at Cambridge,—kind-hearted, companionable, gentlemanly young fellows, like himself;—and, incapable of imagining that youths in most other matters so generous, and so honorable, could uphold any mean and cruel institution, he had half fallen in with them into upholding their institution himself; for he had not considered that there probably never was a tyranny yet, which had not the party-spirit of much such lively, agreeable, kind-hearted, wrong-headed sons and grandsons of tyrants, to defend it.

One seldom knows the power of any force until he has been opposed to it. Stand beside the engineer on the front of a *locomotive*, and it may seem to you a harmless, tractable, and softly-moving thing. Spring before it, to push it back from the wayfarer whom it is going to grind down on the high-road, if you want to know its horrid and destructive energy. Edward slid along smoothly enough with the Juggernaut of slavery, and never guessed how hard it was to turn or stop, until he saw his brother in its way and rushed to save him, but saw his bright young head laid low in the dust at his Master's very feet, and felt his own heart crushed. When he came back from Bondage for the first time, leaving Herman there, he was in the state of some surprised wild beast which, while basking in lazy fearless strength in its hitherto unapproached fastnesses, suddenly sees its young writhing in the gripe of the hunters, and leaps up roused to unappeasable fury by

their barbarities. His hatred to slavery, and all that
belonged to it, took thenceforth the form of a bitter
personal resentment,—not the purest, certainly, but
one of the mightiest weapons which it is the doom of
Oppression to forge for its own suicide. He ferreted
out its enormities with the skill of a policeman, and
had them attested with the precision of a notary. He
studied the Black Codes of each of the slave States and
knew them by heart, or by hatred, as few jurists do.
He proclaimed his hideous discoveries and his brother's
wrongs in all companies, with a passionate and vehe-
ment, not scurrilous, eloquence which compelled attention, as his facts did amazement; until the very school-
girls, in many of whose eyes he was a " bright particular
star," told one another Herman's story in *recess*, or as
they walked home together. Of course, the young
men who liked to share his good dinners, cigars, and
trotting-horses with him, were forced to share his
orations likewise. They were soon agreed among
themselves that, Arden seemed terribly cut up about
that poor little brother of his; and no wonder! It
seemed to have been an abominably hard case! Those
Southern fellows were getting to carry matters with
too high a hand, and would have to be seen to before
long, if they didn't look out; and the country down
there was hardly fit for a Northern gentleman to travel
in, if Arden's luck was a fair specimen.

Clara and Edward Arden were not people whom it
was possible to *drop*. Mrs. Mydass tried it, and left
them out at a ball, but soon found that she had made
a mistake, and gave a dinner on purpose to repair it.
Clara neither observed the omission nor accepted the
invitation. Availing herself of the opportunity afford-
ed by the timely demise of a cousin whom she had

never seen, at the West, she went into mourning, kept out of company, and devoted herself chiefly to Constance, whose remorse and misery were like a long-drawn death. When Edward went home, the black dresses and red eyes were apt to send him out again the next time in fresh indignation. Thus, altogether, a very general feeling, compounded of curiosity, admiration, and pity, had been excited in Herman's behalf.

Herman was a hearty lover of concord when he could enjoy it honestly, and, besides, welcomed the change of feeling towards himself as a good political symptom. He received all the explanations and recantations graciously and cordially.

Not so Clara. For almost the first time in her life, she felt herself *crustaceous* inwardly. "What do these men mean?" cried she. "They were all rude and savage to you, were they, and slandered you, and thwarted you in every way they could, when you were trying to do your duty to your country and theirs? Oh, Herman, you would never tell me how much you suffered!"

"I never could," said he, involuntarily.

"And now they come smiling and bowing up to you, and pluming themselves mightily on their magnanimity in seeing that they have made mistakes after it is too late to repair them,—as if it was the prettiest thing in the world!—and telling me, in the most congratulatory way, that they have found out you were 'pretty near right, after all;' as if I had not known you were quite right all the time! Abominable! isn't it, Constance?"

Constance blushed painfully, hesitated, and faltered, "You know I can't censure them without condemning myself."

15*

"I beg your pardon!" exclaimed Clara, raising carnations on her own account.

"For showing how you can forgive and forget? Granted. I wish all my offences had been of that kind. Oh, Herman, I can never, never tell you half how good she is!"

"Then I don't believe anybody can; and therefore, how lucky it is that I don't need to be told!"

"She is tolerably good," said Edward; "but she will be perfect, if she will move us all down to Sea Farm next week."

"Sea Farm!" exclaimed Herman. "Why, isn't it rather early and chilly to go there yet?"

"You shall have a buffalo-robe and a poker to take with you. I want to. brace you up a little, my boy." The echo of a whisper had already reached Edward, that his brother's still too evident languor and feebleness were "put on for effect." (When the highest and holiest of sufferers flagged under the weight of his cross, if there were any Pharisees present, can we doubt that they pronounced that he languished for effect?) Edward was jealous for his brother, and wished to get him out of sight, where he could rest and refresh himself at his leisure, away from under the evil eye. Besides, he had just come from a secret consultation with an eminent physician whom he had persuaded Herman to see once or twice, and whom he found inclined to agree with the latter in thinking, that his was "one of those cases of merely nervous prostration, for which letting alone and fresh air are the best remedies, and about which, 'least said is soonest mended,' " but with himself, in considering fatigue and excitement very bad for his patient.

But it did not suit Herman to consider himself anybody's patient. It can hardly be a comfortable thing to a young athlete, accustomed to take an honest pride in the vigor and hardihood which were in great part the blessing of Heaven upon his own brave, active, and temperate life, to own his vigor gone before his youth, and himself a puny, delicate invalid. "At it again!" cried he, in mirthful wrath and wrathful mirth. "What an old raven! Don't listen to him, girls! He'd croak the Queen's beaf-eaters into a regiment of hypochondriacs. How horribly out of practice he must be, to try so hard to get hold of one case!—I am not going off for a month!"

"Take your time, sir," said Clara; "but Ned and I are going next Wednesday or Thursday; and so is Constance. I always thought I should like to be perfect; and if I have a chance to become so, so easily, you may be very sure I shall not let it slip."

"Very well. If you're all against me, I shall have to compromise the matter. If I allow myself to be carried off next week, I must be allowed to go out this, without ejaculation or molestation. Why, I have hardly seen the Great Elm yet, or the Mall!"

"You saw them too long, yesterday," replied Rhadamanthus. "You stood in the east wind, ogling the Frog-Pond and talking to old Mr. Hunckor, full fifteen minutes."

"Not five, by Park-street clock; I looked at it."

"So did I; it had stopped, finding in your example a better excuse than it usually has for its doings. N. B. Somebody coughed disagreeably last night, and kept me awake for a whole hour. I suppose that must have been Patrick. Patrick shall imbibe a large dose of squills, if it happens again."

"Nonsense!—When you go down to the stable, tell

your fellow to saddle Bay, then ; and let us take a trot round Milton Hill. I sha'n't stop on his back to talk, nor take cold either."

"I wouldn't use Bay just now. He stumbles."

. "Humph ! Wants bracing too, perhaps."

"Exactly. By the time he has had three or four weeks of pasturing, and you of bark, you'll be fitter to hold each other up."

"Your bark is worse than your bite.—There are some people I must go to see, at any rate."

"In the autumn."

"To-morrow morning, to begin with."

"Oh, Herman !" said Clara, "I thought that Constance and you and I,—and Edward, if we could get him,—would have a coach to-morrow morning, and take a boy-and-girl drive together, for the sake of old times, round Milton Hill."

"After we come back, then, before dinner."

"Herman," said Constance, "Clara and I have been learning some of Mendelssohn's duets to sing to you. Perhaps you would like to hear them to-morrow before dinner, while you rest after your drive."

"I can't deny that I should.—On Sunday, then."

"Why, Dr. Lovel was coming to preach, and spend the day with us on purpose to see you quietly," said Clara.

"A manifest conspiracy ! Come, Ned, now it is your turn. Have you any cause to show, why I should not make a few calls on Monday ?"

"To be sure I have."

"Ah ? you surprise me. May I ask what it is ?"

"When Dr. Brodie went abroad, I gave him a commission to buy you a ton of the best medical works to be had in Paris and London, you ungrateful and obstinate puppy. The boxes are in the custom-house now, and will be up here by Monday afternoon at the furthest; and if you walk or talk yourself dead beforehand, it is plain that you will have no voice left to tell me how and where to bestow the books, before we go."

"Another bribe, and a brother, worth having! If anybody was ever killed with kindness, my situation *is* precarious; and you shall, all three of you, have your way with me; as you deserve. But, indeed, there are a few persons who might well feel hurt, and misunderstand it, if I went out of town without giving them a chance to see me. So, if I do not visit them all myself, you must connive at my taking a chaise on Tuesday or Wednesday and going to two or three of them, who probably cannot come to me, and receiving any others who happen to hear of my return and come of themselves. Patrick will know them well enough by their threadbare coats; and I will try to listen as much and say as little as I can."

CHAPTER XXVII.

THE KNIGHT ON THE SHORE.

"Fatal oracle d'Épidaure,
Tu m'as dit, 'Les feuilles du bois
À tes yeux jauniront encore;
Mais c'est pour la dernière fois.
Le fatal cyprès t'environne,
Plus pâle que le pâle automne,
Tu descends vers le tombeau!
Ta jeunesse sera flétrie,
Avant l'herbe de la prairie,—
Avant la vigne du côteau!'"

MILLEVOYE.

It was a lovely Sunday evening in August. The sun was going down through an atmosphere of aerial amber under a canopy of purple and gold, and filling all the deeply-dyed and gilded ocean under it with the gorgeous glories of an inverted sky. Herman had not been at church. He was lounging on an improvised couch made of Edward's, Clara's, and Constance's plaid shawls, under a tent pitched on a cliff and open to the water, looking less at the sunset than at Constance, who was leaning against a rock at a little distance, and making Clara give him an account of the sermon which she had just heard. It had been one of those,—unsatisfactory always,—upon that most interesting of themes, our future state.

"Is that your idea of heaven, Herman?" asked she, as she finished.

"No," said he. "Scarcely any man's own original idea of it is that of any other man; and that, I suppose, may be the reason why no other man's is satisfactory, or even otherwise than somewhat *dis*satisfactory and disagreeable to me.—I have had beautiful dreams of it sometimes,—such beautiful dreams that trying to tell any one else about them, who has not been blessed,—thrice-blessed,—with something like them, is like trying to describe Constance's face to a blind man, or her singing to the deaf." Talking seemed to tire Herman this afternoon; as it did sometimes. His eyelids dropped; and his lips closed for a few moments; and then he spoke again with pauses, filling up the spaces between his fragmentary words with his own thoughts; as if he stopped to look through his own clear soul into the life of the blessed, then described something of the glimpse which he had had, and then broke off to look again.

"It seems to me," he continued, "that there the soul marches or soars on through scenery as much more grand and beautiful than that of Switzerland or Italy, as theirs is than that of the common earth, lighted up with more than the splendor of noonday, the tenderness of moonlight, and the solemn joy of the stars. The emotions which could be excited in it in this life only now and then, in some rare moment, by the noblest poetry, music, or architecture, have passed into its habitual mood. Life is lifted into heroism. The service of the King of kings is carried on forever with a passion as sublime as that with which a warrior thrusts himself before his prince, to die in his stead,—as glorious and triumphant as that with which he lays down the enemy's taken flag at his prince's feet.— Good conquers evil visibly all around, far and near, through the unriddled mystery of the transparent universe, and conquers still to conquer.—The risen disciples sit visibly again at the feet of the risen Christ. They see the glory which his God and their God has given him; and he shows them plainly of the Father.—No angel's foot crosses his neighbour's path; each angel's hand helps on his neighbour's work.—From system to system, through endless cycles of space and time, Newton flies after Galileo, and Galileo looks on before Newton, that each may know and rejoice over the other's last discovery.—Moses walks with St. Paul, telling the untold story of the awful converse and visions of the mount.—Joshua and Washington sit resting side by side.—Raphael, with a reverent pencil filled from the palette of the Sunset, tints the designs of Michael Angelo; while he, with his nervous and sinewy strength and the lantern that burns on his head, helps the tender hands of Sabina to hew out her designs clearly and perfectly in the hard, dark, quarries of thought in which every one, male or female, must go down deep and labor patiently and mightily, who would bring out any new and perfect thing before men and angels.—David teaches Dante to play upon his Tuscan harp the old airs of Judah.—Each voice chants a call to every other voice, to swell and complete the general chorus of thanksgiving and of victory. Gabriel's tenor cries out for Michael's bass; and both will have Cecilia's soft *soprano* to sing beside them. Each spirit has, and longs to share with every other, something that every other wants. No soul is there alone, unprized, unsought. Each is a larger or a smaller block or atom, *unique* in shape and color, whose absence would make a gap or flaw in the grand mosaic pavement of seraphic glory over which God walks,—on which He shines!"

"Herman," asked Edward, "is not yours a heaven which only an intellectual person could enjoy, and find himself at home in?" It was noticeable, that he spoke very gently and gravely, and with no disposition to ridicule what had been said.

"Every person has an intellect," answered Herman. "The difference between what we call an intellectual and what we call an unintellectual man, is chiefly that in one his intellect is developed, and that in the other it is not;—sometimes for want of education;—sometimes, I think, from the heavy, sluggish physical structure which he has inherited from uneducated, unthinking, *animal* ancestors;—in the spiritual body it can work better.—And well-educated persons are almost always, more or less, manifestly intellectual and different in their intellectual powers. As they go on in their developement, they separate further. No two great (or, in other words, well-developed) men are really alike, even if we call them by the same names of "artists," "philosophers," or "saints." They start like divergent lines from one common point, the birth. At ten months old, the difference between them may still be microscopic, but it can, commonly, already be seen by sharp observers; at the end of ten years, they are at least a foot apart; at twenty, a yard; at forty, a mile; and when they leave the world, and we lose sight of them, often a league. Only imagine, then, what the difference must be between the intellectual powers and qualities of even common men, whose developement has gone on under all the favorable influences of the heavenly state,—sympathy, example, encouragement, assistance, and the most judicious and affectionate guidance,—for thousands of ages!"

The argument did not interest Clara. She was still

dwelling upon the picture of heaven, and him who had drawn it. "Herman," said she, with her blue eyes swimming in tears, as he paused, "it seems to me as if, feeling as you do about the other world, you must almost long to die."

"And leave you?" said he, smiling, but drawing her cool hand to him and laying it upon his forehead, which was too hot. "I am very well contented to wait where I am, and enjoy the distant prospect. One must not be too impatient. Even at the banquet of eternity, I do not want the fruits before I have had my second course."

He looked too tired to talk any more, and called Constance to come and sing to him the "Psalm of Life," which she and Clara had arranged as a duet to a beautiful air of Handel's. Herman was very much in love with life. He had taken its altitudes and sounded its depths already, as few men have at his or any age.

He had not yet begun to gain strength as fast as he or they had hoped. In May, the weather was raw, damp, windy, and altogether unfavorable to his passing so much time as he would have wished to do in the open air; for he was not sufficiently vigorous to take exercise active enough to keep him warm out of doors. In June, there was no cold to complain of; but the heat came on so suddenly and violently that "it was enough," so Edward declared, "to melt down a bronze Hercules;" and Herman, at least, was like the bronze Hercules in respect to its effect upon him, if not so at that time in any other respect. It continued through July; and Herman was not yet rallying in any good degree from the prostration which it had caused in him; though for a week past,—ever since

August came in,—both atmosphere and temperature had seemed made for him, dry and bright, but as cool and bracing as September. If he was disappointed, however, in the rapidity of his convalescence, he showed scarcely any sign of noticing its delay; except, indeed, that whereas in May all his little plans for rides, walks, or long drives, to show Constance old favorite views and haunts in the neighbourhood, were made for "to-morrow or the day after," and in June, for "next week," they were now fixed for "next month."

Scarcely any such plans had yet been carried out. Eager as he was for exertion, he looked so utterly unfit for it and was sometimes so unwell after it that Edward, in his professional capacity, had forbidden it for the present with some peremptoriness; and the young athlete's daily exercise was now little more than a short airing in a *barouche* in the afternoon, and, in the morning, a saunter across the road and up the barberry-crested bank to the bars of the paddock, where poor old Bayard, fast falling into the dotage of his short-lived kind, hobbled along at sight of his master, putting his best foot (which was by no means a good one) foremost, to receive a bunch of pink and white clover-blossoms. Thither Constance following Herman one day, heard him condoling with the venerable steed and saying, as he patted his nose, "'*Sic transit*,'—*sic transimus*,—poor fine old fellow. So the most glorious bays of this world must soon droop and perish!" But it must have been merely a general reflection; for, though there was tenderness in his voice, there was no sadness; and, at the sound of her light step behind him, he turned round with a smile as bright as the morning, and, dividing his flowers between Bay's mouth and her hair, playfully crowned her forehead with a rosy diadem.

"The summer is very apt to be a trying time to any one who is not strong, particularly a summer like this. A little bracing, breezy, autumn weather will set him up, you'll find;" so Edward said; so Herman thought; and Constance believed; and Clara hoped. In the meanwhile, if the summer had been "a trying time" to him, it had also apparently been, thus far, a season of enjoyment almost unalloyed and unearthly. The messages of remembrance, the kind inquiries of one after another old acquaintance of his family, of which Edward had reports to bring back every time he went to Boston, the beauty and tranquillity of the fair wild Nature about him, and the attendance of Constance and Clara, were daily and hourly feasts to him. The greater part of their days they spent in the tent, pitched in one or another dry, airy, and picturesque spot, in order that he might enjoy the scenery, and be constantly breathing in the pure salt breath of the brine, without fatigue, without exposure, and with them. He heard them read; he saw them work, and talked with them; or, when too tired to speak or hear another word, he stretched himself at their feet; and they thought he slept; while he "felt their presence," and enjoyed the memory of past sorrow, the hope of coming joy, and the soft, lulling whispers of the rippling waves beneath them, that murmured of "Eternity, Eternity!" while the young man dreamed of life.

He was so happy, that it seemed hard to run the risk of disturbing him by word, look, or sign; but after a second week passed by, bringing seven bright suns and, day by day, clear, fresh breezes, but still no visible amendment in him, Edward's anxiety at last broke through the fear of exciting Herman's, (which hitherto had kept him silent since the first few days after his return,) so far that he suggested to him that he might hasten his recovery by having further advice. Herman was not disturbed by this proposal. On the contrary, he caught at it with some eagerness; and it appeared, that he had been kept from making it himself only by the fear of hurting his brother's professional feelings.

Therefore, week after week, one eminent physician after another came to Sea Farm; and to one after another he repeated, with the same kind of calm, clear earnestness, the same story of " not one single pain, or *bad feeling* even, that" he was "conscious of; but such strange weakness and sluggishness, fatigue without exertion, *sinking* without hunger, and drowsiness without power to sleep." They, singly and severally, answered that he had been living on his nerves too long and must allow himself time to rally, and recommended rest and stimulants; but these he had already been trying for months, as thoroughly and perseveringly as he did everything else which he undertook to do. Bark and wine made him feverish, but did not make him strong or hungry. He was worse if he exerted himself; but so he was if he rested. It was not merely that he did not gain ground. He had lost it, of late particularly. He slept less than he did in the spring, ate less, and weighed less. His loss of flesh was even more than in proportion to his loss of appetite. They spoke for the most part cheerfully, though vaguely; but he knew the secrets of their craft by this time too well to be deceived by them; though he had been, by himself. In the spring he had said, "I give myself three months, to get myself into perfect condition again." He said now, "I give myself a year."

He was surprised, and at first somewhat disconcerted, at finding himself a sick man. It interfered very much with his long-cherished plans, which had seemed to him upon the very eve of fulfilment,—plans of winning a field of wide usefulness for himself, and a pinnacle of prosperity on which to enthrone his lady-love. But, young as he, was, he had already had experience enough to lead him to think that, when God makes any great change in our condition, it is often less His purpose to make us suffer, even in this world, than to make us enjoy in some new way. Those are apt to be happy, who are always willing to be happy after a fashion of His choosing. On such occasions Herman often said, "If I had not been shot by a Border Ruffian, remember, I should not have been taken pity on by a Sister of Charity."

His mind soon turned to the blessings of sickness; and from this, chiefly, Clara knew that he did consider himself a sick man; for to her he talked a little of the blessings, though not of the sickness. She was sitting beside him in the tent, with one of her hands in both of his, and with the other, bathing his temples with Cologne-water; for he acknowledged that they ached, after Constance left him, forced away by a conspiracy between all the others to take a ride with Edward. Herman spoke then of the perfect luxury of repose, stillness, and the care of those one loved.—No well person could know it, except in infancy. It was one of the blessings of infancy, which only sickness could restore to maturity.—Clara must be ill some time,—a very little so, after she had cured him,—that he might show her how very sweet it was.—No one could be a thoroughly-trained physician, who had never needed one. This would be a good apprenticeship for him. He should be able to do twice as much good after it, as he had ever done before,—as he ever could have done without it.—"Psyche,—do you recollect how our Lord said to his Apostles, after they had been trying to do a little work for him, 'Come ye apart into a desert place, and rest a while'? It seems to me continually that, in this sickness, he is saying so to me. The thought that he or his Father has provided this retirement and refreshment and opportunity for quiet self-recollection, preparation, and communion with Him, before I go back to my work, is very soothing to me;—one of the very sweetest drops in the cup of life which God has mixed for me is the thought, that He had already planned all this rest and dear companionship and tender care for me,—when I was—at the South,—and it seemed,—at times,—so doubtful whether I should ever be one of you again. It would have been sad to be ill there;—very hard to die."

He seldom inclined at this time to speak much of himself,—never so fully as upon this occasion, and to her;—but when he did so at all,—except to his physicians, to whom he gave simple technical statements, untinged by any sentiment of any kind,—it was always hopefully. He talked, when he had breath, with a kind of exhilaration, of church and state, the poor, the country, and the world,—the world of letters, of religion, of science, and of art. Everything interested him that concerned his fellow men. There was "so much to be done!"—he should soon be able to do so much!

How often are such prophecies heard from fading young lips in silent anguish, or reported afterwards, by those more distant relatives and friends who can command their voices to repeat them, with shakes of the head and interjections of "Ah, poor fellow! How little he knows!" But who does know, or can? Is it so certainly the prophets, who are deceived,—or our-selves? May not their predictions spring from the felt stirrings within them of the might of their near immor-tality? Very bitter it is, to stand by and listen to such utterances from the tongues of those whose past life has been thrown away, useless to God and man,—for whom we can only hope against hope, that their career in the other world may prove to be the utter contradiction and refutation of every sign and omen of their career in this,—to whom an honorable, noble, and holy course amongst breathing men has become for-ever an impossibility,—and who have not time left on earth for reformation,—that stamp of repentance which alone can prove the coin genuine and current, and not the mere base counterfeit of fright, impotence, and shame! Bitter enough it still is to listen to such pre-dictions, when the life of the speaker has been so lofty, beautiful, true, and kind, that we are persuaded that neither death, nor angels, nor principalities, nor things present nor things to come, nor height nor depth, nor any creature, can ever separate it from the love of God, which is in Christ Jesus our Lord,—yet know not how our own life can live on without it, and know that it is passing away.

As was natural, those most constantly about Her-man saw the change in him less than those who saw him rarely; and how much the former saw, they did not say to one another, and scarcely, perhaps, owned to themselves. Edward was one of those men, who, if they had a party of ladies to conduct across a ground undermined,—with a match in the mine, and a light at the match,—would do so with cheerfulness and *bon-hommie* to the last possible moment, *keeping step*, and talking of the last new opera. Clara, though she

had not quite broken loose from her beautiful reve-
ries,—she would not have been Clara Arden without
them,—was never now blinded by them to the sufferings or situation of those about her; but her temperament and sympathies always inclined her to hope the
best; and Constance's spirit, always excitable, had not
yet exhausted the reaction of ecstacy and thankfulness
which Herman's return had produced, after the misery
of his imprisonment. She was romantic still; and
romantic minds always fancy, that the story of their
life, like any story of fiction, must of necessity culmi-
nate in some unchangeable climax of bliss or woe.
During Herman's absence, she was convinced that the
latter was to be her fate; upon his return, the former. But this our transitory life is itself a series of
transitions. There is in it much joy, but little unchanging joy; and much sorrow, but little unchanging
sorrow.

It is probable, however, that before the end of the
month of August, they all began to fear that Herman's
vigor might never be restored, and that he must resign
himself to lead henceforth only the life of an invalid.
For, the next time that Dr. Lovel came to see him, he
asked the girls with some solicitude after he left him,
what they thought of him; Constance, her face quite
haggard with expectation, waited for Clara to answer;
and Clara said, gently, "We think he is not yet looking so well as we hoped he would, but that the cold
weather may do more for him."

The color flushed over Constance's cheek and brow.
The old man, who had seen much of her during Herman's absence, and become very fond of her, looked
wistfully at her as if he longed to comfort her. "How

16

peaceful he seems, my dear," said he; "how free from any kind of suffering!"

"The peace is with him," said Constance; "the pain,—where it should be!" and she abruptly left the room. Recollecting herself notwithstanding, she presently came back and went up to him, though with her handkerchief at her eyes. "Forgive me," whispered she; "thank you. Don't think me ungrateful, because I cannot talk about it yet. It is so dreadful to think, that I may have cut him off from all the good that he would have been so happy in doing,—perhaps for his whole life,—and then to have them all so forgiving and so kind and good to me! But I know that he will be very happy still, in other ways; and so shall I,—in helping him to be so,—after we have got over our first disappointment. His loss will be my gain; for now I shall always have him with me. It is such a blessing to have him to take care of! Come again and talk with me, when I can behave better!"

She struggled with herself, gave him a sweet and grateful, though tearful, look, and again left the room.

"Poor child!" said the old clergyman; "poor dear child!" but he said no more.

Dr. Brodie was the last physician consulted. He returned from Europe near the end of September, and was summoned at once. Herman had an interview of an hour with him, within closed doors. Edward met him in the passage when he came out, and was about to question him; but he only cried, "Poor lad! poor lad!" shook hands hastily, pushed by him, sprang into his gig refusing all offers of hospitality, and drove off without seeing Constance or Clara.

All the rest of that day, Herman, exhausted, lay like a dead man, his hands folded on his breast, his fixed white face upturned, and eyelids closed. He was looking into his own tomb. It looked somewhat black to him; as it is wont to do when it gapes suddenly for the onward foot of a man, young, and rich in happiness, hope, and promise, until his eyes become accustomed· to it. He did not sleep a great deal through the night, but still lay quietly; and Edward, who had shared his chamber since his weakness increased, thought he perceived by the uncertain glimmer of the night-lamp, whenever he awoke, that his brother's lips were moving silently, as if in prayer.

The next morning he was better, spoke cheerfully, rose, and dressed as usual. When he had sent the two girls out to walk, as he did every day, he had his easy-chair rolled up to a large old wooden sea-chest which, to his high delight, had been given him for a treasury when he first came to the farm-house as a child. Herman was always a creature of observances; and it had been his whim to lay up here some characteristic token of every one of his afterwards yearly pilgrimages to the sea-shore. There was throughout in him, as there always is in full and complete natures, a remarkable mixture of youth and age. He had been, as soon as he had a fair chance to be so, a manly child. He was a child-like man.

The key of the chest was on his split-ring. He unlocked and opened it, while Edward stood beside him, and took out the dated relics one by one, reading pensively in the associations which clung to them, as if in a hieroglyphic record, the annals of his brief past life. There were the shells, picked up on the beaches the first summer, in a many-colored paper-box of Clara's making; the bow and arrows of the next; the geological specimens of the third; and the boyish pencil-sketches of the fourth. There was a duet for tenor and *soprano*, bearing the autograph of Constance, and the date of his twenty-first year,—the very year in which he first knew her, and at whose close the joint tragedy of their two young lives began! There was the huge elk-horn of the next, brought from the West;—and so on, in due order, to the bullet which came so near his life in Kansas; but for the last two summers, and for this one as yet, there was an omission.

He proceeded to supply it. Edward, at his request, brought him his dressing-case. He took from it a twisted paper, which proved to contain two small sticks of ash-wood, richly and curiously carved and ornamented with a pen-knife. "From the window-frame of my cell in the penitentiary," said he quietly, looking up at his brother. "They repaired it while I was there; and I begged enough of the old wood for these. I carved one of them each year." The longer of the sticks bore, in black-letter characters, the inscription, "*Venni per martirio*," and the shorter, "*In questa pace*," besides the respective dates, on each, of the two years of his imprisonment. Leaning back at his ease in his chair, he addressed himself leisurely, with his transparent, slender, blue-veined hands, to the task of fitting and riveting the two pieces together in the form of a cross. He added to the foot of this the words "*Laus Deo!*" with the date of the current year, and laid it with the former relics in the chest. Next he took out a bunch of withered roses in a cornucopiæ of manuscript that lay in a corner by itself, locked the box, and said to Edward, "The tide is high, is it not? The water sounds near. Will you go out with me? I should like a row."

The tide was very high. Though the blue and diamond-sprinkled water was calm and smooth, it

plashed among the flat, oval, bluish-gray pebbles
within a few yards of the back-door, and along half
the length of the boat; so that Edward had no difficulty in supporting his brother's few unsteady steps to
it, and embarking him in it.

There had been an early frost; and the shores were
gorgeously tapestried with leaves dying gloriously.
The crickets were peacefully singing the dirge of the
year. The day was one of perfect Indian summer,
warm, soft, and bright, though misty and tender; and
the very soul of such a day seemed living in the young
man's wasting, but transfigured, face as he turned,
after a long gaze before and around him, to exclaim,
" Dear Edward, what a pleasure you are giving me!
How good it is to have suffered, ['to *have* suffered'
does he say, already? thought Edward,] and then to
have one's troubles clear away, and yield one back to
freedom and friendship and such scenes as this! How
sweet and bright and calm and happy, it all looks!"

"'How sweet and bright and calm and happy,' you
look yourself!" thought Edward bitterly. "You know
how it will be, in another month, with the scene you
revel in. How, think you, will it be with you?" He
groaned involuntarily.

"Are you in pain? Unwell? I must not keep
you rowing too long. Time flies fastest over the
waves; and I forget how it goes. Turn back, if you
are tired; or, better still, draw in the oars and let us
float."

"My dear fellow, do you suppose I could be tired
of rowing you all day long, while I saw you enjoy
it so?"

"God bless you, no! I do not. Don't be too kind
to me, Ned. You are all quite dear enough to me,

already; and you, in particular, must take care not to wear yourself out; for one man sometimes finds himself suddenly called upon to fill the place of two."

"What do you mean, my dear boy?"

"Not to trouble you until I must, at any rate; and I did *not* mean to say that. Never mind. If you are really not tired, let us go over there to Rose-Rock. I set my heart upon it before I came out, and came out on purpose; but the weather and the day and the delight of being on the water once more with you, in the air and sunshine, put everything else out of my head."

Rose-Rock was, at low-water, a peninsula; at high-tide, an island about forty feet long. The sides were hung with dripping sea-weeds; but on the top there was a sprinkling of thin soil beneath the crisp lichens and green velvet moss. In July, wild rose-bushes blossomed there. They were now full of scarlet berries, and interspersed with lilac asters, and golden-rod. It had been, in old times, Herman's custom to climb to the summit of an afternoon, and read or more frequently muse there as long as he pleased, and then to walk or, as the case might be, wade or swim back with his towels and clothes in an oil-cloth bag, and to carry off a rose every year, to be preserved as a pledge that he should be hospitably received there again on the next. This latter practice he afterwards kept up, though secretly, out of a kind of fantastic sentiment, as a homage paid by his manhood to the feelings of his boyhood. The boat grated at the foot of the rock. "I should like to climb up," said he, "if you will lend me your arm."

"Aren't you exerting yourself altogether too much?"

"If I make you anxious, yes; otherwise, I believe

not. Dr. Brodie agrees with me in thinking that a little exercise, now and then, can do me no serious harm."

Edward leapt from the boat, and made it fast to the gnarled trunk of a tough little cedar. He then put his arm round Herman's waist, helped him to rise, and almost carried him up the short pathway, spread his own shawl on the stone to which his brother pointed, seated him upon it and, resting one knee against it, stood behind him supporting him; for his breath panted fast. Recovering himself presently, Herman took the withered roses from the paper, looked at it, and said, "Will you read it to me, Edward? My eyes seem rather dim."

This paper bore the date of Herman's eighteenth summer. Edward took it and read the gay young lines, written as boys do write of life and death before they have tasted of the bitterness of either:

"ROSE-ROCK.

" Wild rock 'mid wild roses, I climb thee once more.
My steps crush the lichens that pave thy rough floor.
Stretching far into silence, I see the white reach,—
That roars 'neath my feet,—of the foam-girdled beach.
Again thy white sea-gulls ride high o'er my head;
Thy pennons of dulse gleam below, wet and red.
I hear thy free gales round thee pipe as of old,
And breathe their salt breath, and the crimson-and-gold,
Floating sunset behold, that has dropped from the sky,
From its still twin above, on the sea's lap to lie
And, weary of quiet, to roll and be tossed
Till its gay ruddy play in the twilight is lost.
While, searching the distance, my furthest long look
Can scarcely discover the dim cloud of smoke,—
The emblem, wherewith the horizon doth frown,
Of labor and care left behind with the town,—
The old beacon his torch 'gins to flourish aright,
And anew tears the fog with its sharp point of light;

And mine every fibre is thrilled with the wild,
Yet innocent, joy of a passionate child.

  "Oh, say not that Eden was shut to our race,
When Adam and Eve first fell into disgrace,
Forever and wholly!   Through Infancy's door
Each soul gets its glimpse of the glories of yore!
Each soul has its own dim, sweet eld, and its share
Of a pure world's green youth, like that mischievous pair;
There's for each some charmed spot, by rock, lake, wood, or rill,
Where his childhood outgrown keeps its tryst with him still.
Who, who does not know how the pilgrim's heart burns,
When from new haunts and mates by himself he returns,
Like one thread drawn out straight from the tangle of life,
To his playground of old, of old memories rife?
Returning to this from the dry beaten track,
His Infancy's Eden it renders him back.

  "One seeks the flat inland and, bosomed in trees
And dotted with hay-cocks, his paradise sees,—
With an orchard and hedge choked and choking with green
The soft, pretty, drowsy and spiritless scene.
All is still, save the apples that drop over-ripe;
But, to show where the farm-house lies smoking its pipe,
There's a chimney half-seen, and some blue wreaths that pass
Through the leaves, like a toper's who smokes in long grass
Disposed on his back; and unseen cattle keep
Up a sound like his breath when his slumber is deep.
White clouds sleep o'erhead in a still, azure sky;
And a slow, shady brook purls a lullaby by.
While I'm able, my flight let me prudently take,
Lest I sink in a stupor, and never awake.
But look!   Who goes there?   What a fire from his eyes
Flashes on the tame landscape around him that lies
'Tis the pilgrim; sly Memory is casting her spell
For him, o'er hedge, hay-cock, and moss-covered well.
He cries, 'Earth can show no more exquisite spot!'
I *know* it is lovely; though I love it not.

  "One goes back, to look for his light-hearted joy,
To the lone, lofty dell whence he rushed when a boy.
I have met him emerging; and lo! it was plain,
From the glow on his cheek, that he looked not in vain.
But his mountains are jailers, and build up their walls

To shut in the fancy; their chill shadow falls
On my heart pent within them; their white mists to me
Are but vapors, and blue ones; I chafe to break free;—
My soul's boundless being cries out for a place
Where, unpinched, it may widen in limitless space;—
But if shivering I climb them, since they are so high,
How hopelessly distant appeareth the sky!

" Here no harsh line divides us; the bowing heavens sink
To kiss Earth's round cheek by the sea's brimming brink.
The ship, through the moonlight that glides over there,—
In water or sky,—well might swim through the air,
For aught that I see, and my spirit to rest
Waft away, with its sails to the home of the blest,
Or on, in a long voyage never to cease,
Bear me, 'twixt earth and heaven in moonlight and peace.

" Wild king crowned with roses, I sit on thy throne,
And make thy sweet sceptre of mullein mine own,
And thank the kind Fates, that the rush and the roar,
The sweep and the surge, of the much-shouting shore,
Gave my boyhood, and thee for my memory's shrine!
Once more salt my lips with the breath of thy brine.
Let thy wild romping wind in my face fling thy foam;
'Tis my old nurse's rough kiss that still welcomes me home.
The old blossoms, that thou to my childhood didst lend,—
See!—I've kept like a lock of the hair of a friend;
They have grown to a heap, that would burst from the hand
Which the first gray old stems, in their verdure, first spanned;
Yet, covetous still, let me add to the store,
For the sake of old times, still one more and one more.
Since we met, thou alone and forsaken hast stood,—
Unshaken, unworn,—winter, tempest, and flood;
At thy bald, hoary head, sleet and hailstones were hurled,
While I played the deserter. The much-abused world,
Howe'er with its servants or slaves it may be,
Has never been cruel or treacherous to me.
I've mused by the lamp; I have mixed with the throng;
I've shared in the feast; I have joined in the song;
I've laughed with the gayest; but naught could I find,
Believe me, old playfellow, more to my mind
Than to sit down once more, by the side of the sea,
Alone with glad Nature, Hope, Memory, and thee.

16*

"Whether, sunken and shrunk, thou dost wade or dost swim
In the waves when the ocean is full to the brim,
Or risest to make, at the turn of the tide,
Thy dripping dark garments' low borders all wide
With a fringe of black sea-weed,—old Pharisee!—here
Receive me on pilgrimage year after year,
In peace to look back on the year that is gone,—
Its battles all over, its victories won,—
To count o'er its wounds but by glorious scars;—
Then send me back, armed with fresh strength, to the wars.
While thou keep'st thy roses, bid me keep my truth;
So shall age, in us both, wear the crown of our youth.
Taught by thee, I will smile,—with as equal a front,—
At the sun, and anon of the storm bide the brunt,
As thou dost through all my strong manhood; but when
I'm pushed to the edge of my three-score and ten;
When the sum of my sunbeams and starbeams is told,
And this foot, fleet and sure, totters down to the mould;
When Death comes to bring me his hellebore-cup,
On this mossy altar, Earth, offer me up;
For my spirit,—through no gloomy valley,—would go
To its bright heaven above from its bright heaven below."

Few years had passed since those lines were written; but where was Herman's "strong manhood" now?

But if those few years had done the work of a lifetime on him, had he not done the work of a lifetime in them? He listened in silence, with his slender fingers clasped around his knee and his large, spiritual eyes looking off to the horizon or beyond. When the last words were ended, he bowed his head; and Edward thought he dozed. Then he stirred once more and, gazing round him dreamily, murmured, "It is very strange. It is very solemn. God strengthen us all!"

"What is it, Herman?" said Edward, taking his hand and longing to sooth him, but not knowing how. "Do you think there is any occasion for fear?"

Herman's bony hand closed around his, with a

cordial and reassuring grasp. Letting his head fall back upon his bosom, like a child's on the breast of its mother, that he might raise his eyes to his, he said, with an irradiation of countenance almost too solemn in its brightness to be called a smile, "No, dear Edward; I am *certain* that there is no occasion for fear. Did I say anything? Perhaps I was dreaming. I am drowsy and cold. We must go home;—but first, my roses. Oh, they are dead!—it is too late. No matter. They have left plenty of beautiful berries." He stretched out his hand for a twig of them. Edward broke it for him. He placed it with the faded flowers. Then, tottering to his feet, he turned himself slowly all round on the same spot, with a fond, lingering gaze, which seemed to mark and cling to every familiar inlet, stone, shrub, and stalk, within its range. He half sighed, but recollected himself and, looking up cheerfully into his brother's face, clasped his hands round his arm and said, "Come; they will wonder at the farm-house what has become of us."

Edward laid him at his full length in the boat, carefully muffled in all their shawls and cloaks; and he slept all the way home. When established there on his sofa, he merely kept his eyes open long enough to give Edward his roses, and desire him to replace them with the coral berries in the chest, whispering, "If — I am not here next summer, give the key to Clara. Those trifles may have an interest for her; for the record of my years is the record of her kindnesses." Then he slept again, with a placid, satisfied look, all the rest of that day, and the following night.

The morrow, and the remainder of the week, were harsh, raw, and rainy. Perhaps the weather affected his spirits. They were fitful and, though sometimes apparently natural, sometimes forced and sometimes depressed. He often called Constance to come and talk with him, but, after saying a few abstracted words while . he studied her exquisite face, would remark anxiously upon her paleness and send her away, begging Clara to wrap her up warmly and take the air with her.

And Constance? Constance held her breath. There are times,—times of spiritual as well as of bodily anguish,—when the sufferer does so, and feels as if it was all that he could do and as if, if he ceased to do so, he must cease to exist.

The following Sunday, however, was another golden day; and Herman revived. In the afternoon, while Clara and Edward were on the steps of the open door, reading respectively Vaughan's Poems and the newspaper, Herman sat at the window, drinking in the soft south-wind, as it panted upon his pale brow with the sweetened breath of the ocean. He took Constance's hand, drew her into a chair beside him, and pointed out to her the bright, dreamy, mysterious beauty in which land and sea were basking. "My dear heart," said he, "how blessed a thing it is, for us to sit side by side here, and enjoy the wonderful loveliness of even this changeful, dying earth together, and at the same time to look forward to sitting side by side again, before many years have passed, to enjoy together the undying loveliness of heaven!" He stopped, and felt her pulse. "How it flutters! I wish it was not so faint. But there is no use in waiting for that, I am afraid. Poor little heart! it beats in too true a unison with mine. My poor, dear girl, do you feel strong enough to-day to hear me tell you something?"

"No, no, Herman, don't!" cried she, with all her

old impetuosity, and a spring and stare like that of a dart-stricken antelope.

But he knew her and had nerved himself, for her sake, to go on. One would have said, from his aspect of calmness and hers, of despair, that it was her sentence of death, not his own, which he was about to pronounce.

"My poor darling, it is bitterly hard for you, I know; but it must come; and therefore I must soften it for you as much as I can; else how shall you be able to bear it by and by? Face it bravely now, Constance; and let me, while I can, bear it with you and comfort you."

The tender authority of his manner produced something of its usual effect upon her. She hesitated an instant; then crossing herself involuntarily, (according to a habit which still clung to her when in any great strait,) she resumed the seat to which he steadily pointed, and gasped rather than said, "I should be strong enough, indeed, to hear what you are strong enough to say! Go on, Herman. Tell me that I have cut off your glorious young life; and let me die with you."

Water, glasses, and hartshorn, were on a small mahogany table by his side. Before he spoke he, with a steady hand, dropped a certain number of drops of the hartshorn into a wine-glass-full of water, and made her swallow it. Then leaning back again in his easy-chair, taking her hand again in his, and fixing his earnest eyes compassionately upon hers, he answered, "What I supposed you would say. I wished to answer it. Constance, never, as you love me, let me hear you say it again,—not even in your own heart, when my disembodied soul looks down on yours, and sees and knows it as only the disembodied spirit can know a spirit. Constance, my inexpressibly beloved, have I ever, from the first words I ever spoke to you, spoken to you anything but the truth,—the kindly, the honest, or, as just now, the cruel truth ?"

She bowed her head : "Never !"

"Then you will believe me now. Yours is not a presence to lie in; nor am I, I trust, a man to lie in any presence; and I stand, besides, now on the very threshold of God's presence-chamber. Constance, look me in the face. As if with my latest breath, I tell you that you have been, from first to last, one of the greatest blessings of my greatly blessed life. Dearest Constance, except for your sake, I could scarcely wish that the circumstances of my life, so far as you had them in your power, had been decided otherwise. If I am now in any degree worthy of your love, it was your withdrawal of that inestimable love which, by God's grace, made me so. You withdrew it, for a little while, from a weak, self-indulgent, visionary boy. If you bestowed it again upon a man, as you think not altogether weak, self-indulgent, and visionary, you must thank for him the blessed sorrow which, like a thunderbolt, hallowed and fired as it struck him. Then you gave yourself back to me, nobler and sweeter even than before,—dearer I do not say, for that could scarcely be. Then,—once for all we will go on to the end without flinching,—then you confessed to me your youthful fault. Observe; I do not palliate it. I speak the whole truth still. I call it a fault. By confessing it, as you did, frankly and nobly and like yourself, as soon as you perceived that it was a fault, you put it in my power to peril myself to rescue you from peril. Can *I* be sorry for that, except for your sake ? You also inspired me, by my love for you, to turn twenty beasts of burden into men and women. *Can* I be sorry for that? There your agency ended, Constance, in that whole matter, excepting that the thought of your tenderness and sympathy supported me under the cruelty of others. Look at it, my dear love; and try to see that it is as I tell you.—

" Oh, Constance, I am telling you the whole truth still, as it looks to me;—indeed I am! I don't deny that I am sorry to die so young. I am sorry to die, and leave nothing written that will live after me,— nothing that men will stand by my grave and bless me for when I shall be no more.—I am more sorry than I can tell, to make you so unhappy by my death;—I hoped to make you so happy by my life! But don't you see that, in inflicting all this sorrow on me,—on us both,—you had no part or lot? Was it you, who made the laws which conflict with God's law? Was it you, who made brotherly kindness a crime? Was it you,—poor, terrified, broken-hearted child that. you were!—who shut me up from you to live in a prison, and let me out only to die at your side? My poor darling, it was not. Don't you see that it was not? Oh, don't sob so!—

" Constance, we have both of us been, from first to last,—you even more than I,—the victims of a bar- barous tyranny, that blasts the bodies and souls of both masters and slaves,—blacks and whites! Oh, my God!" cried he with a burst of irrepressible feeling, lifting her hand still clasped in both of his, and his hollow piteous eyes, towards heaven, " Against that tyranny, I appeal to thee with my dying lips,—in the name of our blighted youth and hopes,—in the name of this poor, lovely, helpless, desolated thing! Oh, my

God, look upon her!—look down in mercy upon her, and on how many other weeping girls as helpless, desolate, and despairing, as she! Oh, my God, how long!—how long,—Father,—shall manhood be trampled to death, and womanhood be left to writhe and agonize alone, under the cloven hoof of Satan sitting in the judge's seat, or standing in the statesman's place?" His unusually loud and rapid utterance suddenly stopped.

She raised her head; and her fright instantly turned the current of her feelings and stopped her tears, as she saw how pale he was. She would have flown to call Edward, who was in sight, walking up and down the beach with Clara; but Herman had caught her dress, and held it fast.

After a moment, he partially recovered himself, and went on, though in a whisper, still more rapidly than before; as if he feared not to have time or breath enough for all that he had still to say: "I do not think that I am really to be separated from you; for—' are they not all ministering spirits?' I shall be allowed to come continually and minister to you,—better, perhaps, than I could have done if I had lived.—Constance,—must I weep in heaven over your tears on earth? Constance, will you not—try, for my sake, to be comforted?"

She knelt at his feet: "Yes, yes,—I will!—I will try!—Oh, my God, help us!—Herman, if you will only rest, I will,—I can!—I will!"

He went on, faster and fainter: "Yes, pray, sweet soul, and God *will* help us, and give you strength and peace, and joy at last.—Constance,—you can go to the closet or the altar, now, and there remember no brother or sister hath aught against you.—No blood nor tears are appealing to heaven against you.—You have ennobled my life!—You cheer—my death! You will gladden—my eternity!" He bowed his head upon her hands on his knees. His lips were very cold. He had fainted.

They carried him to his bed. For an hour he gasped and swooned, and swooned and gasped. Edward was almost as pale as he. The least further agitation, and he might never gasp again. It was then that the true nobleness of Constance showed itself. His swimming eyes opened and asked for her. The creature bent over him, and actually smiled. A tinge of color came into his lips; they moved. She stooped closer and just caught, with eye and ear together, the words, "'Forgetting the things that are behind,'"—She took them up from him eagerly, with a clear sweet tone exclaiming, "Yes! 'Forgetting the things that are behind, we *will* press onward to those which are before, to the mark of our high calling in Christ Jesus!'" He thanked her with a look of unspeakable admiraration, gratitude, and relief. Before long, his limbs grew warm. He turned on his side towards her. Again she smiled; and he slept.

He awoke somewhat better; but he was very ill. The week, which followed, was a dreadful one to them all. He never left his bed; and they did not expect that he would ever leave it again, except for his coffin. He suffered, too,—he who seemed so much too weak, so much too dear, not to be sheltered from all suffering! Every evening a delirium came on, in which not even the sight which had always, hitherto, been ecstacy to him could bring him any comfort; for when Constance bent over him and told him that she was there, and smiled to sooth him, he called her "America," cried to her, that she had cherished a viper in her breast, which would sting her to the heart, and shrieked to her in agony to tear it out; so that she was forced to leave him. It was a piteous proof, how the young lover and patriot had enshrined together in his soul two of the earthly objects which were the dearest to it, his love and his country.

And when at last his outcries had been stilled by opiates, and they took watch and watch one after another, at his side, Edward, unable to sleep, would pace the long, bleak beach and think. What the nature of his thoughts was, we can in part conjecture from the course of his after-life; but their poignancy can be known only by those of us who, like him, have left some loyal, loving comrade and brother to fight the battle of life alone, and ranged ourselves fairly by his side not until he has received his mortal wound. Still, by the great mercy of God, the strait gate is unbolted to us; the narrow way is open; and still our heavenly Father is ready to give the holy spirit to us who ask him; but the human spirit which once, in its dear visible form, would have walked and prayed and striven at our side, has vanished. It has borne its cross alone,—alone borne the burden and heat of its day;—it has marched its march, uninspirited by any music of ours. We could have been fellow-soldiers once; but he is promoted to the legions of the angels; and we must follow after him,—as he went before us,— alone.

Or Clara knelt and wept so fast before God that she could scarcely pray for her more than brother,— her foster-son and foster-father, her nurseling, and her guide,—but gained, she knew not how, strength to strengthen them all. Her trial was a hard one; but hers was the lightest; because she had been so faithful to him from the first,—faithful, as it seemed, even unto death.

Or Constance, in her turn sent unwillingly to her sleepless bed, dared not to think or weep, but wrung her hands before God, and prayed that He would give her strength while Herman needed her strength, and then,—that His will might be done; for Herman had bidden her to pray for that, — Herman, who might never lay upon her any injunction more. Her sorrow was the keenest; she believed herself to be the cause of the sorrow of them all; and in her misery she felt herself alone. Clara could go to Edward for comfort, or Edward to Clara; but to Herman she must not go. Oh, what is more terrible than to turn instinctively from habit, when some stunning blow has made our hearts reel, to one to whom we have hitherto turned for support under every shock, and never turned in vain, and to see that it is through him that that blow has reached us. It is precisely by our shivered prop that we are pierced; and we dare no more to lean upon it, lest we should break it quite off at once.

But if Constance reproached herself not altogether unjustly for her lover's sufferings, she compressed even into those few days the devotion and self-sacrifice of a lifetime. If her grief was inconceivable, so were her fortitude and disinterestedness; for they triumphed over her grief, and enabled her to go every morning to his chamber with cheerful composure.

"This is unnatural," said Edward; "she will do herself harm by it. Clara, you must talk to her, and make her talk to you. This sort of tearless, dumb grief is dangerous."

Clara had not waited for this exhortation; but

Constance, considering herself, as we have seen, the cause of the sorrow of the rest and supposing that they must consider her so, too, had felt her self-reproachful anguish to be peculiarly her own, and beyond the reach of the sympathy of either of them. She had hitherto even almost repelled Clara's, with an unconscious relapse into her former impenetrable reserve of manner; for in our manners we are often, without our knowledge, haunted by the avenging ghosts of our old faults.* We willingly sinned once, against our neighbours and Christian charity; and now, in our tones and looks unwittingly, we are overhung by the following shadows of those old errors, and they come between us and the kind offices of Christian charity and our neighbours' hearts.

Clara, notwithstanding, was not to be easily baffled, and obediently tried again, when Edward left her to go to Herman. She led Constance by the hand into her own chamber and sobbed, out of her own full heart, "Dearest blessing, you are the greatest comfort to Herman and help to us all; but Edward says that you are behaving *too* well; it makes us anxious about you. You must not control yourself too much. Herman would not wish it. You must not deny yourself the relief of weeping here. If you can keep your smiles for him, you must bring your tears to me."

Constance was on her knees before her, with her arms around her waist and her averted face upon her lap. "I dare not," answered she, in a calm, hollow, hopeless voice. "If I began, I could not stop, perhaps. That relief I must never have, even after— He believes that he shall still be near me. I would not grieve his spirit away by a sigh nor a thought.

---

* Mrs. Sherwood

I have caused him sorrow enough; I will cause him no more. While he was in this world, he thought only of God and me. When he is in the other, I will think only of God and him. God is doing His best for us both. I begin to understand it now. Nothing but the matchless agony of losing Herman for a time, in this life, could have made me fit for the ecstacy of a place beside him forever in the other. What would one not bear for that? God is good." Arising, she pressed Clara's head to her bosom, kissed her brow with a long, loving kiss, and went again to Herman.

She had her reward for her resignation and composure; for the sight of it did him more good than anything else, and soon enabled him to give her the aid and encouragement for which she forebore to appeal to him. Fear for himself cast no shadow upon him. His early morbid conscientiousness had been so superseded by his after active and healthy conscientiousness, that in his self-devoting life he had almost entirely lost the habit of thinking about himself; and there is this to be said in favor of striving to reach a standard of divine excellence: that if there was only one of all the sons of men who could attain to it on earth, still the perpetual effort after and uplifting of one's-self towards it, is apt to keep a man from any gross lapses, and to prevent the overgrowth of any giant sins to stand at his last hour between him and his Father. Nothing showed more clearly how perfect was the love to which Herman had attained, than that it was rapidly casting out fear even for the tender, loving, and most beloved creature, whom he appeared to be about to leave alone in the hands of God. For her present suffering, he felt indeed only too deeply; but he was sure that all would be well with her in the end. And Constance made haste to think so too, for his sake, that she might show him that she did.

"Don't look back to your parting with me," he said; "look forward to your meeting with me. Hours are short that are spent in good works; as yours will be, my own. Do not think of lonely years. They may not be in store for you; and sufficient unto the day is the evil. You are young and well, though worn and weary. Husband your strength for my sake, that you may do the good I have left undone, and supply the imperfections of your lover's service; but do not fear that God will want messengers to summon you, through all your health and strength, when it is time for you to go. He has many ministers as strong and sudden as his flaming lightnings, to open the gates of Death, in spite of all the powers of Life, to your imprisoned, longing spirit. If you miss me in the morning, say to yourself, 'He has gone out for a little while; but he may be with me again at noon.' Or at noon, say, 'He is spending the day in our King's palace; but he will come for me,—perhaps this evening, or to-morrow,— and present me at that Court.' Some day,—when you least expect it perhaps,—it will prove true."

Constance listened with the meek and tender serenity of a pitying, but unsuffering, angel hovering over a death-bed, yet with her hands often clasped as if in prayer. She promised all that he wished; and he knew that with her, to promise was to perform. The endless week ended at last; and he was better.

His delirium returned no more. He was able to take a little more food; and it did him good. He could sit up for a little while, without faintness. He was able to hear them read a little in the Bible; (and, though he never made any such personal application of it to himself, they could not but feel how full of hope and peace it must be to him, and how literally many or most of its promises and benedictions belonged to him. How had he loved righteousness and hated iniquity! how visited those sick and in prison! how clothed the naked, fed the hungry, and welcomed the stranger and taken him in to his charity!) He was able to talk with Edward, and to use his influence over him,—the powerful influence of one speaking from the brink of the grave,—to moderate his hatred of the upholders of the fatal institution which had destroyed his happiness, (as it has done the happiness of how many!) and to endeavour to direct it only against the institution itself.

"Brothers all—brothers all!" he said. "Where should we be now, upon this subject, if we had been born and bred where they were? They have the worst of it, poor fellows! Remember, the time is very near, when every soul of them will own slaves no longer, or *own* them only among his transgressions.—'Tis the sin of the fathers visited upon the children. If one generation says of a thing, 'It is wrong; but it can't be helped,' what can you expect, but that the next will say of it, 'It is right; and it sha'n't be helped'? Put down their wrongs, Ned, with one hand,—you can do a great deal towards it, if you will;—but help them up with the other. They're as good-hearted as they are wrong-headed, many of them. God bless and undeceive them!"

"How noble he is!" said Dr. Lovel, one day as they left his chamber, to Edward. "I have lived through what many think will prove to have been the palmiest days of our country, and known, both before and behind the scenes, many of her most famous sons;

but my deliberate opinion is, that taking one thing with another,—parts, acquirements, spirit, and years,—I have not known a greater man than Herman Arden!"

"How much greater, too," said Edward gloomily, "he is than anything that he has had time to say or write! 'The world knows nothing of her greatest men!'"

"But her greatest men," returned the old clergyman earnestly, "least need for their glory, that she should know of them; and yet I prophesy that, if the young man dies for this cause, out of his grave a tree of liberty will spring, that shall flourish over all this continent!"

CHAPTER XXVIII.

THE WEDDING-NIGHT.

" The world goes up and the world goes down;
And the sunshine follows the rain;
And yesterday's sneer and yesterday's frown
Can never come back again, sweet wife,
Can never come back again." KINGSLEY.

DR. BRODIE, after his next consultation with Edward, no longer avoided the girls; though he spoke with caution. He told them, that he thought Herman's late severe illness might have been a crisis in his disease, after which he would be better than he had been for a long time. His case had been, from first to last, a very peculiar and perplexing one; but there was certainly, for the present, a marked improvement in his pulse and other symptoms. "Let him try, now," he concluded, " doing as he likes, and having his own way. He is prudent. He won't hurt himself. It was loneliness, privation, and confinement, that made him ill in the first place. Now let him read and see and hear and do, everything, and everybody, that he pleases."

This was advice which they were by no means sorry to follow. Clara knelt for a moment in her chamber, in tears of joy where she had so often of late knelt in tears of sorrow. She then went to Herman, and found him pillowed up in his easy-chair, and arranging with Constance,—whose pale face was blushing and smiling, oh, how differently !—a very charming

17

plan, which waited only for his brother's and sister's concurrence.

They were to move up to town in a few days. They could go in a steamboat with little fatigue; and a change always did him good. He thought, indeed, that he had exerted himself too little through the summer, and that it would be better for him, as soon as he could, to try somewhat more exercise, and variety in his way of living. Then his wedding was to take place. Then, as soon as the few necessary preparations could be made, they were all to go to Europe for a few months. Edward and Clara must be of the expedition, that they might help the other two to enjoy it, and themselves enjoy the contrast which it would present to their former trip. Herman's stocks had risen greatly within the last three years; and his fortune, under the judicious and faithful management of Mr. Flint, amounted again nearly to what it was when he set out upon his *quest*. He could very well afford for a while to lie upon his oars, as he said; and if he was not, as he hoped to be, restored at once by the voyage and the sight-seeing, Constance and he would establish themselves quietly in some healthy, airy little home among the Alps or the Apennines, and stay abroad for a year or two. Those are fortunate who, in never playing when they should work, and in working as hard as Herman had been, do not forget how to play; they have a hundred pleasant resources left, even when they can work no longer. His exhilaration and gratitude, in view of this project, drew the tears of thankfulness again to Clara's blue eyes.

They moved him to Boston. He bore it well, and seemed to gain ground surely though slowly. His appetite became good; and his muscular strength was in his favor. He drove daily, and a little further each day, but husbanded his powers very carefully for the wedding. "I am like David Copperfield," he said,—"afraid that I shall break my leg before the holidays." He ventured to receive few visiters; but, as he lay upon his sofa, he looked over, and over again, all the cards with old familiar names upon them, and appeared never weary of hearing the messages of kind inquiry and interest which were left for him, and sometimes scarcely able to control his emotion in dictating his replies to the latter. These tokens of remembrance were very many. Death, the peace-maker, shelters from prejudice and jealousy those who sit under the shadow of his wings, and pleads for them both with warm enemies and with cool friends. It is well when the tributes of the late remorse brought about by his mediation are brought in time to be laid even at the feet of the dying, and not on the tomb of the dead. If we could all but remember, at all times, that we were dying creatures in a dying world, we should, almost all of us, lead more forbearing and forgiving lives.

Herman set his heart upon seeing all the friends of his family at his wedding, even if it were only for a few moments. Edward and Clara agreed with him in this wish. They desired that a complete reconciliation should take place, in the present high tide of mutual kind feeling, between him and his native city, and that his departure from his country should be a dignified and becoming one, not looking like a flight. They decreed him a triumph, in their house at least.

Thus, in happy, quiet thought and hope and sweet domestic intercourse, the wedding-day drew on. It came; and Herman had not broken his leg, nor even lain awake all night. On the contrary, when Clara went into his chamber to give him his breakfast, he told her that he had not felt so well before for months; and not even the news, which Patrick incautiously blurted out before him, that his favorite, old Bay, had been found dead in his stall, could dash his spirits for an instant.

In order to avoid any unnecessary fatigue, and perhaps also from a little boyish impatience, he dressed for the evening when he first rose in the forenoon, and begged of his indulgent keepers leave to go below at once, that he might see what they were all about. All day long, while the festive bustle went on through the house, he lay still, but supremely happy as it was easy to see, on an ottoman in the library, seeming to find his own thoughts sufficient company; though Edward, the girls, Sally, or the faithful Gummage, looked in upon him as often as they could, to see that he was warm enough and wanted nothing. After dinner, however, he declared that he would not have all his cake cut by the hired waiters, and made Sally bring in one loaf, and spare time to slice it before him, with Clara's help, in the good old-fashioned way. In the meanwhile, with his own pencil, he directed a few boxes of it to some of his humbler friends, and dictated the names of others to his brother, smiling at all Ned's jokes, though saying very little himself, as if he was still on his guard to reserve himself for the reception.

At half-past seven, the door-bell began to ring a marriage-peal; and Patrick, with a face of hearty Irish welcome and a white favor in his button-hole, to ply between it and his black colleagues at the foot of the stairs and the entrance of the front drawing-room, in which Clara in her beautiful bridesmaid's costume,—

having put the last touches to Constance's dress above, not forgetting the long put-off point-lace veil and orange-blossoms,—assisted Edward to receive their guests.

At eight, both withdrew. Clara brought the bride down from her chamber, and joined her brothers in the library. Herman rose and stood leaning slightly on the arm of Edward, his groomsman. They took their places silently, side by side. The folding-doors were pushed back by the attendants. A little murmur of sympathy and admiration ran through the company, as they pressed forward and closer together. Dr. Lovel advanced and, with all the feeling, which, for the invalid's sake, he dared not express, trembling through his old voice, in a very few simple and solemn words made Herman and Constance one.

A chair was then brought for the bridegroom; and he sat, the centre of a throng, while the young, the old, and the middle-aged, crowded around him, welcoming him back, congratulating him, praising his bride, or wishing him happiness, health, and a long life to carry out the upright and patriotic course which he had begun.

> " Again his soul he interchanged
> With friends whose hearts were long estranged. * * *
> As warm each hand, each brow as gay,
> As if they parted yesterday;
> And doubt distracts him at the view;
> Oh ! were his senses false or true ?"

And it was no dream, but a blessed reality!—a reality that a Timon might have sneered at, indeed;—a reality which, as his own penetration taught by hard Experience showed him, was insecure and might be very fleeting without any fault of his;—but still a reality which a generous and forgiving heart, like his, could very thoroughly enjoy while it lasted.

Fearing lest he might be indulging himself in it too long for prudence, however, he managed to slip out of a door behind him, in the stir of pairing-off to go to supper, which was on his account ordered very early, and had himself carried in a chair, as usual, to his own room. Missing him, the girls became anxious; and Clara followed him as soon as she could. He immediately remanded her to the merry-making, saying that he was resting delightfully; she might send old Sally to him, if that would be any relief to her mind; but he was doing very well; in fact, he felt quite strangely well and comfortable.

The company soon dispersed. Constance found Herman on the sofa before his fire, basking, as it were, in the light of the broad-faced hunter's moon which, hanging on the window-sill, shone all over him. He put out his hand to her fondly, and drew her down to give him her first kiss, saying, "Thank you, love, for the happiest day of all my life. Thank God! I have been thinking, as I have been lying here, that I scarcely ever formed a wish worth having which He has not granted me sooner or later, and you to crown all,—the best for the last!"

"Dear Herman," said she, "the moon is shining directly into your eyes. Does not it dazzle them? Shall not I draw down that shade, and light your lamp?"

"Not on my account. You don't dislike it, do you?"

"N–no;—except that it makes you look so pale." ·

"Screen me yourself, then; take your harp,— will you not?—and sit in the window, so that I can see the outline of your features and your veiled head against it; and sing me to sleep. Sing one of Schubert's songs."

Without consideration, she began the first one that she remembered,—one which had been a favorite with him in the first months of their acquaintance. As she played the low, weeping prelude, faint and broken as sobs around a death-bed, the words came to her.* They struck her as ominous; but, unwilling to disappoint him, she instinctively and mechanically went on:

"Oh, 'tis our last, last moment!—
O thou, my only love!—
The moment of our parting!
Without me soar above.
Death cometh as a friend,
That gives thee liberty;
In heaven receive thy life,
And for eternity.

"Farewell! to wait for me
Thou goest. Soon I come.
Within my faithful heart,
Thy memory keeps thy home.
Farewell, until the dawn
Of that blest day I see,—
The day I trust in,—sure
To give me back to thee!"

She sang to him; and he slept. She spoke to him; and he did not awaken.

---

* Translated from *Béranger's* "*Voici l'instant suprême,*" &c.

THE END.

NOTE TO VOLUME II.

NOTE A., *to page* 239.—"All that."—Of this assertion, as to the "raw back and iron collar," the reader may find confirmation on pages 35 and 89 of "A Key to Uncle Tom's Cabin." I do not know whether or not Mr. Broadstone meant to declare that the iron prongs of the collar were also lawful, or, if so, what were his grounds for the declaration; but for the use of such prongs, at least, the inquirer may find a precedent, on the authority of a Southern lady, *ad loc. cit.*